MONI

BY THE SAME AUTHOR

House of Dolls

KA-TZETNIK 135633

MONI

A Novel of Auschwitz

Citadel Press Secaucus, N.J.

Published by Citadel Press
A division of Lyle Stuart Inc.
120 Enterprise Ave., Secaucus, N.J. 07094
In Canada: Musson Book Company
A division of General Publishing Co. Limited

Queries regarding rights and permissions
should be addressed to the publisher
Lyle Stuart Inc.
120 Enterprise Ave., Secaucus, N.J. 07094

Originally published in the United States
under the title *Atrocity*.

Edited by Lyle Stuart

ISBN 0-8065-1022-6

Manufactured in the United States of America

A *Piepel* was a boy whom the Block Chiefs of Auschwitz selected for their sexual orgies. The recorder of this account does not know the origin of the name "Piepel," who coined it, or in what language it originates. Be that as it may, in Auschwitz the name was as familiar as the names for Bread and Crematorium.

K.Z. (German-pronounced Ka-tzet) are the initials of the German term for concentration camp. Every K.Z. inmate was nicknamed "Ka-tzetnik Number . . ." the personal number branded into the flesh of the left arm. The writer of *Atrocity* was Ka-tzetnik 135633.

E. D'M. A.

THE HIERARCHY AT AUSCHWITZ

S.S. Camp Commandant:
Rudolph Hoess

S.S. Officials:
S.S. Camp Doctor (Dr. Mengele)
S.S. Camp Chef

Camp Senior:
Ludwig Tiene

Block Chiefs:
Franzl, Werner, Willi, Bruno, Robert

Piepels:
Eddie, Jackie, Moni, Golden Lolek, Bobo, Benyek

Chief Block Orderly:
Zygmunt

Vatzek – Kapo of the Peelery
Schmulik – Kapo of the Bread Store
Food porters
Barrel washers
Block orderlies
Block cooks

Camplings

Mussulmen

BOOK ONE

1

"This is what I call a present!" Franzl said as he stared at the boy. The electric bulb above them was sheathed in pleated red crepe paper and gave a ruddy dull glow.

The man sat on a chair in the center of the block cubicle, holding the boy's upper arms in a viselike grip that forced his shoulders up to his ears. The boy, imprisoned between Franzl's knees, gaped.

"Mo-ni." Franzl savored the sound with his tongue. "Moni." He smiled. "You're a little doll. Even your name has appeal. Mo-ni. And look at these eyes!"

Rostek, Franzl's private cook, leaned against the closed door, watching silently. His shoelaces were untied, sleep was still in them. He held his eyelids open with some effort; it would be unpolitic to reveal the indifference he felt for the scrawny creature in Franzl's grip.

"What do you think, eh, Rostek? The sweetest little Piepel you've ever seen, eh?" Franzl laughed gleefully. "What a prize! What a present!" He pinched Moni's cheek.

Two block orderlies stood a few feet away, their backs to the scene. Not even the sound of breathing came from them as they went about their chore. Only their hands moved, preparing the bread rations for the prisoners. One ran a nail across the back of the oblong dark bread loaf and the other sliced along the nail marks.

Outside, a shout was carried with the wind: "Block chiefs to the Camp Senior! Spread the good word! Block chiefs to the Camp Senior!"

The command flashed through the barracks like a non-stop express train. Franzl must report immediately.

He hesitated, moving his hands down the boy's back until they encompassed his skinny rump. He pinched the boy and abruptly stood up, reaching out for his cap which he slapped onto his head.

Franzl's muscular arm shot out and his fingers gripped Rostek by the ear. "See that my Piepel gets some meat on him, you understand? No skinny mussulmen[1] for me, Rostek. Fatten him up, or it'll be your ass!"

Not waiting for a reply, he bolted from the room.

The boy stood in front of Franzl's empty chair and now he began to tremble. In the thick redness of the light, the corners of the room were only dark blurs.

Rostek walked to the table where the bread was being cut and took the rations for which he'd come. His tiny pig-eyes stared for a flickering moment at Moni, and then he trudged past him and out of the cubicle without a word.

Outside, the darkness still hung heavy on the ground. The camplings had been driven from the blockhouses an hour ago; it was their clean-up time. It was safer that way for everyone, for it would be to nobody's advantage to watch a bread being cut into ten or twelve rations instead of the four called for by camp regulations. Nor would it be healthy to see the storage place where the surplus loaves were hidden.

Franzl's black boots stood next to his bed, their upper parts gleaming. In the narrow locker, everything was arranged with precision: clothes brushes, shoe brushes and polish on the highest shelf—underwear, clean, freshly laun-

[1] *Mussulmen*: camplings whose bones were all that held them together.

dered, neatly folded as if it had been ironed, on the bottom shelf. One could sense the hand of a former Piepel, the way a second wife, coming into her husband's home, could feel the hand of her predecessor.

Moni ran his tongue along his delicate bottom lip. Then he reached for a shoe brush and polish. "A Piepel must attend to all the Block Chief's comforts," he'd been told. He closed the locker. Franzl's striped jacket hung on a hanger from the outside door. It was freshly laundered and ironed. On the breast, where a medal could have been, was sewn the green triangle that designated a criminal inmate. Beneath the triangle was stitched Franzl's Auschwitz camp number. Two digits. Franzl had been one of the pioneers at Auschwitz.

The cubicle door swung open for Zygmunt, the Chief Block Orderly. Noticing Moni, his face flashed an obsequious smile, which faded as quickly as it had appeared. He went to the breadcutting table and thrust his head between the two silent men. "You bastards!" he roared. "You dirty sons of whores! I want twenty-five loaves left over today or you'll eat your own skins for dessert! Twenty-five—and not a one less!"

Zygmunt turned to Moni. "In the shithouse they want two loaves for just one pack of cigarettes. Can you imagine? And Franzl hasn't a single smoke to his name!"

He glanced at the twin shadows as if waiting for protest, but they remained silent. You can only slice bread so thin, no thinner. Their arms worked faster and faster but they could only cut the bread, not create it.

Zygmunt again faced Moni. The boy stood as if petrified, one hand clutching the shoe brush and the other deep inside the boot.

The rim of it reached almost to his neck. Zygmunt went over to Moni, bending his head close to him. The pockmarks on Zygmunt's face looked as if they had been carefully stippled, one beside the other, by an exacting craftsman. The red light filled them like tiny bowls. Zygmunt spoke softly to Moni, almost in a tone of fatherly reprimand:

"What do you think you're doing, Piepel?" he said, pointing at the boot. "That's no job for you. Don't you know who Franzl is? He's king! And if Franzl is king, that makes you queen! You, shining boots? For one single spoonful of soup a thousand camplings will not only shine this boot for you, they'll lick it with their tongues all day. Being Piepel is the highest *Funktion* in the block, if you know what I mean. And if a Piepel's got a head on his shoulders and not only an ass"—he pointed at Moni's posterior—"he can get anything he wants out of his Block Chief. Get what I mean, Piepel? In bed they're all like little lambs."

Zygmunt returned to the breadslicers, and as if to show that the job of Chief Orderly was nothing to take lightly, he brought the truncheon heavily down on the shoulder of one of the orderlies. The mute shadow snatched at the shoulder with a throttled groan, but immediately pulled himself together. It isn't proper for a block orderly to let out groans like a common campling. "Bastards!" Zygmunt again shouted at them, "I want twenty-five breads today!" His hand on the doorknob, he turned another fawning smile on Moni. "You're all right in my book, Piepel. I see we're going to get along fine." He winked at Moni, nodded, and left the cubicle.

Hardly had the door closed when the orderly at the table took off his jacket. Both heads looked at the bruise where the truncheon had landed. Suddenly the eyes of the beaten man met Moni's. For a moment the orderly's profile assumed a sheepish smile, as though he had been caught at some indecent act. The two returned to their work.

Moni sank down on the bed. Near his feet lay the Block Chief's boot. The red light sharpened the gleam of the tall upper. The crimson density of the cubicle stifled him. Where could he go? To whom could he turn? An agony of fear and loneliness choked him. He went out of the cubicle.

From his eyes the empty block streamed dim, unending. On either side, up to the rafters, the three-tiered hutches rose vacant. He passed into the hollow darkness of the vast block. From the rafters hung an electric bulb which barely lit several hutches. He sought refuge in the drab and empty darkness from everything that engulfed him. He had not yet fully grasped where he was or what had happened to him. He could still feel his hand held tight in his father's palm. His eyes could still see the sealed wagon doors sliding open and the herds of people tumbling out onto the Auschwitz unloading platform. They were lined up in a long row. An S.S. man at the head of the row, only his hand ordering: Right! Left! Right! Left! He felt Papa tighten his grip.

They stand together. The line moves forward quickly. Huge lorries waiting on the left. Men in striped uniforms snatching people out of the masses pushed to the left, and shoving them onto the lorries. Just a handful of people on the right. Papa presses him to his side. Everything happening without a sound. So terribly fast. Left! Right! No one knows which side is good and which is bad. The row moves forward. Now they are both at the head of the row. The German's eyes pause on him for a moment, smile, and suddenly Papa is torn from him. Their clasped hands break apart. Papa is dragged off to the lorries but his glance does not let go of him. Papa calls to him: "I'll be waiting for you at the gate!" What did Papa mean by that? In the wagons, Papa promised that the war would soon be over. There will probably be an awful crush getting out of camp. People will trample each other the way they did at the collection points in the ghetto. In the sealed wagons, on the floor, people lay underfoot, trampled by those standing on them. If he hadn't been riding on Papa's shoulders he would have been trampled too. Papa was thrown into one of the lorries among all those feet, hands, heads—with his eyes still fastened on his own from afar. The Germans kept tossing and shoving the people onto the lorries. Until Papa's gaze was lost among them. Gone.

The front gate of the block swung open. The red light streaming through the cubicle window illuminated Zygmunt's stormy entrance. Moni made for an aisle between two hutches. Zygmunt climbed to a top tier. The orderlies handed breads up to him, and he stowed them away. The open cubicle door fed the red band of light to the top tier, and back and forth in this redness the block orderlies passed, bringing bread from the cubicle. Zygmunt's hands dangled down to them from above.

Moni wanted to get out of the aisle, but his feet would not obey him. From the kitchen came the smell of frying sausage. The smell mingled with the terror of his loneliness and the memory of Franzl's stare and made him want to retch.

He walked to the front gate. No one was there. He pushed the gate open and walked to the main path.

"Piepel! Piepel!"

Like a far-off echo came the call. Moni turned. From behind the corner of the block, near the assembly ground, the crown of a boy's head jutted. The boy repeated his frightened cry: "Piepel! Piepel!"

Moni went over to him. The boy's teeth chattered with the cold; his body trembled. "Let's go to the back where Franzl won't see us together . . ." The words clicked out through the boy's teeth.

Walking side by side, they entered the assembly area between two blocks. His companion was shorter than Moni. Suddenly Moni felt a desire to put his arm around the other's bony shoulders and to comfort him. He had not yet had a good look at the boy; he didn't even know what the lad wanted to say to him. But a strong surge of affection overcame him, as if for a brother found in a moment of loneliness. The boy kept turning his head, glancing fearfully in every direction to be certain that no one was watching them from the main path. His arms crossed his chest and his fingers were tucked deep into his armpits to warm them. They reached a path in the back, where a gray mass of myriad skeletons huddled, skulls drawn into shoulders: those cast out from the block. The boy slipped into the skull-stream as if this were where he belonged.

The two of them stood face to face. "I was Franzl's Piepel," the boy said to Moni. "If you just give me a piece of bread, I'll teach you tricks that Franzl likes, and he'll treat you right when you're good with him."

Moni understood nothing. He looked around him, and saw backs rubbing against backs to produce a little warmth. The boy's teeth were chattering with cold. He kept lifting one shoulder to his ear, and then the other shoulder to the other ear, rubbing the shoulders against the ears to keep them warm, and at the same time hopping from foot to foot, as if to detach his body from the cold earth.

"I know just what Franzl likes," the other boy was saying through his chattering. "I know just what he likes. And you'll make out all right with him."

Moni felt tears come to his eyes. He trembled and shivered. The blurred skeleton-mass around him came into focus in the boy's face. It was a face just like Moni's own—and both of their faces were from Franzl's cubicle. Suddenly Moni felt he'd committed a terrible crime against the boy; he had displaced him as Piepel.

"Why aren't you Piepel any more?" Moni asked.

"Franzl had enough of me," the boy replied. "He tired of me. I knew he'd pick a fresh Piepel from the platform. But I didn't wait for him to get rid of me. I got away first."

Moni ached to throw his arms around the boy and hug him. "I'll go get you some bread," he said. "They just finished slicing the rations."

"No! No!" the boy cried out. "Not rations. They'll be watching you. I ought to know. Then they'll follow you and get me when you bring me the rations." The boy's body moved closer to Moni. "You're all right," he continued. "You're all right. My name is Berele."

It was as if Berele were embracing him, Moni thought, even though the other's hands were thrust deep into his armpits. "Never touch the rations," Berele continued. "Better from the stash. Then they won't notice. Besides, you're the boss there. I'll wait for you in the latrine, behind the water-pump partition." He paused, and then added:

"I knew you'd be all right."

Out of Berele's eyes, Moni's own destiny stared at him. He was frightened. "How could you tell that the Block Chief was getting tired of you?" he asked.

"I could see it in Franzl's eyes. A Piepel knows. The heart of a Piepel can tell right away. The Block Chief just waits until he can bring back a new Piepel from the platform. That night he takes the old Piepel into the cubicle, lays him on the floor, and puts a cane across his throat. Then he steps on the cane—one boot on each end—and he does a seesaw. And that's all—that the end of the old Piepel. I saw Franzl do it to the Piepel before me, so I didn't wait. I got away first."

Moni could see Franzl's mouth, carefully, slowly murmuring: *"You're a little doll. Even your name has appeal."*

"Did Franzl get you at the platform, too?"

"No," Berele replied. "He spotted me while we were marching from the platform to the camp, and he picked me out right away. I wanted to run after my father when I was on the platform, but the S.S. man put me in the group going to camp. When they opened the train door, my mother fell to the ground, dead. Or maybe she was still alive, the way her eyes kept staring out at me."

Before them the gates were opening: the camplings could now enter the blocks. They all stampeded at once. Each one wanted to be first. Berele did not move.

Daylight now bared to Moni the countless wired borders of Auschwitz.

"Your father probably is in one of those camps," Moni said suddenly.

Berele shook his head. "When my mother fell out of the train dead, and my father was taken off in the lorry, I didn't know that I should have been happy for them. I just didn't know how lucky they were not to be alive." The two boys gazed at the myriad skeletons shoving their way into the blocks, surging ahead as if on their way to freedom.

2

Moni wrapped his hands around his midriff. He could feel the fingertips of both hands meet. "I'm strong, Papa," he wept. "I'll hold out, Papa. I will."

It was dark in the block kitchenette and he was alone. He stood by the window watching for the front gate of the block to open. Franzl is due any minute. His supper is ready. He will have to serve Franzl. Then he'll have to pull Franzl's boots off his feet. Then, with Franzl in bed.

Today more than ever he felt smothered by the terrible loneliness of his first Auschwitz days. Lately the loneliness had abated somewhat. He thought it had gone. Because he was always keeping busy.

He did not know whether night had just begun or whether it was midnight. A big *Selektion*[1] had taken place in camp that day, and Franzl had had to go to the crematorium to help herd the lot in for the gassing.

Opposite, in Franzl's cubicle, the table was set. But he was afraid to go inside. Ludwig Tiene, the Camp Senior, knows who is Crematorium Chief-of-the-Day. Often he drops in at the cubicles of the absent Block Chiefs, to poke around for a

[1] *Selektion*: the weeding out of weaklings sent to the crematorium.

hidden bottle of schnapps. And if he happens to find the Piepel too, that's the end of the Piepel. Everybody knows that Ludwig Tiene's lovemaking means death to the Piepel. To Ludwig Tiene, loving isn't loving unless he has topped it off by choking the life out of the Piepel.

Moni fixed his eyes on the front gate of the block. It was quiet in the block. In the triple-tiered hutches, entangled in each other, the camplings lay shrouded in their Auschwitz sleep. Not a breath was heard. As though they were not there. Only an agony of pain issued from them like a vapor into the vacuum of the block. Soon it, too, would be rooted out of here and into the crematorium.

The dense red light from the window of Franzl's cubicle fell on the front gate. But when he gazed back into the darkness of the kitchen, his eyes again saw the procession—just as he had seen it at sundown: endless rows of naked Mussulmen from the *Selektion*, shoulder bones stark in their pallor. Backs. Spindle-legs. Marching tongueless to the open gate, on to the crematorium.

Now he could see them more clearly than he had earlier. Now he could see also the barbed wire meshing the horizon behind their marching skulls; the aching twilight of the day between the wires drawn along on the nude pallor of shoulder bones.

He hadn't had the time to notice all these details before. It was block curfew when they were being marched to the crematorium. The left-behinds were not allowed outside the blocks then. Fearfully he had opened the gate ever so slightly —he couldn't control himself: what if Berele is among the marchers?

He did not see the beginning and he did not see the end. Only a skeletal vastness in naked profile march. Going. Going. Only now he can see his fear joining the fear of their nude backs, marching together with them, although he is still standing here in the dark kitchenette within the block. Like them, he will go marching through the open gate; like them, he will arrive where they are now; where Franzl is now. Then Franzl will come back to his block, just as he will come back tonight. Only he himself will no longer be here. Another Piepel will be here. A fat Piepel. A Piepel who will give Franzl what he wants during the lovemaking.

Through the window of Franzl's cubicle opposite, he saw the table set for supper. Everything was in place there. Cleaned up. Tidy. It was all his work. His hand had handled it all. He, the Piepel. But now more than ever he knew with terrifying certainty that he did not belong there. None of that was his. The red stillness in there glowered at him with Auschwitz eyes of kapos and Block Chiefs.

He knew that he was still around only thanks to Franzl. But he also knew that Franzl was not satisfied with him. *I'm not having any Mussulman in bed!* Block Chiefs like a good, fleshy Piepel to make love to after a spell of hustling Mussulmen to the crematorium. What would happen to him when Franzl was through with him?

All alone he stood there in the dark of the kitchen, sodden with the agony of those lying in the hutches. All at once he stood face to face with the unspeakable loneliness of Auschwitz. He was afraid to move a limb. The loneliness was everywhere. All around him and as far as his thoughts could reach. He flattened himself against the wall. His eyes tore open with terror. The darkness projected at him the receding lorry into which Papa had been tossed. He cannot hear what Papa is crying out to him from there, but he knows that Papa is telling him just what he managed to blurt to him when they were torn apart. "Moni, wait at the camp gate when liberation comes. We'll meet there!" Oh, Pa, why did you leave me?

He spoke weeping into the dark: if we were together, I would be able to give you bread now. I'm Piepel. Every day I could bring you marmalade in your hutch, and whatever was left on Franzl's plate I would keep just for you. I could take care of you here. You mean it, Papa, you won't go away from your block naked in a *Selektion*? You're strong, Papa! Pa, take care of yourself there! I'm terribly lonely here all by myself. Please, Pa! Hold on to yourself, and then I'll be able to hold out, too. Franzl yells at me that I'm a skinny Piepel. You're the only one who knows how strong I really am. Remember in school how they always used to say: "For his height, Moni could use another few pounds," and how you always told them: "We Preleshniks are that way. At Moni's age, I could touch fingers around my waist." He raised his jacket, wrapping his hands around his bare midriff. Look, Papa. See how my fingertips touch? But I'm strong. You'll see, I'll hold out. Promise you'll hold out in your camp! Don't miss me the way I miss you, because that will make you weak. When you miss somebody the way I do, you have to cry. And I don't want you to cry. Don't worry about me, Pa . . . Do you hear what I'm saying? You're not to worry. The war won't last long. I'll be waiting for you behind the bars of the open gate. It's going to be very crowded. Everybody will be pushing to get out to freedom at once. But I won't budge from there till you come for me. I know what—I'll climb up to the top of the iron post at the gate so you can see me. You know what a good climber I am—

The gate swung open. Franzl strode into the block. "Piepel!" he roared.

The latrine was packed with camplings. It was altogether impossible to recognize it as a latrine. The long rows of holes down the center of the block were covered with camplings who were invisible because of the waiting throngs surrounded by throngs waiting for them.

"I just couldn't get to you," Moni said. "I tried and tried for two days. You do believe me, Berele, don't you?"

They were standing in the corner near the water-pump partition. Berele gulped snatches of the bread Moni had brought him. He crumpled it to bits in his pocket, holding each scrap in his hand as in a bowl. His frame shook all over, and his hand shivered, too. He ate rapidly, lest a crumb drop to the ground. In this crush you could never get back such a crumb, and you could never find it under so many feet. He ate feverishly, feeling that he was committing a crime against the bread by gulping it so. But he was also aware of the menace of all the eyes around. The latrine is crawling with merchants. The camp is full of them. All he needs is for an orderly from block 12 to catch him with a portion of bread after Moni has gone. Now where does a lowdown campling come off having a bread ration in the middle of the day? Better get it down fast.

He licked the palm which had cupped the scrap of bread, the way you lick a bowl which had contained a soup ration. In his pocket his hand felt quite a bit of the ration. He knew that afterwards there would be a whole hoard of crumbs there. He looked up at Moni. "You don't have to make excuses to me," Berele said. "Last time, when you came to my block early in the morning to see whether I'd gone off with the *Selektion*, I was really worried about you afterwards. Zbichev saw you leave me, and then he saw me eating bread. Bread, right in the morning! You know that the Chief Orderlies are all in cahoots about things like that. Zbichev and Zygmunt are best buddies. I was afraid to go and meet you afterwards. I told you not to come to my block. They know you're Piepel. You mean a lot to me, Moni."

"After that night with Franzl I just had to come to you. I'm terribly lonely here, Berele. I was afraid you'd gone off with the *Selektion*." His eyes halted mutely on Berele. His friend's face looked no better than those crematorium-marchers. Berele could have been one of them then, just as he is fit for the next batch. Moni reached out his hand, cupping Berele's little hand in his. Both their hands shivered. "You mean even more to me, Berele. I really love you, Berele."

Behind them throbbed the motor of the water pump. Breast to breast the two boys stood, Moni's back to the latrine block, so none of the merchants should see his face. The crush around them was great. Mussulmen wiped with their hands the feces trickling down their drawn-off trousers, as camplings kept shoving them away and passing them on to each other. Moni's arm embraced Berele's shoulders. He let his head down on Berele's shoulder.

"I'm scared, Berele. Franzl hasn't used me in bed for two straight nights. I'm really scared, Berele."

"Sh-h-h! Don't talk so loud," Berele whispered. "Did you do everything I told you?"

"He won't let my body touch him. He kicked me out of bed. He says I've got the bones of a Mussulman."

"I told you not to undress. Just let your hands do the whole job. Franzl likes that. Get him hot in all the places I told you. Then he'll go right at you."

"I do, I do, Berele. But the minute he lays eyes on my body—"

"I told you to turn out the light."

"Franzl yells: 'I want to see those eyes of yours, Mussulman!' Oh, Berele, why can't I be fat? Back home once, when Miss Emilie was feeding me, she called me skinnymerink. But just in the children's room, so nobody should hear. My pa liked me just the way I was. He said I was a Tarzan. All of them liked me the way I was. Help me, Berele. I don't want Franzl to do a seesaw on my neck with his cane!"

Berele's body shivered as though from cold. He felt Moni's tears hot on his throat. In his pocket he still had the bread remains and a trove of crumbs. But at the moment his mind was not on that at all. The hunger which leeched him asleep and awake now suddenly seemed to have petrified in him. He knew what was in store for him if Moni lost his *Funktion*. Just as he knew the meaning of a Piepel's foreboding that his Block Chief was preparing to do a seesaw across his throat. He clung to the corner of Moni's jacket, as though by clinging he would safeguard Moni's life. He now loved Moni with the rare love that could manifest itself only in Auschwitz. Before his eyes, the camplings dissolved to a hostile infinity, insatiably consuming human bodies without cease, without cease. Now he was ready to offer himself to it, only that Moni should be spared. His jaws chattered as he said:

"I meant to tell you, Golden Lolek has been making eyes at Franzl lately. Whenever Franzl leaves the block, Golden Lolek is there waiting for him. What does your heart tell you, Moni? What does your heart tell you?"

They regarded each other. They knew that both their fates hinged on the answer. When a Piepel's heart tells him even at the height of lovemaking that his Block Chief is thinking of a seesaw across his throat—it is time for him to flee for his life. Not one more night in such a cubicle. The ear merely has to be attuned to the heart's signal. "What does your heart tell you?" As tremblingly as Berele, Moni awaited his own reply.

"Franzl says my eyes have him hooked. He says that even after he's had a hundred Piepels he'll never forget my eyes. But he wants me fat, Berele, why can't I be fat?"

Two Corpse Kommando men—the crematorium's corpse disposal crew—came barging into the water-pump compartment, followed by two merchants. One of the corpse collectors drew off his body an elegant woolen pullover he had "organized" at the crematorium, while the others counted cigarettes into each other's hands like banknotes. Berele mutely jabbed Moni to leave. With a last hug he whispered feverishly into his ear: "A good angel protect you!"

Moni moved off into the swarm of camplings. Berele remained standing there. Moni turned his head to him from afar. His velvety eyes glistening with tears, Berele sent a soft, sad smile to Moni, his lips again breathing the prayer with which his mother used to soothe him to sleep in the ghetto:

A good angel protect you, my sweet Moni . . .

Moni's eyes bulged from their sockets. "No, not magic, but a maidenhead!" he rattled the reply.

Gradually, as though the mollifying answer had needed time to pass through the ears to the brain, Franzl's fingers relaxed their hold on Moni's throat. Franzl slumped back in the chair, propping half his body on the table, one booted foot slung over the arm of the chair. "Thass-right, not magic!" he said groggily.

Franzl's stranglehold had forced Moni to his knees. He got up and reached out both his hands again to grasp the boot of the dangling foot, and again he began to tug in vain. This is the thousandth time Franzl has grabbed him by the throat, screeching the same question into his face: "What's in those bloody eyes of yours that's got me hooked, magic or a maidenhead?" And for the thousandth time the same reply. Always the same reply. Franzl waits for his reply as though it were some formula to drive away spells. Moni does not really know the meaning of "maidenhead." He does know that this word alone has the power to set his throat free from Franzl's stranglehold.

It was well into the night. Long after the final gong. The block was deep in Auschwitz slumber. Only the night guard, wrapped in a dark blanket, sat on one end of the brick oven as though on a night vigil beside the black-shrouded body on the ground the eve of burial, in the way of the Jews.

It is worst when Franzl returns from a night tour of duty at the crematorium. Even Rostek and Zygmunt—the cook and the Chief Orderly—keep out of Franzl's sight then, scurrying off to their bunks. Only he, the Piepel, mustn't be absent. He is Piepel, Queen of the block.

He, Moni, for whom the danger is at such times a thousandfold greater, and the fear a thousandfold more terrible.

He gripped the boot, one hand by the heel and one hand by the toe, but simply could not budge it. The foot dangled over the arm of the chair. Franzl did not make the least move to help him. He let the last of the schnapps drip from the bottle into his mouth, his bleary eyes on Moni. "You're a softy!" he declared. "But that's all right. That's what I like about you is that maidenhead in your eyes."

Franzl swung his foot off the arm of the chair. He seized him between his hands, training his drunken eyes on Moni's eyes, his mouth drooling the words: "I like you soft. A pussy like you is got to be soft. That's just the way I want you. Ain't a Block Chief here that's got a Piepel with eyes like yours. Eat their hearts out. But you're mine. All mine. Just stay put the way you are so I can go right on looking into those eyes of yours. Ah-h, that's sweet . . . m-m-mm, yeah . . . yeah . . . That's it . . . Right into the eyes—" . . . .

. . . the whole family is seated around the dinner-table in the large dining-room. A festive dinner. Harry and Sanya are here to say goodbye before leaving for Palestine. Harry is taking pictures. "Jump into my arms, little monkey saint!" Pa says to him. Harry is standing opposite. He focuses his camera. "Only Moni has exactly Ma's look," Sanya says. Pa nuzzles Moni's face. "From your rabbi grandpa's. Right, little saint?"

"Every Block Chief in Auschwitz is mad about my Piepel. Isn't a Piepel in Auschwitz with eyes like that!" the slobbering of the drunken mouth opposite Moni startled him awake.

All at once he felt his father's arms carrying him in the dark to bed in his room. *Little monkey saint!* He so wanted to feel himself being carried in Pa's arms just once more. He ached to hold on to Pa's head as he put him down in bed and never ever let go. "Pa," his heart cried out, "take me in your arms again! Tell me just once more that I'm your little monkey saint! Pa, I'll be waiting for you at the camp gate, so don't forget to come! I don't know what I'll do if I wait at the gate, and everybody is gone from camp, and you never come to me—"

Sparks exploded in his eyes. He did not feel the slightest

pain. Franzl had landed a stunning blow in his face. "Get out of here!" he shrieked at him. "You've gone and shot my girl's maidenhead full of tears!"

Outside, the night guard's head rose drowsy-eyed: why is the Piepel scooting up to a top hutch in the middle of the night?

3

Rostek sat on a low crate. He was peeling potatoes, preparing lunch for the Block Chief. More drunk than sober he sat there, elbows propped on his knees, his paunch bulging almost to his elbows. The potato turned lazily in his fat fingers, and the long band of peel—succulently white and parched brown—snaked down from the knife. He did his best to keep it from snapping. He did not lift his eyes from the paring, and the words drawling from his mouth seemed directed not at Moni but at the potato between his fingers. "Screw it all," he mumbled, "just so's a man gets his nip."

Moni stood at the side of the kitchen window. Weeks had gone by here. Auschwitz weeks. With a white towel he wiped the Block Chief's eating utensils. He tried to keep out of range of the cubicle window opposite, so that Franzl should not see him.

In Franzl's cubicle Dental Call was on. Every time a new transport arrives in the block, there is a rush for gold teeth in the mouths of the new arrivals.

The curtain on the window is pushed aside to increase the light in the cubicle. The campling is made to kneel on the ground, his mouth wide open to the light of the window. Piotr—"Holy Dad"—pulls the teeth.

No one in Auschwitz knows what made Death lend Piotr his hands. Block Chiefs take lessons from him. Whenever a Block Chief feels like providing some distinguished victim with an exclusive death, he turns him over to Piotr. Because it is a known fact that Holy Dad can draw his victim's death agonies out indefinitely, or that he is able to snuff out a life like the flame of a candle between two moist fingertips. Made to order.

They say Piotr is a German from Lower Silesia. But he was brought to Auschwitz from the Ukraine and he does not know a word of German. It is also not clear for just what crime he was committed to the concentration camp. He is a dwarf, with a face flat and stretched as though by a distorting mirror. No forehead, no chin, a toothless, insucked mouth like a knife scar, and in the center a nose like a wrinkled old potato. But most important of all—his two long hands. The famous Piotr hands, with which he does his work silently, conscientiously, solemnly, as he turns unctuous eyes on his victim. That is why he was titled Holy Dad.

A thrill of terror runs through the block every time the Block Chief cries: "Orderly, tell Holy Dad to drop by!" Just the other day Zygmunt got wind that a campling had smuggled a diamond into camp. But by the time Zygmunt got to him, it was down in his stomach. Zygmunt went straight away to the cubicle. Franzl came out. Halting beside the campling he studied him a while, his eyes suddenly lighting up with a green smile. "Hey!" Franzl called to the orderly standing near by, "Get me Holy Dad!" Piotr was there in a flash, caught what it was all about. Then, not saying a word, he offered the fullgrown campling his hand, the way a child offers his hand to an adult to be led. Piotr went along with him to the pump compartment in the latrine, went inside, and was there only a short while before he reappeared with the diamond sparkling between two fingers rinsed with blood. A large diamond. Block orderlies later carried the campling with the slit stomach to the corpse heap behind the block, and shoved him, still warm, in among the cold, dry skeletons.

A thousand camplings are now lined up the entire length of the stove bisecting the block. It is forbidden for anyone to be in the hutches now. Pocksy Zygmunt and his block orderlies patrol the top of the stove, wielding truncheons. The campling-skulls stand, mouths agape. Zygmunt cranes down from the stove, peering into every open mouth to check for gold teeth. If there are none, the campling gets a truncheon across his skull, telling him that he may now beat it back to his hutch. But if there is the least hint of yellow in a mouth, Zygmunt bestows a fatherly caress across his pate: it's the cubicle line for you, boy. The block orderlies pace up and down the top of the long brick oven, vigilant lest anyone get the nasty idea of vanishing amid the hutches.

Inside the cubicle, the table is away from the window. Zalke—chief "organizer" and camp fence—is writing on a sheet of paper the kind and number of the teeth extracted and tossed to him: platinum, gold crowns, half-crowns, gold bridges. Behind the campling's back, Franzl sprawls in his chair, his booted legs slung across the table. Moni looked at them from the window opposite. More than once had those very feet kicked him out of bed. *I don't want any Mussulman in bed!* But a few minutes later Franzl took him back in again and looked deep into his eyes: *Those eyes of yours have got me hooked.* Berele had taught him what Franzl likes, and again it turned out all right. Franzl got what he wanted.

Berele is waiting for him in the latrine, Moni mused. It is several days since he has brought him anything. The block orderlies are around all day. Nothing is done in the block without the Piepel. He is the Block Chief's trusty. They're always looking for him, always calling to him from every side. *Piepel, the smokes dealer is here.... Piepel, bread for the margarine dealer. . . . . Piepel, bread for Vatzek at the potato peelery. . . .* It is dangerous to go wandering around with a bread portion in your pocket. The sharp crust shows up clearly in the pocket. Now for whom would a Piepel be carrying bread around? Everybody knows that a Piepel isn't short of bread himself. If only he could eat what he is served at the table! He can't understand what the devil is the matter with him. Why can the block orderlies go on eating all day, while he—as soon as he's had his fill, he can't get another bite down? Other Piepels will even eat the common campling soup from the barrels—anything to keep fat, and he, he can't even stand the smell of frying sausage. He can't stand the camp bread. His gullet locks as soon as he swallows one slice. It burns away inside his stomach. He knows that Piepels have to be fat. His heart tells him that it will all end bad with him. He keeps telling himself off: Save your life! Eat! Being fat is your job! Everybody knows a Piepel must be fat. Last night Franzl kicked him out of bed again. He saw such a mean glint in Franzl's green eyes that he ran out of the cubicle and hid in a hutch. Is it possible that his eyes no longer excite Franzl? Can it be that Franzl has had enough of him? He must talk it over with Berele. Soon. Berele will tell him whether he sees any change in his eyes. Berele will tell him what to do.

This could be the best moment to sneak off to the latrine. Berele must be on pins and needles there. This morning he hid a bread ration behind Franzl's locker. How was he to know they would go and have Dental Call? It's too risky to go in there now. Franzl will see him digging something out from behind the locker. Better wait for the tooth-pulling to end. He mustn't come to Berele empty-handed.

The campling in the cubicle kneels on the floor so the hands of Holy Dad should be above him. His mouth gapes upward, his skull bent back all the way to the nape. He pulls his mouth open wider, harder: Aa-a-a . . . Take the gold!

Take it! Just leave me my life. Even the hair of his body has been taken off him. He really did not remember that he still owned anything. Aa-a-a . . .

As though gazing into the view-finder of a camera pressed up against the belly, Piotr lowers his glance into the open mouth-cavity, aims a thumb and forefinger like pincers into the open mouth, looking up at the ceiling—then, out of the campling's mouth crop the two fingers clawing a dull yellow chunk. He holds it high for a moment, for all to behold the cunning of his two fingers. Let's see anyone else in camp pull something like that off! But as soon as Zalke cups two prodding palms at him, Piotr's fingertips part and the yellow chunk comes dropping into Zalke's impatient hands. Oh, Zalke knows all the stunts. He knows what a bloody liar Holy Dad is. He knows that Piotr has stashed away in his long sleeve a little forceps with which he pulls the teeth. Before every pull Piotr shoves the prisoner's head down to the floor so that no one should see the forceps dropping back into his sleeve. Those suckers. Ha, Zalke knows all the sharpster tricks of that bloody runt, that butcher, that hot-air artist who likes to puff about knowing things that no one else in camp does. But Zalke's got his number. So what! Let them think Piotr really hoists teeth out of mouths like wild mushrooms. Business—that's what counts.

The row before the cubicle grows shorter. It won't be long now. Zalke's bag is filling quickly. He wears it under his jacket, hung diagonally by a cord, and it humps up the jacket. How will Zalke get it up the main path? Ludwig Tiene, the Camp Senior, is as keen on gold as he is on Piepels.

A white china plate, just like at home. Where on earth did the Block Chiefs dig up such a thing in Auschwitz? Moni kept wiping it with the white napkin, to appear busy. In the gloss of the white china he saw the hope of *Funktion* and Prominentship, just as the Auschwitz despair of skeleton piles at the back gate glittered in Franzl's black boots on the table opposite. He did not know what to do. Who would help him? He so wanted to serve Franzl with all his heart. He wants to be devoted to him, shine his boots, serve him his meals, see to it that there are always fresh underwear, clean socks in his locker, the bed neatly made. He so wants Franzl to like him in bed. He is ready to let Franzl try anything he wants on him. At first it had hurt him terribly. Those first nights in the cubicle with Franzl, he hadn't been able to lift a foot afterwards. He had to lie down all day. He lost his appetite and couldn't touch a bite. He had choked down his tears. But after a while he got used to it. Only his appetite never came back. Oh, how he wishes he could give Franzl what he wants in bed. He doesn't let out the slightest groan any more during the lovemaking. Why won't Franzl understand? Why does he kick him out of bed? Moni raised his eyes from the plate and looked around the kitchen. Auschwitz sadness welled in him at the thought that he might lose out on all this.

Rostek stood at the stove holding a griddle in his hand over a low flame, frying slices of sausage. His bulk swayed to and fro, the griddle circling along over the flame. With the flat of his knife he lifted the fried sausage rounds, all the while slobbering monotonously at the griddle: "Three packs of smokes . . . Screw it all . . . Just so's a man gets his nip . . ."

There had not been a cigarette to be got in the latrine that morning. Franzl had been ready to slaughter every last block orderly. So Zygmunt winked a hint at Franzl that Rostek had all his wealth in cigarettes. That was all the hint Franzl needed. And right then and there Rostek knew: if Franzl helped himself to three packs today, he won't lay off him now until he's squeezed every last fag out of him. To drown his despair Rostek went off to the Office cook and splurged the rest of his cigarettes on half a bottle of schnapps.

"The real stuff," Rostek just could not stop raving. "Where did that whoreson learn to make such schnapps?" Rostek's pork-eyes seemed now like two raw wounds. And come to think of it, there really was something to rave about: whisky in Auschwitz! How does that fellow manage it? A religious boy. Brought here from Hungary. He had almost become a Mussulman. Suddenly he let fall in the presence of his Chief Orderly that he was an expert at making liquor. They would not believe him. On the chance that he might turn out to be a quack, the Block Chiefs concocted a really rare death for Holy Dad to serve him. Meanwhile, Vatzek, kapo of the potato peelery, made available any ingredient the boy asked for. Just imagine: schnapps! Home brew. Made in Auschwitz! Tension ran high. Finally—the great moment. Festively all the Block Chiefs parked themselves in a semicircle around the skeleton. No one breathed. The honor of the first swig went to Ludwig Tiene. The Camp Senior swallowed, then let out a yelp: "Schnapps!"

"Real schnapps, Piepel! He's a wizard, that son of a whore from block 1. That Piotr knows shit. Big deal, hoisting teeth out of dry gumbones! They bring them here from the ghettos out-and-out Mussulmen. Let's see Piotr pull a schnapps out of his sleeve. Right, Piepel?"

With the flat of the knife Rostek flipped sausage rounds into the air and caught them with his mouth. Not one missed. He could go on stuffing himself all the time. "It's Franzl that runs the show here," Rostek went on, "so he ups and lifts all your fags. Why not, Piepel? Wasn't there always a sequestrator coming to you out there, in the world? Screw the liberation. What good's the liberation to you without a kitchen like this? Out there they won't even give you a wooden coffin. Here at least they'll shove you into the crematorium like on a griddle and the Mussulmen will fry in you like in a whole pack of margarine. Every camp has its camplings and Funktioners, Mussulmen and Prominents. And if you've been lucky to land a *Funktion,* keep your ass put. But you, Piepel—you're in for a bad end. So help me —bad. In camp, if you know what I mean, it's the fat and the skinny. The fat belong to life; the skinny—to death. Piepel—you belong to the skinny."

"I want to live, Rostek. Teach me, Rostek. Make me fat," Moni pleaded.

"Beats me why Franzl goes for the likes of you."

"I want to do everything, Rostek. Please teach me, Rostek," Moni pleaded.

"There's just six hours between a full belly and a hungry one in camp. And once you lose your *Funktion,* inside of six hours you're just as hungry as the rest of them. And you know where the hungry go in Auschwitz, Piepel. Six hours is all you need to tell you."

Opposite, inside the cubicle, Piotr is holding up the tooth between his two fingers. The campling is still kneeling at his feet, mouth agape. Till Franzl suddenly swings his white cane at him behind his back. The campling's skull echoes to the blow like a hollow, upturned pot. The block orderly opens the door for him. Running out he collides on the threshold with the one coming in. The one does not see the other. The incomer's eyes overflow with the black sheen of Franzl's boots sprawling on the table. The eyes of the one running out gape, seeing so very much yet seeing nothing. His feet run of their own accord to the boards of his hutch. His mouth still gapes wide, though he is now permitted to close it.

Only one campling, the last, is left before the entrance to the cubicle. He looks as though he would like to hide inside his own naked skeleton. One alone he stands there, exposed to the eyes of all the block orderlies. The eyes, which had previously roved helter-skelter over a thousand skeletons, were all now trained on one alone: him.

Zalke's bag is full, but his face doesn't look happy yet. Not much of a haul today, judging by his list. Small pickings in pure gold for him. The rest of it is cheap muck. Still, the teeth should get him at least five packs of smokes. One thing, though: they can croak, for all he cares, but he's charging Pocksy Zygmunt and Holy Dad to Franzl this time.

The name Zalke stands for something in camp. King of the Merchants. Product of the Balut underworld district of Lodz. Comes an argument, and Zalke aims a pair of eyes at his adversary, rapping out: "I'm a Balut boy, I am." Enough said. In this terse declaration, it has been made clear to the challenger that he is not dealing here with some fly-by-night peddler who made his career in Auschwitz. Sweetheart, it's a Balut boy you're dealing with! This is a pedigree anteceding Germans and Auschwitz, evoking the greatest respect in camp. And Zalke really is a blue blood. His father before him had been the leading fence in Balut. Zalke had made a fortune during the war. There was not a border he could not steal across. Finally, the Germans not only took away his entire fortune, they also sent him to Auschwitz. But Zalke is not one to quit under pressure. The camp wags say that even when they are slamming the furnace door on him, Zalke will strike a deal for the empty gas containers. Here in Auschwitz he hardly takes the time to eat. Eat? There is business to be done! He loves to boast of the way he launched his Auschwitz business career with a pair of socks he "organized" right out of Bloody Robert's pocket. At the time, Robert, Chief of block 16, had been ready to murder every last campling in his block. But when Zalke—after he had already become Zalke—described the way he had done it, Robert fairly exploded with laughter: that was a good one on him!

Inside the cubicle Franzl rose from his chair. They should be gone soon now, Moni mused. *No one in camp has a Piepel like this.* He has often heard Franzl boasting this way to his colleagues. All the Block Chiefs came to look into his eyes. Maybe Franzl will make up with him again tonight. It has happened before. It's Berele who taught him the kind of lovemaking Franzl likes. He must bring Berele his bread right away. Where are the bread rations from behind the water pump disappearing to? There's nobody in the latrine when he is stashing the bread away behind the generator. All the camplings are locked up in the blocks then. He hides it carefully. But Berele hasn't been finding it lately. Maybe he'd better find another stash. Who could have thought of looking for bread there? As though an invisible hand had discovered their hiding place.

The first to come out of the cubicle was Franzl. Zalke carried a filthy shirt for the laundry on his arm, to camouflage the bag humping up his jacket. Holy Dad followed, a cigarette pegged in his mouth slit, his cheeks sinking into deep cavities with every draw. They must be going to the gold assessor in Zalke's block, where they will divide up the loot. In passing, Zygmunt caught Moni's glance in the kitchen window. Zygmunt turned back into the kitchen. "Piepel," he bent close to Moni with a fawning smile, "do me a favor, will you? I'm supposed to dash over to the barrel scullery to pick up some margarine for Franzl. But those scum'll screw me proper if I'm not around when they're divying up the teeth. Do a pal a favor, won't you?"

"Why sure, Zygmunt, sure." Moni grasped at the opportunity to take Berele his bread. If they looked for him in the block, why, then, he had had to go to the kitchen for margarine. "Sure, Zygmunt," he repeated.

Hurrying out of the kitchen, Zygmunt tossed at Rostek's burly back: "That shithead screwed you out of your smokes."

Rostek did not turn. Like a hog in mid-feast, he grunted: "Screw 'em all. Just so's a man gets his nip."

The central kitchen block was placed not far from the camp entrance. Unlike all the other blocks it did not stand sideways but full-front to the main path. A painted block, well-groomed, a lord among blocks. It was rich in doors and windows and partitioned into sections. Each section had an entrance of its own. And outside, a spacious stone-paved compound for a carpet at its noble feet: the Kitchen Block! The holiday of the camp, the umbilical cord lavishing the flow of dream-stuff to all the other blocks in camp. Out of their hutch supinity, myriad campling eyes are longingly raised to it—not daring to approach its presence. Till they are cleared off to the crematorium, and take along with them only the soup-dream which had glimmered at them from this kitchen block.

The first door opens on the most important section of all, the cauldron section—where the soup is cooked. The second door leads to the barrel scullery—the barrels which receive the soup ready from the cauldrons and are then taken into the blocks for distribution. The third door opens on the potato peelery, which is "potato peelery" in name only. As yet no one in camp has found even a clue to a potato in his soup. Vatzek, kapo of the peelery, sells the potatoes to the personal cooks of the Block Chiefs, and the cauldrons here get only turnip and pumpkin rot. The last door leads to the warehouse, where the lorries deliver the turnips and potatoes. That is actually Vatzek's trading station. A narrow passage running down the entire length of the kitchen block connects the various sections.

At each cauldron stands the cook in charge. Within, brew the desires of camplings and cooks. Standing at his cauldron the cook muses: and if that pack of margarine does get into the cauldron—then what? Is that going to save the camplings? Margarine or no margarine it's the crematorium for them. Now take himself, it'll buy him five smokes! The good Lord knows he can't get along without the smokes. When he's got a yen for a drag, he feels he just won't be able to hold out at the cauldron another second unless he sneaks off to the latrine to light up. But if you don't come across with some grease, those dogs won't even show you the short end of a fag. Catch anyone thinking of the next fellow in Auschwitz.

But sometimes there is a hitch: the black-uniformed S.S. chef comes touring among the cauldrons. Then it's bad: any second now the pack of margarine will be thrown in. The lid of the steaming cauldron is up. The soup is done. The S.S. chef passes silently from cauldron to cauldron, hands clasped on the small of his back. Stepping along behind him is the kapo of the cauldron section. The fold of the kapo's white apron, loaded with packs of margarine, is gathered into his left hand, and with his right hand he sows pack after pack, wrapper and all, into the steaming cauldrons. This way he knows that the pack of margarine, all of it, will remain there. The cook is drawn up at his open cauldron like an honor guard at a fresh grave, his nerves racing around from head to toe as though galvanized. The pack of margarine lies on the seething water surface inside the open cauldron. What the devil is he going to do now? Only seconds to go! In all that heat the wrapper opened, spreading out like a madly sizzling sky with a yellow sun-ball melting in its center. The receding back of the S.S. chef infuses irresistible daring into his arteries. Now?...Go for it now? No! ... There's the profile. Easy. In a second Blackie there will turn into the next row of cauldrons. The cook holds ready the filthy rag which he uses to polish the cauldron. It'll only be a second. Easy ... In just a second you'll get to drop the rag on the melting margarine. But what if Blackie suddenly turns around? The chance sends his blood erupting towards the brain like the steam billowing out of the cauldron to the ceiling. Yellow fatty eyes inside the cauldron bob in warning. Now! It's five smokes against the crematorium. But he isn't thinking of the odds now. Out of the cauldron there now glares at him a maddening yellow sun-ball. Will he get the margarine before it melts, or will Blackie swing around to catch his hand in mid-air over the kettle? Every second counts. All at once, as though a steel spring had snapped in his muscles, he flings the rag at the yellow melt. The rag scalds his hands. Yellow drippings run off the rag on to the concrete floor. He can't run to the latrine this way now, and there's nowhere to hide the goods. So he makes a dash for the scullery next door and lets out the mortal fear pent up in him: "Hey, you whoresons! Where are those clean barrels? The soup's nearly ready to pour!"

The barrels, rinsed clean, are stacked in two rows along the wall. The cook dashes over, bends his eyes into one of the barrels as though to check it for cleanliness, tossing the rag with the margarine into the bottom barrel. "Clean, goddamn it?" he cries as he replaces the upper barrel. "In a couple of minutes I'm opening the cauldron tap, and it's your ass if the barrels aren't ready!"

And he rushes back out to his kettle.

Every cook has his steady "grease" fence among the barrel washers. Dashing in with his mock imprecations, each cook in the process roars out the name of his fence: "Hey, whoreson Moshiko, where are those clean barrels?" Which is to say: As soon as he's taken off, Moshiko should drop whatever he's doing, get over to the barrel, fish out the hot rag, dunk it in the cold water basin to get the "grease" hard again, and take off with it for the latrine. The cook doesn't care what the barrel washer gets for it there, just so he gets the five smokes coming to him! Needless to say, the barrel washer fixes his price as high as he pleases, because getting rid of the "grease" in the latrine is also a risky business. That is why it is better to come and get the merchandise in the kitchen. No middlemen to pay off.

Outside the scullery entrance stands a long row of barrels returned from the blocks. Inside, at water-filled basins in which barrels are soaking under open taps, stand the barrel washers: husky lads, sleeves rolled up, brawny wet arms, reddish rubber aprons around their hips; some with brushes in their hands, some holding whisk brooms, some in the center of the concrete floor, others at the window—all of them scrubbing away at the barrel planks, inside and out. The water splashes on every side and from all the taps into the drain gutters on the floor, running along the walls to the central drain pipe of the kitchen block.

"Hey, Piepel!" Their faces light up when Moni appears in the scullery. In Auschwitz, *Funktion* people feel themselves a closed family circle, like a clique of whites ruling a continent. And the family pet is the Piepel. All cosset him. All ears await every utterance of his lips. THE PIEPEL. The joy of the Funktioners in Auschwitz. The fondling.

One of the barrel washers passes near him as though just happening by. "There'll be some fresh grease along right away. You won't have to wait long," he lets fall out of the corner of his mouth, and goes off.

The window of the scullery frames the barbed-wire walls of the adjacent camp. A Czech transport has just been brought from Theresienstadt. A queer transport: whole families. Here, they have long forgotten what a whole family looks like. Outside, camplings keep bringing back barrels and planting them at the scullery entrance. Why do they scrub the barrels so hard? Moni mused. Everybody knows that before the barrels are brought back from the blocks the camplings lick them clean, inside and out. Wherever as much as the smell of the soup can possibly stick to the barrel, campling tongues penetrate. Cunning tongues of Mussulmen even know the art of getting under the iron hoops around the barrels. That is exactly why the barrel washers demand that the block orderlies watch out for barrel lickers. First of all, it really isn't hygienic! And then, it's bad for the *Funktion*! Because if the S.S. chef sees the barrels brought back so clean from the blocks, then why will he need all that gang of barrel washers? So: murder anyone who dares to come licking! More than one Mussulman has been clubbed to death by block orderlies beside an empty barrel. Nevertheless, whenever a barrel is being carried back to the kitchen, tongue-darting Mussulmen scurry along behind to snatch that one more lick at its wood.

The food porters park the empty barrels on their shoulders

beside the entrance, and flee for their lives. By the main path bordering on the kitchen compound stand the Mussulmen who had dogged the barrels, staring at the scullery entrance. Oh, there was so much licking left in those barrels standing there!

In the scullery, a row of basins is built into the walls. In two of them the barrels are washed, and in the two others soak the heaps of turnips which have been cut up for the cooks in the peelery next door. The washers scrub the wood of the barrels, all the while turning fawning glances on the Piepel. Vatzek, kapo of the peelery, comes in from the cauldron section carrying a white bowl covered with an overturned bowl. Everybody knows that Vatzek, the young Polish peasant, isn't much of a talker. Either he is silent, or else he screams bloody murder at you. You never know whether he is screaming because he is angry. Because in Auschwitz, Vatzek had learned from his masters, you must do as your betters do. In his style of speaking, Vatzek's model is Ludwig Tiene, the Camp Senior. That much is clear. It is not clear whom Ludwig Tiene is imitating.

Passing, Vatzek noticed Moni and halted beside him with the closed bowls in his hands. Lowering his eyes to the boot tips of his two firmly planted feet, like a bull about to charge, he erupted with a scream: "That whoreson, damn his mother, he better not send to me for any more spuds! That Franzl is starving you! What a way for a Piepel to look in camp! Drop him, Piepel! Drop him, I tell you! Any Block Chief will be tickled pink to have the Piepel with the pretty eyes. That whoreson better not dare send to me for spuds!" Done with his scream, he strode off to the potato store.

Although the bowl was covered, the aroma of roast meat lingered in the air of the scullery. The barrel washers enjoy Vatzek's jesting in high Auschwitz fashion. They know his style. They laugh. For a moment they have been diverted. They are surfeited with boredom. It is obvious that they hunger for a little diversion.

Near the scullery door, a campling lowers a barrel from his shoulder. In the process his glance falls on the sliced turnips brimming over the top of the basin. The campling keeps his two hands on the barrel, not withdrawing them, as though he has only just brought it. He stands there, back to the basin . . . nothing wrong with that, is there . . . he is just leaning the barrel over on its side . . . there seems to be a hole there . . . that's all that bothers him . . . maybe the hole should be mended . . . it's camp property! But the sly glances of the barrel washers see all, though they are now bent low over the barrels, scrubbing and rubbing industriously away. One of them approaches Moni.

"Don't look at the door, Piepel! There's soon going to be some fun here." The barrel washer's face is flushed with anticipation. His eyes are all a-glitter. He struggles hard to keep from exploding with laughter: mustn't look at the door. The quarry is moving right into the trap. If you look, you'll scare him off.

With rare industry they all work away. The bowed skeleton quakes over the barrel as though in a malarial seizure. He knows what a chance he is about to take. But the turnip flesh beckons to him from the basin: just a step, a reach, a snatch —and off. A thousand bells clang inside his brain. See how busy they all are. They don't even see you; they're not even thinking about you. You've been standing at the barrel all this time and nobody even knows whether it's now or before that you brought it. Put it back up on your shoulder. There. Nothing wrong with that. See? Nobody even bothers to glance at you.

The barrel washers feel that they are going to explode. They bury their heads in their work. The tension mounts. What fun. No ordinary quarry today. The campling again puts the barrel down on the ground. But this time just a little closer to the basin. How is he supposed to know that's forbidden? The basin? He isn't even looking at it. Never even occurred to him. But the barrel washers aren t paying any attention to you. Quick. Reach—

Whoops and yells. The work in which everybody was so immersed is cast aside. Brushes, brooms, barrels, scattered all over the concrete floor. The scullery is empty. All have hurried out to the compound. They are now hot in pursuit of a barefooted skeleton racing off on long spindle-legs. Long, bony hands, one of them clutching a chunk of yellow turnip stolen from the basin.

They lead him back. Upsleeved, brawny hands lead a human by his skeleton arms. They lead him across the spacious kitchen compound. Their eyes sparkle festively. A bright, translucent sky canopies the compound. The captive between their arms seems to be hovering in the air. He is now being accorded a great honor. Every man is accorded such an honor just once in his lifetime, when His Majesty Death offers him his hand and leads him off.

"It's turnips you wanted? . . . Turnips? . . . Now you'll get your turnips!"

Two bring a bench from the potato-peelery. A third comes along with Vatzek's truncheon. The fun is about to begin. What a bore scrubbing sucked barrels all day long! They knew that stinking Mussulman was going to reach for the basin.

"Well, come and get your turnips!"

The long body is slung across the bench. There is not a sound out of him. As though not the body of a human were lying here but a filthy long kitchen rag, flung across the bench to dry. But soon he will sound off: it's "twenty-five in the ass" for him. *Turnips! Was it turnips you wanted?*

At the first blow of the truncheon, the long rag starts up from the chair—and the fun is on. His eyes are abysses of Auschwitz fear. The hands of Death again take him by the arm and lead him wordlessly back to the bench. Slowly, carefully, he lies down across the bench again. Now the blows are no longer directed at the long skeleton of the campling, but at the invisible essence of a human life.

Vatzek comes in from the peelery. The bowl in his hand is now uncovered. One bowl is inside the other. He is carrying them back to the cauldron section. He passes by the execution rite without noticing it. Vatzek has had his fill of this sort of thing and he lets his apprentices have their little fun. As he passes, Moni looked up at him. "Kapo Vatzek," he called softly, "make them stop."

Vatzek cast a glance at the body prostrate on the bench and the truncheon poised in the hand of the flogger. "Turnips! . . . Turnips?! . . ." Only now Vatzek heard the words. His own words. It's from him they learned them. That is the way he screamed at camplings in his Auschwitz beginnings, when he used to catch them at this crime. Meanwhile, millions of them have passed through here and he has had his fill of flogging.

"Scum, damn your mother's hole!" Vatzek lashed at them. "Don't you know the Piepel wants the flogging stopped? Don't you know what a Piepel is in camp? I'll soon teach you to jump at a Piepel's command!"

The truncheon in the barrel washer's hand dropped sheepishly. The party is over. The barrel washers turn disappointed glances on the Piepel. Aw, Piepel! . . .

But they would not forgo the finale: the dumping of the flogged skeleton into the basin of cold water.

The campling is still flung across the bench. He heard Vatzek shout something, but he does not know what it is all about. The hands of the barrel washers seize him, lift him into the air, swing him forward, back, and into the basin full of cold water. The creature leaps right out. Opposite his eyes the doorway glares like a white splotch. He scampers out. The water drips from his frame. He runs across the kitchen compound more briskly than he had come here with the barrel. The vitality of his years never more to be lived now propels him towards his final hours. And on he runs.

"Whoresons! Where are those clean barrels?" One after the other the cooks come into the cauldron section. One after the other they peer into the row of clean barrels by the window. *"Moshiko! It's your ass if the barrels aren't ready. In a couple of minutes I'm opening the cauldron tap."*

Moshiko dashes over to the barrel which the cook has just inspected. He snatches the roll of scalding rag out of there and drops it into the very basin in which, just a moment ago, a human skeleton had been dunked.

Two seething desires: a cook's and a Mussulman's. Cooled and gelled in the same basin.

"Piepel, four breads or eight smokes?" the barrel washer makes his offer. "In this rag you've got nearly a whole pack of margarine."

From the direction of the camp gate the cart of the Corpse Kommando comes to haul away the piles of corpses from behind the back gates of the blocks. Two Kommando men pull the cart in front, and two push from behind. That cart up the road is being loaded and at any moment will leave for the crematorium full, and the cart just arriving is already back for another load. The piles grow by the hour.

Moni walked to the backpath. In his trouser pocket he carried the bread ration for Berele. He had deliberately taken a flat center piece, so it wouldn't show as he carried it. It has been several days since he has given him anything. Berele must be waiting desperately for him in the latrine. Thank God he is now able to give him something.

Both gate sections of the bread store were wide open. Block orderlies stood in line before the gate according to their block numbers, some holding long wooden bins, others carrying dark blankets. Shmulik, the kapo of the bread store, stood in the doorway with a pencil and paper in his hands. His assistants counted off the breads for each block according to the number of camplings who were still alive at morning roll call. Inside the store the breads were stacked from floor to ceiling like wide, high brick walls.

A short distance from the bread store the merchants waited. This is the best time to collect debts. Better now, before the breads are taken to the cubicles. It's risky to let a Block Chief pile up too big a debt with you. More than once a Block Chief had dragged a merchant into his cubicle and cooled him off: merchant liquidated—debt canceled.

Hundreds of human shadows drag by Moni, this way and that. Their blank stares collide with him as they seek something, not remembering what. They crawl down from their hutches, go out of their blocks to the latrine, but they no longer know the way. They cannot tell the front of the camp from the rear, where the latrine is located. All blocks look alike. Everywhere are the same rows of barbed wire and the same block gates. They no longer know the way, just as they no longer know that, before they felt the need to go to the latrine, the slimy excreta had already run out of them; it drips from their trouser hems onto their bare feet, without their even feeling it.

Thousands upon thousands. Merchants with breads inside their trousers cut a path through them. With contraband it is best to go amidst Mussulmen. No one pays attention. It is for them that Auschwitz was created: from the smokestacks to the barbed-wire walls, from the blocks to the sentries in the watchtowers. But here, on the backpath, it would seem that the real purpose for which they have been brought here is to provide cover for merchants and bread carriers and their like.

Moni's feet halted. At the end of a block Golden Lolek stood whispering with the camp's chief clerk. The clerk leaned sideways against the wall, with Lolek very close to him. Lolek was smiling coquettishly at him, with the side-glance he always turns on a Block Chief whenever he wants to get something out of him. The two of them looked as though nothing else existed around them, as though they were two lovers alone in Auschwitz.

If the clerk were not standing there with Lolek now, this would be the best time to go over and ask him to stay away from Franzl. A long while back he had been warned that Golden Lolek is playing up to Franzl. Why? What does Lolek need Franzl for? Moni halted in a corner of the assembly area: maybe the clerk will leave soon.

In the clear daylight, the golden bristles on Lolek's closely cropped nape glimmered at Moni's eyes. Lolek is blond and fleshy. His custom-fit riding breeches are tucked into small elegant boots. "Lolek!" Moni would have pleaded with him now, "you'll always be Piepel. You'll live to the liberation for sure. Don't play up to Franzl. Don't you have it good enough in block 7?"

Moni's eyes fell to the shoes on his feet: dusty, cracked, oversize. This is the first time he is examining them. *Is that a way for a Piepel to look in camp?* Vatzek's words now thundered anew in his ears and with a different meaning. Before, he had taken them for just another one of Vatzek's jests. Now they gave off the same smell as the German outcries in the ghetto during a flush of the bunkers.

Franzl is starving you! Moni flared up at himself. Everybody knows that Block Chiefs in Auschwitz don't starve their Piepels. He, only he is to blame for the way he looks! He snarled at himself: All right, so you can't eat, you were born that way, you're skinny by nature. But can't you at least dress like a *Funktion* man? Just look at yourself! Look at your pants, your jacket, rotting and wrinkled like a Musulman's! You want to be a Piepel looking like that? Look at Lolek and see what a Piepel is supposed to look like! Franzl needs you to clean the cubicle? Franzl doesn't even want you in his bed at night. You're going to burn in the crematorium, I tell you, and I won't feel one bit sorry for you, you stinking Mussulman!

He bent down to his feet. His trousers were short, not reaching to his shoes. His bony legs showed. He pulled up the red socks which he had never for a moment taken off. Mama had knitted them for him from her red wool shawl. At the collection point, before they were loaded into the wagons, she had taken them out of her rucksack. "Monkele," she said, "they're a present for your eleventh birthday." He smoothed them. They were torn inside. He folded and straightened their white border. He felt them with his fingers. Mama's. And suddenly, with his head bent to them, his eyes began to give tears: Mama. Mama, tell him not to threaten me with crematorium. I want to live. I want to get out of here. Mama. Don't let Lolek take my *Funktion* away from me. Make him stop playing up to Franzl.

The cart of the Corpse Kommando approached. Two kommando men lifted a skeleton, one by the head, the other by the feet. They swung the corpse in the air, forward, back, and heaved it on to the cart.

Naked corpses. In the hutches their neighbors had stripped them of their rags. Often, eyes in the hutch regard each other: Can we strip the rags off you already?

Mussulmen drag by, bumping into the cart and deflecting around it as though it were something that had no connection with them at all. Tomorrow, those same bearers will toss them: heave—onto the cart!

From the assembly area a third member of the Corpse Kommando came hurrying over, making straight for the corpse pile. The first two interrupted their work. The newcomer rummaged through the pile, selecting a corpse, turned it face up, pried its mouth open, peering into the cavity to make certain that it suited his purpose, and shoved a piece of paper deep inside it. The skull's mouth was frozen in skyward gasp. The kommando man took a fistful of white and yellow gold tooth crowns out of his trouser pocket, poured them into a rag, wrapped them into a little parcel, shoved it into the rigid mouth-cavity of the skeleton, and slammed the two rows of teeth shut. The kommando men picked this corpse up gingerly. They did not swing him in the air, they did not toss him, but laid him respectfully on the wagon. They tied a rag around his foot for identification later on. Now let the S.S. sentry at the gate search their pockets when they go out of camp. He'll find the pox, not gold.

The gold-hoarding skeleton vanished under the upper layer of corpses, as though he had never existed. He was no longer visible. At last he had fulfilled his destiny. As though for this alone he had been created. For this alone father's and mother's hands had tended him; for this he had grown into a man. For this he'd been sent to Auschwitz and turned into a skeleton—just so the cavity of his mouth should be spacious, fleshless, fit to serve as a stash for a fistful of gold crowns.

All at once pandemonium broke on the backpath. Merchants, Funktioners tore for the block gates to hide. "The Camp Senior! The Camp Senior!" No one knows better than a veteran campling the urgency of keeping out of Ludwig Tiene's sight. In a flash it was empty outside. The Camp Senior was stalking the block area!

Moni tore away from where he stood waiting for Lolek and made for his block—before anything else he must get rid of the margarine. Then he will go to the latrine to give Berele the bread portion.

"The Camp Senior! . . . The Camp Senior!" Only the stripe of red paint on the back of his jacket and on his cap testify that he, the vampire, is just another campling. Tall black boots, black trousers, a black jacket, a black cap on a rectangular tallowy cranium. You cannot see his eyes, just as you cannot see the eyes of the death's-head emblem on the S.S. cap. And just as there is no telling the age of the death's-head emblem, there is no telling how old Ludwig Tiene is.

Even before the Hitler period he had been sentenced to life imprisonment as a child killer and sex criminal. The Gestapo had scoured all the prisons of Germany to find the right man for the job of Camp Senior in Auschwitz, a man who would set the example for all the Auschwitz Block Chiefs. And the Gestapo knew whom they were looking for, because they knew what Auschwitz was intended for.

The moment Moni opened the front gate of his block and put a foot inside, an ominous silence hit him in the face. The block was empty, as though not a living soul were in it, and empty were the long passages on either side of the brick stove. From right and left of him the triple-tiered hutches exuded at him the fear stopping a thousand breaths. From the top Mussulman hutch, near the front gate, Rostek's oblong head peered at him. With a violent waving of his finger he summoned Moni.

"The Camp Senior is in the cubicle!" he whispered.

In the third tier, opposite the stash, lie only out-and-out Mussulmen. It is Zygmunt who put them there, as a charm against the evil eye and as guardians of his treasure opposite. For this purpose, Zygmunt always chooses Mussulmen in whom the nasty urge to eat has atrophied, who no longer even eat their own rations. He orders them to keep a sharp eye out for anyone who thinks he's going to steal into the stash at night. He is as sure of them as one can be sure of eunuchs in a harem. Zygmunt pays them off by promising not to ship them to the crematorium. And guard they do. Not to escape the crematorium—that no longer registers with them. They guard because they have been told to guard. Everything in their brains has dried out, except the single urge to carry out Zygmunt's command which still pulses in their unconscious. More than once an uncanny infantile cheeping rends the night silence. The night guard dashes over. What's happened? Nothing. One of the comatose Mussulmen had hallucinated a thousand-headed campling crawling up to the stash.

As soon as Ludwig Tiene had swept past the kitchen on his way to the cubicle *with Berele between his hands,* Rostek left his cooking and ran to hide in the Mussulman hutch. The block orderlies all lie hidden in their holes. They know who is in the block now. It is a game with Black Death Ludwig. Better to keep out of sight.

Rostek's pork-eyes stare furiously at the cubicle window. "Jesus Mary, why was the little bastard hanging around the block entrance? Didn't he know Franzl would toss him right into Tiene's trap? That little idiot didn't get into camp just yesterday! Whom was he looking for near Franzl's block? What did he think he was going to find here?"

After Dental Call, Ludwig Tiene turned up to collect his share from Franzl. But the gold was already hidden in the mouth of the dead Mussulman on the corpse cart. Franzl was in a predicament. They walked silently along. How would he make it good to Tiene? Arriving at block 12, Franzl suddenly saw Berele, his former Piepel, standing there like a frightened mouse, his eyes fixed on the front gate of his block. Franzl crept up on Berele from behind, swept him into the air, flung him writhing to Tiene, the way a chunk of meat is flung to the beast raging in its cage, and left.

Tiene carried Berele to Franzl's cubicle, like a black cat going off to a dark corner with its prey between its teeth.

Inside the cubicle, on the ground, a corner of Tiene's downflung black jacket lay like the back of some monstrous bug. Beneath it—a little boy's trousers: Berele's. The red streak of paint running down the center of the jacket seemed like an ooze of blood from Berele's trousers.

Moni shivered. He lay on his stomach in the third-tier hutch beside Rostek, both looking at the cubicle window.

Whom was the bastard looking for near the block? The hard crust of the bread in his trouser pocket now cut into his thigh.

"That's the way all Piepels peg out," Rostek snarled. "Either the Block Chiefs croak them, or they wind up in the claws of that vampire. He should have known."

From the cubicle came uncanny laughter. The laughter rattled like a heavy iron chain dragging across the floor of an empty factory. "Khi-khi-khi-khi-khi-khik . . . Piepel! . . . Kho-kho-kho . . . Piepel! . . . Piep-pel-l-l! . . ." The shrill laughter muffled the boy's ebbing moans for help.

In the hutches of the block lie a thousand camplings, disgorged from wagon exits towards crematorium entrances. They do not know and they do not care what is going on inside the cubicle. They are merely transients here, and whatever goes on there, at the front of the block, does not interest them. They only know that dread, Auschwitz dread, now pervades the block. And that is normal. That is self-evident. So each of them can go on spinning the golden dream of them all. As soon as they stop that laughing in the cubicle, they will probably start handing out the soup from the barrels.

Rostek is furious. How the hell much longer is it going to take? The potatoes are going to get burned on him in the kitchen. Why did that little whoreson have to bring the black death in now? It's all that bastard's fault.

The door of the cubicle swung open. The death's-head stood in the doorway. "Block orderlies!!!" came the roar.

Out of all their hiding-places they came leaping. Ludwig Tiene pointed into the cubicle. "Get rid of it!" he commanded.

As soon as the front gate had closed on Tiene, Rostek sent a mouthful of spit arching from the top hutch to the gate. He heaved himself up off his belly, snatched the rag with the margarine which Moni had brought, let his bulk down from the hutch, and went off to the kitchenette.

Four block orderlies carried a black blanket out of the cubicle, two by the front corners, two by the rear corners. A longish mass—it might have been several camp breads—weighed down the blanket. They passed down the entire length of the block to the back gate. Of the thousand in the hutches, no one looked to see. They shoved open the gate to the backpath, and dumped Berele from the blanket on to the corpse pile.

The boy's belly still breathed, slowly rising and falling. Moni stood quivering near the pile, eyes distended. He did not know whether Berele was alive or dead. The boy lay motionless on the corpse pile, as though the fear of death in strangulation were still scurrying about within his open eyes. All at once, Moni no longer saw the bones of the Mussulman pile beneath Berele. They were now a part of the Auschwitz commonplace which the eye no longer notices for its everydayness. Except that now, suddenly, someone dead lay on them, someone really dead.

Moni's legs buckled. He sank to the ground. His hand pressed the bread relic in his pocket. Now he was all alone in camp. Berele, his only friend, will soon be loaded on the corpse cart.

A terror of loneliness seized him.

SAN YSIDRO RANCH ■ 900 SAN YSIDRO LANE ■ MONTECITO, CALIFORNIA 93108
TELEPHONE (805) 969-5046 ■ FAX (805) 565-1995

4

It was only the day before yesterday.

Everybody had run out of the blocks. Everybody had dashed to the barbed wire by the backpath to behold the marvelous sight, the miracle.

Block Chiefs hurried from their cubicles without their truncheons, shoving arms into sleeves of hastily snatched jackets. Cooks in aprons, sleeves uprolled, had left the steaming cauldrons just before the margarine was to be thrown in; smooth-faced clerks had hastened from the Camp Office; potato peelers with paring knives in muddy fingers; merchants just closing major latrine deals—all streamed to the barbed wire by the backpath. And like in a torrent sweeping everything with it, the Mussulmen, too, were carried along. They swirled amidst the hurrying mass as upright straws in a whirlwind, gaping glassy-eyed at what was going on here. Everybody shoved to look. All faces were turned to the adjacent camp just the other side of the barbed wire. Short ones stood on tiptoe, craning their necks this way and that to catch a good view between shoulders, above heads.

"Children!"

"Children are playing here!" mouths breathed ecstatically.

"They've been brought from Theresienstadt!"

"Whole kindergartens with the teachers!"

"Boys!"

"Girls!"

They caper about there as in a large schoolyard. Boys in short trousers, girls in little frocks. Hair! . . . Not bare skeleton-heads, but hair under this Auschwitz sky! . . . Wide ribbon bows woven into brunette hair, blonde hair, chestnut hair; bounding hair—braided, curled, pony-tailed. A sun has burst over Auschwitz.

Sated faces of well-dressed Prominents, whose presence none dared approach, now mingled with campling riffraff and gaped with the same moist-eyed fascination as they—and the common camplings—they stared, stared, as though suddenly they, too, had become people. Together they stood, lowly campling skull by Block Chief shoulder. The Millennium.

Young kindergarten teachers, silk stockings on shapely legs, ran after children who in the excitement of the game of tag had dashed to the forbidden zone near the barbed wire. S.S. sentries in the watchtowers, who usually itched to let go a bullet at such strays, waved their fingers before their noses in fatherly warning to the youngsters: "Now—now. *Verboten!* . . ." The teachers seized the children by their little hands, drawing them away from the forbidden zone, and with shy, sisterly smiles returned the greetings of the male camplings watching them from the other side of the wire wall. The girls were just as startled at this incredible surprise of Auschwitz.

Why, there's life here! . . .

A sun had splashed upon Auschwitz. Children clambered up the rungs of the play ladder. Reaching the top, they shouted gleefully as they zoomed down the long slide into the yellow sand as into a soft lap. On the seesaw, bare little girlish thighs revealed themselves as short dresses parasoled open and shut in the blue-skied breeze: see, saw, see, saw. Why had it all been set up? Where had it all sprouted from?

Men, women. Coming out of the blocks there as in a summer resort. Whole families. Here and there a mother approaches her child in the playground, unwraps a goodie, feeding it into the little mouth, holding the wrapper for a saucer under the chin. Mustn't let the crumbs go to waste. Children form a circle, and with their hands go clap-clap-clap. Inside the circle a little girl dances near the feet of her circlemates, piping a song—*just like in Miss Zoshka's kindergarten,* Moni's heart quivered.

. . . . Only the day before yesterday.

Now the block gates there gape empty. Silent. You do not see a living soul there; there is none.

They took the whole camp of them last night. An entire camp—all at once. All night the lorries pulled out for the crematorium. Mothers and fathers together. Children with their kindergarteners. All together. Out of the bowels of the dark, far, far off, carried the stridor of the Auschwitz brass band, and the cymbals sucked up the wailing of infants at the crematorium.

Empty blocks. Only the day before yesterday they had been full; just two days ago people were sitting inside them writing letters all day, as though by command: to acquaintances, to friends, to family. All over Europe these letters are now being delivered—the letters of the Theresienstadters, all bearing the same message:

"Life goes on in Auschwitz! . . ."

This is why they had been brought here; this is why they had not been taken directly from the wagons to the crematorium—to write the letters first, in their own hand.

It is all emptiness there, now. The open blocks are airing themselves of the din of the outside life which they had left behind like a strange after-smell. Only the play ladder and its slide stand in the center of the compound. Tiny footprints in the yellow sand. Silence . . .

Only the day before yesterday. Lungs of Funktioners had suddenly inhaled the air of a human world: Auschwitz was no longer a lost planet spinning away in oblivion. Auschwitz had suddenly landed on earth to become a part of it. Orderlies and Block Chiefs had suddenly discovered human feelings in themselves—and they were staggered. The feelings had overwhelmed them like oxygen which they had not breathed so long they had forgotten its savor.

Moni tore his glance from the emptiness of the camp on the other side of the barbed wire. His eyes halted on the shut door of the Camp Office. Why doesn't Lolek come out? Lolek won't dare stay there more than a minute or two. It's a very dangerous place for Piepels. Everybody knows that Ludwig Tiene is liable to turn up there suddenly.

A few minutes ago, when Moni noticed Lolek walking along in the distance, he did not call out to him, but set out after him so it should appear to Lolek that they just happened to run into each other. Now Moni was ready to have it out with him. Just let him remember, more than one doublecrossing Piepel has got the seesaw from Holy Dad! Everybody knows it's the Piepel's life if he cheats on his Block Chief! Moni had almost caught up with him when Lolek suddenly swerved off the main path and disappeared into the Office.

What business does Lolek have in the Office now anyway? What makes him keep switching Block Chiefs? What's he trying to get out of them? What drives him to them? He is always flirting with somebody else's Block Chief. Stands together with his new lover staring somewhere across the barbed wire, whispering with him, giving him that cute sidesmile of his. If only Lolek hasn't gone in there to get switched to another block again! What goes on inside that Lolek? What are his eyes always looking for on the other side of the wire?

Swarms of skeletons drifted aimlessly about. Here and there amidst their naked skulls jutted an empty barrel riding on a campling's shoulder. Mussulmen scurrying after the barrel, rising on tiptoes, darting desiccated tongues to lick. Lick.

Suddenly, the Office door opened. Moni leaped back. The first to come out was his Block Chief, Franzl; behind him—Lolek. Arm in arm they walked in step up the main path. *Where can they be going? Only not to block 12!*

He tagged after them. All at once he felt superfluous, cast out of the camp, dumped into the stream of Mussulman refuse sloshing by him.

With a shock the reality of the camp hit him. As though he had just arrived; as though a moment ago he had not been here at all. All those milling around him became a vortex sucking him in like a drop in a raging current. Soon, he will be swept along with them.

From the adjacent camp on the other side of the barbed wire, the mute emptiness blared at him. Only now he felt the people's being there yesterday and their overnight disappearance. He now felt his own body and skin in their disappearance.

The day before yesterday a kindergarten had been there, just like Miss Zoshka's kindergarten in Kongressia. How long is it since he was in Miss Zoshka's kindergarten? The days he loved most were when Ma used to come to fetch him from kindergarten. It was always so bright and sunny outside. Hand-in-hand they would stroll home between the two rows of trees on Park Street. "Ma, why is everybody looking at you?" he used to ask. "Because I'm walking with the prettiest little boy in the world," Ma would smile.

You mustn't walk behind them, he warned himself. If Franzl suddenly turns his head and sees you, he'll be sure that the only way of getting rid of you is to take you into the cubicle and seesaw you. Moni knew he was risking his life by following them. But he could not tear his eyes from Lolek's back. A moment ago he had been ready to lay it on him. Now he felt so inferior, so shabby against the blue elegance of the woollen pullover hugging Lolek's round shoulders; against the little Prominent's cap cocked so coquettishly on Lolek's head.

His feet could not restrain themselves from following them. Now he knew for certain that he would never have it out with Lolek. So he prayed at the back of Lolek walking along with Franzl: "Lolek, don't go into block 2! Please, please don't! You're pretty. You'll never be hard up for a *Funktion*. After the war I'll take you to my house and I'll tell my whole family. See? This is Golden Lolek! My best friend in Auschwitz. Franzl wanted him to be his Piepel, but he wouldn't. Just as I wouldn't be Piepel for Willi in block 7, because I knew that Willi would seesaw Shimmek, his Piepel, because of me. You'll see, Lolek, I'll take you riding on my bike, and we'll—No, Lolek! Don't! Don't go into the block! . . ."

"Oh, Lolek, why did you do this to me? . . ."

5

"Block Chiefs to the Camp Senior! Pass the word!" The cry flashed along the empty main path in the early morning darkness.

The red night bulbs burning on the long wire wall merged in Moni's eyes to a fiery streak. "Block Chiefs to the Camp Senior! Pass the word! . . ." the gate of block 7 tore open. Willi hurried out to report to the Camp Senior. Moni quickly pressed himself against the wall of block 7 so that Willi should not catch sight of him.

This hour before dawn is the best time for the Block Chiefs to divide the loot of the transport brought in the previous night. Directly from the wagons, before taken to the "Sauna,"[1] the newcomers are marched into a huge block, where they are commanded to strip. Those who have brought their valuables hidden away in their clothing make rapid calculations: what if they search the clothing while they are gone? The brain is on fire. There is no time to think. Eyes scurry around, feverishly seeking: a long block, without a thing in it— just bare brick walls enclosing half-naked people. They

[1] *Sauna:* Auschwitz designation for the gas chamber, which was built like a shower room.

mill around you, shove you, look through you with the same feverish eyes, just as you look at them and do not see them. All at once, right under your feet, you feel the tilt of a floor tile. Swiftly you stoop, ostensibly to put down your bundle of clothing, and you lift the tile: empty underneath! A god-sent hiding-place right under your feet. Quickly you dig your valuables out of your clothes: a multi-carat blue-white diamond; or a pearl necklace; or just a keepsake from a beloved, more precious than any gem. Your hands replace the tile which fits the hole perfectly. No eye will notice the slightest crack. You place your clothes on top of it, to mark the spot, and, relieved, you march naked to the Sauna.

Afterwards, the Block Chiefs do not have to search through myriad items of clothing. They go directly to the stashes beneath the tiles which they themselves had prepared in advance or reach right in behind the wall bricks which they had previously loosened, and pile by pile rake in the last guarded heirlooms of plundered Europe. *All Block Chiefs to the Camp Senior!* Now it is split-up time.

Moni peered out of his hiding-place at the front gate of block 7. Something had told him yesterday that Willi would bring himself a fresh Piepel from the platform. He saw it in Willi's eyes and immediately ran away from the block. And he had not been wrong. He never waits till the last minute. Not like the other Piepels. He is always just a moment ahead, and this moment always turns out to be the one that saves him from sure death.

His eyes were riveted on the front gate. Perhaps the Piepel who took his place will come out and he'll be able to call him right over. The new Piepel won't turn him down. His heart tells him the new Piepel will be all right. They'll go out to the backpath together so Willi shouldn't see him, Moni, hanging around his block. It's best on the backpath now. There all the skeletons are waiting for "clean-up" time to end. He will promise the new Piepel: "I'll teach you new love-tricks. I know exactly what Willi likes. You'll be good with him at night." He will tell him: "I knew right off you were all right. My heart told me." He always "knows." His heart always "tells him." But somehow it always turns out otherwise. Not a single Piepel is ready to risk his *Funktion* for you. Nobody will give you a hand in Auschwitz. He has already been Piepel to most of the Block Chiefs in camp. *The Piepel with the maidenhead eyes* . . . At first, they can't wait to get a taste of you, but next thing you know it's all over. Good thing Berele told him how to give them the slip in time. Otherwise, he would long ago have gone flying out of the smokestack.

On the main path opposite him Funktioners hurried along. Merchants rushed to the latrine with loaves of bread inside their trousers. *In Auschwitz there are just six hours between a full belly and an empty one* . . . When you're Piepel, everybody honeys you. The Piepel—Queen of the Block. The highest *Funktion.* He just could not understand: Why, when he has everything for the taking, is he unable to eat? Why, when he can have all the bread, margarine, sausage and soup he wants, is he full, but the minute he loses his *Funktion* he goes wild with hunger? Now, he could gorge himself all day and night without stopping. Let God just help him get back on *Funktion,* and he'll know what to do this time. He swears he'll be good. He'll eat and eat and never stop. But oh, he knows that as soon as he manages to get back on *Funktion* in some new block, and as soon as he has eaten his fill just once again, he won't be able to stand the sight of food. It's always that way. He knows it's suicide. But he can't help himself. Almost all the Block Chiefs have tried him already. And every time he runs away from another cubicle, it is that much harder for him to get back on *Funktion.* But he just can't help himself.

He sat in the sand packed against the side of the block. They must still be cutting the bread into rations inside, he mused. His glance fell on his shoes. All at once he saw them as a revelation: the shoes. He still has shoes. On account of them he doesn't belong with the backpath lot. The shoes and the cap still give him the right to go out to the main path even now if he feels like. Those there are barefooted. They mustn't be on the main path now. No, you don't belong with the backpathers! You're an old campbird. The lot of them were still nothings in their ghettos when you were already an old-time Piepel in Auschwitz. "See that number on your arm, Moni?" Holy Dad once told him. "That makes you an old campbird. But you botched it all up yourself. A Piepel's got to pack a load of meat on his ass." Everybody tells him the same thing. Every single one of them.

He looked wistfully out to the main path. Funktioners, merchants, all hurrying busily on their rounds. He could not bear the knowledge that he was no longer one of them. They don't even have the time to remember they are in camp. They breathe a different air—the air of *Funktion* and main path. His heart grabbled for this air, like someone in a last desperate effort to hang on to the edge of the precipice. Will he ever be one of them again? Or will he now drop off into the swarming abyss of the backpath and there, together with the rest of them, stream off to the crematorium?

He looked back to the front gate. Maybe the Piepel will come out now the way he, Moni, came out of there the first time. Maybe the new Piepel is like him. Maybe Willi has also put the new Piepel in the light of the red lamp in the cubicle, looked him deep in the eyes, and said: "Like a maidenhead..." Maybe the new Piepel now feels exactly as he felt then. Maybe the new Piepel is as lonely in there as he was the first time. Maybe the front gate will open in a minute, and the new Piepel will come out because he can no longer stand it there—in the depressing red-lit cubicle and the frightening emptiness of the long, dark block. He'll come out. Moni will quietly call to him: Piepel! Piepel! They'll be friends. Real pals. He'll have a pal in Auschwitz. A pal to look after him in case he doesn't get back on *Funktion*. A pal to bring him bread in the latrine, the way he used to bring bread to Berele—

Berele . . . A cold shiver ran through Moni. Isn't it his fault that Berele is dead? Berele came to block 12 because he thought that he, Moni, his best pal, had forgotten all about him. He leaped up in panic. Just as Franzl stole up on Berele, Willi might come back any moment from the Camp Senior, sweep him up from behind and toss him right into Ludwig Tiene's hands—

He fled across the assembly area to the backpath. He was sucked into the mass of camplings like a drop returning to sea.

He stood near a heap of naked Mussulman bones which had been tossed out of the blocks during the night. He looked at the heap of bones and they did not seem to be there at all. He saw only the naked body of Berele, his pal Berele, who hadn't been around for months now. He saw him as he had seen him then, dumped onto just such a heap, Berele gazing at him with open eyes. And as he did then, Moni let himself down towards him beside the pile of dead Mussulmen.

"I'm very lonely, Berele," Moni spoke to him. "I have no *Funktion,* Berele. Almost all the Block Chiefs have tried me. Remember, Berele, how you taught me: 'A Piepel's heart feels.' That's exactly what I do. I always run away beforehand. But no Piepel comes to me through the main gate in the morning the way I used to come to you. I always wait by the gates the way you waited for me. But nobody comes. Why? Why don't they come out, Berele?" He wept into the pile of dead bones. Around him thousands of skeletons fidgeted. They did not notice him, just as they did not notice the mound of dead bones before their eyes. "I'm afraid when I'm by the gates. I'm afraid the Block Chief will hand me over to Tiene. I don't want them to carry me out of the cubicle in a dark blanket. Help me, Berele. Tell me what to do. The Block Chiefs don't want me any more. Tell me how to make them want me. Oh, Berele, what do I have to do so they should want me?"

6

"As for me, sir, I'm not asking anything for myself," Heller excitedly declared, with the magnanimous air of a public-spirited citizen. "I haven't come pleading for myself. You probably don't realize, sir, that the Rabbi of Shilev is in your block! What a miracle that he has happened to come under your charge!"

Fruchtenbaum, Chief Orderly of block 10, stood with one hand in his trouser pocket, looking the Jew in the eye. He let him finish his piece. He was accustomed to this. It never failed every time a new transport arrived.

Behind him stood the block orderlies. The spectacle about to take place here already reflected itself in the knowing twinkle in their eyes. That big-talking greenhorn, so cock-sure of himself—in nothing flat he's going to find himself out there on top of the corpse pile! The very thought startled even them, the Auschwitz block orderlies. Killing a campling? Nothing to it! So you squash a cockroach. But that fellow! He just got here. He's still human.

Heller had been a leading citizen of Metropoli, a man of property, an active Zionist. When he arrived in Auschwitz today and learned that the Chief Orderly of block 10 was the son of the Zionist leader, Fruchtenbaum, he could not contain himself and rushed directly to him. "Young man!" Heller addressed Fruchtenbaum amiably, as he would have back in his own elegant prewar office. "Do you see that cot there, the one I'm pointing to? Well, that is the Rabbi of Shilev in there. And that red-skinned one near him is the well-known Zionist writer, Ferber. Your father, sir, certainly knew of him. Now don't you think for a moment that I am a follower of rabbis or that I ever was. But we must help! It goes without saying, young man, they must be helped! It's simply a miracle that the Rabbi of Shilev was put in your block."

Unruffled, Fruchtenbaum went on standing there, hand in pocket, paunch projecting more than there actually was belly —Fruchtenbaum's favorite pose. As though it lent him importance. When at last Heller was through, Fruchtenbaum leisurely sent the cane leaping up in his hand to the center, then lazily, amiably tapped the cane's steel axe-handle on the chest of the excited messenger as he asked casually, nonchalantly, one might say almost phlegmatically!

"You know me, bud?"

"I know your father, sir." *Bud? Why should he say "Bud" to him? After all, he, Heller, has sons older than that one. And even if this is Auschwitz why shouldn't Fruchtenbaum's son respect his elders?* "Do I know you, sir? Of course I know you. You're Fruchtenbaum's son. What a question, whether I knew Fruchtenbaum! At many a rally I had the honor of sitting on the platform during one of your father's addresses. The Rabbi of Shilev had his followers, and Fruchtenbaum had his. I, for one, was a follower of your father's. Still, if the Rabbi of Shilev is in Auschwitz, it is the solemn duty of each and every one of us to save him. One thing has nothing to do with the other."

"So what did you say my name was, bud?" Fruchtenbaum resumed tapping the axe-handle against Heller's chest.

Heller's eyelids began to blink nervously, racing open and shut without cease. Foreboding began to form in his heart. In Auschwitz you can tangibly feel Death casting His shroud over you. Heller began to wonder whether he had not made a mistake. A terrible suspicion dawned on him. No! He had been expressly told: *Fruchtenbaum's son!* "Your name? Fruchtenbaum is your name. Fruchtenbaum. Fruchtenbaum's son."

Too swiftly for the eye to follow, the sharp edge of the little steel axe landed in Heller's head, like a hatchet splitting a tree trunk, then another stroke, another, and another. Inside of seconds he was transformed from a human shape into a shredded masque of gore, with blood spouts for eyes. Just seconds.

Fruchtenbaum stood there impassive, hand in trouser pocket, waiting patiently for the wobbly, retreating feet to hit the pillar of the hutch and halt. On Heller's right and on his left the block orderlies stood in two rows. Fruchtenbaum's eyes followed the buckling retreat like a billiard player watching the ball after he has cued off.

When the masque at last stood as though nailed to the pillar, Fruchtenbaum came up at him and again tapped the axe-handle against the bloodied chest, tapped casually, nonchalantly, one might almost say indifferently.

"What did you say my name was, bud?" he asked.

Orbs of blood peered out of the masque. The uprooted mouth was now a pulp of shredded flesh dangling by strands, not moving, merely panting heavily, like a dog's dangling tongue.

"So what did you say my name was?" Again the question remained hanging in the air.

One of the block orderlies standing near the hutch tried to coach him. "Say *Herr* Chief Orderly!"

Fruchtenbaum snapped his eyes at the orderly. He snarled: "Don't coach him, you whoreson. Nobody asked you!" And into the air flashed the steel axe-handle, up and down, up and down.

A mangled, featureless mass of flesh writhed on the floor. An uncanny voice shrieked out of it without cease: "*Herr* Chief Orderly! . . . *Herr* Chief Orderly! . . . Jews, help! . . . *Herr* Chief Orderly! . . . Help! Jews, help! . . ."

But Fruchtenbaum no longer heard. He was in the grip of a murderous frenzy—the frenzy which seized him whenever anyone reminded him of his origins. "Take him inside!" Fruchtenbaum commanded his orderlies.

From the cubicle came several throttled cries for help. "*Herr* Chief Orderly!" Then it was still. Several minutes later, the door opened. Block orderlies dragged a dead man to the pile behind the block.

A rage of madness seizes Fruchtenbaum every time anybody utters his surname. He would destroy root and all anybody knowing who he is. There is no telling what drives Fruchtenbaum to seek to drown his name in a sea of blood. Perhaps he fears that his aristocratic birth will hinder his career in Auschwitz; or perhaps he does not want anyone to survive who might later bear witness to his deeds in Auschwitz. In any case, mere utterance of the name Fruchtenbaum sends him into a bloodthirsty rage. He is to be called "*Herr* Chief Orderly." That, and only that. Block Chiefs, to be sure, call him simply Fruchtenbaum. But Fruchtenbaum holds Prominents in even greater awe than the lowest of camplings. He is overjoyed that they deign to address him at all.

Almost every new transport to Auschwitz brings several who are dazzled by the name Fruchtenbaum, and are drawn to him like flies to the sweet poison. From each transport Fruchtenbaum selects a victim as an example to the rest: "*Herr* Chief Orderly."

Fruchtenbaum especially detests religious Jews. His eyes flare with especial fire whenever a religious Jew falls into his hands. Not to speak of a rabbi! So as soon as he had done with Heller, he summoned the two would-be protégés from their hutch. At the first glance he knew which was the Rabbi. The head of one of them was covered with a torn piece of Auschwitz jacket sleeve for a skull-cap. With utter loathing Fruchtenbaum sized the two of them up. His face contorted in genuine pain at the fact that the likes of these were still alive. Although Fruchtenbaum usually spoke Polish, he addressed the Rabbi of Shilev in burlesque Yiddish. Hand in trouser pocket he stood there eyeing the Rabbi, while his clenched teeth ground out the "R" in anti-Semitic fashion: "*R-r-r-rebbetzin!* Mrs. R-r-r-rabbi!"

His mind now set to work concocting a death to serve them.

Moni came out of the latrine. He carried the pack of cigarettes in his armpit. He was pleased. Since becoming Piepel in block 10 he had changed completely. He was a new person. Not the way he used to be. No Block Chief will have cigarettes today except Bruno, his Block Chief. Because he, Moni, always plans ahead. And if there is just a single pack of cigarettes left in camp, Zalke doesn't sell it to any orderly or Chief Orderly. Just to him. Moni doesn't trust anyone else to take care of his Block Chief. He sees to everything himself. He is in charge of all the block business, and he runs it so that Bruno has everything he wants. Meals, laundry, afternoon nap—everything right on the dot.

Other Piepels are spoiled dolls, leaving everything to merchants and sub-merchants to take care of. And their Block Chiefs are often left without a cigarette. Those dolls don't know that sooner or later they pay for their sloppiness. A sad thought suddenly darkened Moni's gloating: Bruno hasn't been using him much at night. Lately, Bruno has been hungrily eyeing other Piepels. Moni pressed the pack of cigarettes in his armpit. The Chief Orderlies were running around the latrine like poisoned rats trying to beg cigarettes for their Block Chiefs. Good for that trash, those whoresons! He was having his sweet revenge. Today Bruno will be satisfied with *him.* No one else could have got Bruno a cigarette today. Certainly not Fruchtenbaum, his Chief Orderly. The merchants can't stand him. And they're right, too. Fruchtenbaum is a conceited lickspittle. He makes you want to vomit the way he bootlicks his betters and tramples those below him. He often makes you cringe the way he honeys you in block 10.

He walked along the main path. Food porters with carrying rods in their hands rushed out of the blocks to the kitchen to bring the soup barrels. They will now bring the dream of the past twenty-four hours to the blocks: two food porters in front, two food porters in the rear, the soup barrel on its perch of rods like a sultana in her palanquin.

Moni continued towards the assembly area. There two camplings were doing *Sport:* knee-bends. They squatted—Auschwitz regulation-style—their rumps precisely two inches from the ground, each holding a brick in his hands high overhead, skipping bird-like from one end of the assembly area to the other, back and forth, back and forth. To keep up the skipping, Fruchtenbaum stood over them hand in trouser pocket, flaunting his paunch, cane handle tapping against boot upper.

"Piepel!" he called cheerily as he caught sight of Moni. "Get a load of the *R-r-r-rebbetzin!* Know what *R-r-r-rebbetzin* means? And that's his sexton. A red sexton. If these two cruds aren't in the pile after one hour of *Sport,* then nothing is ever going to happen to them in Auschwitz."

As he skipped, the eyes of the Rabbi of Shilev looked up to Moni. Moni went on. This is nothing new. In every assembly area you can see Chief Orderlies putting camplings through *Sport.* Frequently a whole block does *Sport* in the middle of the night. Just so; no special reason. Particularly when it is freezing cold, or when there is a lashing downpour. Several groups are doing their *Sport* separately in the same assembly area, as in a schoolyard. The Chief Orderlies thus try to show their Block Chiefs, the Camp Senior and the watchtowers that they are doing their job. No idlers they.

Moni left the assembly area behind him. He opened the block gate. The cubicle was empty. Bruno's Auschwitz uniform, freshly laundered and ironed, hung on the outside of the closet door. Moni took the pack of cigarettes out from under his armpit. He smoothed it and put it in the pocket of the hanging jacket. At roll-call, when Bruno puts on the clean jacket and sticks his hand into the pocket, won't he be surprised to find the cigarettes! A whole pack of cigarettes! Bruno will certainly smile to himself as usual, and he will be satisfied. Moni took a few steps back to examine the jacket from a distance. The opening of the pocket containing the cigarettes was slightly ajar. He did not want Bruno to know right off that there was something in there. He took out the pack of cigarettes, replacing it horizontally, and with his hand smoothed the pocket opening. Now you couldn't tell there was anything in the pocket. But out of the stripes of Bruno's Auschwitz uniform the Rabbi's eyes did not cease gazing at him. He could not shake their gaze. *That's a R-r-r-rebbetzin.* And the eyes gaze at him. Moni turns his glance from Bruno's uniform and the eyes continue to look at him. From the open window, from the shut door—wherever he turns his head they gaze at him. Whose are those eyes? Where has he seen them before? *Moni has Ma's eyes, velvet black like Grandpa the Rabbi* . . . Ma's look . . . Ma's eyes . . .

He dashed out of the block. He passed the assembly area where the two camplings were still hopping. He wanted to say something. But since when does a Piepel interfere in such matters? His feet carried him on. All the Chief Orderlies do the same. Does he think he's going to change things at Auschwitz? Suddenly he veered around and strode to the assembly area. "Fruchtenbaum!" he commanded. He was amazed at the firmness of his "Fruchtenbaum!" But everybody knows that Fruchtenbaum falls all over himself before higher-ranking Prominents. "Get rid of them first. I've got a deal for you."

"For you, Piepel, anything! Scram, worms!" Fruchtenbaum snarled at them. "Get out of my sight!"

"The camp is out of potatoes today," Moni whispered confidentially to him. "Double over to Vatzek at the peelery and let him give you the last of his potatoes. I thought I'd make Bruno some pancakes for lunch today. Get me, Fruchtenbaum? He'll come across. And how!" Moni said, thrusting into Fruchtenbaum's pocket the pack of cigarettes he had brought from the latrine. "And how he'll come across!"

Bruno drained the bottle of schnapps into his mouth, then hurled it at the locker, where everything lay in perfect order. With a crash the glass of the bottle splattered all over the cubicle. "I need a Piepel!" he shouted. "A fat-assed Piepel!"

Moni backed slowly towards the cubicle door. His hands were loaded with the dishes he had just removed from the table after Bruno had finished eating. He went out with the dishes, took them into the kitchenette. He put them down, the call of his heart roaring alarm in his ears: "Run, Moni! Run for your life!" But how? Bruno is in the cubicle. He might call him suddenly: "Piepel!" What will he do then? . . . The white tablecloth is still spread on the table in the cubicle. He must go on and take it off. And in his ears hammered: *I need a Piepel! . . . Run, Moni! . . . I need a Piepel! . . . Moni, run for your life!* He knew that he had to run away, but he knew that his life now lay in the area between the kitchenette window and the cubicle window. His life is not his own, but his Block Chief's. By what right can he take it and run off? Steal something that belongs to the Block Chief and run away?

"Run, Moni!" his heart pounded at him.

Stealthily he pressed open the knob of the kitchen door, and as stealthily let it close back into place. Bruno's window glinted opposite. He turned to the main gate. A horizontal patch of daylight through the chink above the gate illuminated the area which he now had to cross. If the gate lets out its usual creak when he opens it, Bruno will hear it in the cubicle, and he will be right there on the threshold, firing at his back: "Piepel!"

"Run away, Moni!" his heart shrieked at him.

Moni snatched up his life. Caching it away in his person like a stolen article, he gingerly stepped towards the rear gate. On both sides, along the walls, a thousand camplings lay in their hutches. Silence filled the block. He did not run, so as not to arouse suspicion. A long way. He will now have to pass down the entire length of the block. He mustn't turn his head because the door of the cubicle might suddenly open, and Bruno will come out, and notice the emptiness in the spot where something of his had been a moment ago. The spoors of the absent Piepel are still there like the outlines of a missing article in the dust. Bruno will run his glance from the empty spot to Moni's receding back. He will connect the two. "Piepel!" he will shout–

Mietchu, the Piepel of 17, had also wanted to escape at the last moment. He had opened the main gate–and run smack into the chest of the entering Block Chief. "Where you off to, Mietchu? Too late to run away from your sweetheart." The Block Chief took him by the hand and led him back into the cubicle. He had already been pledged to the Camp Senior as a personal gift. Soon Ludwig Tiene arrived in the cubicle.

Moni knew that behind him his back was now exposed to the Block Chief's eye. He walked on feet nakedly crossing a bed of hot coals.

Suddenly: "Piepel! . . . Piepel! . . ." from behind him.

He froze in mid-step. The call "Piepel" clamped iron fingers on his shoulder, the hand of Auschwitz law. He stood there petrified, facing the rear gate.

"Piepel! Piepel!" came the call.

Tautly Moni turned his head, like one condemned to the hands tightening the noose around his neck. From a hutch behind him, a bony arm reached out. "Piepel," someone in there called to him. He knew that he must not move another step lest the call "Piepel" be repeated. Quickly he turned around and entered the narrow aisle to the hutch.

"Piepel, the Rabbi of Shilev wishes to thank you for saving his life."

On the boards in the center of the hutch sat the Rabbi of Shilev, the piece of torn sleeve capping his skull. Silent skeletons sat cross-legged in a semicircle around him—his devotees Their eyes were raptures of devotion, their silence not the silence of Mussulmen. It was as though in the boards of this hutch there were no Auschwitz. *If those two cruds aren't on the pile behind the block today, nothing is ever going to happen to them . . .* Many weeks have since passed. Auschwitz weeks. He had long forgotten all about it. He had not seen them since. Common camplings don't get the chance to come in contact with his class of Prominents. The pale, bony arm which had summoned him was pointing to the one seated in the center. "Piepel, the Rabbi of Shilev says thank you."

The eyes of the Rabbi of Shilev rested on him. Deep, soft as velvet. He felt like nestling his head there as in a mother's bosom, to just stay there, always. "Run away, Moni!" the alarm of his heart shrieked in him again. "Moni, run for your life!" But the eyes of the Rabbi caressed him, as though they were Ma gazing at him; as though they were Ma reaching her arms out to him, asking: "What's wrong, my precious?" And, like long ago, he again felt her outstretched arms. "Oh, Mommy!"

What's the matter, my baby? Who said nasty things to my little boy out there on Park Street?

Mommy, they say I'm an old whore. Mommy, tell them I'm your little boy. Tell them, Mommy.

Oh, my baby! My little boy! I'm taking a walk with the prettiest little boy in the world.

Mommy, tell them you love me. Tell them you knitted the red socks for me. They don't think anybody loves me.

I love you, Monkele! I'll shout it for everybody to hear.

Hug me tight, Mommy. I'm afraid of Bruno. Bruno wants to cool me off; I'm running away to a different block. Bruno doesn't want me any more either. Mommy, tell them I can still be a good Piepel.

The outstretched arm points to the one seated in the center. "The Rabbi of Shilev says thank you."

"Moni, run! Save yourself!" His heart sent the alarm racing to every nerve.

He tore himself away from the hutch aisle. He walked with urgent steps. Almost at a run. Incoming camplings jumped aside at the rear gate. Reverently they made way for him.

The Block Piepel!

7

Hunger seared his entrails like a raw wound. And the peel of the potato came snaking down from between Rostek's fingers right into his mouth—

Moni tore his eyes open. He found himself lying amid camplings somewhere in a hutch. In a block whose number he did not know. The murky light falling from the rafters coated the sleeping camplings as with a layer of earth. Deep stillness. The block was sunk in slumber. He could still feel the band of peel snaking out from between the knife and the potato in Rostek's hands, one side succulent, white, the other side dry, dark, snaking right into his mouth as he swallows and swallows without cease.

Fits of nightmare sleep pounced upon him, abruptly withdrew, and again he dozed off—

"There's only six hours between a full belly and a hungry one," Rostek berates him, his face looking like his governess Miss Emily's. She rails at him: "If you lose your *Funktion*, inside of six hours you'll starve like all the rest of them." She spoon-feeds him. The whole family is seated around the table in the large dining room. He had promised Miss Emily that he would eat up everything if she let him sit at the table with the whole family, and not make him sit alone in the children's room. He knows he must eat. He'd better eat. Because if he loses the *Funktion,* inside of six hours he'll be as hungry as all the rest of them in Auschwitz. But he feels that no matter how much he eats, he'll never stop being hungry. On the table stand many, many plates full of Auschwitz soup. He is sitting in a grown-up's chair, his mouth reaching right up to the edge of the white-covered table. Everybody slides the plates of soup at his mouth. Miss Emily tilts them so the soup should pour straight into his throat, one plate after another. But not a drop of it collects in his stomach. The hunger burns away at his insides. His eyes tear open. And the nightmare of hunger pounces on him as he wakes. He dozes off again, and finds himself standing in the soup line. It is his turn at the barrel with the bowl, with the rest of the camplings. The Block Chief draws a ladleful from the barrel, emptying it not into Moni's bowl but into his open mouth. Behind him a long row of camplings, bowls in hands, snakes toward the barrel. Moni turns to air. Disembodied he stands by the barrel as campling after campling passes through him to the barrel. The Block Chief draws ladlefuls of soup for them, emptying them not into their bowls but into Moni's throat. Campling after campling passes through him as the ladles pour soup into his open mouth. But in the void of his stomach there is nothing. The hunger rages on. A whole barrel of soup has gone into him and his stomach is as empty as ever, and the hunger laps away at his entrails with tongues of fire. He woke with a start.

It was close around him. He was lying on a strange arm. He could not remove it because of the congestion in the hutch. He did not know whether there was still a pulse beating in that arm. From his open-mouthed neighbor not a breath was to be heard. That is the way everybody in Auschwitz sleeps. You never can tell at night who is alive and who is dead. Only at dawn, when the orderlies yell, "Up!"—you know: whoever did not then and there jump down will never jump from the boards again. Soon they will drag him out to the corpse pile behind the block.

All around him they lay, as far as his eye could reach in the dark: camplings above him, below him, to his right, and to his left. He lay amidst them like a single particle of sand bearing the seed of a huge mountain.

Not a sound from them. They are asleep. More than one will never wake again. Here and there, in such final moments of sleep, a smile will sometimes flutter on a face, like the smile of a baby asleep. They pass from this world illuminated with the pure, immaculate reflex of the first smile.

Softly, night moves among the long, dark hutch rows, with gentle hand brushing into the up-gathered train of her robe the crumbs of final breath of those asleep, on whose brow the Auschwitz sky will at daybreak plant a final kiss, outside, on the corpse pile.

Moni turned his eyes to the cubicle window. The red light was streaming through the window. All the Block Chiefs like red crepe paper around their lamps. It is the same in all the cubicles. At one end of the brick stove the night watchman sits dozing, cowled in a dark blanket. Everywhere the same. All blocks are alike, outside and inside. Yesterday evening, at the final gong, Ludwig Tiene's voice suddenly roared through the camp. They all made for the blocks, including Moni, into this block, the nearest, whose number he does not even know. All the blocks are identical. Everywhere the same triple-tiered hutches along the walls. Everywhere the same long brick oven bisecting the entire length of the block, the same skeletons, five hundred on the right, five hundred on the left. You could never tell the skeletons of one block from the skeletons of another, just as you could never tell the hutch boards of the left side from the hutch boards of the right. All the boards of all the Auschwitz hutches are identical, just like the skeletons lying on them.

Moni was watching the cubicle. If the Piepel would come out, he could tell which block he is in. Not a Piepel has ever lifted a finger for him when he has been out of *Funktion*. Tomorrow, first thing in the morning, right after roll call, he is going to Camp Office to ask for transfer to Robert in block 16. Robert is the only Block Chief left who hasn't had him for Piepel yet. Robert is your last chance, he warned himself. You've got to look after yourself and stop counting on the other Piepels. Not one of them has ever given you a hand. They think they've got it made. They would never dream that those boots they polish for all they're worth every morning will suddenly one night go seesawing across their own necks. They can't imagine that the same hands which play with their bodies would ever come to murder them. Try and tell it to a Piepel; he won't believe you. Every Piepel thinks: Maybe other Block Chiefs. But mine? Never! *His* Block Chief is not like the rest. Every Piepel harbors an intimate secret in his heart—the secret of the love which his Block Chief makes to him at night. The Piepel is certain that he is unique in possessing this secret, and he guards it from alien eyes in the belief that he, and he alone, has been initiated.

All around the camplings lay pressed against each other, a mass. No! I'm not one of them! Moni resolved. I am an old campbird. Tomorrow, the day after, I'm going to be Piepel in block 16. No, I'm not one of them. Everybody in camp knows that "Moni" means "old campbird."

"And how do you know Robert will want you?" a voice spoke up within him.

"I know he will!" Moni retorted. "No Block Chief in camp has ever turned me down when I've offered him my body. 'Drop in tonight, Moni. Drop in,' they say right off."

"Until they see you naked," the voice said. "Werner in block 25 wouldn't even come near you."

"Lay off," Moni snapped. "I know the look of a Block Chief. I'm sure Robert wants me. I know it."

"And do you also know that you'll leave Robert alive?"

"I'm not a numbskull like the other Piepels. I won't sit around till the last minute. I've got their lovemaking down pat. I didn't just pull into Auschwitz last night. I know how they run after you till they've had you. But me—the moment I step inside the cubicle of a new Block Chief, I know right off just when I'll have to beat it out of that same door to save my life. I'm not like other Piepels. At the first touch of a Block Chief's hands I know just how many days I'm going to last with him. Oh, no, I'm not a sucker like the other Piepels. They believe in the love of their Block Chiefs, that's why they don't run away. That's why before you know it they're gone—one after the other. Suddenly you ask yourself: Where's Jackie, the Piepel of 17? You haven't seen him for quite a while. But you know you'll never see him again. Or, walking along the blocks you suddenly remember: Eddie was Piepel here, in block 5. Where's Eddie? Your pal, Eddie, whom Hoess himself picked out of a Czech transport. Where's Eddie? But you know you'll never see him again, either. You don't even know when, what night, it happened. That's the way it is with all the Piepels. Every single one of them. Because they're all a bunch of dumb fools, that's what they are: stupid, fat hunks of meat, every last one of them. When you warn them, they laugh in your face. They don't believe you. They're sure it's only because you're jealous of them."

He lay with his eyes focused on the stream of red light at the front of the block. Along his glance were many, many hutches packed tight with skeletons. No, you aren't one of them, he promised himself. They're nothings. Just camplings. Just the dumpings from the platform to the crematorium. They can't even say they're in Auschwitz, because they're just floating through. But you—you're Moni, Moni the Piepel! The oldtimer in Auschwitz! No, you're not one of them! You're just hiding among them for a while, so you shouldn't be noticed. Tomorrow, or the day after, you'll stick your head out again. The Block Chief of 22 has probably forgotten all about you. He probably has a new Piepel by now. And you'll get back on *Funktion* again. With Robert this time. Robert is your last chance! Oh, God, make Robert want me! Please give me just one more chance! Just this one chance! This time I promise I'll—

The main gate suddenly tore open. Heads stood framed in the doorway against the black of night. Forward, as in bold relief, the rectangular skull of Tiene. Behind him—the heads of his confrères. The red glow from the cubicle window dyed their silhouettes as with fresh blood.

They stood fixed in the doorway.

Suddenly, out of Ludwig a chain of uncanny laughter rumbled in heavy soldered links. He did not move, but sent his chain of cackles rattling from his death's head into the farthest recesses of the block: "Hi-hi-hi-hi..." "Light!!!" he roared.

"Everybody down!!!"

Ludwig Tiene's ferocious roar shattered the darkness of the block like a sackful of seeds bursting in mid-air. Down from the hutches, under the lit lamps, spilled skeletons—skeletons—skeletons. From all sides they came spilling, from every crack and hole, Ludwig's decree quivering on their lips. They rehearsed it to themselves without cease, quaking with terror as they recited: *Everybody down!...Everybody down!...*As though they themselves were now spurring their own limbs with the command: *Faster! Faster! Everybody down!...Everybody down!...*From the boards poured arm bones tangled in leg bones; spindle-fingers scrambled across skeleton heads, dribbling down backs, dropping outspread from above as into a chasm. Teeth chattered against teeth with a hollow, chilly chatter, grinding the words of the command, *Everybody down!* as they spilled down into the block.

Atop the long brick stove, Ludwig Tiene darted and wheeled, arms outspread like a black monster on the swoop. From the hutches on either side the skeletons kept coming down. Down, down. Above them, as though soaring to swoop at their bones, Ludwig Tiene raced to and fro convulsed with ribald laughter. "Oho...Oho...Hi-hi-hi-hi-hikh..."

"Everybody, knee-bend!" he shrilled.

And the skeletons: they do not weep, they do not groan, they do not cry out. They array themselves. Bones array themselves on the ground on both sides of the brick oven. Dropping to their knees. Voicelessly, instantaneously. There is only a sound of night wind rustling dry leaves on parched earth.

"Knee-bend! Hi-hi-hi-hi!—"

Ludwig's henchmen leap on to the oven, to see to it that the skeletons knee-bend properly. Whoever raises himself so much as an inch because his lower frame can no longer sustain the burden of his upper frame, his skull immediately rings out like an empty pot struck by a rod.

"Skip!" the monster screeches, winging and wheeling about, to the rasping accompaniment of his cackling command: "Hi-hi-hi-hi-hi!" . . . Skip!"

Feeble birdlings, they barely manage to skip. Their mouths hang open. They want to breathe, but the air will not pass their throats. They skip, skip.

"Blow! Hi-hi-hi-hi!" Ludwig Tiene's command suddenly lashes out.

In a flash the block is empty. The skeletons have vanished into the hutches. Only here and there on the ground is a trampled scrap. Block orderlies immediately clear it out.

All at once:

"Down! Hi-hi-hi-hi!"

"Skip! Hi-hi-hi-hi!"

All at once:

"Blow!"

All at once:

"Down!"

And so on. Again the same round. And again. *Sport!* Auschwitz night calisthenics. Nobody must ever be second.

All must be first. The *Sport* will go on until they are all one to "Blow!" and till they are all one "Down!" Even if, of the thousand, there will remain only one—the last.

Moni, save yourself! the voice cried out within him. He knew that Ludwig Tiene would not end his *Sport* till all of them were laid out for all time on the ground of the block. *Moni, save yourself while you still have the strength!*

At the next "Blow!" Moni snatched the Prominent's cap from his pocket and furtively thrust it on his head. He did not "blow" into the hutches along with the rest, but remained below as though he were an orderly. Keeping his head down he seized the remains of a trampled Mussulman by the feet. "Whoreson!" he shouted at a startled orderly. "Grab the head!" The orderlies, befuddled with terror, were frantically dragging the trampled carcasses into corners. Every one of them knew that to Ludwig Tiene an orderly was just as tasty a bit as a common campling.

"Get that Mussulman to the pile!" Moni shouted at the orderly.

The night shed a blue light on the bone pile behind the block. The backpath lurked dark and empty. The orderly dumped the Mussulman and dashed terrified back into his block. From inside Ludwig's shrieks carried to Moni's ears. The shrieking seemed to be directed at him. He broke into a run. He turned off to the assembly area. The shrieking seemed to be hot on his heels. He fled to the main path. He opened the door of the first block on which his eyes fell. And just as he did not know from which block he had escaped, he did not know into which block he had run.

Almost every night one of the Block Chiefs gives a party in honor of the Camp Senior. It was the thing to do in Auschwitz. By then the camplings are already in the throes of Auschwitz sleep. They do not know what is happening in their own block, and it does not concern them, just as servants do not concern themselves with what goes on in their masters' bedrooms. It is as normal and reasonable as everything else around them here. Part of this world order called . . . Auschwitz. The hubbub of the preparations for the feast mingles in their ears with the rumble of the lorries riding ceaselessly on the highway to the crematorium.

Normal and self-evident.

Tonight it is the turn of block 12. Rostek is in a dither. The orderlies have their hands full: frying, cooking, baking away. Franzl's cubicle is as keyed up as a village preparing for its squire's wedding. And while the last-minute touches are being put in block 12, Ludwig Tiene has stopped off in block 11 next door to work up an appetite with some *Sport*.

When Moni opened the gate, his momentum carried him right into the fluster of the Funktioners. He was swept into the thick of it as though he were part of it all. And by the time he had turned to flee the new danger he had stumbled into, it was too late—

Pocksy Zygmunt appeared out of Rostek's kitchenette, halting in the red light of the cubicle opposite to issue orders to his subordinates.

Moni leaped back into the darkness of an aisle between the front and second hutches. But he knew the danger he was in standing there. He was now neither of the bustlers nor of the camplings. An outsider, suspect. Orderlies rushed to and fro between the kitchenette and the cubicle, seeming afloat in the density of the red light. Zygmunt stood between him and the gate, blocking his way out.

He felt the danger of standing there. His glance darted to the top tier, the hutch of Zygmunt's Mussulmen, the guardians of the food stash opposite.

Moni climbed in amongst them. The smell of Mussulman bones overwhelmed him. They were neither asleep nor awake; they neither lay nor sat. They were piled up, like the tangle of dead bones behind the block. Those stare vapid-eyed at the Auschwitz sky, and these stare with the same vapid eyes at the stash opposite.

Bones astir. He crawled in amongst them.

They received him the way the pile behind the block receives a skeleton just dumped by the block orderlies. Here no one utters a word. Here speech is extinct. They themselves have forgotten the shade of their own voice. The red stream of light from the cubicle window spotlights the aisle to the stash. Only the block Piepel and Zygmunt are permitted in this pale. The Mussulman sentries sniff them with a special Mussulmanic sense, the way creatures in a zoo know the scent of their keeper.

More than once, as Zygmunt comes crawling back down from the stash, his hand reaches out in grateful caress to one of the skulls. Zygmunt knows that if a stranger were to steal into the stash, the block would immediately be a frenzy of twittering like a nest invaded by a hawk.

Moni dug himself in under their skeletons. They lay on his body, covering him. He could feel them upon him, and he could feel them deep within him. The agony of their Mussulmanity filled his being to suffocation. He felt he was going to be one of them. He wanted to save himself. He thrust his head out from under them, like a drowner's mouth struggling to break through the water clogging his breath. His eyes desperately sought the Auschwitz mainland where life was still going on, that hard soil of *Funktion*. But he could not make it. He felt himself going under in the Mussulmanic deep.

The cubicle window framed the table, festively laid out. From time to time Golden Lolek showed in the window. He fussed around the head of the table as though the rest did not exist at all. The napkin at the head of the table did not seem to please him. He kept manipulating it: it must stand point up, like a sail. Lolek knows that such a silly trifle can turn the party into a death-feast. All the Block

Chiefs like to feel in Auschwitz that they have been invited to dine in an elegant restaurant.

A set table. The lives of a thousand camplings will now be served on this table. How many breads have to be stolen from them in order to be exchanged for a pack of margarine; and how many packs of margarine have to be withheld from them to be traded for gold dental crowns; and how many fistfuls of dental crowns have to be hacked out of their mouths so that, in exchange, one such jigger of schnapps can be served. Just one jigger.

Lolek's arms are round and fleshy. His full cheeks gleam like copper in the red light of the cubicle. The woolen pullover is snug around his full shoulders. Golden Lolek! The only Piepel still holding out in camp. Not a trace is left of any of the Piepels who got here after Moni. They all just evaporated, leaving no trace of having been here, as though they had never existed to begin with.

Moni sought some hatred in his heart for Lolek but could find none. He wanted to hate him but he could not. Instead, his mother's face rose to his eyes, blocking the hatred for Lolek with her body. Moni knew that if some Block Chief were to tell him: "Moni, I'll fix it so you can come with me to the Sauna, and when we pass the Women's Camp you can take a look at your ma through the barbed wire," he would jump right into bed with that Block Chief, without a second thought about the Piepel whose death this would bring about.

Lolek is sure that his mother is alive in the Women's Camp. No one can get this notion out of his head. Every Block Chief in camp has promised Lolek to take him past the Women's Camp, leading him on until they get what they want out of him. Actually, Lolek knows there isn't a chance. But let one of them just suggest it and Lolek is his, body and soul. Oh, how Lolek must love his ma. By what right can Moni hold it against him? At first he couldn't understand why Lolek was behaving that way, why he kept going from Block Chief to Block Chief. This is the second time Lolek is Piepel with Franzl. This time Franzl guarantees Lolek that his mother is getting the food packages he is sending her through the Corpse Kommando. But if she really is getting them, why doesn't she ever send word in her own writing? No, he can't hate him. Lolek wants to see his mother at least once more in his life. And maybe he *is* seeing her. Maybe she *is* getting his food packages, but Lolek doesn't want to let on. In that case, why does he keep going to the cubicles of other Block Chiefs at night? Actually, why not? Lolek wants to live. Maybe his ma and he also agreed to meet at the camp gate when the war is over. Lolek wants to live. And it's this going from one Block Chief to the other that keeps him alive. So how can he hold it against him? He wants to live and so does Lolek. That's why he's signing up for Robert's block. He'll be a good, faithful Piepel. He'll eat and eat. He'll be just as fat as Lolek. But how did he ever end up in this block now? All at once his heart shrieked alarm: "Moni, run for your life! This block is a death-trap now!"

He wanted to get down into the dark between the hutches. If the back gate is locked, he's done for. He knew that he must not use the main gate now. It was outside that main gate that Franzl handed Berele over to Ludwig Tiene. Just as he had been handed over at the platform by Commandant Hoess. "Just look at those eyes," he had told Franzl. Outside, in the world, Moni never knew he had such special eyes. So far it's those eyes that have saved him from death. It's thanks to them that he is still alive. Yet, if he hadn't run away from this block in the nick of time, Franzl would either have seesawed him with the white cane or handed him over to Ludwig Tiene. In that case it isn't the eyes that have saved him after all, but the fact that he has always taken the cue from his heart. Only the back gate better not be locked now! If it is, the night watchman is sure to catch him in his dash back. He must make it good! He poked his head out. He was about to leap down from the hutch—

Before his eyes pandemonium broke loose. All the orderlies were scurrying to cover. Ludwig Tiene's approach carried through the wooden wall of the block. In front of the block, by the main gate, they left a wake of red emptiness.

Moni hid among the Mussulmen. Once more he felt that an invisible hand was safeguarding him in Auschwitz. There had been only a step between him and Ludwig Tiene. If he had made a run for it just one second sooner, he would have landed right between two fires. Behind his eyelids, which had reflexively shut, he again saw Papa's head turned to him as he was being dragged to the lorry; Papa's eyes disappear behind the mass being shoved onto the lorry. Even later, when the lorry was gone, Papa's eyes were still there, alive. He had felt then that Papa was saying something to him in that glance, and he could still hear it now, though he was unable to put it in words.

Moni's eyes opened. Inside the cubicle, Ludwig Tiene was draining a bottle right into his mouth. There will be a tall pile of corpses behind block 11 next door tomorrow, Moni mused. In another two or three days, no one will be left of all those who just took part in Ludwig Tiene's night *Sport*. He could feel the invisible hand that was safeguarding him in Auschwitz.

"Schnapps, Franzl. Let's have another bottle of schnapps!" Ludwig Tiene bellowed in the cubicle

Even Franzl was frightened at the pools of red bleariness in Ludwig's eyes. "Hey, orderly. Schnapps, on the double!" he howled into the block through the cubicle window. "A bottle of schnapps, on the double!"

The block orderlies were all stuck away, each in his hole, every one waiting for the other to crawl out and deliver the schnapps to the cubicle. They knew this was a life-and-death gamble.

"Schnapps!! Franzl, schnapps!!" the rectangular death's head screamed.

In his hideaway, Lolek could not bear it. Franzl's outcries were driving him frantic. He knows that the orderlies are all in their holes now, waiting for each other to come out. Meanwhile, his Block Chief is liable to pay for it. Lolek is a devoted, grateful Piepel. Franzl helps him to get the food packages to the Women's Camp. Quickly Lolek crawled out of his hideaway and scampered up to the stash.

Lolek's full face was red in the window light spotlighting the stash. Lolek's head leaned over into the stash as his hands rummaged for a bottle of schnapps. His back was turned to Moni in the Mussulman hutch. The same blank, cold-hearted, fat back. The back which he had once begged: *Lolek, please don't steal Franzl away from me!*

Holding the bottle of schnapps in his hand, Lolek turned to bring it into the cubicle. Mutely Moni's eyes followed the receding back. As at that time on the back path, Moni was afraid lest the back turn around and see him. And just as at that time Lolek had vanished into the gate of this block, he now vanished into the cubicle. The very cubicle Lolek had snitched from him. Only at that time he had not known why Lolek was doing it. Now he knows, and he cannot hold it against him.

"Oho! . . . Oho! . . ." Ludwig's vampiric screech suddenly came through the cubicle window. "Oho, Franzl, what a piece you've been keeping from me. What a treasure!"

Ludwig's black boot rose to the table edge. A shove, and the table capsized with all it held. "What a treasure, Franzl. What a treasure."

Lolek's chubby face turned in panic to Franzl. His eyes sought haven in him. The full red lips of his boyish mouth parted in spasms of terror.

"My treasure! Hi-hi-hi . . . Come into my arms, my treasure!"

Franzl knew that right then and there he had lost his Piepel. It was all settled. So he sent his laughter chiming in with the Camp Senior's. As though the whole thing were indifferent to him. Lolek felt that he was now utterly defenseless. No one here would help him. Step by step he backed away, opened the door and dashed out.

"My treasure! My treasure!" The Camp Senior set out after him.

Lolek did not know which way to run. He took several steps towards the main gate, but immediately recoiled. Just the other day the Chief Orderly of 18 had run away from Ludwig. The S.S. men in the watchtowers had seen him and shot him on the run. Just then the door of the cubicle tore open. The red light spewed forth a black monster. Lolek made a dash for the aisle nearby, scrambled up to the stash and cowered in a corner.

On all fours Ludwig crawled across after him. 'Hi-hi-hi. My treasure!"

Moni felt his flesh crawl with horror. *That's the way all Piepels peg out. Either the Block Chiefs croak them or they wind up in the claws of Ludwig Tiene.* It was right here, where he is lying now, that Rostek had uttered these very words. Ludwig Tiene was now opposite his eyes. Almost within reach. Moni felt terror freeze and nail him to the hutch boards: if the Mussulmen set up a cry now, he's done for. Has fear frozen them, too? They stare ahead: in the stash lies their Block Piepel, and the Camp Senior is peeling the little riding breeches off him . . . The pullover . .

"My treasure Hi-hi-hi . . . Hi-hi-hi . . ."

Lolek's voice gasping: "*Herr* Camp Senior . . . *Herr* Camp Senior . . . It hurts . . . Oh-h. *Herr* Camp Senior . . ."

"My treasure. Hi-hi-hi-hi. . . Hi-hi-hi. . ."

"*Herr* Camp Senior! . . . *Herr* C—"

The smothered voice of the Piepel dwindled amid Ludwig Tiene's hoarse cackles rasping through the block like a dull saw. The red band of light from the cubicle shattered to smithereens in the savage tangle of Ludwig Tiene's love-making with the Piepel.

"Oh, my tr-r-reasure! Hi-hi-hi . . ." Ludwig wrapped himself around the Piepel, baring a cavernous mouth at him. Huge, bristling fangs emerged. Ludwig clutched the Piepel opposite the fangs, staring, staring. All at once he sank the fangs into the naked little body.

Lolek's last cries for help abruptly ceased. The Piepel's throttled groaning was no longer heard. From the stash now carried only a demoniac snorting, as though chaos were now grappling with itself.

The doorway was red with the light of the cubicle. Inside Franzl sprawled in his chair, one booted foot on the edge of the upended table, his head slung over the back of the chair, his hand holding the bottle Lolek had brought, draining the schnapps right into his mouth. He knows that now he has no Lolek and he is furious: why did it have to be his Piepel? And just when he could use a Piepel himself? He flung the bottle to the ground and stamped out of the block.

In the morning the news got around: during the night, Franzl had given the Piepel of block 11 tit for tat for what Ludwig had done to his Piepel, Lolek.

Ludwig came down from the stash, leaving behind him a dead emptiness. "Night guard!" he screeched into the block. "Sweep it up!"

"*Jawohl, Herr* Camp Senior!" came the quavering reply.

Moni lay submerged among the Mussulmen, his eyes gaping with terror. The dread of the Piepel's death in the stash opposite closed in on him like a snare. It became part of him. He felt this death within him. *That's the way all Piepels wind up.* It might have been him lying there now instead of Lolek. He could not take his eyes from the stash. Out of the stash, a red menace, familiar yet unknown, rose to engulf him. His own fate now lay in the stash—an irrevocable fate.

All at once the camp seemed to him like a tiny bird cage in Ludwig Tiene's clutch, with no way to escape and no place to hide. Campling or Piepel, you are always exposed to the stalking eye of Auschwitz death.

He could not bear to go on lying there. He wanted to go down; quickly, quickly get up and run out of this block. He'll run off to any block. In with the camplings. Any hutch. Because it's all one Auschwitz. On the main path or on the backpath Auschwitz with no way to escape and no place to hide. Suddenly it came back to him: tomorrow he wants to be Robert's Piepel in block 16.

He was about to start down from the hutch when Pocksy Zygmunt rushed out of hiding and made for his stash to see what had befallen it. Moni did not dare stir.

Up in the stash, a terrible sight met Zygmunt's eyes. He clutched at his head: what a calamity! All his packs of margarine had been opened and smeared all over the naked body of the strangled Piepel.

Zygmunt beat his head with his fists, spitting out a chain of savage curses, at Piepel and Camp Senior all in one breath: they've gone and bitched up all he owned in this world! Two years of hard saving gone down the drain! They've wiped him out! He dropped to his knees beside the naked body of the Piepel and dissolved in tears. With a knife he scraped the margarine from between Lolek's legs, weeping bitterly:

"What a blow! What a catastrophe!"

An orderly's head rose to the boards of the stash. Murderously Zygmunt kicked him, sending him flying like a football into the Mussulman hutch opposite. Just a little farther and he would have been smashed on the brick stove.

Zygmunt spread Lolek's undershirt out on the boards and scooped into it the mess of margarine he had managed to scrape together. In the light of the cubicle the Piepel's white shirt seemed crimson with blood. Then Zygmunt collected Lolek's clothes one by one: the blue pullover, the little riding breeches, the tall boots. Things like this are worth something in camp. You've got to pick up whatever you can. Zygmunt wrapped them into a bundle, and climbing back down to the aisle between the hutches, he barked at the orderlies: "Get over here, whoresons!"

The block orderlies lined up in two rows near the aisle to the stash. Back and forth Zygmunt paced between them like a beast in a narrow cage. He could not speak for fury. Back and forth he paced. Only yesterday Zalke had begged him to sell him the margarine—half for diamonds and half for cigarettes. Diamonds the size of walnuts. The best. And he, damn fool, wouldn't hear of it for fear Franzl would mooch all the smokes off him the way he had done to Rostek. So now look at him! What a blow! Zygmunt beat his head with his fists. "I'm not staying in this damned block!" he screamed. "Robert is begging me to be his Chief Orderly. I'm shifting to block 16, but first I'm squaring things here."

The night guard fearfully approached, and in a quavering voice blurted Ludwig Tiene's command to clear the Piepel out. Finishing, he dashed off, in order to avert the tip of Zygmunt's boot in his crotch. The orderlies did not dare breathe.

All at once Zygmunt's feet halted their savage pacing. What a brainstorm! He seized hold of one of the orderlies. "Get over to block 2 and bring me Holy Dad! And you," he shouted at another, "wake Zalke and tell him to hotfoot it over here; I've got a deal for him. On the double!"

Zygmunt's face beamed at his own ingenuity. Oh, he's going to make good his losses, all right! And just as soon as he does he's shifting right over to Robert in block 16. That's final. He's not staying another minute in this damned block!

When Holy Dad appeared, Zygmunt first of all pegged a cigarette into his mouth-slit. Then placing his arm around

Piotr's angular shoulders, he told him the long and short of it: ". . . so you see, Piotr boy? The main thing you have to remember is: small portions. Now there's a deal for you. A fat deal! Take him into the water-pump compartment. Just remember, small portions!"

Zygmunt's words reverberated in Moni's ears. *Small portions.* The very words he had heard Zygmunt say the day after he got into camp. The two block orderlies had stood facing the table, cutting the breads into portions. Zygmunt had come in with his truncheon. He had let one of them have it on the shoulder. *Whoresons! Cut those portions small! Franzl is out of fags!* It's almost a year now. A whole year in Auschwitz. Sometimes it seems like only yesterday. There —in that very cubicle. What are they going to do with dead Lolek? *Small portions.* What are they going to do to him in the pump compartment in the latrine?

"Well, there you have it, Piotr boy!" Zygmunt repeated agreeably. "Fat deal, eh?"

Holy Dad did not say a word. He merely listened. Then without a word he climbed up to the stash, slung the Piepel over his shoulder, and without a word he climbed down, opened the gate, and like a butcher carrying off a slaughtered lamb he went with him out into the dark of the Auschwitz night.

8

"Fall in!" "Fall in!"

The block gates were shut. "Fall in! Fall in!" The commands shook the hutches. Orderlies wielding truncheons dashed back and forth on the brick stove ranging like a long, narrow sidewalk through the center of the block. They swung the truncheons in the air, howling savagely as they rained blows on skulls: "Fall in! Fall in!"

Down from the three tiers of hutches spilled the camplings. They lined up in two rows, face to back, separated by the oven. At the hub of emptiness, between cubicle and kitchenette, a chair was placed in readiness for the Camp Doctor. There the *Selektion* will take place. The main gate will be thrust open to the full width of its two panels. Naked the skeletons will pass one by one before his eyes, everyone with his left arm extended to display clearly the number branded into the flesh. On reaching the chair, each will turn a full circle, like a mannequin, before his eyes. And should the Doctor's bamboo rod tap the extended arm, the number will immediately be noted down by the clerks arrayed behind the chair, and tomorrow, by the numbers, those listed will be marched off to the crematorium.

"Fall in! Fall in!"

It was only that morning that Moni had hurried to Camp Office to be transferred here, to block 16. "Moni," the chief clerk had complimented him, "you've really got a sharp eye! You always know when to beat it from a block." Last week at this time he had still been Piepel with Bruno in block 10. But his heart had warned him: "Moni, don't spend the night in block 10! Bruno has had his fill of you. He's croaking you tonight." Always, the morning after he has taken off, there is a new Piepel operating in the block. His heart has never yet steered him wrong. *Moni, you've really got a sharp eye.* They always wonder at Camp Office how he knows. But this time, how come he walked right into a *Selektion?*

He jumped down from the hutch boards together with the rest of the camplings and got into line, doing his best to keep out of sight of the orderlies. He had signed up for this block because he knew there was an opening here for a Piepel. He wondered how he would get close to the Block Chief. Because once these orderlies see him among the common camplings, he has no chance of being a Piepel here.

In making a getaway from a Block Chief, it is best to hide among the common camplings. After a day or two, when the Block Chief is all spoony over his new Piepel and has forgotten you ever existed—then you show up again to look for a new *Funktion.* This way, since nobody ever sees you down with the Mussulmen, you never lose out on your right to belong to the Prominents' family. Because once the Funktioners do see you dragged off into the bone stream —that's it; as far as they're concerned you're nothing but crematorium fodder. And then you might as well forget about ever getting back into the family.

Block curfew! All camplings must now be locked inside their blocks. Outside, Ludwig Tiene and his crew are scouring the camp for camplings trying to get out of the *Selektion*. There's nowhere in Auschwitz you can hide, Moni mused. True, you can sometimes stick yourself away in the corpse piles behind the blocks, but if they take them off to the crematorium first, you're finished. The best place in camp to hide is the stream of living bodies of the camplings. Yet whenever there's a *Selektion* coming on some of the newcomers hide behind the open latrine gate, or in the compartment inside the latrine where the pump is grinding away. Two hiding places that seem to have been ready-made for clever camplings to hide, so that Ludwig Tiene can get his kick heading straight there to find them. First of all, he gorges himself on the panic in their eyes. Then he shoves their heads deep into the muck in the latrine holes, cackling all the while: "Lap it up! Hi-hi-hi-hi! . . . Lap it up!" Until the suffocating man's legs stop writhing and hang limp in the air, motionless, dead.

Yesterday at this time he was still Piepel in block 18. The camplings there are also lined up for the *Selektion* now, but there, as Gunther's Piepel, it would have been all right for him to stay in the cubicle. He would have had a lot to do, there. On a day like this you must do a thorough housecleaning in the cubicle and kitchenette, to get rid of every trace of the cooking and frying that has been done for the Block Chief. (The Camp Doctor has a sharp nose.) There would be a lot for him to do there now. He would be issuing rapid-fire orders to the orderlies. He can see their fawning smiles as they report to him, their "Yes, Piepel!" as they leave him to carry out his orders.

Yesterday at this time he was still Piepel in block 18. But now he knows that he did not dare stay there. If he had stayed to spend the night, he would now be on the pile behind the block.

The camplings were all lined up. The triple tiers were empty. Moni tried to keep his face low. He felt that he had to do something—anything—and now—if he is to get out of this one alive. When the command comes, "Everybody strip!" it will be too late. Now he still has the shoes on his feet and the Prominent's cap in his pocket. Now he can still make one last try—by mingling with the Funktioners. If he's lucky, they'll be so busy they won't even notice there is an outsider among them. And actually, with his shoes and cap, he *is* almost one of them. But if they do catch him, that's the end of him. Then he will have to pass through the *Selektion* like all the common camplings, naked. And naked, there is no question that he goes on the list. He knows that his body is all bones. His brain hasn't gone dry on him yet like the rest of the camplings, to think that there has been no change in his body. Well, do something! Fast! . . .

He slumped to the ground as in a swoon. Flattening himself, he crawled into the narrow space between the ground and the nearest bottom hutch. Prostrate he lay there, cheek pressed to the ground, as though a black steam roller had flattened him into place. He felt that he was going to choke. Air! Air! Opposite his eyes, all the way to the front of the block, stretched a narrow tunnel of light, barred like a narrow cage by the succession of nude legs, spindly as goose-feet. His eyes no sooner had adjusted to the sub-hutch darkness than he realized that the area all around was laid out with many others like him, belly flat, arms and legs outstretched. And he had thought he would be the only one here.

It was clear that he must not go on lying there another second. As soon as the first half of the row has gone through the *Selektion,* the orderlies will get down to search under the hutches, and those dragged out will be handed right over for Ludwig Tiene to have his way with them.

Moni decided to crawl quickly through to the front of the block, as near as possible to the cubicle, where all the Funktioners and block orderlies were fussing, right in the thick of all the commotion. There it will be easier for him to lose himself among them as though he belongs with them.

He crawled and twisted his way through the sprawl of bodies. Faster. Faster. Before the Camp Doctor comes in! Although he did not know when it would be best for him to pop up behind the shoulders—after the Camp Doctor is seated in the chair, or before he appears. He did know that the sooner he was at the front of the block the better!

A group of Prominents' feet in mountain-climbing shoes stood in the aisle by the front hutch. The metal ski-hooks glittered against the darkness of the ground. Sturdy shoes. Solid feet. The block clerk's, or the Chief Orderly's. There goes his plan. He mustn't get up now. If the stash in this block is also in the third hutch right above him, his last chance to get up behind their backs and scoot up into the stash will be when the tips of the shoes turn towards the center of the block. Up there he would stretch flat on his belly and pull a blanket over his head, and it would never occur to anyone that somebody was hiding in the stash among the contraband breads.

Many shoes were moving back and forth before the empty chair set for the Camp Doctor. Here, at the front of the block, you can see them. Here the nude goose-feet do not block the view. Here it is bright. The shoes keep jumping on and off the brick stove. Different shoes all the time. Prowling and supervising: there mustn't be any skeletons in the hutch aisles now, only in the center of the block.

The gate swung open. Into the area between the cubicle and the kitchenette came the Block Chief's black boots. With rapid steps they approached almost to Moni's eyes, leaping on to the brick stove. "Everybody strip!" his voice shouted, followed by a volley of bludgeons on naked skulls. "Strip! Strip! On the double!" The Prominent-shoes darted out of the aisle into the center of the block. Around the feet of the chair—emptiness. All the shoes now prowled at the back of the long brick stove.

Now! Moni edged towards the mouth of the tunnel. He was trembling all over. Carefully he poked his head out. No one was at the front of the block. He could now tangibly see his life suspended, naked and exposed, before his eyes. He knew: now—or never. "Courage, Moni! You're not one of those standing in line there!" his lips murmured to him. He eased out and got up on his knees, snatching the striped cap from his pocket and thrusting it on his head. He stood up, shook the dust from himself, and went out of the hutch aisle, head erect, as though on his way to the main gate. He did not look back to see whether he was noticed. And like a Piepel hurrying busily about his work, he reached for the knob of the cubicle door, opened it, and closed it behind him. He was inside.

The stillness of the cubicle enveloped him. He felt his heart panting with sledge-hammer blows against his ribs. In every nook and cranny here the absence of a Piepel was obvious. Nothing was in place. With quaking hands he began to tidy up, like a burglar trying to straighten up a strange house into which he has just broken. He folded the underwear and outer clothes in separate piles. All at once the door behind him opened: Robert, the Block Chief, stood before him.

Moni bared his eyes to Robert's gaze. He knew: now it is all up to his eyes—life or crematorium. *Maidenhead eyes.* He must now open them wide, wide, with all the tease in them.

Robert moved towards him—closer, closer, gripped him by the shoulders, gazing directly into the eyes. Now the verdict will come. Any second and he will hear it. Just then the main gate screeched open. A patch of Auschwitz sky with the Camp Doctor's S.S. cap in the center flooded the cubicle window. Robert swung around, leaving Moni standing there, and hurried out into the block.

The two gate panels now stood wide open to the main path. A profusion of light sprawled on the site of the *Selek-*

tion. Moni stood far back inside the cubicle opposite the window, his hands again and again laying out and folding the Block Chief's jacket. As though once the hands finish the work, he will have to go out into the block and line up with the others for the *Selektion.* So he did not stop working for a moment, but again and again he stroked and smoothed the green criminal triangle on the breast of the jacket, his eyes never leaving the window, his body quaking all over.

Outside, the chair filled with the black back of the Camp Doctor. To his right and to his left stood backs of clerks with sheets of paper in their hands.

The *Selektion* was in full swing. One by one the skeletons made their appearance—pallid, nude. Their naked steps were inaudible. Each with his left arm displayed before the eyes of the Camp Doctor, exactly as the orderlies had fixed it as they shoved him forward from the line. Thus each held it— the clear knowledge imprinted on the pupils of his eyes—

A human being. There he stands. Bearing his life on his left arm, now. His life and he—shivering, naked. He proffers it to the black S.S. uniform of the physician of Auschwitz.

So much sky pouring in through the gap of the wide-open gate. So much light in the grooves between the skeletal ribs. So much light between his two legs. They stand apart, right and left of his genital nudity, as though nailed to his frame from without.

Uncommanded, the skeleton turns about. He has also to show off his back. He knows that now, thus naked, there is nothing he can conceal. The light of day is upon everything. Instead of mounds of buttock are two rump cavities brimming with light; and a fullness of light in the dazzling emptiness between the legs. His life is ashamed to face him, and his heart twinges with the pity of it all, but he has no solace to offer. Perhaps the eyes beneath the S.S. visor will see his life that way too, and take pity.

He hurries, therefore, to get his circuit over with. He completes the full circle, like a mannequin. A glare of light on the bamboo rod reaching out to him from the Camp Doctor's hand. Ever so gently the rod touches his outstreched left arm, there, at the start of the blue numerical tattoo, where his life perches naked, pure as a snuggling dove.

The long pencils in the hands of the clerks briskly make notations on their sheets. Swiftly. One coming as the other goes. He is already outside the block, on the main path, but he continues to hold his left arm extended the way the block orderlies had set it for him.

Thus one after the other they flit by the cubicle window. Naked skeletons. All alike. No telling one from the other. Like threads in some weird weaving machine they file rapidly past the Camp Doctor, in unbroken succession: a naked body arrives—line; he does a circuit before the Camp Doctor—loop; continues out to the main path—line. Thus without letup: line-loop-line. Line-loop-line.

Robert's back appears, blocking the window. His head bends down to look at the list in the clerk's hands. Immediately he swings around. His face is now fully in the window. He looks at Moni. Their glances meet: will he order him to leave the cubicle and line up naked for the *Selektion?* Their glances lock. With all his might he holds on to Robert's glance, to keep him from tearing away. All of him now abandons itself to Robert's eyes: Take me, Robert, take me . . . You'll be satisfied with me . . . You'll see, I know lots of things . . . See my eyes? They're just like a maidenhead . . . Take them, Robert, take them . . .

His hands which had just fluttered in the folding of Robert's jacket continued to hold on to it. Only they no longer folded. Not a limb in him stirred. As though he had petrified in the process of folding the jacket—he and his gaping eyes together.

The face in the window broke into a smile, vanished, and immediately appeared inside the cubicle. Robert softly closed the door behind him. He called him over close. "You're staying here, old whore. Tonight we'll see what you can do." And he was gone.

Outside the skeleton weave continued past the window. Line-loop-line. But Moni had stopped paying attention. With a sweep of the hand he toppled the pile of clothing and began to rearrange it. But thoroughly this time, not superficially as before. Everything in the cubicle is his now. His. He is Piepel!

Again he toppled the pile and again he rearranged it. The vigor now sang in his limbs to the lilt of his hands.

"Oh, Ma," his lips prayed, "let God make me be a good Piepel to Robert! Let God make my eyes never stop exciting him! Why did he say 'old whore'?..."

9

All the world knows what latrines are for. Doubtless, that is what they were set up for in Auschwitz, too. But here everybody knows that "latrine" means "stock exchange."

Here deals of every variety are carried out, from major bloodsoaked transactions to such petty straightforward trades as a bit of iron wire to hold broken spectacles together in exchange for some string to hold the jacket in place and keep the wind off the bare abdomen. Here is the rendezvous of organizers and Prominents of every sort; the meeting place of wholesalers and retailers. Here block orderlies trade breads for cigarettes with the electricians who come from the adjacent camp to check the electricity in the barbed wire. The men of the Corpse Kommando who come daily to cart the cadaver piles off to the crematorium stop off here between loadings, quickly divest themselves of expensive woolen pullovers whose owners were taken directly from the wagons to the crematorium and sell them for fistfuls of gold teeth which Block Chiefs have just hacked out of mouths; here Poles sell food mold, potato peels, apple rot—at the rate of half a portion of camp bread for three fistfuls of potato peel.

Moni dragged towards the latrine. Day had just risen over camp. A day blue-yellow as the bones of the corpses piled behind the blocks. Wearily he dragged along the backpath, his thoughts apathetic. Every time he took a few steps forward it seemed to him that his thoughts were lagging behind somewhere, and that he had to turn back, take his thoughts by the hand, and lead them like fagged children.

From somewhere at the edge of his memory a fluttering shadow of thought propelled his feet forward. He remembered only that he had come down from the hutch intending to go to the latrine to take care of something important, but trudging along he couldn't remember what. Blankly he gazed at the horizon strung out on the barbed wire. The horizon now surged like a sea heaving javelin waves at a coastland. Someone drowning there was crying out for help. He could recognize the voice. It was his own voice, crying at him to save himself.

But how? Hasn't he done everything to fatten up? What else can he do to keep his frame from turning Mussulman?

"Robert was your last chance. I warned you," someone inside him came back at him.

"Didn't I try everything to keep Robert satisfied? I shoved the food into myself—only because I remembered."

"No, you didn't remember," the voice within retorted.

"Every time I warned you you sent me packing. I told you a thousand times if I told you once: get another soup down in you. Swallow a piece of margarine. Remember, block 16 is your last chance! And you—what did you always tell me? 'Right, right away.' You felt like vomiting, you said. Oh, sure, you always had an excuse. Well, isn't it true? You can kid anybody you want except me. You have no kicks coming against anyone but yourself!"

"How can I fatten up if they won't give me a chance?" Moni tried to justify himself. "How can a man get fat just like that? If they would just leave me alone for a little while, I'd get fat even on what I do eat. Why won't you see my side of it? They never gave me time to get fat. I always had to run away beforehand. Don't you know that if I had stayed with him another night I wouldn't be alive now? Didn't you see in Robert's eyes what he was planning to do to me that night? Why do you keep saying it's all my fault? Why is it my fault? Could you get fat just like that?"

"Yes! Yes! Just like that! All the Piepels here are fat. You don't see any other rattleboned Piepel in camp, do you? This time you should have done everything. I warned you over and over again. Now you pretend you've forgotten. Now you want to put the blame on the Block Chiefs. How many times have you put the soup away after only a lick? 'I'll finish it later,' you always promise. Oh, sure. Always excuses. You always happened to remember 'something to do' just when you were eating. Everything was more important to you than eating: cigarettes for Robert, laundry to be given out, accounts to settle with the organizers, accounts with the traders from the next camp, accounts with the Corpse Kommando. Anything. Anything but eat. Whose bowl was always left standing full on the kitchenette window? Yours! And who always finished it for you? All of them! All of them! Anybody who could get at the window. Anybody, just so long as it didn't have to be you! The orderlies knew that if they waited they would get the bowl of soup you put down, and the bread rations which you always put off eating and then never finished. Maybe you're going to tell me it isn't so? I spoke to you man to man: Moni, I said, look what you're doing again! Every time you lose your *Funktion* you swear that this time you're *really* going to change; this time you'll *really* know how to behave. Look, Moni, I said, Robert is the only Block Chief left in camp who hasn't had you. Hang on to him for all you're worth. And what did you answer me? Yes, yes, you know I'm right; of course I'm right; but in just a second; you just want to get over to the latrine to pick up a pair of new woolen socks for Robert from the Corpse Kommando before anybody else grabs them. As though Robert needed you for socks. As though that were a Piepel's main job in Auschwitz. But then who finished your food? Who finished your soup? So where do you get off complaining about the Block Chiefs not giving you a chance to get fat? Why, they're saints! What Piepel in Auschwitz has had as many chances as you? What other Piepel has been given a whole year in camp? What Piepel has been handed around as much as you? Which Piepel has had a go at all the beds of all the cubicles? They're saints, I tell you! Don't you dare say a word against any single one of them. Saints, I tell you, every mother's son of them!"

Tottering, he made his way through the Mussulman masses to the latrine. He felt very tired. He remembered that he had some very urgent matter to attend to there, but the matter lagged somewhere behind him and he did not have the strength to reach out and fetch it from the fog of his memory. The arguments of the censor within landed with hammer blows on him. With all his strength he tried to vindicate himself to the other. As though, if it turned out that he and not the other were right, his situation in Auschwitz would take a turn for the better. He was now like a man on trial, with the last word to say in his own defense before the verdict, trying with all his might to sway the jury. All the evidence is against him. His guilt is as clear as this rising Auschwitz day. He has but one witness in his favor; the pure and excruciating knowledge of innocence. But will he be able to put this feeling into words to refute the evidence against him? He makes another try:

"Don't you know of my nights in the block cubicles?" his lips murmured. "The others don't know, but you do! Who else should know what I went through in the beds of the Block Chiefs? You tell me—after such a night in a Block Chief's bed—where am I supposed to get the appetite for food? Even for the finest food! If you won't try to understand me, who will? I admit, I tried to fool you. Now I see that when I didn't touch the soup and ran off on all sorts of errands for the Block Chiefs, it was only an excuse because I couldn't swallow a thing. But if you won't see it, who will? In the Block Chief's bed I had no choice. In fact, there I went all out so the Block Chief should be satisfied with me. And you know that often this love-making went on all through the night. All night death was staring me right in the eyes and still I dozed off in the middle of the lovemaking. The Block Chief would grab me by the throat, and only when my eyes tore open I realized that I had dozed off a moment ago. I knew that if it weren't for the fact that the Block Chief was all worked up just then, my eyes would never have opened again. He kept me alive just so he could shoot his load. And then, with the last ounce of strength in you, you try to keep the lovemaking going and to keep the Block Chief's mind off your life with all the love-tricks you learned in your year in Auschwitz. Fear hugs you and rocks you in his arms. Rocks you, till he, Fear, dozes off together with you. And again you tear open your eyes. Again your throat is in the clamp of the Block Chief's hands. Don't *you* know what the Block Chief screams then? Is it only once that you've heard it? By that time you've stopped knowing what you're in for when the Block Chief has shot his load. Then you're torn between two fears; if you draw out the loveplay, you're terrified at the thought of dozing off in the middle; if you end the petting and fondling too soon, you're terrified at the thought that the Block Chief will croak you for it as soon as he's done. Oh, those nights in the beds of the Auschwitz Block Chiefs! Nobody, nobody knows about them. And nobody ever will. But you? You do know! So why do you throw it at me for not eating? How *could* I eat after such nights? How, you tell me, how? Would you have been able to? Why do I understand you, but you won't see my side of it?"

The vicinity of the latrine block was like a beehive in high season. It was impossible to get through to it. Business was going on at a feverish pitch. Poles moved around peddling the greasy cartons under their arms—two slices of moldy bread for one ration of camp bread. Jewish camplings, shrewd bankers of time past, make calculations and snatch up bargains. Mold, rot—who cares? The main thing is for the eye to get its fill.

The latrine block is packed from wall to wall. Especially around the rear gate. Near the water taps, all along the walls, stand Mussulmen holding their trousers in their hands, wiping from their nude legs the feces which had oozed out of them on the way to the latrine. In their armpits they hug yesterday's bread ration which they are no longer capable of eating and never will eat. Their trunks are swathed in a motley of tatters and strings—all the wealth they had managed to amass in the course of their Auschwitz life. The spindlelegs jutting nakedly down from the tatterbatch trunks give them the appearance of toy ostriches with tall steel filaments for legs.

Mussulmen. Only the instinct to snuggle up to the bread ration in the armpit is still quick in them. If a transport leaves their block for the crematorium today, they will not part with the bread ration but hug it along to the crematorium.

Transport to the crematorium. All at once it struck Moni why he had come here now. *A transport to the crematorium.* That's it. He had come on the chance that here, in the latrine, he might meet someone he knows from the Camp Office who will tell him from which block a transport is leaving for the crematorium today. Because before the list of the left-behinds reaches the kitchen, such a block has an extra barrel of soup. I must save myself! he cried to himself. I won't be a Mussulman! I'm an old campbird here in Auschwitz— not like those standing there by the walls! But deep within him he knew that this deliverance his mind was spinning was like a flimsy thread being scrambled to dust by the wind before his very eyes. He reaches out to this thread, to hold onto it for dear life, but his hand closes on empty Auschwitz air.

A crush. A surge. Mussulmen. Skeletons. Skeletons. You do not see them. Just as you do not see the paper, but the words written on it. They are merely the Auschwitz backdrop against which you see only Prominents.

In a corner near the water-pump compartment, one of the Corpse Kommando draws off his shirt. His white fleshiness gleams as over his head he draws a hand-knit pullover of rich, white wool for which he has already lined up a customer. Meanwhile, his partner counts from one hand into the other the gold teeth they were paid for the pullover. He divides the gold into four—two shares for the two other partners, who are now outside, loading up the cart with dead Mussulmen.

Yesterday at this time there was still a human being in this pullover. A human heart was still beating in it, at this time yesterday. A white pullover. Perhaps a sweetheart's hands had knit it as a present for her beloved; measured it on adored shoulders, measured the back, measured the chest, as they stood bosom to bosom. Breaths in caress. Now the clothing bundles are laid out on the ground at the crematorium entrance. Each day a new transport divests itself of its clothing there. Everyone neatly arranges his little pile of clothes on the ground so that afterwards, when he has come out of the Sauna, he will not have to search long, and so that his garments should not get mixed up with his neighbor's.

Only yesterday a man still wore the pullover. Now, it is being sold here. Where is the man who wore the pullover yesterday?

"Hey, Piepel!" Moni turned his head to the voice. Holy Dad Piotr stood behind him. They were almost the same height. "You seen Zalke, goddamn his hide?" Piotr's voice rasped with steely assonance. "I pulled off a mucky little caper for him last night, and if that whoreson doesn't bring me that fag now, my name ain't Piotr if I don't string his gizzards like barbed wire around this shithouse."

Moni said: "Zalke is the biggest merchant in Auschwitz. If he promised you a cigarette, he'll keep his word."

"You know, Piepel, you look to me like you're lounging

around here like Christ on holiday." Piotr's voice grated monotonously on Moni's ear. "Lost your *Funktion,* eh? Well, it's you that buggered it up."

Pride of seniority kept Moni from owning that he really was off *Funktion.* Yet he knew that no Piepel worthy of his name would be dawdling about at such a time. "I quit Robert because I felt like it," he said. "I left him. Why do you say it's my fault?"

"O.K. So pipe that number on your arm," Piotr's voice rasped fatherly reproof. "Look. Those bastards there were still pulling their little gyps in the ghettos when you were already a Piepel in Auschwitz. You're an old campbird here, Moni. And as an old campbird you should have known that a Piepel has got to pack more meat on his ass than you do."

A hand suddenly reached out from behind Piotr's head and nimbly pegged a white cigarette into his mouth-slit. Zalke's lightning eyes appeared. He let fall a slap on Piotr's pygmy back. "Hey, Holy Little Croaker," Zalke spoke at Piotr's eyes. "What say after the war I lead you around the world on a chain together with the Führer? God, what a box-office draw that'll be! A gold mine!"

"Goddamn son—" Piotr never got out the rest of the curse.

Zalke, the biggest merchant and true-penny in Auschwitz, vanished the way he had turned up.

When Piotr draws on his cigarette, his cheeks are sucked like two deep caverns into his toothless mouth. He sheathes the cigarette in his cupped hand, and at every draw the fanned flame shows between his fingers. "They give me a pain, those Piepels," Piotr spoke as though to himself. "They flap around the blocks like butterflies. Green, and still stinking with outside air. First thing you know, there they are like swells with their flashy boots, wiggling their poky little asses inside their skin-tight breeches. Goddamn whores! I'll lay you odds, Piepel, that there's a butterfly like that fresh out of the cocoon flapping around in Robert's block right now. But goddamn, let me lay my hands on him! See these hands,

Moni? I can't stand them. You, Moni, you're an old campbird. I like old campbirds. Take it from me, Moni, I'm your last pal in Auschwitz."

Moni felt his flesh crawl. He could see Piotr carelessly swaying to and fro on the cane across the throat of Max's Piepel: seesaw, seesaw. Up and down. Max had discovered that his Piepel was cuckolding him with one of the cooks from the central kitchen. The presence of the Piepels of all the blocks is mandatory at these ceremonies. Let them see, and let them remember: a Piepel must be faithful to his Block Chief! The white naked body of the Piepel writhed in a convulsive belly dance on the ground to the rhythm of Piotr's weird movements on the cane across his throat. One of Piotr's shows in honor of his distinguished clientele—the Block Chiefs. *I'm your last pal in Auschwitz* . . . Just a hint from Robert and Piotr would do to him exactly what he did to Max's Piepel. Moni felt that he could not stand Holy Dad another second. He barged out of the latrine.

The day had unfurled over Auschwitz. A new Auschwitz day, but familiar in every scent and hue. One just like it was here yesterday, and one just like it will be here tomorrow—after you. Besides it, there is nothing here. Everywhere —Auschwitz. As far as the eye can see—an Auschwitz-latticed sky.

Who will tell him which block is headed for the crematorium today? Moni mused.

The block gates to the backpath were shut. The campling masses were already locked back inside the blocks. They lie there ten to a hutch. A thousand to a block. Myriads in just one of the many camps in Auschwitz. And in each of them, all now spin a common weave, each working his thread into the weave. Shut-mouthed they lie, eyeballs staring at the boards of the hutch overhead, spinning the wondrous iridescent dream of a piece of bread. A little piece. Black bread. The kind they will be issued in the evening.

Their imagination can no longer visualize any other sort of bread. Their memory can no longer conjure any other kind of delicacy. The Auschwitz weave covers everything. Everything. Sky. Sun. Earth. Gone wife and child. Gone beloved God. No more world, and even no more crematorium. Only an outspread weave. The colors of the rainbow are drab and banal as against the splendor of the piece of bread at its center. A little piece. Black. Hard. The very kind they are going to be issued this evening.

Thousand to a block.

No! Moni determined. He is not one of them! But where will he find someone from the Camp Office? It's dangerous to go into block 1. There you're liable to fall right into Ludwig Tiene's hands. Who will tell him which block is headed for the crematorium today?

A new Auschwitz day. Mussulmen lie scattered all over the ground, in corners of the assembly areas, by the block walls. At a distance there is no telling whether they are alive, or whether they are ready for the corpse cart. A new day. Ordinary and familiar. All at once he had the feeling that for him this day would be different—

He gazed at the camp as though seeing it for the first time. A new sadness, one he had never felt, now emanated from the locked rear gates of the blocks. He looked at them. He knew exactly what was beyond them: long rows of hutches filled with Mussulmen. Five hundred on the right, five hundred on the left, a gate to the backpath for the common camplings, and a main gate opening on the main path for the Prominents. His place had always been at the front, between the cubicle and the kitchenette. Always among Prominents and Funktioners. There they had all looked up to him. Chief Orderlies, the worst cut-throats of all, had treated him like butcher boys in the marketplace chucking the fine lady's pet dog under the chin with their blood-moist fingers. They had all pampered him. The day had passed quickly there. A year gone by. He had been in camp, but not in Auschwitz.

He looked at the blocks. He has been Piepel in every one of them. In every one of them he had managed to dodge death in the nick of time. Would he continue to dodge this normal Auschwitz death which is everywhere his eye turns?

He gazed at the camp as though he were seeing it for the first time. Screams carried from the main path where kapos were dashing about, with truncheons flying. A Labor Kommando of a thousand camplings was lining up to march off to work. In the evening, they would carry back on their shoulders the dead and the half-dead. Now all size themselves and each other up: will he carry or be carried?

Mussulmen dragged past him. From every direction they come, from all the assembly areas. They no longer fear the kapos' bludgeons. Absently they straggle to the latrine holding in their hands trousers freshly befouled with feces. Their limp mouths display gumless teeth, fleshless and long as piano keys. Merchants cut their way through them to the exchange, bread bulging inside their trousers against the bellies.

When all those bastards were still pulling their gyps in the ghettos, you were already set up as a Piepel in Auschwitz, Moni repeated Holy Dad's words to himself. And wasn't Holy Dad right? Never! he determined. Not me! I'm not giving up! I'm an old campbird, and old campbirds don't turn Mussulman. They know me in the camp. I'll think of something. Come to think of it, why shouldn't I offer myself again to the Block Chiefs for whom I worked at the beginning? Golden Lolek took Franzl away from me, didn't he? So why shouldn't I do the same to another Piepel? What's it to me what happens to the other Piepel? Am I supposed to look out for other Piepels? Did they ever look out for me? A fat lot Golden Lolek worried about me! *If you want to stay alive in Auschwitz, you've got to kill someone else.* The first commandment of Auschwitz. He wondered why it hadn't occurred to him before. He could kick himself for always thinking of the other Piepel's neck whenever a Block Chief asked him to become his Piepel. If you want to stay alive in Auschwitz, you musn't think about the next fellow, he snarled at himself. It would seem that after a year in Auschwitz, you'd know better.

Now, listen carefully, he told himself, here's the plan. Go through the assembly area to the main path. There you'll keep a sharp eye out for one of the first Block Chiefs for whom you worked. When he shows up, you'll walk briskly by him as though you just happened to be on your way some place. Naturally, the Block Chief will notice you. He'll call: "Say, Moni, I was just thinking about you. How are those pretty velvet eyes of yours?" At this you're to open your eyes wide, very wide. Do you hear? You're to stare at him for all you're worth so he can get a good, long look at them. And your eyes are to hold on to that look of his so that he just won't be able to let go. He'll say: "Moni, how come I don't see you in my block any more? Don't be a stranger."

"I'm very busy," you'll answer him. "My Block Chief has nothing to worry about with me around. I see to it that he gets everything on the dot: cigarettes, meals—fresh cooked and baked. Spotless underwear. Everything laundered, pressed, shined. That's in the daytime. At night? Well, *I* know just what a Block Chief likes. You don't catch me dozing off in the middle of lovemaking the way other Piepels do. There's no recognizing me since that time I worked for you. Oh no, I'm not the same person. You'll never guess how many new tricks I know. Why am I a stranger, you ask? Well, it just so happens that I'm very busy. I take very special care of my Block Chief. My Block Chief is my life."

That's they way you're going to talk to him. You're going to use your brains. And your eyes. Don't you dare forget that: the whole time—wide open! Right at his eyes! He'll say to you: "Moni, what do you say you come back and be my Piepel again? Well—I guess I *didn't* treat you so good that time. But your eyes are driving me mad again. So what if you're skinny? This time I'll keep you with me till you've had a chance to fatten up. Fat Piepels? The place is crawling with them. But eyes like yours! Goddamn! There isn't another Piepel in camp with eyes like that. Promise you'll come back to me?"

"No," you'll answer to start with. "Just now I can't promise a thing. But I must say that you seem all right. I think I can tell you that if I do become your Piepel, I'll be all yours—body and soul. You have no idea how loyal I'll be to you. I could hug you right now. I love you like a brother. After the war you'll come home with me. To my house. I'll introduce you to my whole family. They love me very much, and they'll love you just as much. Because I'm going to tell them: This is my Block Chief from Auschwitz! This is my dearest Block Chief, I'll tell them. He said he didn't care if I was skinny. He said it didn't matter to him if I wasn't fat. Pa said that when he was my age he was also skinny. Pa said the Preleshniks don't get fat no matter how much they eat. I'll show you to all of them. This is my sweet Block Chief from Auschwitz, I'll tell them. He's the one who saved my life. He's the one who said: So what Moni? Just because you're naturally skinny, does that mean you can't be my Piepel? Your eyes are driving me crazy. And there isn't a Piepel in camp who knows what you know about lovemaking. And you do promise, don't you, that you won't doze off in the middle of lovemaking . . . Of course I promise! I know what I'll do: I'll pinch myself. That's the best thing against dozing off. I mustn't ever doze off again right in the middle. The minute I feel myself dozing off I'll dig my nails into my skin and pinch. The best thing is to dig the nails in so deep it hurts and burns, and then you stay awake."

Kapos dealt murderous blows on the skulls of the camplings lined up for the Labor Kommando. They counted the skulls again and again, but the figures did not tally. First there were too many, and then there were too few. That's awful! At the camp gate they will report: "Labor Kommando. A thousand camplings to march out!" Heaven help them if the S.S. sentry checks and the figures don't tally. So they search on the ground, at the feet. Because often, by the time the kapo reaches the last row, someone in a front row has swooned to the ground. He hasn't changed at all. The same open eyes. The same appearance. Only now he is dead. He has to be dragged off to one of the corpse piles, so that he should not mix up the lines.

Moni turned and ran to the bathpath. All he didn't need now was for a kapo to grab him for the Labor Kommando! What excuse will he give him? That he's Robert's Piepel? Sweetheart, a Piepel isn't dragging around camp like a cruddy Mussulman at this time of day. You can tell a Piepel right off, by the nose, by the way he walks! . . . Piepel, ha!

He drew away from the assembly area from which the Kommando was visible. As soon as they are marched out, he will run back to the main path. Which block shall he watch now? Franzl's? Bosker's? One doesn't have to know that he made the same offer to the other. For a moment the Piepels of those blocks leaped to his mind, but he immediately steeled himself. Forget about the Piepels of those blocks! Fat lot they worry about you.

Unconsciously his feet bore him to block 12. Unconsciously his feet so planted themselves that unseen he would be able to watch for Franzl going into or leaving the block.

A familiar voice, gay and glinting as a knife blade, suddenly reached his ears. The voice jarred him out of his reverie like the jangle of bells in a deep, heavy sleep which will not disperse however much the bells shrill in the ears. Turning his head, he saw the two backs: Franzl, his first Block Chief, and Bobo, Franzl's current Piepel.

Everyone can tell Franzl from the distance, because of the white cane which never leaves his hand. He tapped it against the tall, black-gleaming upper of his boot. A white cane. He had taken it out of the hand of a blind man at the Auschwitz unloading platform. Bobo vanished into a nearby block and Franzl stopped to wait for him outside.

Probably on a short errand for Franzl, the voice prodded Moni. So get right over to him! This is your chance! His breath stuck in his throat. He ran his eyes from the tattered toes of his shoes to the top of the jacket beneath his chin. Self-hatred flared up in him. Other Piepels are all primped up—nice boots, snug woolen pullovers. Why couldn't he ever think of such things? He only had to say the word, just snap his fingers, and the merchants would have showered him with such frillery. Now he looks like a stinking Mussulman! Hurry, hurry, the voice within him prodded. There's no time now to think about golden birds that got away. You have maidenhead eyes, remember? Franzl doesn't miss your flashy boots. It's your eyes he itches for. Offer him those eyes now. Remember those nights your eyes used to drive him mad? Sharp, now! Don't be scared! Let him have those eyes. He'll say: "Moni, your eyes are driving me nuts!" He'll say: "I can't forget you." He'll say: "Drop into my cubicle." Now's the time. Hurry ! Hurry! Why are you suddenly so worried about Bobo? What's Bobo to you? God! Forget Bobo, I tell you! You'll bring him a piece of bread every day! And you'll ask Franzl not to seesaw him. Franzl will do that much for you. He'll do anything for you. But hurry up, I tell you, hurry!

Moni's feet moved. He did not feel the ground beneath him. To the left—the long row of barbed-wire strands insulating the new transport; to the right—the long row of apexes of the sloping block roofs. Far, far ahead, at the edge of the earth, the roof of the last block lay virtually on the ground. In the center, the slab of sky over the path bore down on his brow. He did not feel the ground beneath him.

Now he saw his first Block Chief clearly. He stood almost face to face with him. But Franzl's glance lazed far beyond the barbed wire, like a fishing line dipping in a placid lake. Franzl's mouth whistled idyllically to the incessant tapping of his white cane on the boot upper. "Get closer to him! Closer! There's no time!"

Moni now stood directly opposite Franzl. Their glances met. Franzl's green eyes rested blankly on him. Franzl doesn't know him . . . Moni's mouth twisted into a smile. "I'm Moni," he said.

The white cane did not cease tapping against the side of the upper. The criminal triangle on Franzl's jacket was new. The green oil paint had a gloss of freshness. "Oh, Old whore? It's you!" Franzl said, the tip of his white cane pointing at Moni's feet. He snickered boredly. "If not for those red socks on your feet I'd never know you. I thought you'd moved along to the crematorium a long time ago. So you're still around!"

The block gate behind Franzl opened. Bobo came out. "That whoreson tried to pass off a pack of Polak on me," Bobo gloated, triumphantly handing Franzl a pack of quality German cigarettes.

Their backs moved off. The day hurried after them, and with a running leap mounted the black sheen of their boots. It was as though they were carrying the day off with them.

BOOK TWO

1

"Block Curfew!! Block Curfew!!"

The cry swept through the camp like a tempest. Pandemonium at the block entrances. All stampede inside at once. Soon Ludwig Tiene will come out of the Camp Office, and if his eye catches anyone's back outside the threshold, its owner will never again enter a block.

"Block Curfew!! Block Curfew!!"

Hayim-Idl left Moni in mid-sentence, turned and made a dash for his block.

It was silent inside. Dread silence. Pocksy Zygmunt paced up and down the long brick stove as though on an uncultured garden path. Block Curfew. A thousand camplings lie in the hutches, not a sound from them, as though none were there. During each visit of the S.S. inspector, Robert, Block Chief of 16, loves to show off this mock emptiness as the *pièce de résistance* of his block. Always accompanied by the same witticism and the same unsmiling mien: "Why don't they send me camplings? All the blocks are running over with shit. But me"—he sweeps his hand through the lifeless emptiness—"I'm running an empty block." Then, all at once, he roars: "Everybody down!" and a thousand camplings leap as one man from the hutches. Robert chuckles at the S.S. man.

Dread silence. Through the aperture running all along the top of the block for a window between the walls and the ceiling falls the light of day. Only you know: it is neither day, nor light. Here is merely a somewhere into which you were dumped—somehow, once. You do not walk into this somewhere, and you do not drift in it. You *are* in it.

Hayim-Idl lies in his hutch, murmuring over and over to himself: "My luck has run out!" All his life he was a tradesman, buying, selling, and always picking up an honest penny. He cannot recall ever having touched anything without turning a square meal. Even out of the dead ghetto walls he knew how to squeeze the daily bread for his family. He had never been anyone's burden. Not even in the ghetto had Dvortche, his wife, ever had to run to the public kitchen with her pot, like other mothers, to bring home some soup for their little Bella. No luxuries, true, but there was always a bite. In fact, others had even made a living off him. Hadn't Daniella, this Moni's sister, kept alive by smuggling his goods in the ghetto? But here, in Auschwitz, his luck has run out on him.

Others, Hayim-Idl mused, manage somehow: they hang around the latrine, dealing, peddling, and pick up an extra bowl of soup on the side. Oh, if he could pick up just one such extra bowl of soup a week! He's searched in every hole in camp and hasn't found even a rusty nail to get him started. By the time he gets there, someone else has beaten him to it. All kinds of misfits and schlemihls, who hadn't been able to make a go of anything on the outside—in Auschwitz they somehow know how to manage. One does the Chief Orderly's laundry; another gets a Piepel to bring him out the Block Chief's boots to shine. And for this they pick up a soup worth five ordinary rations. Not the mucky top-water, but the real thing left at the bottom of the barrel. And he—everywhere he turns he sees that here, there, there was something to be picked up, but always someone has beaten him to it. And for the life of him he can't think of anything new. His brain has run dry trying to think up things.

As soon as Block Curfew ends he's heading for the latrine. Maybe something will turn up after all. You never know. All the rest of them are doing business there. And they seem to be doing all right. Maybe if he hung around there—Ha! Hung around there! With what? With hands full of air? If he could save up just one bread ration he'd show them all. Now with a piece of bread to work with, he'd know what to do. First of all, he would buy two smokes with it in the latrine. Then he'd trade them to a block orderly for three soups. Two of the soups he would sell right on the spot for a bread ration, and still be one soup ahead. No, wait a minute: he would sell all *three* soups for one-and-a-half bread rations, and keep them till tomorrow's bread distribution. And then, he would eat up the half-bread he had netted, and the next day he would have two whole bread rations to do some business with. Oh, if he could just lay his hands on that *first* bread ration! Ah, pipe-dreams! It will never work! All the times he has tried! He just can't make it! A thousand times a day you die; your eyes pop out of their sockets waiting for the bread to be handed out in the evening. Who can lie there all night hugging a whole bread ration to the heart without taking a nibble, and not go mad? Oh, if only he could save up just one bread ration! Then he would be a merchant in Auschwitz. It's that first ration that counts. Then he would show them all.

If not for the Block Curfew he would run right over to the Rabbi of Shilev's block. Often you feel that you are about to faint from hunger. It would be so good to faint. But that same hunger squeezes your brain with clamps that won't let you faint. At such moments it is best to hurry over to the Rabbi of Shilev. In his presence the tears wash away your misery, and gradually your mind dozes off like a child after a good cry, and you feel better. It would be so much easier for him to bear it all if the Rabbi were with him here in block 16. For the Rabbi, too. First of all, the Rabbi would be rid of that butcher Fruchtenbaum. All the Chief Orderlies are butchers, but none of them comes up to Fruchtenbaum. The hunger pangs are so much easier to bear if you have someone to pour your heart out to. It's this eternal lying flat on your back in the hutch, and the constant blank staring at the hutch boards overhead, that suck the last drop of life out of you. Here, in the hutch, there is no one to have a word with. Professor Rafael, lying beside him, doesn't tire of just lying there day and night, all locked up within himself, not saying a word even to his friends, the Frenchmen lying around him. So they are as silent as he. And even if Professor Rafael did speak, he, Hayim-Idl wouldn't be able to exchange a word with him. They say the Professor knows ten languages fluently. But he doesn't understand a word of Yiddish. Queer Jew. He was brought here from Greece, where he was born. He had lived in Paris and been a professor in Italy. Not even forty yet, and he speaks all of ten languages. But plain Yiddish, the Mother Tongue—not a word! What a gloomy hutch. Full of foreigners—queer as their strange, faraway worlds. Locked within their silence. Just their eyes looking away—one to Italy, the other to France, another to Greece. A man can go out of his mind here!

If not for the Block Curfew he would now head right for the Rabbi of Shilev's block. In the Rabbi's hutch, a man's body and soul are revived. That Moni saved the Rabbi's life. And that's how they found out who the boy was. It would never have occurred to anyone to ask Moni who he is and where he had been brought from. Who asks a Jewish boy in Auschwitz who he is? Why, it's as plain as day: one Jewish boy among a million Jewish boys. Of course every one of them had a father, a mother, a home—that you know without asking. He happened to mention to Ferber that he was Daniella and Harry Preleshnik's brother. The poor thing thinks that Daniella and Harry are in Palestine. No one has told him otherwise, of course. Because it's the hope of seeing his sister and brother after the war that keeps the child going in Auschwitz. And no wonder: not everybody in Auschwitz can say that after the war he will still turn up a sister and a brother. A sweet soul, that boy. Even now that he isn't a Piepel any more, he still faithfully brings the Rabbi a can of tea to his hutch every day.

That's a queer rash the Rabbi's got. The skin of his face is peeling like the bark of a dying tree. They say a little marmalade would cure him. Anything sweet. He needs some sweet in his blood. But where in Auschwitz are you going to get some sweet, when all you get is a spoon-dab of marmalade on the corner of your bread ration once a week? And even that dab is soaked into the bread before your tongue ever gets to it. Otherwise, he would have rushed it right over to the Rabbi. Just a bit of sweet. Abram, the broker, guzzles marmalade every day. Every morning, before the first gong, when the block is still dark, his boy Benyek serves him breakfast in the hutch: two bread rations, sausage, a cup of marmalade, margarine. Just as that Benyek-boy had in the ghetto been able to smuggle six yards of suit material around his belly without ever a German noticing, here he smuggles the breakfast out of the Block Chief's cubicle under his pullover without anyone noticing. Now what would it mean to this swine of an Abram if just once he would give one little spoon of marmalade to the Rabbi of Shilev? If not that squirt of his, Abram would long since have turned Mussulman. But speak of luck: Benyek became Robert's Piepel in Moni's place.

Here, in the block, they all like to crowd around Abram in his hutch. First of all, he is the Piepel's father. It's good rubbing shoulders with such aristocracy. Secondly, Abram is always handing out good news, which immediately runs through the grapevine: "Hitler's finished!" "They're soon opening the camp gates!" No one asks about Abram's sources. "But how do you know?" "Sh-h-h . . . Abram . . ." And that is authority enough. Abram's hutch always has a full audience for his latest "good news." Abram's belly is full. He strolls around in the block as in a resort, abstractly humming away. More than one of Abram's loyal audience is dragged off at night to the corpse pile outside. But his hutch never runs short of replacements from newly arrived transports.

Every so often you find yourself aching for all those faces of the Metropoli ghetto that were transported here together with you. You look around, but you cannot find them any more. One by one they keep disappearing. All that's left of Vevke the cobbler is a shadow. He lies there in the hutch, silent, not stirring. It's not the old Vevke any more, the foreman of the shoe shop in the Metropoli ghetto. Just a shadow of his old self. A lot of them die right before your eyes. You only just spoke to them. You don't remember them complaining about anything special hurting them. They were not hungrier than yesterday or the day before; just a moment ago you had looked at them—and now here they lie in the hutch, just as they were a moment ago—open-eyed. Not a bit of change in their faces. Only—they're dead. You never can tell whether you yourself are not dying this very minute.

Ominous silence in the block. A thousand camplings hold their breath: Robert is about to step forth from his cubicle like an overlord come to mete out justice to his vassals. Pocksy Zygmunt holds the list of numbers scheduled for judgment. No one knows whether the number under the skin of his arm is down on the white chit in Zygmunt's hand. Your heart goes out to the number. Your Auschwitz life cowers there in mute entreaty. But who are you to save it?

Not even the orderlies dare show themselves now. Only Pocksy Zygmunt, the new Chief Orderly, paces around the brick stove. Although he has his hands full here, he is much better off with Robert than he was with Franzl in block 12. With Franzl you never know where you are. Even if you have a thousand smokes he'll squeeze every last one out of you. Oh, one by one, naturally. Just catch you trying to turn him down! Fat fortune you can scare up in Auschwitz anyway! But look, you can't walk out of here after the war empty handed! That's one thing you don't have to worry about with Robert. Robert doesn't smoke.

Robert is a *Reichsdeutsch.* His face gives him away. The aura of death rigs his head like a halo. The very walls of the block defer to him. The ground he walks renders him obeisance. *Robert!* White suède gloves adorn his hands. Just why Robert was sent to Auschwitz no one in camp knows. Unlike his fellow Block Chiefs, he does not boast of a glorious past. On the breast of his immaculate, ironed Auschwitz jacket he wears the green criminal triangle, denoting that already before the war he had been a convict. It is said that he was once a student at the University of Heidelberg. All the Block Chiefs look up to him, because they know that Robert does not bother with trivialities. But when a mass murder is on the agenda and a bottleneck develops at the crematorium, or when several transports of tens of thousands arrive simultaneously and have to be liquidated overnight, Auschwitz Commandant Rudolph Hoess summons Robert to the unloading platform as the experts' expert.

Whenever Robert appears in the block, the warbling of a canary immediately comes piping out of one of the hutches. "The Whistler." A Czech boy. He himself is barely visible. Only a head juts from a top tier, eyes shut, the two skeleton-cheeks inflated as though filled with a walnut each, the blanched lips pursed like a miniature trumpet around the tiny opening in the center.

Always, as Robert roams the block, Liszt's Rhapsody trills on the hollow silence, like the piping of a homesick canary in the woods. Then, on the noon soup line, this same "canary" reaches out his other hand as well, holding an additional bowl. He looks to Robert with tearful entreaty in his eyes: another bowl for the whistling.

The door of the cubicle opens: Robert comes out. There does not seem to be a person in the block. A thousand camplings catch their breaths. There is Zygmunt alone standing atop the long stove-sidewalk, the chit in his hand. Step by step Robert comes on, the creaking of his boots reaching every ear. From a top hutch bends a head, eyes sealed in ecstasy, heart thrashing about beneath the mesh of desiccated ribs like a caged bird in panic, and with the musical genius of all time the "canary" warbles his unending torch song to the second helping of soup.

Pocksy Zygmunt leaps down from the brick oven, sends his cane up and slams it at the sideboard of the hutch beside the craned head of the "canary": "That'll do!" The Whistler's eyes, sealed in a transport of longing, tear open in fright and he gazes at the banal reality into which he has been thrust. Warble unfinished—

Into the block Robert strides like a sovereign about to mount the throne to decree the fate of his subjects. His Chief Orderly Zygmunt holds the chit listing the numbers of the camplings whose manner of death Robert will now pronounce: who shall be hung by his wrists in the center of the block, and who shall get twenty-five in the ass; whose head to be shoved into the excrement inside the latrine hole to suffocation, and who shall be laid out on the ground to be seesawed with a cane across his throat. The solemn hour of judgment. For this Robert has come forth from his cubicle. A thousand hearts now thump to one cadence of terror.

Any second . . . Any second . . .

Suddenly Robert's eyes fall on his Piepel Benyek sitting in a top hutch. Their glances lock, like the eyes of secret lovers happening upon each other in a public place. At this Robert forgets the purpose for which he has just come into the block. Like a lover beneath his sweetheart's window, Robert paces back and forth before Benyek's hutch. Finger by finger Robert tugs at the white suede gloves on his hands. He sends his cane tapping away at the gleaming upper of his boot, his face wreathed in a discreet lover's smile.

Benyek sits on the edge of the top hutch, his little feet swinging coyly into the block. Behind his back Abram, his father, lies prone, sewing a button that had torn off Benyek's little suspender.

Benyek is wearing a snug turtleneck pullover of white wool. Robert brought it to him as a present from the unloading platform. Around his throat the pullover is sportily folded, the way Robert likes it. His handsome riding breeches hug his thighs, down his knees, where they are tucked into elegant little boots. The tailor of Zhichlyn had made the breeches to order for the Piepel. He had completed them just before he was taken to the crematorium.

One of Robert's greatest thrills is to watch his Piepel from afar in just this pose, sitting up there with his chubby angel face, his cherry lips, and the naughty girlish look in his eyes. That look excites Robert most of all. Benyek knows it, and he teases him thus at every opportunity.

Restless with desire Robert paces up and down. He is fairly bursting with pride. Everybody knows that he has the prettiest Piepel in camp.

When Zygmunt hands Robert the chit, a shudder runs through the block. Robert's hand receives the chit. His eyes flit unseeingly over it, and immediately rise back to the Piepel. Again he lowers them to the chit, smiling at it, but obviously the chit and the writing on it are the farthest thing from his mind. His clean-shaven face is cast with a smile of grace. Robert's fingers crumple the chit, which dwindles till it is no longer visible in his clenched fist. As though it were a worthless bit of scrap; a canceled promissory note. For a moment Robert resumes his stern mien. But a thousand hearts know that this is no more than a pose. Campling hearts cannot be deceived. Robert now taps his cane vigorously against his boot uppers, pacing up and down as he declaims into the hutches in a stage baritone:

"Very well, I'm granting you amnesty today! But the next time Zygmunt hands me such a chit, the whole block will do *Sport* under my personal supervision!"

Light floods the block as though suddenly a sun has dawned in it. Benyek swings his booted legs in the air. He catches the smile tossed at him from Robert's eyes and sends one winging back, like a young princess beaming on her knight triumphantly returned from a duel he has just fought for her honor. Abram draws the long thread from a freshly sewn button, darting a furtive side glance at Robert. Behind Benyek's back he basks in contentment. He approves of Robert, like the father of the bride taking delight in his first-rate son-in-law.

Only three words ever break from Professor Rafael's mouth: the names of his wife and two children. The Frenchmen lying silently around him hear, and their silence becomes denser, heavier, more unbearable. Hayim-Idl has nowhere to escape from this accursed hutch. Robert has left the block, but Block Curfew is still on. Names of children. They break Hayim-Idl's heart. Before he had crawled out of the bunker in the ghetto, little Bella had hugged him tight. *Daddy, where are you going?* He had left the bunker to find a way out of the ghetto. He had already escaped once from a burning ghetto together with Dvortche, carrying little Bella on his arm. Then he had managed it. But this time the Germans caught him. What happened to Dvortche and Bella? Could they have saved themselves? They did stay in the bunker. Bella wouldn't cry. The little one is three-and-a-half now. She had never cried during any of the Children's *Aktions* in the ghetto. She lay in a closed crate, and didn't let out a cry. More than once the Germans had stood right beside the crate, and never so much as a whimper out of Bella. By some miracle the little thing knew how to behave during a German *Aktion. Daddy, where are you going?* It was dark in the bunker. He can still feel her face warm against his cheeks, her tiny arms around his neck. With all her might she had clung to him—

Three words—just three—the names of his wife and two children, are all that break from Professor Rafael's mouth.

Hayim-Idl could not bear to go on lying in that hutch.

Abram sits in the center of his hutch. Around him sprawl prone skeletons, heads looking up at him. Between Abram's feet, as on a set table: a cup of marmalade, a large chunk of bread, a sausage end, and a pretty aluminum case with a closed cover, in which Abram stores the margarine. With a miniature knife which he had fashioned from a nail, Abram cuts the bread into little slices; with two fingers he daintily lifts the cover of the aluminum case, lays it aside, then spreads some margarine on the bread and marmalade on the margarine. Then, with the knife he cuts the slices into cubes, spears one of the cubes and consecratedly places it deep inside his mouth, drawing the knife back from between his pressed lips as dozens of eyes accompany his every move, feeling that not only Abram, but they, too, are thus bringing the bread cubes into their mouths—only their teeth chew on nothing but saliva.

Hayim-Idl looks on, beside himself with fury: he could grab that disgusting carcass by his rotten throat and choke him. That scum! Can't he bust his guts at night, when no one is watching? No, he's got to rub it in and stuff himself now! But Hayim-Idl knows that nobody invited him here. It was his own idea to escape here from his hutch because he felt he would go out of his mind there. Everybody is drawn to Abram's hutch. Everybody is curious to see eating. The temples pound away, but no one has the strength to tear himself away from the feast.

God knows how he detests Abram. He reeks of his son's Piepelhood. Yet you can't keep yourself away from his hutch. There is nothing but death around Rafael and the Frenchmen. But in Abram's hutch there is life. Only that crud hasn't a spark of a Jewish heart in him. Once he told him: "Hayim-Idl, pick me up a case for margarine!" Hayim-Idl had rushed to the latrine, hung around there for two days, got it over the head from the kapos, before he finally turned up the aluminum case standing there between Abram's legs. A beauty of a case! The Russian prisoner-of-war had asked two soups for it. With just one bread ration he would have been made right then and there. That carcass would have exploded but would have had to fork over four bread rations for such a case. Benyek-boy doesn't have breads to spare? But he had no choice but to take the Russian directly to Abram. And since that crud dealt with the Russian directly, it seemed only right to him that Hayim-Idl shouldn't be in on the deal. That scum had a piece of good luck. His precious son became Piepel. Otherwise, he would long since have gone flying out through the smokestack.

Abram holds the sausage end in his hands. He speaks leisurely as his teeth nibble bits around the edge of the sausage. Gradually the red meat pyramids in the casing, appearing to jut out of a goblet.

Those lying around him do not hear a word. Their eyes impale the rubicund sausage flesh, which becomes ever steeper towards the center of the casing. Again Abram daintily nibbles a piece with the edges of his teeth and sucks on it as though it were a candy, while the eyes around suck it along with him in unison. But instead of the sausage, they suck the tongue in their mouth.

"If the Theresienstadters heard," Abram sing-songs, "even before they were brought to Auschwitz, about decisive battles in the Crimea—" With one bite Abram nips off the apex of the sausage at the center of the goblet. "Jews! Do you hear? As soon as the front reaches the Polish border we're free!"

Hayim-Idl can no longer contain his loathing. "And as soon as the Joe-boys[1] reach the Crimean Peninsula, then—kkhkhkh . . ." Hayim-Idl brandishes his fist under Abram's nose, letting his tongue dangle as though he were choking. "Then kkhkh . . . kkhkh . . ." And he feels it is not the Germans but Abram that he is throttling.

"Ass, so what are you arguing about?" Abram shouts. "That's exactly what I said! I only forgot to ask how far the Crimea is from the Polish border. If this Crimea place is near, then it's only a matter of a day or two before the camp gates are opened."

The eyes of the skeletons around Abram transfix the empty sausage casing. Among them there may be some who not only know exactly where the Crimea is, but who had even lived in the villas of beautiful Yalta. But now, during the exchange between Hayim-Idl and Abram, they do not take in a word of the discussion. The words "Crimea," "Joe-boys," "Polish border," "open camp gates" echo in their ears as though out of some distant haze; as devoid of content as barrels of noontime soup without a lick left in them. They do not know what all the fuss is about. This they do know: Abram is right! Because Abram is the one eating sausage. This, too, they know: for that empty sausage skin in Abram's hand they would now give everything, anything. If at this moment they were told to go free, they would forego even that for this empty sausage skin.

Hayim-Idl crawled away across the bodies lying in the hutch. He wanted to make his way to Vevke the cobbler's hutch.

Several hutches from Abram lay the Whistler. Hayim-Idl stopped to watch him pick something out of his pocket with

[1] Russians; Joe meaning Joseph Stalin.

two fingertips, hold it up to his eyes, examine it for a moment, then place it between his teeth. Must be bread crumbs. But Hayim-Idl could not fathom how bread crumbs could keep so long in a man's pocket. How can a man know that there are such crumbs in his pocket and yet control himself so long? A whole night! A whole morning! Where does a man get all that will power?

Beside the Whistler two downturned bowls lay side by side, like two living creatures warming themselves at his body. Two bowls. He always carries them with him. That is his exclusive privilege. As though they were his private property. No one in the block is allowed to hold on to a bowl. His pair of bowls are washed, clean. They exude the divine savor of soup. One of them still has white specks of enamel. Relics of their former careers.

That's a lucky fellow, Hayim-Idl mused. In camp you never know what's going to save your life. Here's a man who fixed himself up fine in Auschwitz, and he's going to live. Nothing can touch him now. The block orderlies know that at the soup line-up he is allowed to hold a bowl in each hand. It's legal—the Whistler! When he reaches the barrel he extends one bowl and gets his regular portion along with all the rest. But as soon as that is filled, he extends his left hand with the other bowl. Robert looks up from the barrel. Quiveringly the Whistler looks back. You never can tell how such things will end up. The face around his nose begins to tic. His eyes beseech: it's me, the Whistler! He is ready, standing there with the other bowl in his extended hand, to break into warbling, just like a canary. Right now. This very minute. Let Robert choose any symphony he likes. There isn't a musical creation in the world that he, the Whistler, could not, standing here at the barrel, get out of the little hole his pale lips will now shape. Won't Robert please test him—

But Robert hasn't the slightest intention of testing him. Robert merely raises his eyes to see who it is that dared to hold out a second bowl in his left hand. Ah, the Whistler!

That's all right then. With pleasure. As a matter of fact, now Robert sends the ladle down to the bottom of the barrel, where the fabulous treasures lie: the real essence, not the insipid topwater. The eyes bulge from their sockets when Robert draws the full ladle out. God! Such marvels to behold. As though the legendary Atlantis had risen from the sea. Ah, the Whistler! Welcome to it!

Such a portion of soup has no price. Not once in all his life did Hayim-Idl experience—and he probably never will—the taste of such divine stuff. He doesn't even dare dream of such Prominents' soup. No wonder the Whistler can afford to have bread crumbs lying around in his pocket so long.

Hayim-Idl seated himself on the edge of the hutch. He bent toward the Whistler's feet, like a beaten cur seeking his master's favor. He felt so inferior and poor in the Whistler's presence that he didn't know how to begin. The Whistler was very busy now. Stubbornly he was searching all corners of his pocket. Apparently his two fingertips had not found anything. Hayim-Idl raised his eyes to him. He blurted: "Were you a little boy when you learned to whistle?"

The Whistler concentrated on that something between his fingertips which he had just dug out of his pocket. "No," he replied, at once tenderly and indifferently.

Hayim-Idl did not want the conversation to end there. He wanted to keep the conversation with the Whistler going. There was something he wanted to lead up to.

"I suppose they were all whistlers in your family. Are they still alive?" Hayim-Idl asked.

"No, my friend."

My friend. Hayim-Idl felt a closeness and an odd warmth in his heart. He had something in common with the Whistler, now: his family aren't alive either. A loneliness to be shared. He and the Whistler are equal. One family. Mustering up his courage, he continued:

"Must be a hard trade, whistling. Back home before the war I suppose you gave whistling concerts?"

"Concerts? Yes, my friend. I gave concerts in all the capitals of Europe. But I didn't whistle, then. I played the violin."

The two bowls lay beside him. Hayim-Idl was gazing at them, when—lo and behold: one was filled with the ordinary soup, the same as they all receive, while the other, the enamel-twinkling one, was brimming with the royal essence. Thick. When you stick the spoon in, it stands.

"Teach me to whistle—"

The words erupted all at once from Hayim-Idl's throat. What a moment ago he had not known how to express now came out of him in the simplest of words: *Teach me to whistle* . . . For a moment Hayim-Idl was afraid that he had committed a *faux pas,* that he had spoken too impetuously, without leading up to it as tradesmen do when one wants to do his competitor out of a good bit of merchandise. But Hayim-Idl most of all marveled at the fact that his words had not at all struck the Whistler the way he had been afraid they would. Unperturbed, the Whistler answered gently: "Practice, my friend. All it takes is practice."

Hayim-Idl thought that with these words the Whistler meant to get rid of him. Of course, only he is putting it nicely. You can see he is of good stock. Even though in his fine way he wants to get rid of him. But he doesn't hold it against him. He understands; he even agrees with him. Yet he would like to convince him that he really has no intention of going into competition with him and spoiling his business.

"I swear by all that's dear and holy! May I live to see my wife and my baby Bella as I won't do any whistling in this block! I'll take my whistling to the other blocks!" Tears rose to Hayim-Idl's eyes and clogged his throat. All at once he threw himself at the Whistler's feet, embracing them with his hands and sobbing helplessly into them: "Teach me to whistle. I want to live. Maybe I'll be able to hold my baby in my arms again! Bella! Bella sweet! You'll see, your Daddy's going to learn to whistle . . ."

2

Hayim-Idl halted in his tracks. What's he going to the latrine for? he asked himself.

It was early in the day. Thousands like himself slogged by. The path was full of them. A swarming mass. All identical. Like grains of shifting desert dunes. What's he going to the latrine for if he has nothing to open business with? He has nothing to sell, and he has nothing to buy with. His life tagged after him on the Auschwitz backpath, naked and bone-dry. Worthless. And except for this life he did not have a possession to his name.

He's tried his hand at everything: helped do the laundry for Chief Orderlies; served rich Prominents; polished, swept, washed cutlery, but always, instead of payment, he's gotten a kick for his trouble. Whenever he offered to do the job, the *Funktion* owner agreed. Sure, why not! Much obliged. But when paytime came around, it was a crack on the skull he collected. Does he think he's the only one waiting to get paid off?

Not a *Funktion* to be had.

Let's face it: what's he going to open business with when he has nothing to sell and all of him isn't worth a whistle?

There's all the sky you want here. So many blocks you can't count them. Pillars along the barbed wire, crematorium smoke—and that's the lot. What will he use for buying and what will he sell? The Whistler seems a straight fellow. You can tell right off. Fine stock. He really meant to help him.

He continued slogging along the blocks.

In the assembly area behind block 1 the Greeks were sparring, practicing new numbers. Jewish lads from Salonika. Jews. Now who would ever guess that the likes of these are Jews? They had to send him to Auschwitz so he should find out that tawny skins and muscles like that could belong to brothers of his. His own flesh and blood. They can't speak a word of Yiddish, but that *"Shalom!"* comes out of their mouths like a living verse of Scripture. Every Sunday they put on a boxing tournament in the kitchen compound in honor of the Camp Senior and his gang. *The boxers!* Now they're having a workout. Shmulik, the bread storekeeper, stands on the threshold of the store block watching and beaming at it all. All at once Shmulik swerves around, vanishes into the darkness of the store and immediately reappears with two whole loaves of bread which he tosses at them like a bouquet into a ring. The boxers, bodies intertwined in bout, break hold, interrupt the sparring, snatch the two loaves off the ground, flash their white teeth in a grin at Shmulik, say something in Greek in their hoarse voices, and are gone. So much for the boxing.

So that's why they do their sparring here, Hayim-Idl mused. Right behind the food store! Jewish kids. And what is it they want? Just to live. Greece. Jews everywhere. He had never realized that in Greece the Jews look so Gentile. Jewish kids. They found themselves a livelihood; beating each other with their fists and living off it. You don't find any of them being block orderly here. Not one of them was picked for Block Chief. Though any one of them could lay Fruchtenbaum out for all time with his pinkie. That Fruchtenbaum isn't worth the dirt under the nail of a pinkie of theirs.

Shalom! Can't speak a word of Yiddish, but they always have a hearty *"Shalom!"* for the Jews of the block. Sometimes they show their Jewishness by reciting the *"Hamotzi"* blessing before biting their white teeth into the bread Shmulik tosses at them. Fruchtenbaum. Blast his name and fame! Butcher. Murderer.

Hayim-Idl turned around and trudged towards the front of the camp. But the thought would not leave him: two loaves! Two full-length loaves. If he could talk their language, he would speak to them about it. There is so much goodness in their eyes. Perhaps they need someone to do their shirts. Not that he ever saw them wearing a jacket or shirt. Nothing. Just pants. Bare backs and chests full of muscles. Husky, sunburnt giants. Such a one would never harm him. He would learn boxing from him. Why not? You can learn anything. He has time, doesn't he? He would take off his jacket, sit in the sun and get himself a good tan. If *he* swallowed all of such a loaf in one gulp, he would also have the strength. You get such shoulders by eating. They wouldn't harm him. Together with them he would box. Together with them he would eat. What would it harm them if Shmulik tossed out another bread? But you've got to be able to explain such a delicate matter in plain, simple Yiddish. *Shalom!* That's the only word they seem to know.

Along the barbed-wire wall strolled two electricians, pliers in hands, testing the current in the wires. Hayim-Idl watched them, beside himself with envy: everybody here lands a *Funktion.* See them chatting away there, strolling along as though they were out in the summer woods. Bend every now and then to the lowest rows of wire, as though to pluck a flower. Hard job, that—strolling along the wire with a little pliers in your hand, and nothing to do but tweak and splice. Tweak and splice! All at once it nettled him: why can't he? Why only the others? "Hayim-Idl, God has forsaken you!" the words came hurtling out of him. "Hayim-Idl—"

But immediately he cut himself off. He was frightened at

the blasphemy he had uttered against God in Auschwitz. "Oh, Master of the Universe! Don't punish me for my talk," he begged mercy, gazing all the while at the two electricians. "I wasn't questioning Your ways. But take pity on me and don't forsake me."

From the main path the Corpse Kommando arrived with their cart. Near the back gates of the blocks the cadaver bones were stacked like piles of cordwood which peasants collect behind their huts for winter fuel. A cook came sauntering back from the latrine, sleeves uprolled, everything on him gleaming fat. In one of the assembly areas a campling washed plaid sport socks in a large tub. *Funktions. Funktions. Funktions* everywhere for everyone. This way and that skeletons slogged by, crawling out of every hole in camp, eyes gazing off somewhere. Gazing, gazing–

Not seeing only Auschwitz around them.

Practice, my friend. It seems the Whistler really meant it. He really wanted to help him. *Practice. All it takes is practice!* His jaw bones were at the cracking point, but not a peep came out of his mouth. Well, what do you expect? He never in his life whistled! Polack boys whistled. But they weren't sent to Auschwitz. He thought there was nothing to whistling. But he has stood in every corner of this camp trying to teach himself to whistle. He has blown out his body and soul trying. *Practice.* He was willing. What was he supposed to do that he didn't? The Whistler had a stroke of luck in camp. He's a lucky person. It's all a matter of luck, no getting around that.

Behind block 10 camplings dashed busily about fussing with hutch boards: these dragging whole hutches out of the block and those taking the planks apart. Hayim-Idl drew to a halt. He could tell immediately that this was no forced labor. No kapo stood near to goad them with his bludgeon. In that case, Hayim-Idl's nose told him, there's a new living coming up here. The camplings dashed in and out of the block.

Nearby, one drew diagrams in the air with his hands, showing the other how to build the boards into whatever it was he had in mind. It all looked like Jews living in the same court preparing to put up a common *Sukka* booth. Hayim-Idl could not contain himself. His mind caught fire and his eyes raced hither and thither: what's going on here? In a corner, a campling leaned sideways against the block, silently observing the hubbub. Hayim-Idl hurried over to him.

"What are they making?"

"A stage," the former replied.

"Stage?...Stage?..." Hayim-Idl rolled the word around in his mouth, like someone trying to get the flavor of some unknown delicacy. What is he talking about?

"What do you mean? What's that?" Hayim-Idl asked. The campling did not turn around to him. He went on standing there, in the same attitude, continuing to watch the work raging around the boards, and, neither raising nor dropping his voice, replied:

"There's going to be theatre in block 10 tonight...They're putting on theatre...There are a lot of actors in block 10 ...They're setting up a theatre in Auschwitz..." The campling's mouth told the words as though they were gold sovereigns: "Theatre" and "actors." "Actors" and "theatre." As if he took special delight in lingering on these two words.

Hayim-Idl's brain was already working at top speed. They're setting up a theatre! Something brand new! There he is, in on the birth of a new *Funktion! Theatre!* Theatre!

"Hayim-Idl, it was simply heartbreaking," his mother had told him after they got home, kissing him on the head, her eyes red with weeping. It was Hanukah time, when he was a little boy in heder, after the class had put on "Joseph in the Pit." Hayim-Idl, it was simply heartbreaking.

He had never thought of it again, till now, in Auschwitz. Theatre. They're putting on theatre!

Someone came out of the block. He held a whispered consultation with a foreman, drawing odd designs in the air with his hand. The campling beside Hayim-Idl took in the entire scene. He stared and spoke—perhaps to Hayim-Idl, perhaps to himself—the words coming from his mouth as though not he were uttering them but someone inside him.

"That's the director . . . Used to be director of the Vienna State Theatre . . . Trained a whole generation of stage artists . . . Established a method . . ."

The director! Well, what's there to think about? It's time to act. Mustn't miss out on this chance. He'll have to have a talk with this director fellow. Seems to be a good sort. You can still see the refinement in his skeleton face. Time to act. Time to get down to business. He is in on the birth of a new *Funktion.* Such chances don't come again. God Himself had sent him here now. What did I tell you, Hayam-Idl? he reproached himself. You must never lose faith! You mustn't question God's ways! Everything in good time. The director seems to be an understanding sort. What's it to him if another Jew saves himself? Let's say so-and-so many Jews are on theatre, so there'll be one more. What's it to him? A theatre needs singers, doesn't it? In "Joseph in the Pit" a chorus stood in a semicircle around the actors, singing throughout the show. Bergson, the cantor, is in block 15. Better get together with Bergson. So another Jew will be saved. It will be easier for him to sing together with the cantor. The point is: it's time to act. And fast. Thank God he got here in the nick of time. The only thing is, should he go talk to the director right away or should he first dash over to Bergson? Of course, it's better with the cantor! What an impression it will make when Bergson announces that he is the former cantor of the Metropoli "atheists' " synagogue.

Hayim-Idl was off in a dash to block 15. On the way he kept colliding with the crawling Mussulmen as if they were obstacles which had been laid in his path. He felt as though he had sprouted wings, and he let himself soar. Out of his mouth the words splattered from the thoughts sizzling in his head. "This is no mere choirboy...This is a Cantor...A real Cantor...The Cantor of the 'atheists'' synagogue."

Bergson was lying in the hutch. He looked like a long stalk yellow with blight, whose grains had long since been winnowed. Although he was a *Hassid,* scion of the rabbinical line of Rizhyn, the synagogue elders, detest though they did the *Hassidim,* had elected him their cantor because of the fine figure he cut. Bergson was over six feet tall, and with the top hat appeared still taller. He groomed his chestnut beard in Franz-Josef style, parted at the chin. A model of perfect grooming, always impeccably dressed, he used to stroll majestically along Metropoli's promenade in his soft deerskin shoes, his head towering over the scene like a giraffe's. The congregation prided themselves on their cantor as a prize adornment. "What a royal figure!" women and men alike declaimed. Those who at first had felt that his Hassidic origins were a mark against him eventually changed their minds. As a matter of fact, his Hassidic extraction lent him mystical charm.

Now Bergson resembled a long yellow stalk. His two long leg bones jutted naked from his short trousers, extending far beyond the rim of his hutch. His neck was extraordinarily long, bare as the plucked neck of a gander. At the top of the neck his shriveled head drooped like a tattered flag. His trousers were too low to cover his midriff and too short for his legs. Hard as he tried to draw his trousers up, he never succeeded in bringing them up to the jacket which hung on him like a bolero, and they never covered his naked, tallowy midriff. Bergson soon gave up. He stopped drawing up the trousers, and he allowed hunger and cold to eat away at his "royal figure."

When Hayim-Idl arrived at the hutch, Bergson was dozing, like a beached stick of driftwood. Hayim-Idl had always been short. But now, sitting at Bergson's feet, he resembled a midget riding a log.

"Bergson! Bergson!" Hayim-Idl shook him. "We're saved! . . . They need singers in block 10! . . ."

Not a stir from the log. Bergson's jaundiced eyes gazed at him as from a faraway shore.

"Bergson!" Hayim-Idl went on shaking him. "Bergson, get up! Come while there's time! Two soups a day! One in your own block and another in block 10. You hear me, Bergson?"

Inside Bergson's head everything was already calcified. Things no longer registered with him. Except the word "soup," to which his cells still responded.

Hayim-Idl dragged Bergson from the hutch the way an ant hauls off an object many times its own size.

After much feverish waiting and vain effort, Hayim-Idl finally cornered the director inside block 10. Hayim-Idl held Bergson by the hand. To an observer, it might have seemed that Bergson was leading a little boy by the hand. Actually, Hayim-Idl was holding on to Bergson the way one holds a little child to keep it from going astray in a crowd.

As soon as he laid eyes on the director, Hayim-Idl knew this was not the time or place for bandying words. Some unknown power surged in him, and he came right to the point: "*Herr* Director, take us on in the theatre!"

"Unfortunately, dear colleague, we are glutted with artists. All the parts are filled. Not an opening left." The director spoke like a man who assumes that this reply settles the matter. He wanted to hurry back to his affairs.

"*Herr* Director!" Hayim-Idl did not let him pass. "For us it's a matter of life and death! *Herr* Director . . ."

"Impossible, impossible." The director's face registered pain, as though he were suffering an acute toothache. "Absolutely impossible!"

"Aren't you a Jew?" Hayim-Idl pleaded. "I want to live!

. . . What will it harm you if I save my life? This is my last chance. There isn't another thing I can do. Save me!"

Fairground commotion filled block 10, part of which was in darkness and part lit up. Actors rushed busily about getting things ready. Some ranged near the dark walls of the block mumbling to themselves. Queer words accompanied by odd grimaces.

The director twisted and bent this way and that, wringing his hands as though something really hurt him. He spoke guttural German which did not sound at all Yiddish, and Hayim-Idl could barely make him out. "My friends, what can I do? We are all in great trouble. Great trouble. Look," he pointed to a hutch back in the dark. "There lie the geniuses of European theatre. The glory of the Theatre. There is more Theatre in that one hutch at this moment than in an entire continent. Any continent you choose. Do you hear? Any one! Genius and culture! My dear friends, do I have to tell you?"

"*Herr* Director," Hayim-Idl spoke in a tear-drenched voice. "A human life now lies in your hands. A human being is a whole universe. The theatre is my last hope. Don't send me off with the *Selektion!* Have mercy! Don't send me off to the crematorium! For the rest of your life you'll be able to say that you saved a human being from death. Have mercy . . ."

The director's face suddenly turned yellow as a death-mask. His lips parted as though to gulp air. All at once he began to quake all over. His hands and feet twitched convulsively. The words sputtered from between his clenched teeth. "On my conscience? . . . How dare you place such a thing on my conscience? I am fifty-eight years old, and you wish to lay claim to my conscience?"

"To whom then should I turn? Who can save me now if not you?" Hayim-Idl said heartbrokenly. He felt truly sorry for the director.

"Why did other colleagues understand my situation? Why did the others not lay claim to my conscience? . . ."

"Maybe the others have the strength to go on waiting. I've run out of strength and hope. Only theatre can still save me. Only theatre. God preserved me this long till a theatre turned up. It is the one and last thing I've lived for. Save me! *Herr* Director, save me!"

The director lowered his eyes. He was helpless against this artistic passion which not even Auschwitz could quench. "With which theatre were you connected?" he asked.

Hayim-Idl pointed at Bergson. "We're singers," he said.

Two eyes swelled in the director's head. He was on the verge of tears. Again he began to wring his hands in desperation. "But, my friends, there must be some mistake! A mistake! We are doing drama! Drama without words! Mime! Pantomime. *Ach, Gott!*" The director's face convulsed as though in hysterical weeping. He fled into the darkness of the block, slapping his sides as he ran, as though his whole world had come down around him here, in Auschwitz.

All the while Bergson stood there immobile as a polehook in a clothing shop: unhearing, unseeing, unknowing, merely leaning full-length in a corner waiting to be used. There is nothing more to be done here now, Hayim-Idl mused. The director had gone and left them standing there.

Outside the sky was white and dismal. Camplings took boards apart and laid them out. They are setting up a stage. In Hayim-Idl's head the thoughts began to whirr like the works of a watch whose spring has just snapped.

Bergson dragged along beside him. They did not speak. Bergson's long legs moved off automatically and in no particular direction. An uprooted naked tree, boughless, rootless, sailing along wherever the tempest happens to bear it.

Hayim-Idl did not try to check him. Everything in him rebelled. "Drama! . . ." he argued aloud. "They're putting on Drama. So what? Why should that stickler care if two more Jews save themselves? Would it break him to put on a drama *with* words? Who says it must be without words? What law says that it all must be just so when it's a matter of life and death? Let's say that in Auschwitz he put on a drama with words: so would the sky fall down? Or maybe the public wouldn't buy any tickets? But go try and make a *Yecke* stickler see that! 'Without words!' As a matter of fact," Hayim-Idl argued with the Auschwitz day, "it would be all the easier to act *without* words. No!" he decided. "Mustn't let this chance go! It's a new *Funktion.* A good, cushy *Funktion.* I mustn't let it go! All isn't lost yet. And for the time being no one has lined up anything else. That dried-up beanpole just stood there like crowbait. If only he had spoken up! If at least he had let on that he had been a synagogue cantor. A real cantor. Not a quack!"

In the evening, directly after bread distribution, Hayim-Idl took Bergson and was off with him to block 10.

Out of all the blocks, from every direction, streamed Block Chiefs, merchants, Chief Orderlies, cooks from the camp kitchen, clerks—the camp's Prominents, arm-in-arm with their Piepels, were turning out for the theatre.

Near the rear gate of block 10, Hayim-Idl came upon the campling who had first let him in on the secret of the theatre. Again he stood there leaning sideways against the block wall —exactly as Hayim-Idl had seen him that morning. He might have been standing there looking on all the time.

The red bulbs on the barbed-wire wall glowed eerily. Far off, somewhere beyond the wall from the direction of the crematorium, the wind carried muffled snatches of clashing cymbals of a brass band. At the rear gate of the block preoccupied actors kept barging in and out and stagehands hurried to and fro. The director dashed out soaked with perspiration. His glance fell on Hayim-Idl standing there with Bergson, but he ignored them. He held whispered consultations with camplings—actors, or idea men. Hayim-Idl's feet jerked nervously. He was about to make a dash for the director when the latter again vanished inside the block.

Hayim-Idl felt sadness settle on him like a dustfall. What

rotten luck. There they were dashing in and out like nurses attending the birth of a quivering new life. He envied them. Just two steps away a *Funktion* was taking shape; the *Funktion* which his fancy had hatched and brooded all day long. And he was not in on it.

Hayim-Idl, Bergson, the anonymous campling—three waifs watching wistfully from outside the circus grounds.

Behind them, at their very feet, lay a pile of dead Mussulmen: naked skeletons—cadavers of block 10. The red bulbs cast an uncanny fairy-tale glow on the block roofs. Bergson's long shadow bisected the bone pallor bending towards the other edge of the pile like a narrow black band holding the pile of dead Mussulman together around the center to keep it from caving in.

All at once, Hayim-Idl thought of something: "Wait for me here, Bergson! I'll be right back. Don't you budge from this spot! Do you hear? I'll only be a second." Hayim-Idl dashed across the assembly area to the main path, turned right, and vanished into block 28. His eyes frantically sought the hutch of the Rabbi of Shilev.

The rabbi was sitting in the hutch, the shred of jacket sleeve capping his head, nibbling at the bread ration. The mangy skin of his face iridesced like a weird mosaic.

Hayim-Idl fell upon him. "Rabbi, bless me! Wish me success, Rabbi! Rabbi, I am about to be saved! . . ."

The Rabbi of Shilev interrupted his chewing. The fresh blotches on his face where the skin had just peeled were green as mold. He gazed quizzically at Hayim-Idl.

"Rabbi!" Hayim-Idl continued his hot eruption of words, "*Funktion* in block 10 . . . Extra soup a day . . . Going to do theatre . . Rabbi, bless me!"

Ferber sipped the cold tea, peering over the rim of the wrinkled can, transfixing Hayim-Idl with his eyes. The Rabbi's hand reached into the air opposite Hayim-Idl's head. In one of them lay the remains of the bread ration. He seemed to be offering Hayim-Idl his last bite.

"If you imagine there is any help in me for you, then go ahead, Hayim-Idl. I wish you success." The Rabbi barely managed to breathe the words. It was as though he were offering him the blessing on the palms of his hands.

Hayim-Idl prostrated himself at the Rabbi's gaunt, naked legs, burying his head between them and embracing them with his arms. "Rabbi . . . Rabbi . . ." he sobbed.

"Go, Hayim-Idl. God is also in the Auschwitz theatre—"

The Rabbi's voice cheeped, like a tot startled by the sound of its first utterance.

Ludwig Tiene and his party sat directly before the stage as in a royal loge. The kitchen kapo pulled out of his jacket a bag full of meat cubes; the very bag of meat whose contents were supposed to supply all the cauldrons for the entire camp. Once a week a fistful of such meat cubes is to be dropped into every soup cauldron. But even the kitchen kapo knows how ludicrous that would be: like throwing a cube of sugar into the sea for the fish to find. Neither the camplings nor the Prominents would get anything out of that. On the other hand now, everybody in the party reaches into the bag and helps himself to a fistful of meat cubes which he pops into his mouth like peanuts. That makes sense. That way at least somebody in camp gets to enjoy the meat.

The stage was hung with grey blankets for a curtain, not quite reaching the boards. Through the opening the bare soles of the director could be seen flurrying about the finishing touches. The block darkened. Only on the stage a red bulb remained lit. The blankets parted – two fastened blankets to the right, two to the left, revealing a stage bare except for one actor lying at the center, covered with a dark woolen blanket of a block orderly—he is the corpse. His soul is now to play the main role. And to be sure, from under the blanket a wraithlike form slowly rises, ethereal as a whiff of smoke. How strange. Without seeming to move, hands or feet not touching anything, simply rising like crematorium smoke, wrapped in two aprons of a cook—the soul of the body lying in the center of the stage. He floats about in space, vainly seeking embodiment, until at last he drifts into an empty frame of a mirror and hangs there motionless—the reflection of one who has passed away. Across the stage, neckless and bodiless heads suddenly materialize at a table made of hutch planks, hovering along the table like a row of trunkless jurors. Behind them two actors emerge, heads facing each other, their eyes conducting a horror-dialogue as their feet climb a staircase of air. Queer, mute gesticulations. Speaking shut-mouthed. Towards them come floating two others, announcing something in an esoteric eye-dialect, not moving lips or hands. Their feet really do not seem to be touching the ground. Everything here is happening as though not in the world of man, and not even in the world of Auschwitz, but somewhere in primordial space between Chaos and Creation.

Here is the tribunal. Now the drama will begin. The soul floats out of the mirror frame, drawing up before the tribunal, profile to the audience. Now someone is to be charged with beheading the jurors. Any moment now and Law will materialize in the dock for all to see. But all at once a block of wood came flying at the stage from the first loge and landed on the skull of the "soul." The soul let out a shriek and collapsed to the stage boards. Now isn't that remarkable: the soul's "body," which had lain dead on the ground, covered with the orderly's blanket, started up at the bloodcurdling shriek which had not been in the script and gaped with reincarnated eyes at the loge of the Camp Senior whence the block of wood had come hurtling.

Camp Senior Ludwig Tiene snatched the truncheon from Robert's hand, brandishing it at the stage as he screeched: "Cut that shit! A song! Let's have a song in the theatre!"

Then and there everyone knew that at least one of the actors would shortly hang by his wrists in the center of the stage.

The actors shrank back towards the rear of the stage, their eyes now showing prosaic, unartistic terror. The difference was immediately obvious. They vanished, leaving in their wake the terror of their bulging eyes. The director came out on the stage, bowing deeply to every side, wringing his hands, huddling and twisting as though he were very cold.

"Dear gentlemen! We are here presenting a drama which—" He got no further. Block Chiefs' truncheons came hurtling at his head.

"Bring on the song! Cut the pitch and let's have some singing!"

The rear gateway of the block was open and desolate. The actors had fled for their lives into the Auschwitz night. By the gateway the director raced to and fro, frantically wringing his hands. He did not know whether he should also flee, or whether he was honor-bound to remain with his sinking ship. Never in all his theatrical activity had anything of this sort happened. No one can say he did not do his best, considering the primitive facilities at his disposal. *Ach, Gott! Gott!* What now? He wrung his hands, running around in circles, till finally he tripped over a skeleton foot protruding from the pile of dead Mussulmen and pitched onto the skeleton heap, letting out a wail like a spoiled child who has slipped in the mud, not budging, just lying there shrieking for Mama to come and pick him up.

Through the open gate carried the catcalls:

"Bastards! Let's have some songs! . . ."

"Bring on the play-actors! . . ."

"On with the show! . . ."

The campling beside the wall stood there as apathetically as before, the words stringing from his mouth: "If they'd only let me on the boards. . . I offered. . . I've got five years of radio behind me. . . I know what the Germans like. . . I performed for them in the ghetto. . . I knew immediately this would turn out a fiasco. . . They should have let me on the boards. . ."

Hayim-Idl snatched Bergson by the hand. "Now, Bergson! Now!" he shouted at him. "It's now or never! For the Holy Name of God! We haven't a thing to lose. God is also in the Auschwitz theatre."

Opposite their eyes the director was still sobbing convulsively on the pile of Mussulmen. He had become entangled in the bones and was afraid to touch them with his hands. He was still waiting for his Mommy to come and see what a mess he was in. Hayim-Idl pulled urgently at Bergson's hand. "This is it!" he shouted in a choked voice, as though making the final proclamation of faith before leaping on to the martyrs' pyre.

He was swallowed into the gateway. Two stairs up the stage. No one stood there. They had all fled. Free passage to the stairs. The Rabbi's blessing, *Go, Hayim-Idl, go and succeed,* reverberated in his ears as in a vacuum world.

He dragged Bergson up with him.

A red light flooded his eyes. Opposite, beyond the bank of crimson—pitch darkness punctuated by thousands of heads like a nighttime burst of fireworks. With Bergson he stood in the center of the stage, unaware that he was actually on the stage. Nor did he know that his hand was still gripping Bergson's. Cheers and roars of laughter deafened his ears He stood there as in a trance. White heads like foamy white breakers opening dark maws. Hands raised in applause, spraying white spume. Maws not ceasing to shout and guffaw:

"Pat and Patashon!..."

"Bravo! Bravo!"

"Pat-Patashon!..."

The whooping did not abate. Hayim-Idl knew that he must start singing right away. Anything. He tilted his head up to the cantor, his eyes full of entreaty. Bergson stood erect, motionless, staring indifferently with his Mussulmanic eyes at the dark block and at the uproarious laughter which showed no sign of letting up.

"Bergson, start! Bergson, I beg you, start!" Hayim-Idl spoke up at Bergson, not letting go of his hand as though afraid that as soon as he did the wind would carry Bergson off leaving him, Hayim-Idl, alone on the stage, caged with all those ready-mouthed beasts. "Bergson," Hayim-Idl pleaded up at him out of the corner of his mouth, "you're a real cantor! . . . The Rabbi of Shilev promised that we would succeed! Bergson, open your mouth. Bergson, for pity's sake . . ."

There was not a stir in Bergson, not the batting of an eyelash. And the more Bergson stood there staring as Hayim-Idl sent beseeching looks up at him, the more the block reverberated with cheers: "Bravo, Pat! Bravo, Patashon!"

"Bergson, for pity's sake start! I'll help you along. I won't let you down. If only I knew how to start I'd go first. You're a cantor. A real cantor. Whom are you afraid of? The Rabbi of Shilev promised. Start. For God's sake start!"

When Hayim-Idl realized that the laughter in the block was abating and still not a sound out of Bergson, he knew the situation was desperate. If he hadn't counted on the cantor, he would have prepared something himself. Now he did not know how to begin, and there was no backing out. He would have to start singing himself. But what? . . . His mind was a turmoil of lullabies and snatches of liturgy. What should he start with? . . . From the block the outcries came hurling at him!

"Get a move on, Pat!"

"Come on, Patashon, show your stuff!"

Hayim-Idl shuddered. *In that hutch lie Europe's greatest artists.* He had seen all the artists fleeing out the door as though death were in hot pursuit. *Practice. All it takes is practice.* The director on the Mussulman heap sobbed like a little child. *Go, Hayim-Idl. Go and succeed.* All now seethed in one crucible over the fire of his brain.

"Show your stuff, Patashon!"

Hayim-Idl flexed a cheek, turned his mouth to the side, and out of the corner of his lips spoke up at the cantor: "Bergson, I'm starting! Bergson, don't let me down!"

The more Hayim-Idl spoke thus furtively up at Bergson, the more the loges convulsed with laughter. As though of its own accord Hayim-Idl's hand suddenly rose to signal he was starting. "Sh!"

He cupped his ear in his hand in the cantorial manner, sent his eyes off to the sacred spheres, and laughter once more shook the block. "Sh!...Sh!..." they all shouted, and went on laughing.

Soon dark maws shut. Frothing waves fell calm. And Hayim-Idl's ears heard his own voice quavering!

"Benafsho . . . Benafsho . . . Oy, oy, oy. He risketh his life to bring his bread!"

Suddenly Bergson snapped awake. Something came winging its way back to him from faraway worlds.

He is at the lectern behind his father, prayer leader at the Rizhin congregation in the Galician townlet. It is Rosh Hashana. Papa is conducting the Additional Mussaf Service, and he, just a little boy, is accompanying him.

"Oy, oy, oy, moshol . . . Like unto the shattered pot . . ."

At the sound of Bergson's voice, a thrill of joy coursed through Hayim-Idl. His eyes filled with tears. New life breathed in him. Hayim-Idl sang along, all the while nodding up at Bergson, embracing him with his right arm, snuggling gratefully against him, as their prayer-song merged:

"Oy, oy, oy. Od-om-m . . . Man stemmeth from the dust. . ."

The block surged with applause at the bizarre melody and words tickling them to tears.

"God bless you, Bergson!" Hayim-Idl cuddled up to him like a happy child. "God bless every one of your bones!" But Bergson just went on standing there, as though the whole thing did not involve him at all. And the more he continued to stand there staring vapid-eyed, the more the audience roared.

"Pat-Patashon! . . ."

"Let's have another number! . . ."

"Jazz it up, Pat, jazz it up . . ."

Apparently the campling outside heard how the two singers were hitting it off, for suddenly he was on the stage. Hayim-Idl was delighted to see him. Sure, why not? Let another Jew sing for his life! The more the merrier. Hayim-Idl cheerily signaled to the audience with his hand. "Sh! Now I have the honor to present to you another singer. A real singer, no fake."

And indeed, the singer knew what the Germans liked. It was a sentimental song about a "sweet little kid-o, with two gorgeous tits-o," and all the little details about how such a "kid-o" is to be handled in order to keep "everybody happy." A real hit. Just the thing. The entire block promptly joined in the refrain:

> Yessir, I've got me a baby—Hop-hop-hop-hop-hop.
> A baby who's all mine—Hop-hop-hop-hop-hop.
> And every time I hump her—Hop-hop-hop-hop-hop.
> The juice flows like wine—Hop-hop-hop-hop-hop.
> Let's be merry, let's be gay . . .

From the central camp compound carried the tolls of the gong: playtime is over! Damn, just when things were getting good! Vatzek, the peelery kapo, leaped on to the stage. "Hey, Pat-Patashon!" he roared at them. "Bring your mugs to my peelery tomorrow! You get all the soup you can put away!"

The sky lay like a black blanket low over the camp. The gong tolled for the last time. The main path was empty. Hayim-Idl made for block 16, almost at a run. *All the soup you can put away.* The tears flowed from his eyes. He wept aloud

3

Near the scullery was the potato peelery, where Vatzek was kapo and supreme potentate.

Rows of wooden benches stood in the center of the peelery. Peelers with paring knives in their hands sat there peeling into straw baskets—not really peeling, but cutting the turnip roots and pumpkins, or sometimes just scraping the caked mud off potatoes. Built in along the peelery walls were large basins filled with water. Beside a basin stood "Dziadek" with his pitchfork, raking the potatoes that had been dumped there to rinse them of their mud.

"Dziadek—"

There was an occult rite Vatzek used to perform—select one of the potato peelers, dub him "Dziadek"—"Grandpa"—and treat him as a fetish. It is hard to tell just what inspired Vatzek to this odd custom, just as there is no understanding Vatzek himself. Perhaps it was out of superstition; perhaps out of some other, mysterious motive. For who could fathom the soul of such an old Ka-tzetnik as Vatzek? In any case, it is never clear just what it is Vatzek sees in the face of his elected one, just as there is no comprehending the ceremony that always attends the election. The Dziadek he chooses is generally well along in years, and it makes no difference to him whether he is Jew or non-Jew—although he himself is Christian, and more than once he erupts into such cursing that it seems certain there is a rabid Jew-hater in him. It is plain for all to see that some Higher Power dictates his choice.

The coronation rite—

A Dziadek has been liquidated and there is an opening for a successor. The peelers sit on their benches, eyes lowered to their work, each engrossed in his own thoughts; Vatzek, according to his wont, sits on the chair near the window, eyes musing at the distance. All at once he starts up with a shout at the rows of bowed heads:

"Dziadek! You belong at the basin!"

All eyes come to attention. No one knows whose head the golden scepter has tapped this time. A ray of life has been tossed amidst the rows. Who caught it? Who is the elect? No one dares reach for the crown. But Vatzek immediately sets up a shattering roar, as though someone has struck him in the eye with the potato pitchfork.

"Whoresons! Bastards! Bitches! You should only fry, all of you! I'll dump you all into the crematorium alive! What are you staring at? Can't you see? You there! Yeah, you! Your eyes should only pop! *You!* Let him through, bastards! Let Dziadek through to the basin!"

And so a new Dziadek has been crowned. And always attended by such a ceremony.

There is no fathoming this enigmatic coronation, just as there is no explaining the designation "Dziadek." No one thinks about it. It is as normal and logical as the turnip root in your hand; the watchtower framed in the window like a picture on the wall. As normal and logical as your name "Whoreson"; the names "Crematorium"; "Mussulman"; "Piepel."

This time a Pole is Dziadek. The last time, when the chosen one was a Jew, the peelery was paradise for the Jews. The handful of Poles, who gagged at the very idea of sitting on a bench together with a Jew, gnashed their teeth and felt in the peelery like Jews in exile. But Pocksy Zygmunt gave the last Jewish Dziadek such a murderous beating during the *Selektion* for having failed to steal and smuggle potatoes for him that the man's eyes immediately turned Mussulmanic, and he did not even try to defend himself as Zygmunt led him to the lorry, solicitous as a nurse, pityingly circling his finger at his temple as if to say to the S.S. man: Poor bugger, you'd never know to look at him that he went off his nut . . . That Dziadek was taken off to the crematorium, though there was still plenty of flesh on him.

Now the Poles again rule the roost in the peelery—this Dziadek is a Pole. Although they know that the Jews are in any case marked for the crematorium—whenever the cry comes, "All Jews fall in!" the Jewish potato peelers must immediately put their knives down on the benches and dash off to the *Selektion*—even so the Poles look forward impatiently to each "All Jews fall in!" And bitter is their disappointment at the sight of some of the Jewish peelers, survivors of the *Selektion*, returning to take their places again on the benches. At such times, the faces of the Poles turn sullen at the sloppy way things are run in Auschwitz. They sit there sulking, taking it as a personal insult.

There are not many Poles in this camp. Mainly smugglers or feather merchants who took the place of the Jews in the country's commercial life when the ghettos and transports went into operation. Polish political prisoners are generally sent along by the Gestapo with the Jewish transports taken directly from the wagons to the crematorium.

Most of the Poles in camp have *Funktions*—some of the highest. Only in this camp's office there is not a single Pole. This bastion of the pen is Pole-free. It is also a fact that not one Pole has been sent alive to the crematorium in a *Selek-*

tion. Not even a Polish Mussulman. But then, the Poles rarely turn Mussulman. The Poles receive letters and packages from home. The poor ones at first occupy low-grade *Funktions,* but as the Jews progress into the crematorium, the Poles progress into their vacated *Funktions.* Because when there is a shortage of fresh crematorium-fodder, the Germans do not mind taking even high-ranking Jewish Funktioners. Just so the bones are Jewish. No matter if the bones are covered with flesh, even rolls of flesh; no matter how loyally and assiduously they served the Germans, more loyally and assiduously even than the non-Jews—the crematorium is always at their service. It is only a matter of time and turn.

Only the Poles always stay on. They are not even required to line up for the *Selektions.*

Selektion does not mean Poles.

Burly, big-backed Dziadek stood at the water-basin, gazing boredly out the window, lazily raking the soaking vegetables back and forth with the potato pitchfork. All at once his full face came alive. His eyes had seen something in the window. His taut cheek-puffs lit up with joy, his face widening in a rosy smile. "Vatzek, look!" he called. "Pat and Patashon!"

Hayim-Idl and Bergson stood near the edge of block 1, their eyes riveted on the window of the peelery, in trembling anticipation of the miracle. For although Vatzek himself had explicitly told them last night to come right into the peelery, they were mortally afraid to come any closer to the kitchen. Before they manage to get to Vatzek, anyone—a barrel washer or just some kapo—is apt to crack them across the skull with a truncheon and they will drop dead right at the kitchen entrance.

Dziadek's cry shook Vatzek from his reverie, and turning to look in the direction Dziadek was pointing, he shouted over to them: "Whoring Pat and Patashon! What are you standing there for? Come on in!"

Hayim-Idl stepped gingerly, his bare feet feeling the stone pavement of the kitchen compound. This was the first time his tottering feet had trod on these awesome stones. His heart raced at once in fear and elation. He drew Bergson along by the hand like a child leading his blind father across a teetering bridge. The compound filled him with dread. Hayim-Idl did not take his gaze from Vatzek's eyes. He pressed towards the haven they offered like a foundering boat at night towards the lighthouse, towing Bergson along the beacon of those two eyes.

"Dziadek, get over to the cauldron section and tell the kapo I want a barrel of soup, on the double!" Vatzek commanded.

In the peelery all now felt like children at the arrival of magicians in their courtyard. Hayim-Idl also giggled at the sight of the barrel of steaming soup placed before him. Mucous dribbled from Bergson's mouth and nose without his knowing or feeling it. Hayim-Idl could not believe his eyes. The two of them just stood there, not daring to move a limb. A barrel of soup! A barrel full of soup!

"Lay it in, whoresons, unless you want me to dump the both of you into the barrel!" Vatzek thundered.

Hayim-Idl had not slurped up one bowl when Bergson had already drawn his third. The Poles rolled with laughter.

The Jews, too.

At the height of the hilarity, Vatzek unobtrusively approached Hayim-Idl and under his breath let fall:

"Put the bowl down. You'll get the runs. That's enough the first time." Vatzek's voice was warm and gentle. Hayim-Idl looked up at him. Their eyes met.

The Poles were busy watching Bergson, convulsing with laughter at the sight of bowl after bowl pouring into him without a drop of it all showing in his long hollowness.

Hayim-Idl went over to Bergson, took from his hands the

bowl full of soup he had just drawn and poured the soup back into the barrel. Bergson opened two quizzical eyes on Hayim-Idl. He could not understand. The Poles did not understand, either: why is he spoiling their fun?

"Dziadek!" Vatzek thundered. "Hand them each a knife and let them get peeling. I've got so many freeloaders, whores and sons-of-bitches here, two more won't show."

"Sure, and they'll be good for laughs, too," Dziadek chimed in, his apple-cheeks smiling broadly.

Hayim-Idl was drunk, partly with the soup, partly with joy, partly with the great, wide, wonderful world in which he had the good fortune to live. If he had been told that he was getting out of Auschwitz, he would have believed it sooner than that he would live to sit in the Auschwitz potato peelery. Slowly, carefully he let himself down on the seat. He did not yet have the courage to plant his full posterior on the bench. His heart did not yet believe that all this was really so. And he was still sitting on the edge of the bench when Vatzek's outcry suddenly rent his ears: "Hey, you whoring Pat-Patashon! I'll beat that soup out of you! Where did you leave Hop-Hop? Get Hop-Hop over here on the double!"

A shiver seized Hayim-Idl. He was not yet familiar with Vatzek's idiosyncrasies. He barely managed to stammer: "Hop-Hop was standing with us outside of block 1, but a kapo passed by and grabbed him for work."

"Hop-Hop better be in the peelery tomorrow!" Vatzek thundered. "No kapo out there better grab him for any other bloody work! Get me?"

"Yes, yes, of course." This time Hayim-Idl seated himself more securely on the bench. His hands fairly flew as he cut away at the turnips, his mouth blurting the words: "Tomorrow...First thing in the morning...I'll bring him...Hop-Hop is a real singer...He's no quack..."

4

The rows of camplings marched to the camp gate, ten abreast. All skulls were identical in their round nudity. Dim, yellow apparitions.

A kommando is marching off to work.

As soon as the gate opened, without the camplings knowing just when, how or why, the kapos' truncheons began to rain blows on the aligned skulls. The kapos seemed to be beating a long yellow carpet.

Arriving at the German watchpost, the rows halted, but the truncheons worked all the more industriously, beating the yellow tapestry all the more murderously. And it seems they were right. For all at once the tapestry began to show its true color: an incarnadine mosaic.

Apparently all this was intended for the benefit of the German inside the watchpost—as an exhibition of their devoted labor. Don't let the German think for a moment that the Kapo Bands on their arms are there just for decoration. But the German, stepping forth from the watchpost, did not grace them with as much as a glance. He never turned to see whether the kapos were beating or not. The whole thing did not interest him one bit. It's all shit. Shit. A long, yellow stretch of boredom. All he wants to know is how many shits are passing him and going out the gate now.

The chief kapo snatched the cap off his head, then dashed over to the German, and snapped to soldierly attention: "Reporting—Labor Kommando. A thousand prisoners ready to march out!"

The German gestured with his pencil across the rows, as though he were really counting, entering the total in his report sheet. Immediately the kapos' truncheons resume their rise and fall. Eyes trained on the German, they drub away at the skulls, railing savagely all the while: "Whoresons! Bitches! Mussulmen shit!" *Oh, won't the merciful German confer a glance on the demonstration being put on here for his benefit?* But all the German did was write the total down and vanish back inside the watchpost.

When the German was gone, the truncheons drooped limp again in the kapos' hands. They were like slaves whose master has just dashed into their faces the goblet of wine they served him.

The rows marched forward. The Rabbi of Shilev skipped along in the row beside Ferber like a little boy. Strange: the kapo's truncheon landed on his shoulder, but here he is limping along on his leg. That morning, when the kapo came into the block to pick camplings for the kommando, Fruchtenbaum had pointed first of all to the Rabbi's hutch. "Take that clerical parasite there, who never worked a day in his life! A little fresh air will do him some good, that *R-r-r-rebbetzin*!"

The rows marched out of camp. Outside ranged another electrified barbed-wire wall. Here began the highway leading to all the other camps and sections of Auschwitz, the road along which the lorries sped day and night to the crematorium.

The campling behind the Rabbi kicked and trod on his heels, railing at him all the while: "Mussulman whore! Stop dragging like a corpse! I don't want to suffer because of you. I'll tell the kapo you're lousing up the line. Keep moving! Come on, keep moving!"

"Rabbi, won't you hold on to my arm," Ferber said.

"No need, Ferber, no need. I'm walking. There. The line is straight."

"Kapo, help yourself to the whole hutch!" Fruchtenbaum had shouted. "And don't forget the Red Sexton!" His father—the Zionist leader, Ferber mused. After the war he will probably be the first to come to Auschwitz to roll in the dust, and the first to throw a stone at his son's hanging carcass. Poor Fruchtenbaum! All his life he'll go on thinking that it was his hands that had wielded his son's truncheon. He won't know how to mourn enough. Surely he will wear sackcloth and ashes the rest of his life—the crematorium ashes of the Jews his son had murdered before their turn. Especially since they were murdered because they mentioned his father's name. How many Jews might still be alive if Chief Orderly Fruchtenbaum's father had been a shopkeeper, a shoemaker, or a synagogue sexton? Who knows how many Jews would still be alive if Fruchtenbaum the Zionist leader had been childless?

"Rabbi, did you have any children?" Ferber suddenly asked.

"What did you say, my son?"

"I asked if you had any children."

"No, Ferber. Fulfilled Commandments and good deeds performed are also accounted as one's children. But I, Ferber, will come to God with nothing. Without children, without good deeds." The Rabbi skipped along on his game leg as though he were hurrying to fulfill some Commandment. Ferber held him back, at the same time straightening the row.

On the right sprawled all the camps of Auschwitz. On the left streamed a wilderness: sky, earth, horizon—all sulphuric, Sodom-like, tubercular. The kapo marching on Ferber's right twirled the truncheon in his fingers like a drum-major's baton. Left! Two-three-four-left! Dust settled on the gleam of his black boots. The striped cap perched at a jaunty angle on his head. His nape was clean-shaven, bulging. Across the road stood a few lone, scraggly trees. They melted the heart. Of all the trees in the world, they have been condemned to grow along this road. They seemed tortured, long-suffering.

Far off along the horizon moved S.S. men in their black uniforms. They walked in single file, leading huge black hounds at their sides. A long black band, like some weird prehistoric centipede crawling along the skyline patrolling the borders of its domain.

"Pick up! Pick up!" the commands shattered the air.

The skulls dispersed beneath the tubercular light of the sky like a lorry-load of yellow turnips scattered on the kitchen compound. The kapos' truncheons rose into the air and landed on desiccated bare skulls. The kapos' outcries came reverberating back from every direction, like the echoes of invisible kapos in the skies shouting down. You no longer knew whether it was the terrestrial kapos roaring and the celestial kapos echoing back, or vice versa.

Near a bare rail-bed, a mountain of boards was stacked on the ground. Sections of block walls and roofs, rafters, sides of hutches. Desiccated bone-hands fingered the edges of the boards and tried in vain to drag them out of the pile. Bending and tugging helplessly they stood there, trembling lest the kapo's truncheon meanwhile slice like an axe into the unattended back. Hands of camplings, sere as the wooden planks before them, tugged in vain, because board clamped board and it was impossible to drag anything out. The shrieking of the kapos resounded from sky and earth. Here they are beside you. Feet and hands scampered up the pile, covering it like a swarm of ants. Now there was no wood to be seen.

Everybody lifted and carried. An endless horde. A ghost procession in an accursed wasteland. Now the camplings were invisible. Only the whiteness of long boards high overhead, stirring the paint in the Auschwitz sky.

Boards. Boards. Boards. They are probably setting up

another camp here. The furnaces are working day and night, but they cannot keep pace with the constant flow of humans fed to them.

The father and son from Amstov together carry a finished hutch side. They look identical. There is no telling the father from the son. The father is one of the steady callers at the hutch of the Rabbi of Shilev. A pious Jew. His house in Amstov was a haven for the needy. Those carrying hutch sides must walk on the fringes of the rows; they are the most vulnerable, completely exposed as they are to the kapos' truncheons. The father hugs one end of the hutch side with both hands under his arm. He walks in front. Behind him his son carries the other end. Ferber found a rafter about a yard long for the Rabbi, and the Rabbi hugs it devoutly in his arms like a Torah Scroll.

Odd. As much as Ferber looks at the Rabbi, he goes on seeing him with his golden beard and side-curls. Just the way he looked in the ghetto when he came to ask for his cooperation in rousing the Jews to revolt against the Germans. Odd. He lies in the same hutch with the Rabbi. His eyes constantly see the skin peeling from the naked bony face. Yet he goes on seeing the face with beard and side-curls. "Life is not ours to dispose," the Rabbi had said in the ghetto. "Life belongs to God. If we wilfully walk into the Germans' fire, we shall be accomplices to the murder. God is everywhere and His will is everywhere. Even in the wilderness God said: 'Make Me a sanctuary and I shall dwell in your midst.'" He can still hear those words of the Rabbi's. Now the Rabbi of Shilev limps along beside him. Carrying a board for the construction of another camp, so that God shall also be able to dwell here, in this wilderness. A swell of fury surged in Ferber. Nobody would listen to him in the ghetto. In the woods, the Polish partisans shot every Jew coming to join them. What choice did he have but to go along with all the others to Auschwitz? Oh, had he let himself be talked into it then! He had thought that if he went to Auschwitz he would live to the day of revenge. Now he sees that he will go to the crematorium first. Vengeance! Vengeance! All of him now cried out for vengeance. "Oh, God!"

The "Oh, God!" erupted from his throat without his even realizing it. The Rabbi looked up at him. "My son," he said. "That is the cry of our people now bound to the altar with the slaughtering knife poised at its throat."

"Shut up! Shut up, *R-r-rebbetzin*!" Ferber screamed at the Rabbi of Shilev. "Carry that board to build a sanctuary! You, *R-r-rebbetzin*! You, and the others of your kind are the slaughterers of our people!"

Ferber ground out the "R" with greater loathing than Fruchtenbaum. Overhead, the planks clattered against each other, and his ears could not hear the words which had exploded from his mouth.

The Rabbi lowered his eyes. The thick board began to slide from his hands and he hastened to hug it tight to his heart to keep it from falling. The skin at his temples peeled in roseate patches, and his cheek cavities were mold-green. Painful, humiliated loneliness of defeat lay on the Rabbi's bowed head. Ferber's heart twinged in remorse and pity.

"Is it heavy, Rabbi?" he asked softly.

"No, no, Ferber. No."

"Try to carry it on your shoulder. Like me."

"No, Ferber. Someone behind me might accidentally hit his head on it."

A truncheon-bearing kapo parked himself to look on as the Jew of Amstov struggled to keep the hutch side under his arm from slipping to the ground. The edge of the plank was already dragging in the dust. His son behind him winced at the dread of the truncheon which would, as a result, any moment now fall on his head, too. His eyes bulged with terror. He shoved the board forward to show the kapo how hard he was working. "Whoreson!" he screamed at his father's back. "Get that board high! They'll murder me here on account of you!"

Ferber shifted his board from one shoulder to the other. That is exactly the way he had just screamed, *"R-r-rebbetzin!"*

"Forgive me, Rabbi," he said.

The Rabbi raised his eyes to Ferber. Infinite compassion, anguish and forgiveness lay in the eyes. He said nothing. He lowered his head again. All was clear once more. Clear and understandable.

And side by side they walked on in the row.

The compound at which they arrived was bare and long. On the left streaked the barbed wire of the last Auschwitz camps. On the right a narrow, crooked path branched off the highway. The dust of the path bore the tracks of the huge lorry tires leading to and from the crematorium. Everybody started depositing the boards in the empty compound. Because of the boards being carried across shoulders, the marching column stretched out to many times its original length. After depositing their loads, they all re-arrayed themselves ten abreast. They stood there, waiting, silently watching the crematorium smokestack jutting up through the trees and sending black and white knots of smoke into the sky.

Suddenly all eyes tore from the smokestack. At the edge of the compound someone had noticed a corner covered with a patch of grass. In a bolt of lust they all threw themselves at the ground and with their mouths ravished the grass. The hands were dead from carrying the planks. The hands could not pluck the grass. So the teeth bit into soil. Heads butted heads away. In a flash the patch was covered with back upon headless back. The kapos dashed over, started swinging their truncheons and grinding their boots as though into an anthill. The row stood up and re-arrayed itself. Eyes gazed longingly from afar at the glimmers of green here and there on the ground.

Again the rows started marching back to the woodpile, this time by a side path. Here and there stood trees, their roots exposed and blighted. A Labor Kommando from the Women's Camp was performing a strange job here. Girls, heads and backs bowed to the ground, moved about picking something. It was impossible to see what they were picking —for what was there on this ground to pick at all? When the rows of men passed by the girls did not raise their heads, but merely darted furtive side glances from the ground at the feet of the marchers. S.S. men with hounds walked by. Silently they passed, surfeited with the kill. They looked at the camplings with the nausea of satiation, like someone who had spoiled his stomach overeating meat, whose glance stumbles on the show window of a meat market. The beefy black hounds walked wearily and languidly alongside them. They, too, apparently had had their fill of this brand of man-flesh. All at once, one of the girls fell on another, beating her and tearing at her scalp as she screeched at her in Yiddish:

"SHIMMEK SALTZMAN OF LODZ! SHIMMEK SALTZMAN OF LODZ! WHO KNOWS SHIMMEK SALTZMAN OF LODZ? GIVE HIM REGARDS FROM HIS SISTER! SHIMMEK SALTZMAN OF LODZ! WHO KNOWS SHIMMEK SALTZMAN OF LODZ?"

She did not let up pummeling the other girl's skull, crying all the while: "Shimmek Saltzman of Lodz!" The other girl let her pummel. She kept silent.

Auschwitz mail.

This is the way news is sometimes learned in Auschwitz: that one's sister is in the Women's Camp; that one's brother is somewhere in one of the many sections of this planet.

Jewish genius.

The S.S. men are certain that the girl is really beating and cursing her comrade. That is permitted. Beating one another is the only thing camplings are allowed in Auschwitz.

The rows march on. Sere, blighted tree roots peer out of the sandy soil. *Shimmek Saltzman of Lodz!* The cry did not cease pounding in Ferber's ears. A cry into the void of a world destroyed. The beaten girl did not even turn her head to the passing rows. She was afraid. Her naked bony hand had wielded a clenched fist on the head of her dearest friend. Her partner allowed herself to be beaten, because soon they will exchange roles. Like her, she will drub and scream for one of the marchers who might know one of her dear ones.

Will this cry reach an ear after we have all passed from the world? A voice cannot be burned. Roots. Mute tree roots on Auschwitz soil. When the time comes will *they* be able to recount one whit of it?

One of the S.S. men approaches a girl bending over with her head to the ground. With the tip of his boot he raises the hem of her camp smock. Two yellow leg bones appear. He lets the dress drop, spitting at the bowed profile, and goes off. He was mistaken. He thought he would find something there.

Here everything wilts. Here no bird ever flies. Poisoned air. Gas and crematorium smoke. Whatever can fly higher than the barbed-wire walls avoids the Auschwitz sky.

The mountain of boards seemed as high and full as before. Not a splinter diminished. Where do the Germans get so much wood in wartime? It seems Auschwitz is no less important to the German General Staff than the battle fronts. Ferber once more selected a light rafter and immediately handed it to the Rabbi of Shilev. Again the rows marched off. Camplings fell prostrate in the middle of the road and begged the kapos to kill them. But at the first blows, they leaped up from the ground revitalized, and with renewed strength went dragging off under their loads.

Ferber felt his strength draining. The ground pulled him down. The burden of his feet was heavier than the load of wood. The Rabbi of Shilev hurried along beside him in the row, like a frightened child carrying a heavy load which might save his mother's life. Where does that wizened body get the stamina?

At the side of the road a campling slumped to the ground.

The plank lay beside him. He and the plank. Both identical. Both unbreathing. You could not tell which had to pick up and carry whom. A thick plank, twice the length of the campling. Kapos dashed over. They recognized him.

"Well, look what we have here! Hop-Hop!" The campling looked up from the ground at them with half-open eyes. One of the kapos began to lay into his head with the truncheon.

"On your feet, Hop-Hop! Back to work, Hop-Hop! This isn't theatre time!"

From the other side of the road the S.S. men were approaching. The column of camplings immediately parted to let the black uniforms through with their hounds. One of them gestured to the kapo to stop pummeling the campling. The S.S. men parked themselves in a circle around him, arms akimbo, the hounds at their feet. Mutely they gazed at the campling lying on the ground as at some freak phenomenon: where does a campling suddenly get the grit to lie down on the Auschwitz highway and refuse to continue carrying the plank?

"Well, then," one of them said, "you don't want to work."

As though by command, the hands of all the S.S. men dropped as one to the throats of the hounds. Automatically their fingers released something there. The nickel clasps at the ends of the leather leashes now dangled empty beside the S.S. boot-uppers. The hounds cocked their mouths open. White fangs gleamed like swords unsheathed from black scabbards. An ominous rumble rose from their bellies. With their claws they scraped the ground behind. They were raring to go. But until they heard the command, they did not dare. German dog discipline. The campling's eyes tore open. His mouth gaped. He gulped streams of fear like a drowning man. In his fear he had obviously forgotten what his duty now was. The plank lay beside him. He no longer saw it. He forgot everything. He saw only the hounds. Human eyes and canine eye stared one another down. Stared, and readied themselves: the hounds—to pounce upon their prey; he—to receive death. The tension of the moment to come coupled them into one. In the ghetto he had more than once given this death the slip. He had sung for the Germans. . .sung. . .sung. . .He will make another try—All at once, uncanny snorts of song erupted from him, like the gurgling cries for help of a drowning man:

"Yessir. . .a baby. . .
Tits. . .
Let's. . .merry. . ."

No one noticed the giving of the signal. The hounds leaped as one from between the S.S. boots. The campling was no longer to be seen. A rumbling bedlam of black demons. A furious wrangle in a cloud of dust where a human being had just knelt. One of the S.S. men signaled with his hand. A kapo's shout was heard:

"Camplings! Forward march!"

The rows hurried forward with newly found vigor. The fearsome rumble of the wrangling hounds gradually faded behind their receding backs. Stillness. Only the edges of the planks clattered woodily as they collided overhead.

Gone is Hop-Hop.

The day westered as they marched back to camp. Instead of planks, the marchers now bore murdered and dying. Everybody must be brought back into camp. The numbers must tally at roll-call. At the camp gate, the kapos' truncheons rose once more. A German appeared at the threshold of the watchpost. A kapo dashed over, whisked the cap from his head, and snapped to attention.

"Reporting! Labor Kommando! Nine hundred and ninety-nine camplings marching in! One—fed to the S.S. hounds."

The rows went in through the gate. As each row passed, the German gestured in the air with a long pencil. He seemed really to be counting.

5

Pat and Patashon sat on the front bench. Vatzek had accorded them the great privilege of being permitted to sit among the élite—the Poles.

Although officially Pat and Patashon were not members of the permanent peelery cadre, they reported to work daily with the others and enjoyed equal privileges with them, as though they actually belonged. Could Hayim-Idl ask for more? What *is* permanent in Auschwitz if you're a Jew? The main thing is not to be in the block inferno during the day; to get through the day in one piece, then another day, and keep as much distance as possible between you and the crematorium line.

A miraculous transformation took place in Bergson's throat within just a few days. His cantorial voice revived, literally returned from the dead. True, it was rusty yet, and creaked like a door on unoiled hinges; but still, the voice of a one-time cantor. The peelery sings in chorus, with Hayim-Idl conducting. This ensemble singing is a godsend for Hayim-Idl. Because if he so desires, he can claim it is his voice carrying so mightily through the peelery windows. A chance in a million. So Hayim-Idl sees to it that everyone is left with the impression that but for his leading off and winding up, no one here would be able to carry a single note. It is he who always sets the key and the rhythm, if not with his mouth then with his true conductor's hand. Many believe it is really so, especially Vatzek. And that, after all, is the point.

Hayim-Idl is off to work well before sunrise every morning. He is always the first one there, because he is never certain that, on entering the peelery, he will not find the bad news awaiting him: "O.K., Pat and Patashon! The joyride is over!" He frequently has nightmares in the hutch at night. Once he dreamt about the first portion of the Bible. A serpent wraps itself around his body. The "villa"—that corner of a room—in which they lived in the ghetto expands into a Garden of Eden. His wife Dvortche keeps tearing off her body all his stock of felt and hatbands till she stands there naked, taking a chunk of peeled turnip out of the crate and feeding it to him. He knows that for this God will banish him from the Garden of Eden as he had in the first portion of the Bible. But Hayim-Idl is unable to control his terrible hunger. The chunk of turnip is yellow and juicy. He bites his teeth into it. The serpent watches, waiting for him and together with him rolling off the stage down into the dark block. Everybody laughs with gaping maws. The serpent's head is like Dziadek's. He feels the beast devouring him to the last shred. Nothing is left of him. Yet, he is alive. He wonders about that. He had felt the beast eating him up, so how come he is alive! And if he is alive, where is his little Bella? Where is Bella? He tears the trammels from his body, but his body has no substance, because the beast ate it up. He screams, with all his might till he wakes.

Strange: till he began working in the peelery he had never had any dreams in Auschwitz, good or bad.

Hayim-Idl leaps awake before daybreak. How he loves that dawn crawl across the bodies still torpid with sleep in the hutch, and then that run out of the block in the dark. All day long he does not set eyes on either the orderlies, or the kapos, or the Block Chiefs. He does not see the infernal agony of the camp, the great emporium of death. Hurrying along the main path to work before dawn, he thanks God for His bounty. He drinks in the goodness of it, guarding it close lest the eye of the rising day put a hex on it.

In addition to the soup which the potato peelers receive at work, each of them is also entitled to his daily block ration. Of course, the peelers forthwith sell that soup for half a bread ration. At noon, Hayim-Idl hurried off like the rest of them to get his soup ration in block 16. But unlike the others, Hayim-Idl does not sell it, but rushes it right over to the Rabbi of Shilev. Bergson takes care of Vevke the cobbler. Bergson has not forgotten that it is Vevke who saved him in the ghetto by getting him into the shoe shop without reporting it to the Germans.

Pat and Patashon sit on the front bench, but this does not please Hayim-Idl as it might. In the first place, why should he sit next to those Jew-haters? And then, you can't snitch a bite here. On the rear benches you get a chance to steal a piece of turnip into your mouth. The lips are sealed. The teeth chew. You swallow, and you've got away with it.

The Poles turn their heads and scowl. The Poles are always turning their heads and scowling, as if it were their birthright the Jews were guzzling. As though the Poles had brought those turnips along from their own larders. That makes Hayim-Idl furious. It's more than he can take. But he knows that he must hold his tongue. He—who sits here only by indulgence. But it burns him up. Auschwitz! Our Auschwitz! *Our* hell! *Our* dead! *Our* crematorium! Didn't those anti-Semites step on us enough out there, in the world? And now here, in hell, too! Here, where it is us they're burning and roasting? Here, in this place earmarked for Jews, and Jews alone, where everything from one end of the barbed wire to the other was created just for us? Everything planned and built and set up with just *us* in mind! Where do they get off horning in? This isn't one of their castle towns where they crucified us with pogroms whenever they felt like! This isn't one of their fairs where they skinned us. Here it's all ours! *Our* wives, *our* fathers, *our* children. All ours! *Our* Auschwitz!

After the war those Polacks will show off the numbers on their arms—martyred saints! They were in Auschwitz! The Jews won't be able to show their arms, because Jews there won't be.

The door of the potato store nearby opens. A merchant puts in a stealthy appearance. Vatzek notices him and hisses towards the basin:

"Dziadek!"

Dziadek lays the potato pitchfork down on the edge of the basin, and sets off for the store like a drowsy shopkeeper going towards a fresh customer. The merchant takes off his jacket and ties the two sleeve ends with string. Dziadek fills the two sleeves with potatoes. That done, the merchant rolls up the jacket so the two full sleeves are tucked inside, places the jacket on his arm, and steals out through the storeroom door. Dziadek returns to his post, picks up the pitchfork, and again lazily rakes the potatoes back and forth, back and forth, his jowly profile glistening in the light of the window.

Every Block Chief has a supplier bringing potatoes to his personal cook. The Office kitchen is the finest of the private kitchens in camp. They found themselves a professional cook, a chef from Hungary who treats them to delicious pastries and makes them quality home-brew liquor.

All day the suppliers keep coming and going through the storeroom door. If Vatzek happens not to notice an incomer, the Poles sitting on the front bench immediately signal him. In doing it they feel like a shopkeeper's children who get a thrill helping Papa out in the shop now and then. And playing shopkeeper's children, they promptly look back to the rear benches to make sure that the hired help aren't robbing Papa.

Hayim-Idl sits bowed over his work, his knife slicing away

at the turnip flesh. He feels it with his fingers. So yellow and succulent. How many Jews in the block would be able to ward off death with just one such piece of turnip! Should he thrust it under his armpit? After work, Dziadek and two Poles park themselves at the door to frisk all the departers. Hayim-Idl always manages to smuggle a piece of turnip out for the Rabbi. He slices a flat oval of turnip which he tucks into his armpit—now let them search! So help him, it's easier to stick a piece of turnip away in the armpit than to eat it at work. Because here either they hear the teeth grinding away at the crisp turnip, or Vatzek suddenly starts up from the window with a scream: "Whoring Pat-Patashon, let's have a song!" It's the end of you if your mouth happens to be working on a turnip just then.

Outside a Labor Kommando is marching towards the camp gate. God was really merciful to him that time, Hayim-Idl mused. The same kapo could have picked on him instead of Hop-Hop. They had been just one short of a thousand. If Hop-Hop hadn't been caught then, he would now be sitting here together with him, alive. *Let's be merry* . . . It could have been him instead of Hop-Hop! Outside the kapos scurry back and forth with flying truncheons, like butchers goading a herd of cattle to the slaughterhouse. Who knows if the Rabbi isn't among them again? If he himself weren't sitting here, he might also be outside among that mass of heads. A weird, grim apathy emanates from the marching heads. The gate must be open. They are moving.

Vatzek arrives from the cauldron section, holding a large white bowl covered with a down-turned bowl. He's a hefty boy, that Vatzek. The ground shakes every time he walks. Tall boots on his feet. He is all muscle and brawn. Probably he was a farmer back home. The bowl is well covered, but you can smell the roast meat. It makes your head burst. Vatzek passes by, making straight for the potato store, sits down there on a crate behind the two reserve cauldrons. The fragrance of the meat is now stronger than ever. Vatzek has probably taken the top bowl off. Hayim-Idl feels a thousand needles pricking away inside his cheeks. After a while Vatzek rises, uncovers one of the cauldrons, puts the bowl inside, returns to the peelery, and lets out a burpy shout: "Dziadek!" Dziadek was primed for the call. He had already set the pitchfork on the edge of the basin. He sets out behind the seated men. Entering the store, he uncovers the cauldron, takes out the bowl and vanishes behind the wall. Sometimes Dziadek, too, replaces the bowl inside the cauldron, comes out of the store, his puffy cheeks gleaming more than ever. He makes the return trip to the basin in front. As he passes along the first bench, he places a pudgy hand on the shoulder of one of the Poles, saying nothing, and goes on. The latter promptly puts the paring knife in the straw basket, rises, enters the store, uncovers the cauldron, and withdraws the bowl. Everybody knows what is inside the bowl and what is being eaten from it. Because of the silence, the mute grinding of teeth against turnips inside sealed mouths is heard, as in a stable on a quiet night. The Poles turn their heads towards the rear rows, their inquisitorial eyes darting warning. Don't you kikes think that the front bench doesn't hear the turnip-guzzling!

"Hey, Pat and Patashon, blast your whoring mothers! Let's have a song!" Vatzek suddenly erupts good-humoredly.

Hayim-Idl leaps up and swings around to the benches, flourishing the paring knife in his muddy hand like a choir leader's baton, and begins:

"Oy, oy, oy, Belz—
My little town Belz—"

"My little town Belz." The song has become the theme song of the peelery. Vatzek does not tire of hearing it day or night. Everybody knows it backwards and forwards. Over and over the song is sung, like a solitary record on an automatic turntable. Endlessly, without Vatzek ever having enough of it. There is no other song he wants to hear. Hayim-Idl had a stroke of luck: the song had caught on throughout Poland before the war—in Polish and Yiddish. Beggars used to sing it in the courtyards. God Himself had prepared the Polish lyrics for him, so he might have it ready for Vatzek.

More than once as Hayim-Idl sings "My little town Belz" his eyes brim with tears. More than once, as his ears suddenly catch what his mouth is singing, he can see the townlet of his birth. Home, Mama, Papa, his sisters. The townlet and its lanes, its buildings, its Jews—here the synagogue, there the marketplace; here the *heder* school, there the river. Jews, Jews, Jews . . . Sabbath-day Jews, workaday Jews. Chmielnik. Chmielnik, my home. My little town of Chmielnik.

"Give it again, whoresons, give it again!" Vatzek thunders, and Hayim-Idl starts all over again:

"Oy, oy, oy, Belz,
My little town Belz . . ."

Vatzek sits forward in his chair, his head leaning against a corner of the window, his eyes in faraway reverie, his husky peasant body not stirring. A few more rounds of the song, and silence. Not a stir from Vatzek.

Hush.

What is it that soothed Vatzek so? Could it be the poignant longing in the melody? Or the Jewish melancholy put to music? Or perhaps the lyrics? And what are Vatzek's eyes seeing there, where the sky is snared in the upper barbs of the wire? And what is it they see in the patch of black earth below the wire wall?

Silence in the peelery. Dziadek no longer rakes with the pitchfork in the basin. The peelers, as they rise to dump their produce into the basin, step on tiptoe, then gently slide it out of the baskets, so there should be no splash. The peelery now seems like the sickroom of a child who has just been lulled to sleep, everybody walking tiptoe so as not to wake him.

Hayim-Idl cannot understand what could possibly be eating that husky peasant. What makes that fellow tick, sitting there motionless with his powerful shoulders bowed, staring hypnotically at the barbed-wire mesh? Everybody knows that Vatzek was brought here from somewhere around Zamoszc. But was his home destroyed on him too? And did he leave behind a Dvortche, and a little girl like his Bella? But his wife and child weren't taken off to the collection center. And they weren't in a ghetto. They didn't hide in any bunkers. They weren't shot at. *His* world isn't in ruins. He is well set here in Auschwitz. Stuffs himself with roast meat. For him it's all one big resort. After the war he'll be going free—back to the wife and child waiting for him, back to his relatives and neighbors. What can possibly be eating that healthy young peasant?

The door of the potato store opens. A merchant! Dziadek hurries over to him and shoves him outside, whispering: "Later, later . . ."

Hours pass. All at once Vatzek jerks out of his trance, leaps from his seat and begins to scream as though possessed!

"Whoresons! Pigs! Sons of bitches! Fry, every last one of you! I'll dump every one of you into the crematorium! Your mothers were whores, and your grandmothers before them were whores! You're all whores, every one of you! I'll... I'll..."

He froths at the mouth, turning purple with rage. The curses roll in a barrage from his mouth. Hell-fire murder rages in him. He storms at them with clenched fists. He'll slaughter them all. He'll personally shove them all into the crematorium furnace! Not one of them will be left! Whores! Pigs! Goddamn bastards! No one looks up. Everybody cuts away at the turnips. They all know that the blaze will shortly abate, as soon as Vatzek has vomited all the curses he has in him. Then he will calm down. That's the way it always is.

When Vatzek has cooled off, he goes over to Dziadek and in a whisper asks him who it was that had come to the potato store a while ago. Dziadek replies in a whisper. Vatzek seems to be unhappy about all those merchants constantly cluttering up his place as if it had no doors. But he says nothing, returns to his place by the window, back to his chair. The atmosphere in the peelery returns to normal. As though nothing had happened.

Outside, in the kitchen compound, Zalke paces back and forth with one of the Camp Office clerks. Vatzek's eyes follow them thoughtfully. All at once he opens the window and shouts: "Hey, Zalke! Get over here!" Zalke signals with his hand that he will be in just as soon as he has closed the deal with the customer from the Office.

As soon as Zalke came into the peelery, Vatzek took him by the arm to a corner and put an odd question to him:

"Who do you think is letting potatoes out of here for the Block Chiefs?"

Zalke turned big, innocent eyes on Vatzek, as though to say—Boy, did you pick the right man to ask such a poser:

"Well, who's letting the potatoes out?" Vatzek persisted.

Now Zalke turned on the opaque look of a born Mussulman. A blind man could see that Zalke hasn't the foggiest notion what this is all about. What, pinch potatoes here? First time he ever heard such a thing. Who you kidding? Fat chance anybody's going to try and pinch spuds out of the store with Vatzek as kapo!

Vatzek took Zalke by the arm and led him to one of the reserve cauldrons inside the storeroom. He opened the oven door underneath the cauldron, shoving Zalke's head deep inside the opening, then pulled down Zalke's trousers.

"For the last time now!" Vatzek thundered. "Who's swiping spuds for the Block Chiefs?"

Zalke's two bare buttock-mounds stared mutely at the peelery walls like the eye-whites of a blind man. He did not answer.

"Dziadek!" Vatzek screamed. "Let's have that pitchfork!"

The water dripped from the iron prongs as Dziadek drew

the pitchfork out of the basin. Vatzek reached for the pitchfork, turning menacingly at the two mute eye-whites of Zalke's posterior protruding as prescribed by Auschwitz regulations

"Now you'll come across. Now you'll sing. Oh, are you going to sing!"

Vatzek went off to the cauldron section, inserting the iron prongs into the fire under one of the cauldrons to heat them. When they were red hot, he returned to the peelery, carrying the glowing pitchfork like a banner in a parade. In festive procession behind him trailed cooks and barrel washers: the fun is on!

"Now he'll sing. Oh, is he going to sing!" Vatzek snarled and, with the white-hot pitchfork, started raking the livid, naked flesh. The eye-whites began to blacken and run. The reserve cauldron howled to the high heavens. The screams shook the peelery walls. Zalke's head was held fast inside the cauldron opening. He shrieked for dear life, but there was one word he did not let out: the name of the potato leaker.

After two hours of incessant torture, when Zalke lay on the ground peeled and scorched and the give-away word "Vatzek" had not left his mouth, as though the word had been cauterized in his throat, Vatzek snatched Zalke up on to his back and carried him off like a blood clot to the K-B Hospital Block.

The doctors fussed with Zalke as with an ailing crown prince. Thrice daily Vatzek brought the patient specially prepared meat soup. And as soon as Zalke recovered and left the K-B, Vatzek dismissed all his merchants and suppliers. Zalke had stood the ordeal of fire, so Vatzek made him his exclusive potato supplier to all the blocks in camp.

"Put it there, Zalke," Vatzek said. "A man can talk turkey to you. You're no cheap whore."

"You bloody bugger!" Zalke shoved the proffered hand aside. "You've striped my ass good and red for the rest of my life!"

II

Hayim-Idl could not sit still on the bench. He twisted and turned as in delirium. On the window of the potato store stood a white cup full of marmalade, and Hayim-Idl felt his head was about to burst. The cup kept jabbing away at his brain. Even shutting his eyes he could see it.

"What's it to Vatzek?" someone inside him argued. "Now for the Rabbi of Shilev it would be a life-saver. Everybody says marmalade is the only cure for his rash. Something sweet. All he needs is a little bit of sweet. The Rabbi will go off to the crematorium any *Selektion* now. Murderer! Who do you think will be responsible if not you? Is that the way you thank God for having fixed you up here? Who saved you if not the Rabbi? They all say he needs something sweet. Just one such cup of marmalade and his skin would stop peeling."

Hayim-Idl felt his face on fire. His temples pounded, his heart racing with fear. And the one inside his conscience would not relent: "Vatzek is sitting with his back to the store. Nobody is watching. Get up and go into the store with the basket as if you have to get some turnips—" No! No! Hayim-Idl recoiled. What can he be thinking of doing? Hayim-Idl turned his back to the store so that he should not see the window or the cup. Whew! What an idea! He had been ready to get up and go. He had been about to cut his own throat. He must be having it too good here! Seems he's forgotten the hard times. This cushy job must have gone to his head. What a loony idea!

"Hayim-Idl," that one came back to him. "So you think you've got God where you want Him, eh? You think just because you're all set in the peelery you've got a lifetime contract with God! Maybe you think that just because you're Pat-Patashon nothing can touch you? In his hutch in the block the Rabbi of Shilev sits like Job, and you sit here between warm walls thinking you're out of God's sight, eh, Hayim-Idl? Do you happen to know that at the next *Selektion* the Rabbi is finished? Will you be able to tell God it wasn t your fault? Do you really think that just because you're Vatzek's crooner God won't know how to settle the score with you? Are you really foolish enough to think that if you don't stand up and wave your hands like a choir leader nobody here will know how to sing 'Belz'? Whom are you trying to fool, Hayim-Idl? *Me?* I'm not Vatzek. You and I know that even when you're rotting away somewhere in a hutch they'll manage to go on singing 'Belz' here. I guess you've forgotten about Rafael's staring all day long at the boards of the hutch above him. When you get back to your block at night it's dark already and your hutch-mates are curled up inside each other like rotten rags and you don't even see them. And in the morning, when you dash out of the block, they're still lying there the way you found them the night before. Maybe you think you're better than them? Is that it, Hayim-Idl? Why, if not for the Rabbi's blessing you'd also be rotting away like them in the hutch, or you would long since have turned to smoke. Maybe you think that God's eye doesn't reach into the peelery? Hayim-Idl, do you remember the words: 'God is also in the Auschwitz theatre'? Remember, Hayim-Idl: 'Bless me, Rabbi, I want to live'? Remember what went on in your heart then? No, you don't! Your belly's full and you've turned as heartless as they. You're no better than them, I tell you! The Rabbi of Shilev is in for a *Selektion.* Vatzek won't croak if he doesn't have this one helping of marmalade. It's a drop in the bucket for him. You can do it without getting caught. Nobody will even miss it. What's a cup of marmalade to them? Nobody will even know it was you who took it. Save yourself, Hayim-Idl! Yes, yourself! It's for this that God sent you here. You are only a messenger. And this mission didn't cost you a thing. God is putting you to the test. Remember the Rabbi's face when he told you: 'Go, Hayim-Idl. Go and succeed'? Oh, Hayim-Idl, Hayim-Idl. If only you haven't sinned already by doubting. You should have run to do it! A man runs to seize the opportunity to do such a good deed! You run with all your heart! With joy! With everything in you! With—"

"Oh, God!" the groan heaved out of Hayim-Idl.

Bergson, sitting beside him, heard the sudden groan. Without looking up, his hands scraping the mud off a potato, he asked:

"What's bothering you, Hayim-Idl? Is it your stomach?"

"Oh, God!" Hayim-Idl twisted and writhed on the bench, as in a seizure of cramps, groaning all the while: "Oh, God . . . God . . ."

"Go to the latrine, Hayim-Idl," Bergson offered. "You'll feel better."

"It'll pass. I feel better already."

Several minutes later Hayim-Idl suddenly spoke up. "Bergson, would you give your life for another Jew?"

"You're talking foolish, Hayim-Idl. Do you really think we have a life left to give?"

"Bergson, don't you think it is the Hand of Providence that put us here?"

Bergson bent down, picked up a turnip, and started slicing. "No," he said caustically, "not the Hand of Providence, but the foot of that *Goy* sitting there at the window. The fool questions you're asking today, Hayim-Idl!"

"I've got the chills, Bergson."

Bergson glanced up at him. "You look as though you've got fever. Your teeth are chattering."

"It'll pass," Hayim-Idl bore up.

"That's all you need now—a case of malaria," Bergson said.

Several minutes later Hayim-Idl spoke up again: "The Rabbi of Shilev is very sick, isn't he, Bergson?"

From Bergson's throat came only a groan.

"He's a righteous pillar of the world!" Hayim-Idl said. "It's by his merit that we're sitting here! Bergson, remember that night at the gate of block 10? Remember my leaving you standing there? Where do you think I ran? It was to the Rabbi of Shilev I ran."

"Often," Bergson said, "I sit here trying to remember how we ever got here, but I just can't remember a thing. I only know that the night of the theatre, I was already a Mussulman. Besides that I can't remember a thing. If we get out of here alive, we won't even be able to tell what happened to us. We won't remember a thing. That is the real tragedy. The world won't even know what happened to us here."

Vatzek stands up and goes off towards the scullery. The light of the window silhouettes the white marmalade cup. By the handle, the enamel is cracked and there is a black spot near the base. The black tin shows through the crack of the enamel. All at once, Hayim-Idl's conscience started up again: "Now, Hayim-Idl! Grab your basket. See, it's even empty now. Listen carefully. Go into the store for some turnips. In passing, just happen to glance out the window. Is there anything wrong with looking out the window? Your back will block everything. But while you're at it, shove the cup of marmalade into your basket. What are you afraid of? Your back has blocked everything. Then go to the turnip pile and fill your basket, meanwhile sticking the cup inside your armpit. Stick it in deep, the way you tuck those turnip slices away in there. But be careful not to spill any. Hold it straight, not tilted. Then come back to the peelery, sit down in your seat and hold the basket in your lap as though you suddenly don't have the strength to bend down. You can even let the basket down to the ground with your right hand. Better ask Bergson to do it. As far as he's concerned, you have a bellyache. Then, at the first chance, get up and leave. That's right, just leave! Just as though you're going to the latrine to relieve yourself. That's not forbidden, is it? Dziadek won't search you. Even after work, during the general inspection, he lets you by. He isn't even frisking you lately. After all, you're Pat and Patashon! And if he doesn't search you after work, what makes you think he's going to search you now? You'll see, you'll make it. And then you'll head straight for the Rabbi. So why are you standing there like a lummox? Get moving! Now! Not another second! That's it. You've forgotten the basket—"

Hayim-Idl did not feel his hand pick up the basket; did not feel himself stand up; did not feel himself walk. The two reserve cauldrons came towards him like a pair of disguised big-bellied demons. As a boy, coming home from *heder* one winter night, he had seen those two very demons, and he had felt then what he now felt. The light from the window dissolved before his eyes to a white glare. He stared outside wondering foggily what could be making the roof of block 1 next door topple onto the watchtower across the road. Suddenly he felt two of his fingers dipping in a cool, moist density, his head still poked out the window and his hand groping for the cup. After this he probably went on doing everything the way he had been commanded. After all, a flawless plan had been worked out for him in advance by that hidden saint-of-a-conscience in him.

When Hayim-Idl returned to his seat, Bergson automatically reached to take the basket. "Why so stingy with the turnips?" Bergson asked.

Hayim-Idl felt the two fingers sticking together. On his right trouser leg, by the knee, gleamed a dark spot. Under his left arm the load dragged like a boulder. The store window looked frighteningly empty now. The spot on his trousers was fresh. It was plainly marmalade. He must have unconsciously wiped his two sticky fingers there. In the front row there is nowhere to hide the foot and nothing to cover the spot. And he must not bend. He must sit up straight. *Now, Hayim-Idl! Get up and leave!—*

Hayim-Idl rose and immediately sank back into his seat. Vatzek returned from the scullery, passing right by him, and again planted himself in his place at the window like a dog before his kennel. *Now, Hayim-Idl! Get up and go!*

He stood up. In his confusion he forgot the directions he had rehearsed earlier: to walk out as though he had a belly-ache. He was nearly at the door when Vatzek's shout seized him from behind.

"Whoring Pat and Patashon—let's have a song!"

Hayim-Idl turned around. His face now contorted involuntarily because of the uproar in his bowels. He looked pleadingly at Vatzek: now he really must run to the latrine.

At the basin Dziadek's bored mien broke into a smile at the sight of Pat holding his stomach with one hand while the other dangled like a cripple's. Hold on there, sonny boy ...You're not kidding this fellow. That's a mighty big turnip under your arm, sticking way out behind your back! All that and no song? No, buddy, you're not pulling that...

Hayim-Idl saw Dziadek's bloated belly near his dangling arm. He saw the trouser belt sectioning off Dziadek's paunch like a tight rope around a pillow. He felt Dziadek's hand crawl up his back inside the jacket, then pull the cup by the handle...Fear swelled in his head like a paralyzing block. The marmalade might spill!...All heads are up...All eyes are watching...Rows of upraised eyes...Why are all the eyes looking like that? The basin on his right is half full of water. Must be very early if they haven't even started dumping turnips in there...Vatzek is holding the cup of marmalade between his hands. How did the cup get to Vatzek's hands? He didn't see anybody hand it to him.

Hayim-Idl no longer knew what was going on about him. He stared without seeing, listened without hearing. Two Poles came carrying the flogging bench in from the store, as though bringing a throne for a state guest, then suddenly carried the bench back, while Dziadek bent down to the oven opening under the reserve cauldron and opened it. Shouts and yelps. Hands propelling him towards the cauldron. Vatzek isn't there for some reason. But as Dziadek hands

Vatzek the pitchfork, Vatzek is there all right. Dziadek's hands are pudgy and white; they don't scrape mud from potatoes. Vatzek's hands are also white, but not as pudgy. Nearby Vatzek screams: "Bitches! Whoresons! Pat-Patashon!..." Hayim-Idl knows that right away Vatzek will stop screaming. He always screams, then stops. Yet he knew that this time he would not stop. It is different, this time. This time he, Hayim-Idl, will first stop living. When Vatzek's screams let up, Hayim-Idl's life will have been pummeled out of him. At the window, Poles draw a piece of turnip out of Bergson's undersize trousers. Bergson never said anything about smuggling turnip in his pants. Suddenly Bergson is there beside him. All heads roar in glee. Just like the time they first showed up here. Hayim-Idl and Bergson are standing together as on a stage... Vatzek turns to Dziadek and whispers something. Dziadek wheels around and fretfully leaves the store, Vatzek opens the door, waving the pitchfork at them. "Whores! Bitches! Don't let me lay eyes on you here again! You'll vomit up your souls if you ever set foot in the kitchen compound again! Get out of here! Get out!..."

Bergson's bare spindle-feet paddle the bright air of the kitchen compound. Hayim-Idl does not know if he is permitted to run along, or if he must wait to be killed. Vatzek doesn't let up screaming, but Hayim-Idl does not hear the words hurled at him. He feels Vatzek's boot land in his posterior. He goes flying through the open door.

The barbed wire, the blocks, the camp—all pounced upon him like ravenous lions at the condemned flung into their pit.

6

A summer gone by in Auschwitz. Hayim-Idl could not grasp it. He dragged his bare feet over the camp and tried to arrange it all in his mind. There was a heat wave when he was taken in the transport from the ghetto, as far as he remembers. Here, in Auschwitz, he has been through several cold spells. In that case, how long has he been in camp? Can it be that he has already spent a winter here without realizing it? He simply could not make things tally. Now it added up to quite a few frosts and scorchers, and then it seemed that he hasn't been here even two months.

Summer's end. Rosh Hashana approaching. Once, the *shofar* was already being sounded now, during the month of Elul. Jews getting up early to attend the *Selikhot* Repentance Services! Yellow leaves covered the ground of the synagogue yard, the autumn branches seeming to tremble at the approach of a great Day of Judgment.

The edges of the camp were invisible. Coils of mist shrouded the upper rows of barbed wire. Now the camp seemed shrunken, again it seemed boundless, covering the entire world. Hayim-Idl did not know which way to go—to the beginning of camp or to the end. The end was also in the beginning and the beginning was held by the end. His bare feet dragged on.

Long gone was even the last vestige of the good days in the potato peelery. As though they had never existed. As a matter of fact, before having been in the peelery, he had adjusted to hunger. But no sooner was he thrown out of there than hunger pounced upon him anew, like a provoked dog at a fresh bone. Now he no longer has his old stamina to fight the hunger. His despondency has become all the more unbearable. The smell of end fills his nostrils. He has never felt it as tangibly as now.

An unfamiliar, gnawing grief pervaded this Auschwitz summer's end. There were no trees to shed yellow leaves, here. Here were yellow bones. A pile to every block. Their yellowness covered all. This was no autumn. This was end. Across this end he dragged his naked feet.

In one of the assembly areas between the blocks sat Moni, one hand tucked deep inside a long black boot, the other dipping the tip of a brush into a can of black polish on the ground at his feet. If they were to set out a tea barrel for distribution now, Hayim-Idl thought, Moni would immediately drop boots and polish and hurry to grab a can of tea for the Rabbi of Shilev. Hayim-Idl walked over and sat down in the sand like a child come to watch an adult at work, and silently observed Moni's movements.

Moni polished the tall uppers of the boots. "You were green in camp!" Moni said to Hayim-Idl, not looking up from his work. "Boy, were you green! You should have asked me. Before you try to pull such a stunt you ask someone who knows the ropes. Where did it get you? And what did it get the Rabbi of Shilev?" Moni expertly smeared the polish around the platform of the boot. "It's a crying shame. A bowl of soup a day. What a crying shame. You've screwed it all up for yourself and for the Rabbi. What am I talking about? That soup kept a whole hutch going."

Hayim-Idl is silent. There is nothing he can say. He knows

be botched it all up. What can he say for himself? Moni is right. What could have got into him? He never in his life stole. He must have been out of his mind. He doesn't even know how it all happened. He didn't know what he was doing. All of a sudden he goes and gets an urge to do a good deed, and there was no controlling the urge. What is there for him to say? No murderer ever fixes a man the way a man sometimes manages to mess himself up.

"In Auschwitz you mustn't go soft-hearted," Moni continued. "You should have asked me. I'm an old campbird here. But no use talking about that now. It's over and done with. You're finished, Hayim-Idl! You've as good as killed yourself and dragged the others along. The Rabbi won't last long now."

Hayim-Idl felt Moni's words lashing away at his body. He could not bear another moment of it. By way of changing the subject he asked:

"For whom are you shining those boots?"

"What do you mean for whom? For the Piepel of block 8! He's too good to polish boots. He's a queen. So he lets me have his Block Chief's boots to shine. And I'm supposed to be tickled pink to get the job from him. When that Piepel got to camp, I'd been Piepel in every one of those blocks. See?" Moni swept the air with his brush. "Every one of those blocks! But you know what? A man never wises up till it's too late."

"What do you get for polishing a pair of boots like that?"

"Shit I get! Bread? A lick of piss from the barrel is what I get."

Piss from the barrel. Hayim-Idl's heart skipped a beat. If only he could get a lick of that piss. "Maybe I can help you?" he said."

"You help me? How are you going to do that?"

"I thought—maybe sometimes you don't feel like having the soup."

"Oho, so that's it. But do you know that sometimes I have to hang around a block all day to get that stinking drop of soup? Do you think it's so easy to get to them? If you're not there at exactly the right second, you're a goner. Empty barrels. Licked dry. You think it's such a cinch? And I can't go kicking to the Block Chief, either. He didn't give me the boots to polish, so he doesn't owe me a thing. And the Piepel —he figures he's got a lifetime contract with his Block Chief. He doesn't know that inside of six hours after losing his *Funktion* he's going to be just as hungry as me."

All around them was the odor of crematorium smoke. The odor sprawled like a heavy fog upon the camp. It came from the ground, from the sky, from the blocks, from the electric mesh and all the winds. All that remained was to envy the Mussulmen dragging blankly past your eyes. They no longer sense or understand. And, apparently, they no longer hurt. But before you reach that stage, you must first die sixty deaths a second—and then not know whether a Mussulman really feels no hunger; whether he really doesn't hurt when the truncheons pound his head like a tongueless bell.

Up the backpath came Holy Dad Piotr, the cigarette hidden in his fist. The cigarette was invisible. Visible only was the cupped fist at the mouth crevice as deep pits were sucked into the cheeks from time to time. Hayim-Idl felt his scalp crawl.

When Gunther, Block Chief of 15, had coveted Robert's Whistler, and Robert had refused to let him have him even for a week, Gunther had sent for Piotr and stuck a cigarette in his mouth. "Daddy," he had said, "tonight I want you to bring me the canary in the Whistler's throat." The next morning the Whistler was found lying behind block 15 with a slit, scoured throat.

"No two ways about it, Hayim-Idl, you were green," Moni said. "You can't be a softy in the Katzet."

"But the heart, Moni, what about the heart! We're Jews,

aren't we? We were born that way and there's nothing we can do about it. Why do you keep bringing the Rabbi tea every day?"

Moni's hands froze in mid-polishing. He sat there, murmuring as though to himself: "I don't know. I just don't know. But whenever the Rabbi looks at me I feel as if my mother were saying to me the way she used to in the ghetto: 'Monkele, bring Papa a glass of tea!' " The boot slumped to the ground, Moni's hand still tucked deep inside it: "I don't know. I just don't. . ."

Moni, the old Auschwitz campbird, suddenly burst out crying like the little boy that he was.

Day and night, night and day the rain lashed away. The main path, the backpath, the assembly areas between the blocks—all flooded. The bulbs along the barbed-wire walls were kept lit day and night. The blocks seemed like floating, transport-laden wagons bound for the crematorium.

Hayim-Idl lay in the hutch. Nothing remained of Rafael's head but the immense black eyes. Any minute now and they will take off from the head like birds from a shattered cage. Liberated they will soar away to their freedom nest, with only the head remaining in the hutch—an empty, derelict cage-wreck.

In the block the air hung like a soggy, filth-laden sack. The camplings lay in the hutches tangled up in each other, dank, decomposing rags. A brotherhood of tatters.

"I must sleep now!" Hayim-Idl told himself. "All I need is to doze off at night."

At night he fills in for the night guard, sometimes getting a bit of soup in payment. That one is a steady Funktioner. "Night Guard." Lives in luxury, like a block orderly. What should he stay up nights for, when for a couple of spoonfuls of soup Hayim-Idl will do the rounds for him all night, dashing to wake him at inspection time and taking off to hide? "*Herr* Camp Senior! Honored to report..." the night guard cries at the top of his voice as though a moment ago he hadn't been fast asleep.

But sleep is now as remote from Hayim-Idl as his world-that-was. Once it had been Yom Kippur today. Jews had prayed for a good new year. After Yom Kippur had come Sukkot, Simhat Torah. What will come after Yom Kippur this time? The grapevine has it that a shoemaking kommando is soon leaving for a labor camp in Germany. *Kommando.* The word gives him the shivers. But can he expect any better in this camp? At the next *Selektion* he'll definitely be off to the crematorium. How much longer will he be able to dodge it? True, he doesn't know a thing about shoemaking, but together with Vevke he'll make out. God won't forsake him. The only question is whether the kommando will leave camp in time to miss the *Selektion* for the crematorium. In any case he has to apply first. Tomorrow he's going into the Office to sign up for shoemaking. If only it weren't called a "kommando"! Something tells him it won't end up well. Those who had joined the kommando to the Bunau factory asphyxiated the very first day. They say they were sent right to the vats to mix chemical gases. But what can happen to a shoemaker working shoes? Tomorrow, God willing, he's applying. Only they shouldn't give him a test to see whether he really is a shoemaker. Or maybe he shouldn't rush to the Office tomorrow. Maybe it would be better to wait for the last moment, then dash in to sign up. At the last minute they won't have time to give him a test. What's more, if he hurries to sign up and then hangs around camp waiting to be sent, someone might give him away as not being a shoemaker. Or who knows, maybe some better deal will come along meantime. Something which won't be called "kommando." The word gives him the creeps. But if he is already listed as a shoemaker he won't be able to sign up for anything else that might come along! Good thing he thought of it in time. It's a wise man who thinks twice before acting. Though you never can be wise enough. He was so clever in the potato peelery, wasn't he! Oh, was he clever! But then he didn't even begin to know what he was doing. Maybe if he had given it a little more thought he wouldn't have done it. He must have been out of his mind. If at least he had first talked it over with Bergson. Bergson was sitting there right beside him. It was just a piece of bad luck. What could he have been thinking! It might be good to talk it over with Vevke the cobbler first. Of course. Of course. He should long since have discussed it with Vevke.

His entangled hutchmates do not stir. Rafael doesn't even look human any more. Rafael! What about himself? God knows what he must look like! Rafael is probably now thinking about him exactly what he's thinking about Rafael. But who can tell what Rafael is thinking? You just can't discuss a thing with him. Ten languages! Imagine a man knowing ten languages, and not a word of Yiddish! Might as well try talking to a deaf mute!

Hayim-Idl crawled on all fours across the hutches. His knees trampled the tangle of bodies, but not one of them stirred. It's a long crawl to Vevke's hutch.

Vevke lay there with his eyes agape like Rafael's. An uncanny loneliness engulfed Hayim-Idl, as though he were roaming a vast world filled with dead; a graveyard in which the dead are not covered with earth because they are not even dead. Here you do not die. Here you are burned. A limbo in which there is no dying. He wanted to cry out and waken the undead. He was too terrified to go on bearing his ghastly loneliness alone.

"Vevke!" Hayim-Idl called. "Have you signed up for shoemaking?" The call shot from his mouth like a cry.

Vevke, the ghetto shoe-shop foreman, who had always looked like an athlete, now lay there in all his skeletal flimsiness—a Mussulman. He did not turn his eyes to him.

"Eh, Vevke?" Hayim-Idl spurred him.

Vevke's body was gutted and sapped dry, but his brain, apparently, not at all. "I'm not going any place any more," Vevke said evenly. "I'm dying here."

"What are you talking about, Vevke? Die, now? Now? When we have a chance to live? Just let's get out of here. The main thing is to get out of here. Everybody says so."

"I'm not going. I don't want to work for the Germans any more," Vevke continued in the same flat tone.

"Vevke!" Hayim-Idl said, his eyes fairly popping from their sockets. "You're ruining me! What will I do now? You're butchering my plan."

"You're young, Hayim-Idl. You go."

"Without you, Vevke? Without you? What kind of advice is that?"

"Nobody is giving you advice. No one dare give anybody advice here."

Vevke lay there frozen-gazed like Rafael. Hayim-Idl saw that this was not the right time to talk to Vevke. First let him settle it with himself, and then Vevke will come around. He knows him only too well. Everybody knows what a heart of gold Vevke has. Never mind. When we get to it, Vevke will be all right. There's still such a thing as justice in the world. There is still such a thing as right and wrong! The Rabbi of Shilev is still in Auschwitz, thank God. And so is Ferber. Vevke doesn't have the final say here yet. Let's just get around to it. First we'll have to see what it's all about. The logic of a Jew! He doesn't want to work for the Germans any more! Who does want to work for them? Is this a work-ride? It's a life-saving ride! Of course, lying here in this graveyard it's no wonder that after a while a man loses sight of things. Here there isn't even Yom Kippur any more. Here a man forgets altogether that he's a Jew. That's something: in Auschwitz, among nothing but Jews, you forget that you're a Jew!

"Yes, Vevke, it seems it's Yom Kippur today," Hayim-Idl suddenly groaned.

Vevke's eyes were fixed somewhere in space, silent.

"Remember, Vevke?" Hayim-Idl continued as though talking to himself. "Remember the synagogues packed with Jews? Women in their white shawls. Jews in their white *kittl* robes. Children. Children in the synagogue yard. Children in their fathers' laps. Children clinging to their mothers' dresses..."

Vevke's glance suddenly came to life. A moist gleam veiled his eyes. The yellow corners of his mouth twitched. His lips moved feebly, contorting in a throttled, hoarse murmur!

"Gittel always left for the synagogue ahead of me on Yom Kippur...Always as she stood at the door she would wish me: 'Vevkeshi, may we soon lead our children to the bridal canopy together'..."

Hush in the block. Awe in the block. Yom Kippur in the hutch of the Rabbi of Shilev.

Hayim-Idl had managed not only to steal out of his block and make a dash for the Rabbi of Shilev's block, but also to drag Vevke along.

The Rabbi sits in the hutch, his two naked bone-legs stretched out alongside each other as though he were standing for the silent *Amidah* Prayer, his eyes sealed. *"Unesaneh tokef*...Let us express the mighty holiness of this day."

In the Poles' hutch opposite the cubicle, Fruchtenbaum sits with the Poles. They are unpacking cartons of food sent them from home. Out of the cartons they pull large red apples, home-baked goodies. Fruchtenbaum is having the time of his life. He lavishes fawning smiles on them, and they all treat him to a bit of something.

The Poles' hutch! You mustn't even come near it. You don't dare pass by there lest you so much as brush against the wood of the hutch. These Poles get blankets, just like block orderlies. Blankets for spreads, blankets for cover, and even blankets for draping the hutch. Whenever they wish, they drape the hutch at night to partition it off, as though they had no connection with the rest of the block; if they feel like, they can pretend at night that they are traveling in a private Pullman compartment, and when they wake up in the morning they'll find the war is over, and they'll get off the train and go home, back to their waiting families, to their world. Fruchtenbaum sees to it that nothing disturbs their illusion. He caters to them all he can, regretting only that they know he is a Jew and that his name is Fruchtenbaum. But there is nothing he can do about it. He cannot take it out on them in *Sport*. To them, he's just another kike.

Vevke's eyes start from their sockets. Jars full of jam! The Poles take the jars from their cartons, examine their contents and colors by the light, remove the lids, dip in their fingers and taste. Exactly the kind of jam Gittel always used to prepare for the children in the winter! The Germans gave them only ten minutes to clear out of their flat. He barely managed to snatch up his shoemaking table and the case of tools. That was when the Germans herded the town Jews into the ghettos. Poles then moved in and took over the Jewish homes. The uprooted Jews left everything behind for the taking. Wasn't it Gittel's hands that prepared these jars of jam now in the hands of the Poles?

Yom Kippur in the hutch of the Rabbi of Shilev. Gone block. Gone Auschwitz. The Rabbi of Shilev is translating himself to sublimer spheres, all seated around rising with him. The last veil of the material world falls away. It is Yom Kippur also in Heaven. Angels and Seraphs shudder there; they veil their faces with dread, declaring to one another: "Let Thy throne be established on Grace, and sit Thou in it in Truth..." And down in the world, in the hutch of Auschwitz, the Rabbi of Shilev's mouth now repeats after them, word for word.

Vevke's eyes shut. A synagogue packed with Jews. Praying

heads wrapped in prayer shawls. Children snuggling against thighs of Papa or Mama. The entire congregation joined in one clamor: "Sit Thou in Truth."

Vevke's eyes open. Uncovered jars in the Poles' hutch. Jars of jam. "Rabbi!" the cry suddenly spurted from his sealed throat. "Where are the Jews? Where are the women? Where are the children?" Vevke leaped down from the hutch and battered the block wall with his fists. "Where are the synagogues full of Jews? Where, Rabbi?"

Fruchtenbaum came dashing over, his mouth full of chew. In one hand he held a half-gnawed apple, and in the other the cane. "Whoreson!" he swallowed, screeching at Vevke. "What are you doing in my block? Get out of here! Get out!" It would be such a pity to lose out on all the good things going in the Poles' hutch, so Fruchtenbaum let Vevke off with only one swipe of the cane's iron handle across his skull, and kicked him bleeding out of the block.

Soup distribution is almost over in block 16. The last of the line are on their way back from the barrel with full bowls in their hands. Those who have gulped down their soup cluster to stare again at the soup in the hands of those just returning from the barrel, as though there were some drug in the soup compelling them, the moment they have swallowed it, to hurry and feed their eyes with others' bowls of soup.

Vevke is sitting in the hutch, the bowl of soup between his folded legs, his palms leaning on his knees, his head bowed. His eyes stare stonily into the soup. The back of his head bears the hole left there by Fruchtenbaum's iron handle. The coagulated blood on the bony nape looks like the cooled dripping of a black candle. But Vevke does not feel any of it. Bent motionless over the bowl of soup he sits there, his eyes inside the bowl like a crystal-gazer. His hutch-mates do not see him. He does not exist for them. It never occurs to them to wonder why Vevke doesn't eat. All thought has ceased. A bowl of soup stands there on the boards—all eyes upon it. The world bates its breath: a bowl of soup!

Vevke does not know he has a hole in his head. He does not feel the coagulated blood on his bent nape. He is aware only of a fire burning somewhere inside him, leaping to his brain, every flash splitting his head asunder. The words swirl within him like sparks in knots of smoke. *Vevkeshi, may we lead our children to the canopy together*...The synagogue packed with Jews joined in clamor: *Sit Thou in Thy throne in Truth!*

All at once Vevke's feet flexed and kicked at the soup. The bowl went flying through the air, struck the board of the hutch opposite, and tumbled to the ground. "See now!" Vevke raised his eyes as though crying protest to Heaven. "I will show You that even in Auschwitz Vevke the cobbler is equal to fasting on Yom Kippur! But You—You are to sit on Your throne in Truth! Do You hear me? IN TRUTH!..."

Like black ghosts camplings leaped from the hutches all around. Open-mouthed they threw themselves at the ground, toppling and trampling all over each other. The soup-splattered hutch sides were strung with bared fangs and darting tongues probing at the wood, licking, sucking.

Vevke lunged out of the block.

Outside, the sky shrouded the block roofs. The rain no longer just fell but seemed to collect in space. Vevke's bare feet floundered in the muddy Auschwitz earth. The rain rinsed the clotted blood from his nape. All at once his hands rose clenched at the Auschwitz heaven. "I am a heinous sinner, I am!" he cried. "But what did my Gittel do to You? And my five sons—did they do You some great wrong? Answer! Answer! Why!"

7

Hayim-Idl set out for the office, his brain feverishly working on the new plan he was about to carry out. His heart wasn't all in it yet. It seemed too full of risks. He could not make up his mind whether it was a good idea. If good—then it's very good indeed. If bad—he could do nothing worse. He kept vacillating, walking in response to every vacillation —alternately dashing forward; wavering and turning about in fright; then dashing forward again lest he lose out on everything.

Since they issued the call for engravers in the block, he hasn't had a moment's peace. Engravers! Actually, he doesn't know exactly what the word means. Very few answered the call, because there aren't many of them, and Hayim-Idl's investigation disclosed that only foreigners applied. Not one of his sort of Jew. Getting right down to it, he doesn't even know how he will talk to them. (Hayim-Idl's feet slow up.) He never had dealings with that sort of Jew. He isn't even sure whether that sort has a real Jewish heart. Take a real sort of Jew like Vevke the cobbler, for example, now *that* sort of Jew would never let a man down. A Jew like that wouldn't stand by and see another Jew hang without trying to do something. Foreigners! Supposedly your own flesh and blood. Brothers. But all the same, lost brothers. You feel about them the way you'd feel at meeting a brother who left home before you were born. Somehow you can't be sure about those foreigners. You don't know them. You don't even know whether you can afford to count on them. Then again, what can you know? Take Abram. He's your sort of Jew, eh? He should only croak instead of Rafael. And Fruchtenbaum! A good homey sort of name—may it be stricken for all time! He isn't worth one drop of the piss of the lowest of those Greek boxers. No, you really can't ever tell. (Hayim-Idl's feet spurt forward.) Picture printing! A silly trade, when you get right down to it. But there's nothing you can't learn. The main thing is the people you'll be working with. Just so you can count on them not to let you down. Then—so what if you never in your life laid eyes on a print shop? When was he supposed to see one? How was he supposed to know that his life would one day depend on it? So he doesn't know what "engraving" is. And does he know the other kind of printing?

What a miracle he didn't sign up for shoemaking that time. That whole kommando turned out to be a dud. They didn't need any more shoemakers. They filled the quota from the other camps. Now they need engravers. If he had signed up for shoemaking, how could he now suddenly turn out to be an engraver? Simply a miracle. Maybe some Jew of his kind will turn up from some other camp as an engraver. He has nothing left to hope for here. The next *Selektion* it's crematorium for him. If only it isn't too late. (Hayim-Idl's feet rush along.) But what if they decide to test him? (The feet halt.) Maybe he should first try to find out how he's supposed to answer their questions. But if he asks one of those foreigners, he might report him to the Office. No! He mustn't ask anybody a thing now! When he gets there, no Jewish heart will be so cruel as to do him any harm. (The feet take off.) God won't forsake you. Where's your faith, Hayim-Idl? So soon you've lost your faith in the Ineffable One? Who told you that you won't find some real Jews of your own sort there? Only they shouldn't tell him at the Office that the list is full up...

His feet broke into a run.

Inside the Office, the clerks sat at a long table. It's warm here. Cozy. Not Auschwitz at all. Just look at those faces. Like in a Polish tax office. Look at those cigarettes they're smoking!

"Why didn't you report sooner?" The clerk glared at him. "Been too busy?"

"I was a bit under the weather." *God, help me! Please don't forsake me!*

The clerk takes a list out of the drawer. The cigarette dangles from a corner of his mouth, half his face screwed upwards. The smoke curls towards his squinting eye.

"So you say you're an engraver?"

"Engraver!" Hayim-Idl hastens to reply. "Of course, engraver." *Please God, don't forsake me now.*

The clerk examines another sheet of paper, with German typewriting. He examines it with one eye, the other squinting against the smoke, one side of his face creased in discomfort of satiation in fat folds of flesh towards the temple. Hayim-Idl had forgotten the look of flesh on skulls. The clerk continues to read, asking questions without looking up.

"Have you done color gravure?"

"I suppose I have," Hayim-Idl dismisses the question. "A man can do anything."

The clerk raises his open eye from the sheet, explaining to Hayim-Idl somewhat apologetically: "Because, you see, we're not looking for ordinary engravers."

"Who said anything about ordinary engravers?" Hayim-Idl comes back.

The clerk lowers his head back to the German-inscribed sheet. "I must ask everything, you see," he says, still apologetic, continuing to read the German instructions.

God, don't forsake me...I have no one left but You... You're a Merciful Father...Don't make me twice an orphan...

Ludwig Tiene comes in. The sound of his voice alone is enough to send the flesh crawling. Ludwig pauses across the table to speak to the clerks. *Don't look there,* Hayim-Idl warns himself.

The clerk returns to the handwritten list. It does not seem to have many names. About two dozen lines at the most.

"In that case," the clerk finally decides, "I guess I'll have to put you first on the list. Nobody on the list has all the qualifications as you do. Let's see the number on your arm."

Hayim-Idl extended his left arm, where the number was tatooed into the flesh. He held the arm bent, as though to be measured for a sleeve. The arm trembles. *God, give me strength!* Ludwig's voice rasps: "Clerk, Muscles there better not conk out on you before the group takes off! Hi-hi-hi..."

The clerk does not look up. He enters Hayim-Idl's number in thick, ornate ciphers. "It would be a shame," he says as he writes. "It's a de luxe kommando. They'll fatten them up proper there."

Outside, the sky appeared bright. Too bright. Hayim-Idl felt his eyes smarting at the brightness. He walked as though drunk. *De luxe kommando.* He's done it. *They'll fatten them up proper there*...There's no turning back now.

Looking up at the sky, he whispered: "Now it's all up to You, God. I've done my share. I've done everything. Even more than that. Engraving! What a queer word. It smells like those foreigners. But what's the difference? So it's 'engraving.' *Color gravure.* Gravure...Gravure...What did he mean by that? They say they're going to print dollars. Queer. If the Germans need dollars, they have to resort to Auschwitz camplings? That's just talk. Still, it might be worth while cultivating that Dutch engraver. He seems to be a Jew with a heart. How does that one know they're going to print dollars? Maybe he's done that sort of work before. Or maybe he guessed from the questions they asked him. *In that case, I'll have to put you first on the list.* He, Hayim-Idl, first on the list! The dazzle of the very notion pricked at his eyes. But what's the difference—first, or last? If the Dutchman gives him a hand, it will make no difference where he is on the list. He has nothing more to lose here, in Auschwitz. *Muscles there better not conk out on you first.* Blast his name and fame! If God only willed it, Ludwig could die a violent death even though he is Camp Senior. He can even croak first, that butcher.

In the assembly area between blocks 4 and 5, Moni stood bent over a large tub of water washing a shirt. Moni is sure his brother and sister are in Palestine, Hayim-Idl mused. Nobody has tried to tell him otherwise. What for? Why tell him the truth? Maybe they really are alive somewhere. Daniella went to a forced labor camp. Harry was also taken from the ghetto. Who knows? Maybe they really are alive. Alive! Just like all the other Jews are alive. Moni is getting skinnier all the time. He is all dry bones.

"Moni, I'd like to talk something over with you," Hayim-Idl said. "You know the camp better than I."

"What is it, Hayim-Idl?"

"I've just done something. Something big."

"The big things you can do in this camp!"

"No, really, I've just done something so big, my heart is running away with me. But I heard with my own ears that you can fatten up. There'll be plenty to eat."

With a groan Moni straightened up, and looking Hayim-Idl straight in the eyes he said:

"Only a Piepel can fatten up here."

"Laugh at me all you like, but if God helps me I won't be sorry."

"Hayim-Idl, I have to finish this shirt. What's up now?"

"I've just signed up as an engraver," Hayim-Idl blurted diffidently.

Moni bent back down towards the tub and resumed washing. "So what are you worried about?" he said. "Very good!"

"You really think I did the right thing, Moni?"

"Why not? Maybe you're resigning from a *Funktion* as cook?"

"What I mean is, do you think I did the smart thing?"

"There's nothing smarter than getting out of Auschwitz. Here you've got only the smoke-stack in store for you. It can't be any worse anywhere. Do *you* think it can be worse, Hayim-Idl? I wish I could get out."

"Do you think I'll make it?" Hayim-Idl feverishly waited for the child's affirmative reply.

"What a question? What are you scared of? You're a printer. I envy you. I wish I were a printer."

Hayim-Idl stood up. He could not bring himself to utter another word. His feet carried him off. He felt as though he were walking into a vacuum. The rows of blocks on either side seemed to be closing in to crush him. Moni's voice reverberated back at him from all the block roofs. *You're a printer! You're a printer!*

His feet carried him to the hutch of the Rabbi of Shilev.

8

Moni sat at the edge of the assembly area on the rampart by the block wall, his eyes gazing across at block 16. He was afraid to come any nearer to the block, lest he run into Robert. But every time the gate opened he leaped up, in case it was Benyek at last, so that he might hurry over and ask him for help.

From his semi-concealment he could not see the gate of block 16. But neither could Robert, if he should come out, see him watching the exit of his block. Moni simply could not understand why a Piepel shouldn't help a friend. True, it isn't Benyek's fault Robert wanted to croak him, but why shouldn't that Benyek help him? At least give him Robert's boots to polish, or Robert's shirt to wash? If a fellow just wants to, there are plenty of ways of helping out an old Piepel.

The main gate of block 16 was not visible from here. Here he could only hear the long, shrill creaking of the gate's hinges whenever it opened or closed. At every creak he leaped up: if it's Robert, he'll make a dash for the backpath; if it's Benyek, he'll rush up to him before he gets away.

Benyek never has time for even a word with him. Always in a hurry. Always the same excuse. "A merchant is waiting with margarine . . ." "A customer for diamonds is waiting . . ." Benyek never has a second for a word with him; it might cost him a slice of bread.

He sat on the bank of earth, his ears and nerves taut. The constant leaping up at every opening of the gate, and the disappointed slumping back again, were sapping the last of his strength. Always after escaping a Block Chief he waits this way to ask the new Piepel to help him out, to keep him going just till he gets back on *Funktion*. For hours on end he waits. For days. But this time he will never get back on *Funktion*. He knows it. This time Benyek will just have to keep him going. Benyek now has the last job he held. Benyek simply must see it. If Benyek doesn't help him now, he'll be off to the crematorium next thing he knows. Moni knows exactly what shape he's in and just how he looks. Not like those Mussulmen there who check their bodies every day like clock dials and don't see any change for the worse. They think they look exactly the way they did the day they were brought here.

Oh, this terrible waiting outside the block gates! He's missed out on more than one soup ration in his own block, only because Piepels like Benyek didn't keep their promises to come out to him. Hours on end you wait for them, always exposed to the danger that the Block Chief is going to sweep up on you from behind and toss you right into Ludwig Tiene's hands while inside the block the likes of that Benyek has long since forgotten his promise to come back out to you. Maybe he never dreamt of keeping the promise even while he was making it. And you sit and wait. Every creak of the gate rips open your brain and your nerves. Every creak of the gate riddles you at once with hope and fear for your life. Is it the Piepel? Or Robert? The creak becomes part of you. You remember it. You recognize it. You can tell whether it's coming from block 16 or from block 15 next door. Every gate has a screech of its own. One is the cry of a campling when his head is being shoved into the brick oven. Another is the first shriek of one hung by his wrists. Each gate hits you with its own special creak. And you know each and every one of them.

Food porters are bringing the barrels of soup from the kitchen. Scurrying along behind each barrel is a swarm of camplings. The barrel is brimful. The soup surface rocks back and forth between the open rims. The eyes of the tag-alongs transfix the barrel opening. They are afraid to come nearer, but they shove and jostle each other. Each pushes to the fore. Their eyes reach out to the whole soup surface swaying this way and that. Perhaps one of the porters will lose his balance, and the soup surface will rise a bit higher on one side, then pitch sharply to the other side, and a chunk of the surface will shatter on the sharp barrel rim, golden drops will trickle on to the sand, and whoever is in front will pounce on the ground, dig his teeth into it, and suck the sand dry.

Inside of six hours after losing your Funktion, you're as hungry as all the rest of them in Auschwitz. For the thousandth time he asked himself: How is it that just when the finest foods in Auschwitz are his for the taking, his throat gags and he cannot touch a bite? He simply can't understand it. At this moment he could eat all day and all night and never stop. Oh, God, why couldn't he fill himself with so much food then that he wouldn't be hungry now? *There are only six hours between a full belly and a hungry one.* When Rostek told him that, he didn't understand. He hadn't felt it yet.

On the other side of the main path, Fruchtenbaum is putting a group of camplings through *Sport.* Must be a new transport. One of them had probably come rushing up to Fruchtenbaum with the good news that he knew him from "outside." It's hard to understand why Fruchtenbaum, of all people, has so many acquaintances from outside. He, who can't stand it. Why does it bother him that they knew his pa. Every Prominent in Auschwitz has some bug of his own. As soon as Fruchtenbaum became a Prominent, he was off with his *R-r-rebbetzin! "R-r-rebbetzin!* What did you do all your life?" Fruchtenbaum had snarled. "Of course you didn't go in for athletics. Well, now you'll do some *Sport* for me. Go on, it's good for you. Hippety-hop, hippety-hop . . ."

This Fruchtenbaum will go places in Auschwitz, Moni mused. When they brought Fruchtenbaum to camp, he was already Piepel in block 28. The very first day Fruchtenbaum came bawling to him: "Outside I was a big shot." In camp they all tell you they were millionaires or somebodies outside. "After the war every door will be open to you if you'll be able to say that you helped me," Fruchtenbaum had assured him. And Moni had hurried to bring him his own soup ration from the cubicle. Not so the doors should be open for him after the war but because he simply couldn't stand Fruchtenbaum's tears. They both moved and nauseated him. Because what sort of campling comes crying for a second helping of soup his first day in Auschwitz? Then Fruchtenbaum buttered up the Block Chief. Without being asked he started beating camplings and organizing the soup distribution. The Block Chief soon saw that here was a born block orderly. Now Fruchtenbaum is Chief Orderly, and he's not stopping there. He is always trying to show Camp Senior Ludwig Tiene that he's fit to be a Block Chief. And he'll make it, too. But the day Fruchtenbaum becomes Block Chief, this camp will be the bloodiest of all the camps in Auschwitz. Because then he'll probably be out to show the Germans that he is fit to serve them as Camp Senior too. It is plain that Fruchtenbaum is out to make a big career for himself in Auschwitz no matter what. And you can see his shiny boots heading straight for his goal.

The gate kept opening and closing. Each time Moni leaped up. But now it was a block orderly with bread inside his trousers. And then a launderer with a Block Chief's shirt in his hand. Or Pocksy Zygmunt. None of them must see how down and out he is. Because here you're either a Prominent or a shit flushing through camp to the crematorium. There is no in-between. The moment they find out the state he is in, they'll squash him underfoot. For the time being he still has the shoes on his feet. That comes in very handy. An ordinary campling doesn't wear shoes. True, his shoes are torn; the tips are coming apart and the toes show. But still he's somebody in Auschwitz with shoes. He's never taking off the red socks. Let them call him "Old Whore with the red socks" all they want! There is almost nothing left of the socks, just the little red bands around the ankles. Whenever he looks at them he sees Mama's head, in the ghetto, wrapped in her red shawl. He's never taking them off his feet. Ma knitted them from her shawl as a present for his eleventh birthday. When is his twelfth birthday? Has it passed already? Or is it to be? Here you don't know whether it's summer or winter. And if he hasn't had his birthday yet, will he still be alive on his twelfth birthday? In the ghetto, at the loading platform, Pa took off his shoes and put the new red socks on him. Ma was standing beside him, hugging his head to her breast, and, like every year, singing into his hair:

Happy birthday, Monkele!
Happy birthday, my little boy!

Then, when they loaded them into the wagons, Mama disappeared and — suddenly the gate squealed open. Benyek! Benyek's white pullover! Benyek is running towards a nearby block. Benyek! Benyek! Moni blocked his way:

"Benyek. Have you got a second? Just one second! I want to tell you something . . ."

Benyek was in a hurry. He knows what Moni wants to tell him; the same thing he tells him every day. "I have no time, Moni. Not now. I'm on an errand for Robert." And he hurried off.

When he returned Moni again blocked his way. He only wants a second with him. Just one second. "It's very important, Benyek. I'm in very bad shape. I can't tell you how bad. Won't you hold on a second, Benyek? Maybe you've got a shirt to wash. Maybe there's—"

The block gate again let out a terrifying shriek: *Robert!*

Moni quickly turned and fled for his life.

Evening.

There were only the two of them in the latrine. Benyek rolled up the white pullover, unbuttoned the suspenders, lowered his riding breeches, and sat down on the hole. Then Moni seated himself on the next hole.

The latrine was empty. Still. Eerie. The rear section was in almost total darkness, and only the section leading to the main road was illuminated with a dim light which barely dispelled the dense dark hush. In the blocks bread distribution is still on. This is the moment of fulfillment of all the Auschwitz dreams. The moment at which everybody in Auschwitz is busy — merchants collecting debts from camplings who at noon had mortgaged to them the present bread ration for an immediate bowl of soup-water; block orderlies maintaining order. The main stock-exchange activity has now shifted to the blocks. Auschwitz brains are in feverish activity. And for a Piepel who is kept busy day and night, this is the best time to make for the latrine and attend to his needs.

Moni sits on the hole next to Benyek. He has not lowered his trousers. That isn't what he came here for. All day he had kept careful watch on Benyek, knowing that this is the best time to pin him down for a talk. That is why he sat down beside him. This is the only chance. Moni wants to speak up, but his throat is plugged. He cannot find the word to begin.

Benyek groaned on the hole. He assumed an attitude as though there were no one beside him at all; as though no one had sat down on the next hole with buttoned trousers for the sole purpose of telling him something. In his hand Benyek held a roll of bandage paper. The kind of paper the K-B doctors withhold even from the seriously wounded, but which Prominents use to wipe themselves in the toilet. How long has it been since he, Moni, was a Prominent, and also used it for toilet paper?

The block seemed endless and vampiric. In the rear corner, the motor of the water pump chugged away inside the compartment. How long is it since he was himself a Prominent? If he doesn't do something quickly, it's the crematorium for him at the next *Selektion.* "Benyek," he suddenly blurted. "Don't let me die . . ."

"What can I do? Robert never lets me out of sight."

"Let me have at least one soup a week," Moni pleaded.

"Loony! How am I supposed to get a bowl of soup out of the block? Bonehead! Everybody will see!"

In the dark of the latrine, the water pump chugged away. Always at this time, Moni mused, he used to steal in here to stash a bread ration behind the generator for Berele.

"I used to be a Piepel, too. So how did I help a buddy out? All you have to do is want to, Benyek . . ."

Benyek pressed into the hole like a chubby toy poodle defecating, his mouth expelling the words: "Don't be a pest, Moni. Don't be a pest . . ."

Moni gnawed at his nails. He did not know what to do. But he did know that it is all up with him now. Benyek is his last hope. But how can he soften Benyek's heart? How can Benyek let him down this way? Can't Benyek see that he'll be gone with the next *Selektion?* He tries again:

"Benyek, I'll teach you love-tricks you never dreamt of. I know what Robert likes. You'll hit it off with him."

"I don't need that stuff!" Benyek said. "Don't you worry, Robert isn't turning me in for any one else. Just in case you're interested, Robert can't live without me. No, thanks. I don't need any of that. Besides, there are things you don't know that I've forgotten already."

Hate flared up in Moni – hate and mortification. It's over a year now that he's in Auschwitz! How did he let himself sink so low? He, the old campbird, who outlived all the Piepels who were here when he got to camp; he, whom Robert had personally asked so many times to be his Piepel – how did he let himself go this way? Who put a hex on him against ever getting fat? If only he could get fat, he would never have to come to the likes of such as Benyek and –

"Oh, Benyek, Benyek," Moni said. "If I had been able to pack those soups in the way you do, you wouldn't be Robert's Piepel now. You would have gone flying out of the smoke-stack a long time ago!"

"Shut up!" Benyek snapped. "Who took Robert away from you? What are you kicking about? You say you know such great tricks. If you're so smart, why did Robert dump you?"

Moni is hungry and Benyek is full. That very fact makes Benyek right. That is an iron-clad law of the *Katzet*. He spoke gently, pleadingly to Benyek: "Remember, Benyek. There are only six hours between you and me. Once you aren't Piepel any more, inside of six hours you're just as hungry as me. And take it from me, Benyek: not a Piepel in Auschwitz has ever signed a lifetime contract with a Block Chief! Do you hear, Benyek? It's *me* telling it to you, the old *Katzetnik*. Just one more thing. You were still making mud pies in some ghetto when I was already Piepel in Auschwitz!"

Benyek gets up. He silently buttons his snug riding breeches. His face shows that he has no intention whatsoever of answering this pest.

Without saying a word Benyek turned and went towards the exit. Moni sat frozen to the hole. Benyek's fleshy back inside the white pullover jabbed at his tear-soaked eyes. All at once he cried out at Benyek's retreating back:

"Remember, whoreson! Prettier dolls than you have been carted out of here!"

He was all alone in the latrine. Benyek had long since gone, but Moni continued to stare at the gate which had closed on his back. He did not have the strength to rise, and he had nowhere to go. Nowhere did the chance of another piece of bread await him. Right and left of him ranged the round latrine holes. There was no one sitting on any of them. In the deep dark the pump ground away, as though the nocturnal heart of Auschwitz were pulsing there. Through the tubular emptiness of the latrine you could hear the pulsations as through a stethoscope.

Benyek had been his last hope. There was no one waiting for him anywhere now, and he no longer had any place to wait for anyone. He knew that in the blocks it was tea distribution time. Everybody is lined up before the barrels of murky water. In each barrel float a few leaves. Lately he has been lining up to get tea for the Rabbi, because whenever Fruchtenbaum, who hands out the tea, sees the Rabbi approach, he fills the ladle, and instead of pouring the tea into the proffered can, he turns it over on the Rabbi's head: let the skin on the Rabbi's rashy face peel a little more. A queer rash. He knew that it was time to bring a can of tea to the Rabbi's hutch, but he did not have the strength to get up and do it. He was completely drained.

Out of the dark along the walls, shadows — Mussulmen — began to emerge one by one. Silently they came from the rear gate on bare, muffled skeleton-feet. Along the walls they stood, wiping the excreta oozing from their trousers. Unheard they stood, as though they had no tongue. All identically occupied, each sealed off within himself. A row of shadows silent beside dark walls. The latrine now seemed emptier and more ominous than before. The stillness, too, was more menacing.

One after the other they arrived and came into the latrine. More Mussulmen, and more. Apparently the blocks are open again. Tea distribution must be over. Ferber will probably share his tea ration with the Rabbi. Ferber and Hayim-Idl both knew Harry and Dani. Hayim-Idl says that with his own eyes he saw Harry and Dani leave Metropoli for Palestine. Too bad Ma couldn't hear Hayim-Idl say it. After the war Harry and Daniella will come back to Kongressia, home to Park Street. Again they'll all sit around the table, not in the nook but in the big dining-room, the way they always used to when there was company. No matter what, he mustn't let himself die in Auschwitz. He must do everything, everything to hold out till the war ends. But what? If he can't turn up at least two bowls of soup a week, he'll be off with the next *Selektion* – just another Mussulman among all the other Mussulmen. Just two soups. *Bonehead! How am I supposed to get soup out of the block to you?* Maybe Benyek is right after all. Maybe his brain really has turned to bone. But why had he been able to get a bowl of soup out of the block to a pal? If only Benyek would let him have at least a shirt to wash, or boots to polish, then he wouldn't have to be afraid to be seen bringing him a bowl of soup for the work he did. Why do they all say he hasn't the strength left to wash a shirt? Why don't they give him a double soup ration every day so he should have the strength? Why do they all send him packing with, "You look beat, Old Whore?"

He got off the hole. He was very weary. He dragged towards the back door. The unplastered brick wall blocking the corner formed a separate doorless and roofless compartment for the water pump, with only an opening to go through. He went inside. It was totally dark there. The motor, as usual, was covered with a tin sheet. He knew well the corner behind the sheet, and he knew well the empty space behind the transformer. He pushed the sheet aside. He bent down, reaching his hand the way he used to deep into the space behind the transformer, his lips moving feebly: "Berele, I always put a portion of bread here for you, didn't I? I'm not really a bonehead, am I, Berele, for asking Benyek to help me out? I'm hungry, Berele, terribly hungry. Help me now, Berele. I'm scared. I'm scared about the *Selektion.* I have a feeling that the next *Selektion* is the end of me. Oh, Berele, maybe Benyek is right. Maybe I really have turned bony. I haven't a drop of strength left. Berele, I'm turning Mussulman! Oh, Berele, I can feel myself turning Mussulman . . ."

He got up off the ground. Tears gushed from his eyes. He wobbled out of the compartment. "Right here you once told me, 'A good angel protect you'. . . Tell it to me again now, Berele! Tell it to me now . . ." He dragged towards the exit. He pushed open the back gate. A long row of red bulbs burned on the electrified barbed-wire wall outside. He dragged past the blocks. He did not know which one to enter. Now he was all alone, lost in the never-ending planet of Auschwitz. All of him ached for the Rabbi's hutch. He so wanted to lay the pain of the loneliness away, unseen, somewhere among those who did not call him "Old Whore with the red socks." He stood at the gate of the Rabbi's block. He desperately wanted to go inside, but guilt deadened his steps. He hadn't brought the Rabbi the can of tea today. He had no excuse for it.

His feet dragged on.

9

He did not know whether a moment ago he had been dozing or awake. He did not know whether it was the beginning of the night, or the end. Hunger pounced on him again with renewed ferocity, like a beast which had been stalking its quarry a full year for just this moment. Moni was terrified. His eyes tore open. He felt: this is the final hunger! Gripping the sideboard of the hutch with both hands, he sank his teeth into the wood. Quickly to swallow something, quickly! His mouth tore to bite into the dark air. It's the final hunger! After this he will never again be hungry. He knew it. Everybody in Auschwitz knows it; every Mussulman feels it just once in his Auschwitz life. He felt he was now crossing a border, every campling's last border. The last borderline of hunger. He was turning Mussulman.

More than once has he seen camplings throw themselves at the ground to sink their teeth into the block gate; more than once has a campling at night chewed off a piece of dried leg from his hutch-mate; more than once does the Corpse Kommando load on to the cart half-chewed skeletons dumped behind the backgate during the night. The first time he saw this after he got to camp, he thought it was just a fit of madness. Soon he learned it was THE LAST HUNGER. One who has just so ravenously bitten into the wood of a hutch does not afterwards eat a thing; not even his own bread ration. Hunger never touches him again.

The last hunger! He wept, but no tears came. Every bit of moisture had long since dried up in him. Fear only pried his eyelids apart. His fingers convulsively pinched at the vacant darkness. He felt blades of hunger scraping the parched walls of his entrails. He shoved a fist between his teeth: to swallow something fast; to rush something to his entrails—anything: a bite of hutch wood! His foot! His sleeve! Hunger flickered madly inside his brain like the wick of an evaporated oil lamp.

He wanted to save his life, but he did not know how.

This is the last hunger for him. Tomorrow the soup will get into his mouth and run right through his backside, as through a hollow pipe. He will no longer have anything inside him to keep what he swallows. Day after day he has seen it happen to the others. Watched it indifferently. Everybody here is indifferent when he sees it happening to others. You suddenly remember only when it's you.

The horror of the oncoming Mussulmanity seized him. All at once he saw his own image as in a slide projection. He was afraid to look. He shut his eyes tight, but the vision would not leave—clinging to his sealed eyelids, or hovering in the dark when he opened them, as on a projection screen. He saw: Moni, the old campbird, drags his feet across the assembly area from block to block—a Mussulman. Somebody snatches the bread ration from under his arm without his knowing or even feeling what is being done to him. This Moni turns, stares blankly, and drags on. He goes, not knowing that he is going. A kapo lets him have the truncheon across his skull. The blow feels as if it had landed on a head not his. He lets out a squeal, freezing there, not running away. A Mussulman never runs away. Nobody recognizes him. Nobody knows who he is. And Moni doesn't recognize anybody either. He dissolves among thousands of Mussulmen. He is a drop in a skeleton river flowing to a sea of ash. He shuffles across the camp, back and forth, back and forth. He does not know where he has come from or where he is going. He does not know who he is.

Moni! Why this is he himself—MONI! He sees his trousers, and below—the red sock bands around his ankles. The one there on the screen opposite his eyes doesn't know that one is—Moni. That one doesn't know anything any more. But he himself knows that one is Moni! They are still two apart. Now he is still capable of seeing that one and knowing that it's himself. But tomorrow, or the day after, they will merge into each other and this Moni will no longer be able to see the other Moni. He will no longer be able to feel sorry for the other, console him, protect him, hang on to him. Because he will no longer know that the other is Moni. He himself; the old campbird, the former Piepel of all the blocks. He will look at the red woolen bands around his ankles and he will no longer know that those are the very socks which Ma knit from her shawl for his eleventh birthday. Always, in the worst moments of terror, he would touch those red socks with his eyes and Ma's face would come out to him. At such moments he felt his ma telling him it would be all right, cradling him to her bosom, protecting him with her warmth. Now, anybody who feels like it will be able to strip them off his feet. He will watch them being stolen from him and he won't say a word. He will no longer know they are from his ma, and they will no longer be his lifesaving talisman.

Beneath one of the rafters at the far end of the block burned a dim bulb. Directly under the bulb, on the edge of the brick oven, sat the night guard, cowled in a dark blanket, his head dozing away on his chest. The oven stretched to Moni's eyes like a long pallid thread. The rows of hutches right and left merged at the end of the block. The empty aisles ranged on either side of the oven like bands of darkness. The bulb near the gate seemed to radiate threads of darkness and silver at his eyes; the web of a spider hooking long threads on to Moni's eyelashes, with the black blob of the blanket-hooded night guard, the spider at the center of its web, not revealing whether he is dozing or stalking.

Several new transports have arrived since Moni has been in block 4. Dutch "Mommy-weewees,"[1] Italians, Belgians. Jews from faraway lands, with foreign languages. Now they all lie on his right and left, soundless. As though no one were here. Long threads radiate from the web, covering all. The block seemed an empty tunnel of night in limbo.

Only from the front of the block, in the barrel washers' hutch, snoring resounded as into an empty block. The barrel washers sleep on quilts and cover themselves with woolen blankets. No one dares approach their hutch. They come into the block after the final gong and leave before the first gong. Nobody ever sees them in the block, but the wood of their hutch is treated with deference. They are Prominents by day and Prominents by night. The only snorers here. It seemed as though the entire block were now holding its breath so as not to encroach on their snoring.

When you get your fill during the day, you snore at night; tomorrow, or the day after, he, Moni, will no longer feel that he must save his life. He won't be running around any more looking for some chore to do for a spoonful of soup. Now he could still save himself. Later it will be too late. Later he won't even feel that it's too late. He won't be able to do a thing about it. Later he won't even be aware that it is too late. Oh, God! Let him at least keep on realizing that he must save himself! How can he make his head hold onto whatever it is that contains this realization? What should he do to keep it from suddenly evaporating? Now it's still inside his head. At noon yesterday he saw a Mussulman let his bread ration out of his hand and crawl over to lick an empty barrel. He knows that he wouldn't do that now. But tomorrow, or the

[1] A child's call to his mother to be helped to the toilet; a nickname applied to the Dutch camplings, possibly because of their simple straightforwardness.

day after? Will he feel the moment, that terrible moment when this realization leaves him?

His hands snatched at his brow. With both hands he covered his head. At the collection points in the ghetto mothers used to shelter their children this way so the Germans shouldn't take them. Realization! That last bit which he must hold onto for dear life. The long, whitewashed brick oven caught on his eyelashes like a pale-silver thread of a spider web. An angular snore in the barrel washers' hutch stopped short, as though someone there had been strangled in the middle of a cry for help, the way Ludwig Tiene had strangled Golden Lolek in the middle of lovemaking. Oh, God! Don't let this realization leave his head! He had got away from all the Block Chiefs in the nick of time. He has outlived the lot of Piepels. And all thanks to this realization of his. It always told him: "Moni, tonight you're hiding in another block!" Or: "Moni, you're not to let this Block Chief ever lay eyes on you again!"

When do you turn Mussulman? Do you feel the moment? He isn't a Mussulman yet! Why, he still realizes with everything in him that he must save himself immediately. It's after the last hunger that you become a Mussulman. This doesn't seem to have been the last hunger. He feels that he's going to be hungry again. He felt good: he's going to be hungry again! These barrel washers got into camp after him. How could he, an old campbird, have let himself go to pot like this? He thought he was doing everything to save himself. Oh no, you weren't! You didn't do everything! You did things you shouldn't have done. Every day you ran after Benyek, waiting hangdog for that doll face to take pity on you and drop you a crumb of bread; every day you hung around the block gates, believing that the likes of Benyek would help you out. Think of all the times that made you miss out on your own soup ration in your own block. Why did you do it? Where were your brains? Why didn't you do something instead of just counting on that doll? It was the hanging around the block gates all day that brought you to this! It sucked you bone-dry. You? You had to become a shirt launderer? It's yourself you washed out at the tub. Now they say: "You're not worth a damn! The shirts you do have to be done over." Now nobody wants to give you work. "Old Whore!" they all say. When you left Robert you should have gone right into business. Didn't you know that block 16 was your last chance as Piepel? Why didn't you see what was coming? That night when you ran away from block 16 — why didn't you at least take some bread along? Just one loaf! Zygmunt wouldn't have noticed that the stash was one bread short. You could have been a merchant now — one of the camp's merchant crowd. Where were your brains?

From behind him, in the first hutch, came the snoring of the barrel washers. He felt that he was not one of them. He was one of those whose breathing is not heard and about whom there is no telling whether they are asleep or dead, like those lying here around him. He is one of these. He is lying among them. Mommy-weewee Dutchmen. Transports. Transports just streaming through camp, and everybody knowing what a shame it is to waste those bread rations on them. The hordes of them keep pouring off the train platform through the camp to the crematorium. Nobody sees them and nobody turns to look at them. Nobody knows them. A floating colorless dumping. Before you know it they have streamed off into the crematorium. In passing, they lie in the hutches. Only those snoring away there in the front hutch are the real permanent camplings, the rocks around which the river of transports washes.

He felt he was helpless. Near him lay camplings. He did not know whether they were asleep or awake. They lay unbreathing, curled up in one another's fate. He did not know their faces. He had never seen them. From the first to the last gong he trudges the camp. His own brother might be lying next to him without his ever knowing. Above — camplings. Below — camplings. On every side — camplings. A year — and now he, too, is in this unending stream.

He felt he was without hope.

With all his might he wanted to save himself, but he did not know how. He saw himself running desperately from block to block tomorrow, looking for work. He must do something, quick. Pick up at least a quarter of a soup. But they all turn him down. Everywhere they avoid him. They don't even want to talk to him any more. He sits behind the blocks waiting. Waiting for nothing at all; his eyes concentrating so hard at the blurry distance it makes him dizzy — and waiting. Maybe some Piepel he knows will pass by. He leaps up and immediately slumps back again, disappointed. Oh, this constant leaping up and the disappointed sagging back! Until the moment he will just find himself slumped on the rampart against some block. Nobody will see. Nobody will know. Nobody will ever turn to look. It will be on him before he knows it, sooner than he imagines: they'll sound the gong. His ears will register the sound, but he won't know in which block he is supposed to get his soup ration. He will stray all over the main path like one of those Mussulmen who leave their blocks for just a moment and never again find their way back. Meanwhile the soup will be handed out. And he will never again know whether he took his day's soup or not. He won't know a thing any more. He will be a Mussulman. Tomorrow. It will come tomorrow —

He struggled. He wanted to tear out of the stream. He wanted to save himself, but he did not know how.

A powerful hatred for Benyek surged in him. *Angel-faced doll!* When Robert first brought Benyek into his cubicle, Moni had been sure Benyek would help him out. With all his heart he had believed that Benyek would treat him the way he had treated others whenever he came into a new *Funktion.* If he hadn't counted so on Benyek's help, he would have taken along some bread. He had free access to the food stash. But his heart had shouted at him: "Moni, get out of block 16 just as fast as you can!" Nobody would have said a word if he had gone up to the stash and helped himself to bread. Nobody knew then what his heart foretold him. All they knew was that he was Piepel. Everybody was still playing up to him. But then he had still believed that doll-face had a heart. And because of that belief he will now go to the crematorium. If not for that, he could now be a merchant. If only he had taken just one loaf of bread that time from the stash—

The stash . . . the stash . . .

Like rings on the rock-punctured surface of a deep pool the word "stash" kept reverberating in his mind; clicking away in his brain as though someone were signaling him: *the stash . . . the stash . . .*

At the far end of the block, on the brick oven, the night guard dozed, head on chest. The night guard in block 16 must also be dozing this way on the oven, Moni mused. *The stash* . . . He will crawl across the upper row of hutches till he reaches the stash. One loaf. They'll never miss it. He has nothing to lose. He must save himself before his brain gives out. He still has a flicker of realization left inside his head. Tomorrow, the next day, will be too late, and he won't even know it's too late. He hasn't a thing left to risk or lose. He only stands to gain, now. Just one chance. The last . . .

Remember, Moni, save yourself! Your last chance!

His eyes smarted as though he were standing over a blazing furnace: *The stash . . . Pocksy Zygmunt . . . Robert . . . his last chance . . . Holy Dad Piotr . . . the final hunger . . .*

He fevered, feeling what everyone in Auschwitz feels on the brink of Mussulmanity.

The long filaments of the spider's web quivered and kept crossing one another. The black blob of the night guard hung motionless at the center. The long whitewashed oven-pavement swayed to and fro before his eyes, like the pendulum of a clock. Dark stripes, silver stripes . . . Back, forth . . . Back, forth . . .

His last chance. Tomorrow will be too late.

He crawled down from the hutch. Below there was not a trace of stripes or of all that his eyes had a moment ago hallucinated. He worked it out that if the night guard does not wake as he passes him, that will be a sign that the night guard in block 16 will not wake, either. Instead of the stripes, two long aisles now ranged on either side of the oven. Dark and empty. In the center of the whitewashed brick oven, the night guard sat shrouded in the blanket like a peasant woman in her winter shawl, his head slumped on his chest. His feet dangled over the side. Moni caught his breath. This isn't a spider. This is the night guard. Only he shouldn't wake! His heart pounded. What is he afraid of? This is block 4. What's he shivering about? He's allowed to go to the latrine in the middle of the night, isn't he? But if the night guard wakes, that will be a sign that the one in block 16 will too. That one must also be sitting there this way dozing. Must be. The stash in block 16 is behind the back of the night guard. There he will do exactly as he is doing here: pass by quietly. There . . .

The night guard went on dozing. Moni did not turn his head to him. As though he were afraid to look. On tiptoe he stole towards the gate. He thought he felt eyes burning into his back. He was afraid to look back.

The gate let out an irretrievable shriek. He froze in the narrow opening as though his body were trapped between the blades of giant shears. He did not know whether he should close the gate or leave it open. He shuddered at the thought of hearing the hinges screech again. He turned around: the eyes of the night guard stared at him out of his dark shroud. The eyes transfixed him. With his whole body he shoved the heavy gate back into place, and before it shut he glimpsed the night guard letting his head drop back to his chest, slowly, indifferently, as though nothing untoward had happened.

Outside the wind charged at his face, fizzling out like a jet of cold water on white-hot iron. In his mouth his teeth chattered, row against row. The earth sank fangs of frost into the naked soles of his feet.

Not a trace of sky was to be seen. Night shrouded the camp with darkness, blotting everything from sight. Out of the bowels of darkness the wind came galloping at him as on ironshod feet, hemmed him in and gave him a shaking as it hissed into his ear: *You're out to steal bread? . . . From Robert? . . . Go on . . . Piotr's hands are ready and waiting . . .*

It's a long way from block 4 to 16. The block numbers barely show in the dim lamps over the gates. Only a few steps from the gate and you are deep in the dark of the main path.

He walked now the way he had once walked from the ghetto to the wagons: behind him – only death outspread. Ahead – wobbly walk amidst the throngs of Jews, on one side clutching Pa's hand and on the other side Ma's.

Now he went: behind him – death outspread. Ahead – quaking walk to dread unknown.

Along the wire walls glowed the red bulbs. Far, far off they tapered to a spear of red engaged in a curtain of black. The white concrete pillars supporting the wire arched into the camp like necks of terrified geese, warning that the barbed wire was charged with electric death.

And death was what everyone in Auschwitz feared most.

He hugged his chest with both arms, tucking his fingers into his armpits. He was very cold. He shivered all over. There was no turning back, now. He walked forward as though a German were marching behind him, commanding: "Move!"

In the ghetto, when the Germans herded them all out to the gallows square to watch Jews being hanged, he had seen one of the Germans whisper in the ears of the condemned men to get over to the gallows. He had watched the obedient feet of the condemned. How promptly they had gone! As if it were not to the gallows the German had told them to go, but just to find another place to stand. A few minutes later he had watched those same feet swinging in the air. That time he had felt not fear, but the way he had felt on his first tram ride – he wanted to vomit.

In the dark before his eyes hovered – bread. A whole Auschwitz loaf. Oblong, with two sides, two ends, and eight rations in between. He knew that what his eyes were seeing was not real. Yet he went towards this unreal thing because there was no going back. He went the way those Jews in the ghetto had gone to the gallows: behind him was the hutch in block 4, ahead – a whole loaf of bread. He knew that Robert was luring him on. Piotr and Zygmunt too lurk somewhere in the dark waiting for him to walk into their trap. They had set a whole bread before his eyes to bait him on. He knew it, yet he could not help going, just as a thirsting man in the desert cannot help charging blindly towards the pool mirage. He went towards this terror because at its hub was bread. He knew it was not bread but death in the form of bread. But behind him too stood death – in the form of a Mussulman.

There was no turning back. Helplessly but fully conscious he went towards this death, because in his hands he also held – bread.

In one of the watchtowers an S.S. sentry sang into the night:

> You are cute, you are sweet, Belle Amie–
> Tralla-la, tralla-la-la . . .

He was very cold. In Auschwitz you never know whether it's winter or summer. Your frame is consumed by the fire of hunger. So, what's the season of the year to you? Here it is the never-changing season of hunger.

Far behind him, somewhere along the Auschwitz highway, lorries sped without cease. He did not know whether they were riding full to the crematorium or empty from the crematorium. He gave it no thought. His ears registered only the steady rumble of their rolling wheels.

Only when he reached block 10, he suddenly began to notice; he stopped in his tracks: what's going on there? Off in the dark, one of the block gates kept opening and closing. A suspicious midnight traffic. He counted the lamps: here, where he is standing, is block 10, then block 11, block 12, 13, 14, 15 — block 16!

Block 16. The gate did not stand still. There was a puzzling coming and going. Singly or in pairs shadows kept gliding out of block 16 and vanishing into the dark of the main path — all making for the latrine. Did the whole block get diarrhea in one night? The night guard can't possibly be dozing now. He was bitterly disappointed, at the same time feeling a nightmare had released him. He shivered, realizing that he was shivering only because he was cold.

There was no sense just standing there that way. The gates of the rest of the blocks also started opening, one after the other. Uncertainty engulfed him. They might start coming from behind him, and they'll take him for a thief. Why else is he standing there on the main path in the middle of the night? Who says standing? He's going. Going like everybody else. Going to the latrine.

The assembly area between the last block and the latrine was a thicket of darkness, except the part bordering on the backpath, which flickered in the dim yellow light of the nearby block. Like disembodied shadows, camplings emerged from the main path. The main path seemed to be dripping long, black drops. Veiled with night and dark mystery the shadows hurried along as though knowing exactly where and why. They dropped into the assembly area as into the cover of a shelter, and immediately dissolved in its darkness.

They stood pressed against the entire length of the outer latrine wall, mute, dark. Rustling shadows. Exuding will. A hectic black will, almost palpable in the dark. Here in the assembly area these shadows had suddenly come to life. Their black will throbbed with the mystery of Auschwitz night.

Nocturnal and silent they stood in line facing the back-path. Orderlies of block 16 hurried about soundlessly, only their hands commanding. In the dim borderland between darkness and flickering yellow, Zalke stood with a pencil in one hand and a sheet of paper in the other. Before crossing that border, each campling first extended his left arm into the yellow light. Zalke bent his head to the arm, scrutinized the digits in the skin, and entered the number on the sheet. Then Zygmunt gripped the shadow by the shoulders, squeezing him between his hands, as he impaled the gaping eyes on his glance. All around, night bated its breath: a mute initiation of terror was about to take place. Silence and eerie attention as Zygmunt's eyes give the pledge to the campling-phantom: you hunk of garbage, you spook of a man, if you ever just happen to get the cute idea that you're not shelling out for what you're about to buy here — it's me you'll be answering to! Look at me! It's the eyes of me, Zygmunt, lord of all the shadows in block 16, talking to you! All right, you can go now.

Zygmunt released him from his clutches, shoving him into the yellow light as though stripping him of a black shroud.

The shadow ran to the backpath, turned left, and through the back gate vanished into the latrine.

. . . what is this market suddenly taking place here? What are they selling here in middle of the night? Moni looked, but could not figure it out. Zygmunt must have organized a whole barrel of soup! Tomorrow they'll have to give Zygmunt their bread rations. The stash will be full of bread tomorrow. Mussulman! Ever since Auschwitz has been Auschwitz camplings give away their own bread here, speeding up their own burning. Stinking Mussulmen! Where are their brains? It's always the same. It's been that way ever since this world here was created. He saw it when he came here, and he still sees it. The stench of Mussulmanity hit his nostrils. He knows what it means to sell tomorrow's bread ration. It disgusts him. It is like dead skeletons, about to be carted away from the bone pile behind the block, pulling their own rotten rags off their bones and handing them to the orderlies to pawn. Hundreds of thousands have already passed through this camp, without one of them realizing that by selling his bread ration he is fixing his own execution. When it dawns on them, it's too late. Only an old campbird knows it. But an old campbird doesn't have to come to that. Old campbirds are organizers. This time, Moni decided once and for all, he is organizing a bread and also going into business. Everybody steals. That's the only way he'll ever become a Prominent again. He'll buy cigarettes and do business with block orderlies. So why does he go on standing here? He doesn't belong with those shits who at night sell their next day's bread ration.

An orderly stood guard at the latrine main gate. Moni did not know what to do next. He isn't one of those here to sell their bread rations, and he isn't one of those dividing up the bread loot tomorrow. Nobody sent for him. Nobody even told him what is being sold here tonight. Merchants don't make deals of this sort with old campbirds. Soup isn't sold to old campbirds. Being an old campbird makes you a Prominent. "And I," he kept repeating the words to himself, "am an old campbird. I'm an old campbird." Yet he felt that he wasn't one of them. He was an outcast. Abandoned to the Auschwitz night. A low-down beggar, with nothing left but the old-campbird pride – and nobody is taking that away from him! He turned around. Putting courage into his steps he strode to the latrine main gate. The block orderly came suspiciously at him, scrutinizing his face closely to identify him. "Old Whore?" he asked.

"Yes," Moni said.

Without another word the orderly opened the gate to let him into the latrine as a member of the camp's Prominent family.

The odor of smoked sausage jarred his nostrils. Inside, he halted at the latrine entrance. He swallowed the odor like something real. Through the pores of his parched skin he sopped it into every limb and organ of his frame. The latrine was dark. Only at the other end the water pump emitted an eerie red flicker, as though the motor inside were aflame.

Fried sausage! They've stolen the whole sausage supply from Shmulik's store! It smells like the sausage the block cooks used to fry for him in the cubicles. Strange: the very smell that always made him want to retch now tantalized him beyond endurance, baiting his former hunger on him. He drank in the odor and it felt rich in his mouth. He began to chew it with his teeth, the chewed odor exuding a sharp, titillating essence. He swallowed the essence, but his hunger was not allayed. It became all the more savage.

Along the wall of the back gate campling-shadows stood in line facing the narrow opening at the pump compartment, simmering with hot anticipation.

He could not just stand there and watch. He was drawn irresistibly to the spot where the sausage was being fried. The odor seethed madly within him. Now he was ready for anything. For a piece of fried sausage he would give Zygmunt all the bread rations he is due to receive in Auschwitz. To hell with being an old campbird! Now he wants to be one of those standing in line there. He'll keep his promise! He'll pay them all the bread rations they ask! Won't they believe him? It's not his fault he's an old campbird. Why should that make him worse than those standing there in line?

Down the entire length of the block, between him and the pump compartment, ranged the latrine holes. Slowly he stole towards the rear of the block.

Through the opening of the compartment a bonfire cast its light into the dark. Holy Dad Piotr sat crosslegged on the ground beside the fire, tossing pieces of wood into it. On his left stood a bin filled with chunks of raw meat. With a long knife Piotr cut the meat into portions, weighing each portion in his hand, and if one seemed larger than necessary he cut it in two, immediately tossing both pieces into the bonfire.

Meat! Portions of meat! They've stolen all the meat from the kitchen. Ever since he started eating the camp soup he never once found a trace of meat in it. Not a campling knows that there is supposed to be meat in the Auschwitz soup. Everything gets stolen here. After a year in camp he thought he knew everything. Now it seems that the Germans do supply meat, but the merchants sell it before it ever reaches the cauldrons. Such a portion of meat could save his life now.

The faces of the camplings were splattered with the red flickers coming at them through the narrow opening of the pump compartment. Their shadows stretched up the wall to the rafters, the heads leaping about high up in time with the capering tongues of flame. It seemed as though high on the wall there were another row of elongated black shadows; they too had come to buy meat portions, and up above they are mutely fidgeting: When will they get their turn to the pump? When are they getting their portion?

Each of them will be charged a full week's bread for such a piece of roast. Tomorrow at noon distribution time, Zygmunt will collect their bread rations, and they will stand watching the dream of twenty-four Auschwitz hours pass into Zygmunt's hands. Even the dream of the day-after-tomorrow's bread will be collected from them, and the dream of the days following. It is not their bread but their dream of bread they are selling here. At bread distribution time they will stand there husked and drained. Before their hands ever again hold a bread ration they will be off to the crematorium. Now they quiver impatiently; they can hardly wait. But not one of them calculates that he is now parting with bread for life. Not one of them considers that before ever he settles his debt with Zygmunt he will be lying on the corpse pile behind the block. No! Moni determined, he isn't doing it! He isn't that bad off. He isn't one of them and he isn't going to be. He still has a brain to think with. Stinking Mussulmen!

The pump motor kept chugging away, drowning out the crackling of the bonfire of fresh meat, blood, fat and wood. Block orderlies scampered around the compartment, scraping red-hot chunks of dripping meat out of the fire and laying them out on the ground for distribution.

The camplings looked on pop-eyed. Their feet would not stay put. Each of them prayed body and soul for his piece to be larger. There, that portion! That's the one! It looks bigger...But speaking is strictly prohibited. The block orderlies are keeping a sharp eye out. For the slightest sound you're liable to lose everything. The size of the portion you get when your turn comes is all a matter of luck.

Each skeleton snatches the searing piece with both hands, presses it to his heart, tucks it away inside the jacket, licks the drippings off the ground, and dashes off to hide somewhere with his piece of regained life.

Tomorrow the stash in block 16 will be full of bread. Everybody steals. In camp nobody helps out the next fellow. There isn't a merchant in camp who didn't have to get started himself. Moni knows it, as he knows what it means to sell one's bread ration. No! He isn't doing it. If he could lay his hands on just one loaf he would be a somebody again. Nobody will help him. He has to help himself. He'll steal bread and he'll join the merchant gang. Then they'll think twice about him. He's to blame for his own bad luck. He went and became a shirt washer. They all began to consider him a bootblack. He'll be a merchant and supply the Block

Chiefs with cigarettes. All the Piepels will buy from him. Benyek will also change his mind about him when he comes to do business with him this time. He'll go up to Benyek as a merchant. He'll offer him cigarettes for Robert. Just one loaf of bread will put him back on his feet. Zygmunt will never miss it from the stash. Tomorrow the stash will be stuffed with bread.

Piotr sat on the ground near the fire, working silently away, an unlighted cigarette leaning from his mouth-slit up towards his nose. *Just one loaf of bread from the stash will save him.* The blade of the knife in Piotr's hand glittered eerily in the fireglow.

The back gate opened: Zygmunt! He hurried over to the pump opening and spoke down at Piotr. Piotr did not look up, but mutely went on slicing and tossing the portions into the fire. Then, groping with his hands behind him, he drew out two long stripped bones, laid them on the ground at Zygmunt's feet, and went on with his work. Zygmunt bent, picked up the two bones, and went off to the dark end of the block.

Moni leaped aside. Only the row of holes now separated him from Zygmunt. All at once Zygmunt halted. He sensed someone who did not belong there in the dark. He peered sharply. Moni held his breath, his eyes freezing on Zygmunt's silhouette.

"Who's that?" Zygmunt said.

Moni did not breathe.

Zygmunt hurdled the row of holes. The two stripped bones phosphoresced like whetted blades in his raised hands.

"Moni, it's me, Moni!" he quavered.

Zygmunt lowered his hands. He probed Moni's face.

"Piepel?...Why didn't you say so in the first place? Another second and you'd have been a goner."

Piepel...Whenever Zygmunt is in a good mood, he calls him by his old official title: "Piepel."

Zygmunt placed a hand on Moni's shoulder and took him

along a few steps. They went like two old friends of equal standing.

"Piepel! Good thing I ran into you now. Look. These are Benyek's bones. Piotr is slicing him up there. If you had any brains, you could get back as Robert's Piepel. The *Funktion* is open. But with a mug like that, Robert won't even want to look at you. Drop in at the block tomorrow. I'll leave you the soup barrels. Help yourself to whatever you find there, and you'll even have a couple of pints left over to sell. I have no time now. I've got to keep an eye on my boys. What a deal this was, Piepel, what a juicy deal! Now I've got to bury the bones so there isn't a trace of them. You know, Piepel, I always did like you. I couldn't stand the sight of Benyek. He rubbed me the wrong way right off. If not for that doll you'd still be our Piepel now. What a lulu of a deal. Don't forget to look me up tomorrow night. Don't be a boob!" Zygmunt squeezed out through the slightly ajar gate, carrying the pair of pallid bones hidden behind his back.

Moni slumped onto one of the latrine holes. In the bonfire, an upright piece of wood crackled and sparked. The motor chugged away. Piotr's hands kept laying out the portions of raw meat. Moni gaped at the fire. His eyes were held fast by the portions of meat roasting in the fire. All at once he saw Benyek standing in its center. In the white of the fire he saw the white wool turtleneck pullover. Above was Benyek's smug round dollface with the cherry lips. Benyek stood there sure and devil-may-care as ever.

Moni did not know where he was. His mind was a maelstrom of thoughts unrelated to what he saw. He felt no fear. Everything now seemed familiar, as though he had already felt it all before. Everything here now was a vampiric epitome of Auschwitz latrine. Even the black shadows high up on the wall seemed familiar. They swayed in mute monotony, like the swaying feet of the hanged in the ghetto.

And as then, he felt like vomiting.

A double row of camplings. One below—on the ground,

its double above—on the wall. Dark-red shadows below, and black capering shadows above. A double row. The gate kept opening and closing. A campling reached out to snatch his meat purchase, and above, on the wall, the shadow followed suit: reached out hands, bent to the ground to lick, dashed out of the latrine.

Two rows. Standing, waiting, watching. The motor chugged away. Benyek floats up in the heart of the fire again —intact, secure. But every time Piotr's hands toss fresh portions into the fire, Benyek disintegrates like a reflection on a rock-shattered water surface. Gradually he comes together again, until Piotr's hand is at him once more, when Benyek shatters and is gone.

Benyek, Robert's Piepel, who had taken his *Funktion* from him and forever finished him as Piepel. *Moni, I bet you there's a new butterfly flapping around in block* 16, *but Christ have mercy on his soul if I lay my hands on him.* It was right here in the latrine that Piotr had told him that.

Moni felt his head swim. He simply could not conceive that those chunks of meat being grabbed up by hands one after the other were pieces of Benyek.

It was right here, where he is sitting now, that he had sat shoulder to shoulder with Benyek. Benyek is buttoning up the riding breeches which the Zhichlyn tailor had made to order for him.

Benyek, don't let me die...

You say you know some sharp tricks. So why did Robert dump you?

Benyek, let me have just a soup a week.

Ah, clear out, bonehead!

Moni's head turned towards the front gate. He saw Benyek's round, full shoulders, wrapped in the white pullover, retreating towards the exit. Benyek is leaving. He is leaving him sitting here frozen to the hole. He can now plainly see the white back. It is sealed, blank, fat...

Remember, Benyek, prettier dolls than you have been hauled out of here!

By the crimson glow, on the wall above the roofless pump compartment, a giant head leaped about—the head of Holy Dad. It looked as though Holy Dad were dancing in the center of the bonfire, while around it, shrouded from head to toe in black, phantoms pranced up and down, up and down.

Why, that's what they did to Golden Lolek! A shock went through Moni. Zygmunt had said: "Daddy-boy, now that's a fat deal. But keep the portions small." Holy Dad had slung Lolek over his shoulder. "Take him to the pump," Zygmunt had said.

The odor of roast which earlier he had gulped so ravenously now turned his stomach and made him want to retch. The essence of the chewed odor coated his mouth thickly, as though, after relishing a dish, he learned that he had been chewing away at vermin. His hands seized at his cramped stomach. He stood there mouth agape, then lurched out of the latrine as though to vomit.

The bulbs above the block numbers dazzled his eyes. He did not feel the ground beneath him as he walked. He went without knowing whether he was walking or standing still. He did not feel his feet move. The camp stretched before his eyes like an extension of a dark latrine block, a long, endless latrine block in which human flesh was going up in flames and in which he, Moni, was walking. The red bulbs above the barbed wire pranced before his eyes like shadows on a black wall. The cold engulfed him, sent him shivering as though in a delirium of fever. The pitch darkness in which the main path floated ran on to the end of the world.

He walked, not knowing where he was or where he was going. Campling-shadows flitted by him—hunched, shrouded, hands clutched to their breasts. They were dashing back from the latrine, hugging their meat bargains to their nakedness inside the jackets. It reminded him of a live bonfire, night-shrouded and crimson. Capering and mute. He knew where he had seen it, but he could not remember when. It might have been once upon a time, and it might be now and forever. Just like the smoke out of the crematorium smokestack. Just like Auschwitz. It was now. And it was forever. Portions of roast meat. Benyek in his white pullover. Red fire on white pullover. Daytime Auschwitz and nighttime Auschwitz. Unbounded and borderless. Day and night in one. All of everything drifted by as in a dark vacuum.

All at once: the main path. Everything around froze. He floated frozen in the vacuum of black congealment. He wanted to lie down on the ground. Someone unseen bent over him and sang into his ear:

You are cute, you are sweet, Belle Amie...

The rampart near one of the blocks was dimly lit. He dragged to the assembly area. He slumped to the rampart, leaning back against the block wall. Suddenly:

...Benyek alongside him. Moni stared at him. He did not wonder why Benyek suddenly had the time to sit on the ground with him; why he wasn't hurrying back to Robert. Benyek's face was wan and sad. Benyek—the prettiest Piepel in camp! Moni now felt about him the way brothers feel about each other during a *Selektion* in Auschwitz.

Then:

...Zygmunt on the other side of the latrine holes with two long, livid bones. *Look, Piepel! These are Benyek's bones...*

The two visions stood equally real and distinct before his eyes. He turned his head towards Benyek. He asked him:

"Why did you treat me that way, Benyek?" His voice was sodden with grief.

"I had to look after my pa," Benyek said. "If you were in the same block together with your pa, would you think of anybody else or would you always only be looking for ways to save him? I wanted to keep my pa alive."

"Why did they do it to you, Benyek?"

"I don't know."

"Robert must have been fed up with you."

"Robert isn't trading me in. He can't live a minute without me."

"There isn't a Piepel here yet who made a lifetime contract with a Block Chief. Remember, Benyek? Remember my warning you?"

"I was a dope. They made a deal out of me."

"Why didn't you run away from block 16? Why didn't you get away from Robert while there was still time? Why didn't you save your life, Benyek? Why didn't you do what I did?"

"Moni? You know what a hell my nights with Robert were. You're an old Piepel. Why didn't you ever tell me about getting away from Block Chiefs in time?"

"I was always after you: 'Benyek, just a second. There's something I want to tell you.' Why did you always run away from me? Why didn't you ever wait?"

"It was bread you were after! And soup! You were always thinking of yourself. You never once thought of me. Tell the truth. Nobody's listening, and besides, you can't fool me."

"Why did I always manage to help out a buddy?"

"Moni, I swear! I was scared of Robert. You're different. You have only yourself to think of. I had my pa to look after. Day and night I went crazy with worry about my pa. Wouldn't you have been the same way? Think about it, Moni. Wouldn't you have been the same in my place?"

"I like you, Benyek. I like you a lot."

"Now you like me because I'm not alive any more. Why did you hate me before?"

"I wanted a piece of bread out of you. I wanted to live. I wanted to save my life."

"Selfish! Why didn't you ever think that I was in the same spot?"

"Don't be sore, Benyek. Don't you see I'm turning Mussulman? Zygmunt told me to drop in at the block tomorrow. He promised me the scrapings of the soup barrel. But I don't trust him. I know Zygmunt only too well. He just happened to be in a good mood. He made a good deal out of your flesh. Tomorrow he probably won't even remember that he saw me tonight."

"Better not set foot in block 16. Zygmunt will hand you over to Piotr. Just like me."

"Piotr told me: *'Piepel, I'm your last buddy in camp.'* Nobody in camp wants to have me any more. Maybe Piotr will want me to be his Piepel?"

"Don't trust him. Stay away from Piotr's hands."

"Benyek, is the stash in block 16 still in the same place?"

"If I were alive, I'd tell you everything now."

"Benyek, I'm planning to pinch some bread."

"They'll make a deal out of you."

"What should I do? I don't want to turn into a Mussulman . . . Oh, Benyek, I'm scared . . . I don't want to be a Mussulman! . . ."

"That's the way all Piepels end up."

"No! I'll jump over the barbed wire and I'll run away. Then I'll just keep going. All day and all night. I won't have to rest. I won't be hungry. I feel the hunger going down into my soles. When I was little I never wanted to walk. Dani always wanted to take me for a walk in the park. But I wouldn't go. Now I'll walk all over the world, till I get into our living-room in Park Street. When I'm tired, Pa will pick me up in his arms the way he always does and carry me to my cot in the children's room. Won't you, Pa? Won't you pick me up in your arms again?"

"But you saw them throw me into the lorry."

"But then I saw you standing in B Camp."

"That wasn't I. Maybe it was Harrik."

"But Harrik is in Palestine!"

"So why do you ask such childish questions? You know that in B Camp all the heads looked alike."

"When are we going to be together again, Pa?"

"After the war we're meeting outside the camp gate. I'll be waiting for you. I won't budge."

"And you'll pick me up in your arms again, won't you Pa!"

"And again I'll say to you: 'My little monkey saint.' "

"See, Pa? They made a deal out of Benyek."

"That's because he didn't know how to get out of Robert's clutches."

"I always felt in advance when it was time to run away."

"Ma always did say you were bright."

"Have you run into Ma any place around here?"

"I don't know."

"Is Ma in the Women's Camp?"

"I don't know."

"Just don't forget to wait for me at the gate. Then we'll go look for our ma together. I guess it's going to be awfully crowded, the way it was getting into the wagons in the ghetto. Then we'll all meet at home, and the whole family will sit around the table in the big dining-room. I won't turn into a Mussulman, will I, Pa?"

"Old campbirds never turn Mussulman."

"But they won't give me work to do any more. To them I'm an old whore—that's what they call me. Pick me up in your arms, Papa! Hug me tight, Papa! Tell them I'm your little monkey saint.

"Pa..."

"Hey, Piepel, why are you sitting there bawling like an old grandma in the middle of the night?"

Moni raised his tear-soaked face. Zygmunt, Piotr, the whole crew of them were on their way back from the latrine after winding up the deal. They all stood around him.

"Better get back into your block before Ludwig Tiene catches you sitting here," Zygmunt said gently.

Zalke bent to help him up. Moni was shivering. He could not stand on his feet. Zalke took two cigarettes from his pocket, joined Moni's two hands and put the cigarettes in them. "Get yourself a hunk of bread tomorrow, Moni," he said.

Moni dragged out to the main path. He saw the group vanish somewhere inside an open block gate. He did not know which block. The camp was long, empty, dark. The same camp. He knew it inside and out. All the blocks are alike. As alike as the camplings in them. He slogged on. He was very cold. He was unable to run or even to walk slowly. The two cigarettes shivered in his hand. He no longer had a pocket in which to hide them, and he was afraid to hold them tight lest he squeeze the tobacco out of the ends. First thing in the morning he's buying a bread ration. Two cigarettes. Zalke had a good night. The two cigarettes are from Benyek's sliced-up flesh. Tomorrow he'll buy a bread ration with them. For the first time Benyek is giving him a whole bread ration.

Outside the barbed wire the lorries rode without cease. He knew there was no "outside." Outside it is the same as inside. Outside—Germans, and inside—Germans. He's been "outside." That's where the Germans brought him from. He knew that "outside" no more home or family existed. Not only his home, and not only his family. Outside there were only Germans. Everything else was here, inside. Everything ended on the inner side, at the barbed wire, at the electric mesh.

In the watchtower the S.S. sentry was still singing: *You are cute, you are sweet, Belle Amie . . .*"

He opened the door of block 4. Everything looked the same as before. Nothing had changed. Except the two cigarettes he now held in his hand. He entered the block, dragging past the mute, wooden hutches and the snores of the barrel washers. The night guard lifted his head and let it back down on his chest. Moni's eyes sought the hutch where he was supposed to lie. All the hutches looked identical. All of them crammed with the identical tangle of bodies. The identical heads. All one color. No young, and no old. A monotonous stream of murk reaching from the platform to the crematorium.

A thousand camplings, brought from diverse lands; diverse languages. All identical now. All drops in the same stream. He went in among them.

He lay among them, side by side with them, body to bodies. He had no way of telling whether the one lying beside him was his age or his father's. He did not know who they were, just as he did not know who the other thousand in the block were; as he did not know who were all the hundreds of thousands who had previously streamed through these very hutches. They were all one thing to him: camplings.

The two cigarettes were in his hand. All at once Benyek stood before his eyes: Benyek! Only now he saw the grief that had always been in Benyek's eyes but which he had never noticed. That same unchanging grief had been in the eyes of all the Piepels he found here when he got to camp, and it is in the eyes of the Piepels now serving in the blocks. But no one notices. No one sees it. Just as the Piepels themselves do not see the look of their own eyes.

Berele. Golden Lolek. Mietchu. Lonny. Every last one of them. Once-famous Piepels who had long since vanished without a trace. All now regarded him with the same sadness in their eyes.

Benyek!

Silent tears. White, innocent tears ran down Benyek's face. Moni reached out his hands. He wanted to embrace him. Hug him tight. He could not endure Benyek's weeping. He reached out his hands—all at once he felt: it is his own face in his palms, and the tears running from his eyes are his own.

Moni wept. The grief of all Piepels lay in his grief, and the tears of all Piepels wept from his eyes.

10

"All Jews fall in! All Jews fall in!"

They were all lined up naked on the main path. Thousands and thousands. Endless rows. The bundles of clothing on the ground lay beside the bare feet. All bundles were folded alike: the trousers, with the jacket on top. Rows of naked bodies above, and rows of clothes bundles below.

Shortly they will march to the crematorium.

"Oh, God!" Hayim-Idl wants to wring his hands, but he does not wring them. Nobody else is wringing hands. All stand straight, facing the shut blocks. Rows of naked skeletons—standing, looking, waiting.

"Oh, God!" Hayim-Idl wants to say Confession, but he cannot say Confession. He does not know what he ought to say. He knows only that at such moments Jews used to say Confession. He had ingested this with his mother's milk. But now the moment has come, he suddenly does not know the words. He had not prepared himself.

What's the prayer you say at Confession? He never saw it in the Prayer Book. He is cold. He shivers. He stands there, a gutted ruin. An eerie tempest howls through him.

"Oh, God!" He wants to cry out "*Shma Yisrael,*" but no

one else is crying "*Shma Yisrael.*" There is no time to cry "*Shma Yisrael*" when you're lined up for burning.

The Rabbi of Shilev is standing with the camplings of block 10. So naked, so puny, like a little boy. He stands as though waiting for the train that is to take him to a place where, when he gets off, his mass of devotees will be waiting for him.

Ferber's skull gleams like antique copper in the sun. The blocks are sealed. So still all around. Nobody cries out. It doesn't hurt. Soon there will come a pain so intense you'll have to die. This time the pain will not let up first. Meanwhile there is nothing on the main path but frost. Everyone shivers. The sun shines and the teeth chatter. Nobody cries out. The bundles of clothing are neatly arranged at the feet. Everybody stands and waits.

Long rows of naked bones. Eyes. Eyes. Withered thistles on a white field of winter. A raw wind blasts them, not bending but freezing them upright.

Robert runs back to the camp gate. He is waiting to greet the S.S. Staff. If Camp Commandant Hoess is along, he won't want to talk to Fruchtenbaum or any of the other Jewish Block Chiefs, though the eagerness and efficiency with which Fruchtenbaum does his job is up to German standards. As a matter of fact, Fruchtenbaum probably supplies more skeletons to the crematorium than Robert. But in spite of that, Hoess won't have a word for him. Hoess prefers the criminal badge on Robert's breast to the Jew badge on Fruchtenbaum's.

High above the block roofs the smoke from the crematorium smokestack rises into the sky, tall and straight. At the edges of the assembly areas stand clusters of Block Chiefs—chatting, smoking away, tapping their truncheons against the shiny uppers of their boots—boredly passing the time like a gang of butchers before the municipal slaughterhouse waiting for their herds to turn up.

From right to left, as far as the eye can reach—rows of

naked bodies. It is all over now. There is no more hope. Hayim-Idl stares, quaking. There is no more consolation in seeing hollower rumps on others. The sight reminds you that you are one of them. They are your mirror. Ridges of backs. Heads. Ears. Any moment now and it will all be burning.

Nobody utters a word to his fellow. As though nobody had any connection with anyone else. They stand together, each alone. Nobody is crying out; so he does not cry out, either. It does not occur to him that he can cry out. All are shivering, so he shivers along with them.

Hayim-Idl's eyes search. There is the Rabbi of Shilev, standing naked beside Ferber. That he is himself standing naked Hayim-Idl does not notice. But seeing the Rabbi of Shilev naked conclusively indicates to him that they are all really standing naked—because they are going to be burnt. The Rabbi's mottled face sets him apart from the rest. He stands out like a colorful flower in a cropped wheatfield.

How can he get over to the Rabbi of Shilev? He would so like to be with the Rabbi now. He does not know whether death will hurt any less if he is with the Rabbi, but he does know that he wants very much to be with the Rabbi afterwards. He does not know what this "afterwards" is. He cannot visualize this "afterwards." He cannot even think about it now. He only doesn't want to lose sight of the Rabbi. After the *Selektion* in the ghetto it was also together with the Rabbi that he was shoved into the wagons. With his body he kept the Rabbi from being trampled. And for that he was himself not asphyxiated. Taking care of the Rabbi had given him strength. He protected the Rabbi, and because of that he was himself protected. He had known then that he was riding to death; he was being taken to Auschwitz. They had all known they were riding to death. Although he had had no idea what sort of death Auschwitz was, just as now he had no idea what sort of death crematorium is. But perhaps crematorium is not yet the last of all Germanic deaths. Just in case—he would like to be in the same hutch with the Rabbi of Shilev, there.

He has seen death often. At the collection points inside the ghetto, and at the wagons during the *Selektions*. He has always seen death the way he is seeing it now. Clearly and face-to-face. But always, after this confrontation, he didn't die but was hurled from limbo to limbo, from these German hands to those German hands. But this time he will be tossed into the crematorium. What is there afterwards? What is after the crematorium?

High up in the blue, the crest of the crematorium smoke dissolved to nothingness.

Matchek went to the latrine. Matchek—the worst Jew-hater of all the potato peelers. The sun sits lanced on the tip of the paring knife jutting from his breast pocket. He does not turn his head to look at the naked rows. He walks straight on, smiling to himself in unconcealed pleasure. He walks close by the naked skeletons as though the main path were empty. He feels the myriad eyes looking at him. His pleased mien says as much. He probably does not need to go to the latrine at all now but is unable to forgo the pleasure of displaying himself to them in their final moments before burning.

Hayim-Idl knows that he must say Confession. But he does not know what one says. He hasn't the time to think about it. It is the last minute. Nobody is saying Confession. Everybody's jaws are shivering with cold. He doesn't remember a thing now, though he remembers so much.

Nobody is saying Confession. A cheep comes slipping out from among the naked skeletons. But you don't know what they are trying so hard to let you know. Why do they look at you? What do they see with their gaping eyeballs? What is each of them thinking? They look at you but do not see you. You look at others but see no one. Round eyes. Skeleton heads. An unending succession of skeletal nakedness, with a column of blue crematorium smoke in the van for a guidon.

Matchek saunters by. He is in no hurry. He walks leisurely. The front bench foreman in the potato peelery.

Nobody will be left here. Matchek will be left. A whole people is being reduced to ash in Auschwitz. Nobody will ever see them again, and nobody will ever think of them again. After the war Matchek will be "Mr. Auschwitz Campling"; the only victim of the Germans. The Rabbi of Shilev will no longer be, but Holy Dad Piotr will be. The sky will go on being here. Everything here will go on being. Except the Jews. There will be no Jewish towns or Jewish townlets. Gone Plonsk and Kielce. Gone Lublin and Ciechanowa. No more classrooms full of young Talmud students, and no more Medem libraries. There will be no more Jewish Sabbath, no more holy day weeks. But there will still be the world and the Germans, cities and villages. Everything. Except Jews.

This hurts him. The pity of it streams through him like a river. He stands there, nude skeletons all around him, heads: a yellow river of pity. All of them, every one of them flowing through him as through a sieve. Jews. Jews. Jews. All going to their burning. No man ever again will call to his father in Yiddish: "Tatenyu!" nor child cry out for his "Mamenyu!"

Hayim-Idl did not remember a thing. He did not remember a word of the holy prayers. He remembered only Chmielnik, townlet of his birth. "My little town Chmielnik—" the words seethed within him. All at once he wanted, just this one last time, to hear with his ears the sound of Yiddish words. But his teeth chattered in his mouth. He cheeped like all the others around him, gaping ball-eyed like all the others. His throat clogged. His ears plugged. But with the back of his eyes he saw the Yiddish words in the deep of his self, afloat on a yellow river together with his boyhood years in Chmielnik, townlet of his birth.

Robert hurries back from the camp gate. Every time Robert comes hurrying back, a rustle runs through the standing skeletons, like a wind brushing across yellow leaves on the forest floor: The S.S. Staff! Are they here yet? Skeletons stare at skeletons and quake. Quake anew. As though until now they had not been shivering. They fever in anticipation like a throng on a barren steppe at the distantly approaching train for which they had been waiting for days and nights. Deep within you someone feverishly gets ready for you. Someone you do not know and never in your life knew. Now, at the last moment, he has bestirred himself like a guardian suddenly concerned about you. Soon they will be uprooted from this spot. All look at the bundles of clothing on the ground. *Shall I pick it up now? . . . Would it be all right now? . . .* Your hands want to reach for the bundle on the ground. Nobody has heard a command. *Wait for the command, or better be ready with the bundle in the hands? In all the fuss afterwards, someone might grab your bundle by mistake.*

Not a skeleton thinks of parting with his bundle of "clothing." More than one has in the latrine given his bread ration for a length of tatter to wrap around his bare throat; his soup for a string to hold the jacket together around his midriff; a piece of decrepit board to tie to the bottom of at least one bare foot, to have it just a bit warmer during the hours long assemblies in the dawnless mornings. Now it all lies on the ground, bundle by bundle. The parting is so hard. Harder than, in the other world, to part with great wealth and valuables. Possibly, if he had eaten the bread then, he would not now be standing here. The bundle lies at his feet. Day and night he had wrapped his life in it. This is no clothing bundle: it is his skin. More than his skin. To it he had entrusted the secret of his skeletonness, so that it should cover up his Mussulmanity — for his skin was no longer capable of doing so. There will be a terrible crush here when the lorries pull up. Should he snatch the bundle into his hands now?

Abram clutches the little aluminum case in one hand, the nail-knifelet in the other. Many are doing so, clutching knick-knacks inside their fists. As soon as Benyek vanished from block 16 Abram turned Mussulman. Zygmunt saw to it. Abram sold everything, but he wouldn't part with the knifelet and the case. To the very end he would every evening, back from the kommando, scrape the dab of marmalade off the bread and into the case, then spread it back on his scrap of bread, stick a crumb on the knifelet, and plunge it deep into his mouth. This eating ceremony gave him the illusive feel of the good old days gone forever. Like a senile actor, his hands shaking as he takes out the motheaten costume of his favorite starring role, puts it on, staring at himself in the mirror, reliving the days when he captivated full houses.

The sun was coming up, but the S.S. Staff had not yet arrived. The lorries aren't free yet. They keep riding from the platform to the crematorium, back to the platform to reload for the crematorium, and then back again. Fruchtenbaum beats away with his cane on the heads of the skeletons in the front row. Why not? If the lorries don't show up fast, the shits will probably have to be herded along to the crematorium on foot. This makes Fruchtenbaum uneasy. He does not care to show himself near the crematorium with the Jew badge on his breast. The farther away the better.

No matter how many times Robert comes hurrying back from the gate, he won't stop for as much as a word with the Jewish Block Chiefs. As though he did not know them. Now they are not his *Kameraden,* although for the night orgies it is the company of these Jewish Block Chiefs he prefers. First of all, they've got it all over him as organizers and are more loaded with gold and diamonds. In the second place, they never seem to run out of schnapps. But now Robert remembers who he is, and who they are. At such festive moments Auschwitz-campling Robert hears and heeds the call of nation and blood. His sense of duty towards the Führer's extermination decree fills him with a grave sense of patriotism. He suddenly feels as pious as an old reprobate who has strayed into church during Mass.

In a rage of frustration Fruchtenbaum goes about caning the skeleton-heads. He knows that it is no use. Cane as he might, he will never be worth as much as the lowest of Poles. And that hurts him. He rankles with inferiority: nobody here appreciates his devoted work. It isn't fair. Robert will go on being Robert without ever having to touch a campling. Fruchtenbaum lets those skeleton heads have it with his cane, and he is embittered.

An odd change has come over Professor Rafael. From the moment he was brought into camp he lay in the hutch day and night, silent, motionless, staring with his big black eyes at the boards of the hutch above. Now, at the very last moment, he can't seem to stand still. His head has suddenly become pointed, like a bird of prey. His eyes are ablaze, his head keeps charging this way and that. What has suddenly come over the Professor?

Around Hayim-Idl stand the Frenchmen. He never spoke to them, though they had lain together in the same hutch. They were strangers to him. He did not understand their language and they did not understand his. Remote sequestered worlds. Now, in their shared nudity, his skeleton and theirs suddenly feel an excruciating kinship, as though one mother had borne them. He ached to embrace each of them, to weep over him.

Robert comes storming back. The camp gate opens wide. A black car rides in.

The S.S. Staff!

An elegant convertible. Riding slowly, as in a festive parade. Silently and obsequiously the sky lowers itself, gleaming reverentially in the black sheen of the car.

All breaths stop.

Death is riding in on whitewall tires.

The car glides into this stillness, halting at its hub. The

Jewish Block Chiefs don't know what to do to make themselves useful. Fruchtenbaum just stands there holding his cane. He isn't sure whether this is a good time to drub Mussulman skulls. His hands dangle uselessly. He can't find a thing to do with them. Actually, this would be an excellent time to give the Germans a sample of his drubbing. But he doesn't know whether it is permitted. He doesn't know whether it's his turn now or theirs. Nobody is beating; and that's the worst of all. Because if there is no beating, what's the use of him here? If there is no beating, then he is no better than those lined up for cremation. Fruchtenbaum feels very ill at ease. More than anyone else he can find no use either for himself or for his hands.

In the car the Germans smoke thick cigars and laugh a fatbellied laughter. They chat, not even casting a glance at the naked array of Mussulmen. As though that were nothing of moment; a banal chore which takes care of itself and does not need special attention. The Camp Doctor sits in front. He does not feel like stepping out of the car to count the rows. He merely runs a glance across the array of shit. The visor of his S.S. cap is deep over his brow. Above the visor is the large death's-head badge, and it is hard to tell whether he is looking through his own eyes or through the two eye-sockets of the death's-head. Puffing away at a thick cigar, he estimates the number of the skeletons. His estimate will be accepted as correct in the medical report he turns in. Why bother counting? He can depend on the Camp Commandant. He wouldn't fool him.

Camp Commandant Hoess passes along the rows, hands folded in the small of his back. Rafael's head with the arched neck reaches out of the front row like a slaughtered fowl straining to fly off but unable to bear the burden of his severed body. Hoess comes stepping towards him.

All at once Rafael leaps out of the row. The wild bird-beak sways right and left as on a spring. He twitters in a strange bird language:

"No! . . . No! . . . I don't want to go to the crematorium! . . ."

Hoess halted in his tracks, and planted himself arms akimbo, sizing up this wild creature who had suddenly got the quaint notion that he didn't want to go to the crematorium. Hoess bursts out laughing:

"MAN!" he calls out to him, "where do you get such ideas?"

The beak of the wild bird of prey becomes more pointed. With its long neck it reaches at the Camp Commandant as though to bite.

Hoess's fingers unbutton the leather holster on his hip. The barrel of the pistol looks like a black pencil. Hoess aims it coolly at Rafael's head. He looks as though he were trying to make a dot with the black pencil at a particular spot on Rafael's temple. The bird beak comes to a stop, not interfering, not moving, just waiting for the tip of the pencil to touch the desired spot—

Like one exhausted Rafael tried to sit down. But his head flopped to the ground beside Hoess's black boots. There was not a sign of a hole. Only from the temple ran a slender, short streak, a dark streak, reaching half way down the cheek.

Hoess replaced the pistol in the holster. He looked down at the thing lying at his boots. His fingers leisurely buttoned the leather holster as he sent his black boot kicking — just for the hell of it — at the face of him who was born in sunny Greece; educated in Paris; was a professor at a university in Italy; was master of ten languages without knowing a word of Yiddish; left behind a wife and twin children whose names he bore on his lips till his final moment; who in Auschwitz turned into a beak-headed bird of prey; and whom Hoess — that true son of the German people — had in his last moment called "MAN!" and immediately, with a pistol spurt, drawn from his temple a short, slender streak, a dark streak. Nothing more. And then sent his boot kicking at that shot head.

The Germans went on sitting in the car smoking their cigars. They had not yet decided whether to herd the shits to the crematorium on foot, or whether to quarantine them in several blocks until the lorries were available. No getting around it — there's a damned day's work to be got over with.

Outside the barbed wire, on the highway, the lorries sped back and forth from the platform to the crematorium, and from crematorium to platform. The smoke gushed in leaping billows out of the crematorium smokestack at the sky.

All at once Ludwig Tiene came dashing up with a list in his hand. Breathlessly scurrying along behind him came the chief clerk. The Block Chiefs quaked as Hoess roared: "Why the goddamn hell didn't the Office report this list?"

Ludwig barked something at the Block Chiefs, who in turn set up a shout:

"All engravers step out!"

The Block Chiefs stormed through the rows of naked bones in search of the engravers. But many on the list had forgotten their numbers standing here; many had forgotten who they were altogether, and many had not waited around to stand here today, for they had long since been dumped on the corpse piles behind their blocks.

"Engravers!"

"Engravers!"

A hunt for engravers in the cemetery. Block Chiefs try to save the day: seeking among the Mussulmen of their blocks, or rummaging through the corpse piles beside the block walls: "Engravers!!! Engravers!!!"

All at once Hayim-Idl finds himself standing outside, apart. Dumbfounded he stands among a handful of other engravers. He does not grasp what is happening to him. Only now, for the first time, he can clearly see the yellow bone-river ranging along the main path there. The miracle is too great for him to grasp. He does not have the strength to comprehend it. He stares at the yellow stream, when suddenly it strikes him with a lightning flash: they — are there! And he — is here! He is apart. Outside. Only now he sees them, and much more distinctly than before, standing in their midst; and he also feels the anguish of standing there the more acutely. For the pain is no longer in him, but opposite his eyes; it no longer numbs his senses but slashes at his pupils. How and when did the change come about? It would seem to have happened a long, long time ago, in another existence. He cannot remember a thing; he is too stunned to grasp a thing. This alone he can feel: he is – outside.

Myriad eyes look at him, and with the same myriad eyes he looks back at them. A yellow river streaming by him, rain lashes punctuating the river with thousands of eye circles fixed on him.

And he at the bank.

He does not remember anything. He does not know whether he is dying or being born. Wondrous things are happening to him now. Things over which he has no control. He is clay. Hands knead him. Hands shape him into something. First Creation. He knows that he ought to want to know what is being done to him. But he knows that he has not yet had the will infused into him with which to want to know. He knows only this: They are ash, he – is clay.

"Engravers! ! . . . Engravers! ! . . ."

The Block Chiefs do not cease yelling for the engravers. The word pours into the dark hollows of his arteries, injecting life into them. *Engravers!* His skeleton quivers, comes to life. The word courses back and forth through his kneaded mold with invisible light rays, blowing the breath of life into him.

He feels that he is being born now. He is standing on a threshold. Not with his back to the world, but with his face to the world. Where has he come from? What is behind him? He cannot remember whether he has already been in the crematorium. He must have been in the crematorium. He remembers seeing the smoke: the smoke of his own body. He remembers feeling himself burn; feeling that he was smoke; feeling himself rise into the sky in a column of smoke. Now it is all gone. From here, where they stood him, there is only horizon to be seen. From here you see neither smokestack nor smoke. Can it be that he is past the crematorium?

From time to time the Block Chiefs drag out another engraver. He doesn't know what is wanted of him or where he is being taken. He has already forgotten that once there was a world in which he had been an engraver. He is shoved into the separate row.

That's all. The black car backs up to the gates of three open blocks. Truncheons of Block Chiefs move between the sky and skulls. From here it all seems to be in some faraway nightmare. The truncheons rise and sink in dull underwater movement. A universe of vacuous stillness.

The skeleton river is channeled into three special blocks. The doors are locked on them from the outside.

Emptiness.

Except the rows of clothing bundles along the main path to the edge of the world – row after long row of miniscule squares, like furrow ridges in a vast, empty field. The black car approaches. Commandant Hoess runs his eyes across the row of engravers, then pauses to consider each of them individually with a fatherly look, growling at Ludwig Tiene:

"My God! What a way for a prisoner leaving Auschwitz to look! I'll teach you! Before they leave this camp the engravers are to be given some good care. These people look like we've been starving them here. My God! The sloppy order I find in my camp!"

Ludwig stands at rigid attention, feeling guilty as a general about to be degraded for treason. Ludwig has often played out this very same farce together with Hoess. Yet one might think Ludwig were hearing these words for the first time, the way he stands there so gravely before Hoess – and before the little string of wretches about to leave Auschwitz.

The car turned towards the exit, ready to ride out. Stepping towards the car, Hoess continued to play out the farce of being beside himself at the terrible disorder he has suddenly turned up in his Auschwitz. Before entering the car, he turned to Ludwig once more: "Sweetheart, am I going to teach you! . . ."

Black spheres of S.S. caps move off in the open car towards the camp exit.

Engravers. Handle with care. Not a hair on their head is to be touched.

They were marched to the K-B block, where everything was neat and spotless. There each of them will get a bed of his own and fresh clothing. There they will be isolated from the rest of the camplings and watched over until they are taken out of Auschwitz.

Like very important personages they marched to the K-B. Near the block gates lay piles of dead skeletons. Now the marchers were as remote from them and alien to them as life is remote from death and alien to death. All at once Hayim-Idl caught Moni's glance peeping out at him from his hiding place behind a pile of skeletons.

11

The day after the *Selektion* a new transport arrived in Auschwitz: the remnants of such German labor camps as Niederwalden, Sacrau, Annaberg—camps without crematoriums of their own, or any of the other vital facilities which entitled a camp to recognition as a German Katzet worthy of the name.

The transport comprised also the last remnants of long-liquidated ghettos which the Germans had kept behind to help them ferret out the treasures which the Jews had taken along in their flight to the bunkers and buried there. For who better than Jews could plumb the ingenious concealment devices which ghetto wits had thought up. And the Jews of these "Search Kommandos" daily accompanied the Germans. Like seasoned bloodhounds they crawled on all fours into holes hidden deep beneath the ruins of the gutted ghettos, their fine sense of smell extracting from the earth another few days of life for themselves.

Moni lay in a top hutch looking down at the new faces: Again the block is packed full! The hundreds of newcomers roamed about on both sides of the brick oven, filling all the hutch aisles. They looked around with query in their eyes: They've been through many camps; survived many fires; eluded many deaths. Now here is Auschwitz. The Katzet Auschwitz! Will they make it here, too?

From his shredded trousers the bones of his legs peered at him. They were like two little yellow stalks, telling him: "Moni, you're a Mussulman." He was ashamed of his body before the newcomers. The disgrace of it mortified him. Soon he will lie behind the block, these yellow leg-strands will protrude from a pile of Mussulman corpses, and not one of these newcomers will know that these are the legs of one who had been Piepel in every one of the camp's blocks.

He was very cold. He felt that he could not go on lying there. He crawled down off the hutch. The block below was a crowded tumult of newcomers. Acquaintances from former camps fought their way to common hutches. They spoke to each other, calling each other by name and shouting towards upper hutches, while from above others called down for them to stop looking—they had found a good hutch! Everybody shoved. Everybody was busy. Everybody was getting himself set up. They created a queer atmosphere—as though they were human beings with human needs. They exuded a pungent, tantalizing air—the air of the outside.

The block was permeated with the familiar smell of newcomers.

For the first time in camp Moni now felt rage at the bovine ignorance of the newcomers. All the new transports he's seen coming in! It's always the same: At their first glimpse of the planet Auschwitz comes the hidden relief: *There is life here!* It is every campling's first reaction on his first day of Auschwitz—that is, if he hasn't been sent directly from the wagons to the crematorium. It had never bothered Moni. But now it infuriated him: What are they making all that fuss about? Why are they so busy getting themselves set up? Don't they see where they are? This is Auschwitz! Auschwitz!

He could tell them a thing or two. Just a few words. Though old campbirds never tell newcomers what's in store for them here. No, not out of pity. It's just that old campbirds don't go in for that kind of sentimental blab. It's beneath the dignity of an old campbird to stand around making talk with a greenhorn. Most old campbirds regard newcomers the way adults boredly regard children at play. In a little while they will in any case be dragged off behind the blocks, or be off with the *Selektions*. So what is there to tell, and who is there here worth wasting talk on? They'll wise up soon enough. In the pile behind the block their eyes will open without anyone's help . . .

He had a powerful urge to stop one of them in the middle of his fussing and tell his dumb face a thing or two. Just a couple of words. For the first time now he was furious about their bovine stupidity. Perhaps because for the first time now he felt that this time, their fate was his fate. To this transport he is linked in death. He isn't outliving these. With them he will be taken to the crematorium.

As he dragged towards the exit, a group of camplings looked down at him from a top hutch, whispering frightenedly among themselves, showing large eye-whites, as though seeing a horrible sight. Moni looked up at them. He could tell them a story now which would stop making them feel disgusted at the way he looks. But old-campbird pride kept him from taking it up with them. At least he hasn't lost his pride yet. He lashed a loathing glance at the packed hutch. "Greeners! Whoresons!" he muttered and dragged towards the exit.

Thousands and thousands of newcomers swarmed outside. Only yesterday it was all empty here. Now it is packed everywhere. The main path and the backpaths; between the blocks and inside the blocks; in the latrine and around the latrine—teeming everywhere. Merchants bustled about. Big organizers and petty dealers. It looks like the busy old times again. But there are all new, strange faces. No one to say a word to. He felt as though he, the Auschwitz old-timer, had suddenly been dropped into a strange camp. As though not they had arrived in his camp today, but he had been dumped into theirs.

He felt forlorn, an outsider.

In clusters—former camp-mates, former ghetto neighbors—the newcomers streamed past him. In every corner they bunched, near all the blocks. All of them had someone to talk to, something to talk about. Each of them still had someone—the way it always is the first day in Auschwitz. Only he was all alone. The only greener here.

All at once he missed the familiar skeleton faces of acquaintances and strangers alike, with whom he had been together only the day before yesterday. He ached for those who had known him and now were gone. He so wanted to be able to line up once more for a can of tea for the Rabbi of Shilev. All at once he was not certain that it would not have been better if he had gone together with them to the crematorium. There, maybe, he would be together with them. It had never occurred to him to wonder what goes on inside the crematorium; what it looks like on the inside. From the ghetto hovels to the last line-up your every second is one long dread of the crematorium, and there is nobody who has been there to tell you what happens to them all after the crematorium. Pa went away in the lorry. He can see him now as distinctly as he saw him then. It isn't possible that after the crematorium Pa stopped being Pa. He must be some place. Otherwise, he could not see him now exactly the way he saw him then.

Up and down, back and across the camp the newcomers streamed like the warp and woof in a loom. The faces coming at his eyes interwove with backs retreating from his eyes. Only he drifted in this weave like a dropstitch.

He could not fathom why, that time at the platform, Rudolf Hoess had separated him from Pa. Why should Hoess have minded his staying together with his pa? Why did he pick him out of all the boys and send him into the camp?

The door of the K-B block was locked. The engravers are being closely guarded in there. Soon they will be sent on a job deep in the heart of Germany. Some very important secret job, it seems. They're washed, fed the best food—like pets. The K-B block has been locked ever since the engravers were put there. They are not allowed outside. They might get lice from the others. Special food is handed in to them. The doctors fuss and fret over them. During roll call they line up separately. They are being put together again and groomed as though for an audience with Hitler himself. Moni came a little nearer to the K-B block. Yesterday, when the engravers were being marched along the main path to the latrine, Hayim-Idl shoved a whole bread ration into his hands. That saved him. It put some light in his eyes. A whole bread ration! If only he could see Hayim-Idl for just a second now. "I've done a terrible thing!" Hayim-Idl had told him. "I've gone and signed up as an engraver." What had Hayim-Idl been so scared about? It went off all right. What a miracle that he's an engraver. He'll get out of Auschwitz. Is it really possible to get out of Auschwitz? In camp you never know what's right and what's worthwhile. If Hayim-Idl hadn't stolen that cup of marmalade for the Rabbi of Shilev he wouldn't have been thrown out of the potato peelery. And if he hadn't been thrown out of the peelery, he wouldn't have signed up as an engraver. And if he hadn't signed up as an engraver, he would have gone off to the crematorium with the Rabbi of Shilev and with Ferber like the rest of them, all of them.

The newcomers standing near the gate of the K-B block suddenly fall silent. Staring at him again! What are they staring at? Haven't they ever seen a Mussulman before? Why are they moving away from him? Do they think they're outlasting him here? Do they think they'll keep their fat looks forever? Cruddy greeners! Whoresons! . . .

The bed of the large truck tilted backwards, dumped the load and slowly settled back into place.

In the kitchen compound, near the open tailgate of the truck, lay a tall mound of turnips. After dumping the load, the truck started up and rode out of camp.

Moni stood leaning with the edge of his shoulder against the corner of block 1. Strange. The day looks different when you see a truck ride out of camp empty. Not piled high with skeletons. Against the bright skyline the day is suddenly—day, and the truck—a truck. You suddenly want to shut your eyes and feel some of what your soul felt in another life it lived once upon a time, long ago.

The potato peelers carried wooden bins full of turnips into the store, without let-up, like two rows of ants: one row—in with full bins, the other—out with empty bins. The potato peelers look as though they are only hired day laborers in camp. All because they get to eat all the turnips they can during the peeling. Who can keep tabs on their hands all day long?

From every direction camplings turn up to gaze at the kitchen compound. They stand and wait: A miracle might happen, and a piece of turnip rot will be left on the ground after the storing. They glare at anybody else coming along to watch with them. Already they are wrangling with their glances over the piece of turnip rot which their mind's eye sees lying in the center of the compound.

In the scullery, the sliced turnips lie in two large basins ready to be taken to the soup barrels. If he could get in there for only just one second, Moni thought, he could organize a piece of turnip from the basin. The very thought of a yellow piece of turnip sent the teeth in his mouth weeping with lust. Inside his stomach, hunger has long since died. But the teeth! Hunger is a thousand times more excruciating when it gets into your teeth. They are hunger's last stand. There life and death fight their last battle.

With his cane Vatzek patrols the area near the kitchen, keeping an eye on the mound of turnips. The peelers keep carrying bins heaped high with large turnips into the store. Whenever they return with an empty bin, a full bin awaits them. Matchek stands there armed with a little cane, helping to guard, shouting away in mock-Yiddish: "Ikay-kikey! Work! Work! *Oy-vay, oy-vay, tataleh, mamaleh...*"

A piece of yellow turnip! To get just one such yellow chunk in between his teeth! But too many eyes are watching at the kitchen now. He turns away. He cannot bear to go on looking. His feet drag him back toward the blocks.

If he could get hold of Hayim-Idl for just one second now.

A whole barrel of soup was brought in to them. What are they going to do with a whole barrel of soup?

Food porters carried empty lunch barrels back to the kitchen. Nothing left to lick there. Even the rusty hoops have been licked clean by tongues. That's the first thing newcomers learn in all the camps. The wood of the barrels looks moist with sucking, like the dummy of a baby so cute with all his new front teeth. All at once he had an idea. He dashed over, and with an outstreched bony hand seized the bottom of a barrel: He will help them carry.

"Beat it! Get away from that barrel! There's nothing to lick!" the porter shouted at him.

Moni looked up at the new food porters: Greener bastards! All of a sudden they're big shots in his camp! He could tell them just who and what he is around here. He would only tell them that block orderlies used to snap to before him. He would only tell them that when they were still out in that bloody free of theirs, he was already Piepel in Auschwitz! He could also tell them a thing or two about organizing a piece of turnip in camp. Let them learn from him! Might even do them some good. It won't be long now and they'll be ready to offer their eye-teeth to know what he knows. But he isn't going to stand here making talk with a bunch of green whoreson bastards! Oh no. He's not that hard up yet. Instead, he gritted his teeth, hissing at them:

"Up your whoring mother! Who do you think you're talking to, bastard? How would you like to go popping through the smokestack?!"

At the sound of this true Katzet talk, the new food porter felt puny and insignificant. He better hold his tongue. Let that fellow carry the barrel if he gets such a kick out of it. There's nothing left to lick, anyway. Besides, you can see that that old Katzetnik doesn't really give a hang about carrying the barrel but has something else in mind. Better not say anything.

Usually the barrels are carried to the scullery and parked

by the door. It is only a few steps to the basin. If you're lucky, all you have to do is reach out and you've got yourself a piece of turnip. The main thing is that no one should notice you coming in. You've got to play it smart, casually, without even looking at the basin.

Actually, everybody there watches. Maybe the barrel washers will pretend not to notice. They know him. Maybe they'll even want to help him out. Must take a chance. He's not standing any *Selektion* with those greeners. Oh no! He's not crawling into the lorries with them! Anything, anything, but that! He isn't one of those mommy-weewee whores!

Food porters parked barrels near the scullery entrance and immediately fled to avoid getting a cane across the skull. The kitchen compound was a beehive of activity. Dziadek stood with his paunch billowing out over his trouser belt like a feather pillow held together with a cord. His pudgy hands dangled impotently from his sleeves like boxing gloves. Inside the peelery he holds the pitchfork in his hands, raking lazily back and forth like a pendulum. But here, under the open sky, he is restless as a seal out of water. Potato peelers dashed back and forth with the bins, and Matchek did not cease taunting: *"Oy-vay, oy-vay, tataleh, mamaleh . . ."* Oh, Matchek was fit to be tied. What a shame Vatzek didn't make him Dziadek. He's dying to club. He'd give his life for a chance to do some clubbing. Club openly. Before everyone's eyes. Whomever he feels like and whenever he feels like. Ah, if only *he* were kapo of the peelery!

The food porters planted another barrel on the ground and rushed off. Moni rolled it over the threshold of the scullery. He fussed with the barrel, bending it this way and that, all the while sending his eyes racing in every direction. At the window, the barrel washers scrubbed the barrels with whisk brooms. Water gushed onto the concrete floor from all the taps. It all looked like a bathhouse. Moni turned his back to the basin, as if it did not interest him one bit. He is only attending to this barrel he's just brought in. He's just parking it. There, it's parked. No, it isn't quite parked yet. In just a second he'll take it off his shoulder and it'll stand. Only a second. There, he's putting it down now. All right, it's parked. So if it is, what's he looking for? He isn't looking for a thing. He's just checking the barrel on all sides, to make sure it's standing straight. Not crooked. After all, a barrel is a precious thing in camp. A barrel isn't a campling. A barrel is wood! You can burn a campling. You can burn ten thousand camplings, a hundred thousand, you can even burn a million camplings. But a barrel? Everybody in camp knows what a barrel is. But here, in the scullery, they know all those sharpster tricks only too well. They're old hat. They pretend not to notice. They wait. It's interesting to watch a Mussulman's back trying to put something over on them. Here they know that in just a moment the back will turn around and a bony hand will reach for the basin. It never fails. Still, for a minute it takes your mind off the boring routine of scrubbing empty, dry-sucked barrels. So the barrel washers say nothing and wait for the gay climax.

The game is especially interesting for the S.S. chef now roaming the cauldron section. His eye immediately caught the little back of a small Mussulman in the window, hunched over an empty barrel, tilting the barrel this way and that, picking it up and parking it again. And with every manipulation coming a step closer to the turnip-filled basin.

The S.S. chef stood there saying nothing. What fun to watch those little shoulders tremble; those black eyes darting every which way in the skeleton skull—just like a fly caught in a spider's web. Interesting to see how the fly is going to get out of it. Only nobody in the scullery should frighten him off and spoil the fun. Just look at that creature checking the barrel so carefully to see that there isn't a broken stave. A loyal Mussulman. Concerned about German property. Wants to do the kitchen a good turn. He wants—

"Halt! Halt! Get him, Vatzek!"

Naked little spindle-legs scampered along the main path

like a fawn fleeing a leopard—the piece of turnip pressed to his heart.

The S.S. chef stood at the edge of the kitchen compound, black boots outspread, urging Vatzek on: "Get him, Vatzek! Get him! . . ."

Moni clutched the piece of turnip in his hand, not remembering it. The campling throngs on the main path gave way, like upright citizens before an armed bandit fleeing his pursuers through a busy street. Where should he run? Where can you run—in Auschwitz? Better the electrified barbed wire should get him now.

"Get him, Vatzek!"

Vatzek reached out his cane, and Moni's throat was caught in the curved handle like a puppy's head in the dog-catcher's lariat.

Trapped.

Vatzek's powerful grip led Moni along by his shoulder bone. At the end of the road, near the kitchen compound, stood the black figure of the S.S. chef, booted legs astride, hands folded on chest, waiting.

Vatzek knew whom he was now leading along. He also knew how it would end up. And by the way of trying to answer his own conscience—after all, he was now leading an old campbird—he hissed, looking straight ahead:

"That black whoreson standing there and watching . . ."

Moni heard yet did not hear. The piece of turnip was still pressed to his heart. Opposite his eyes the black figure of the S.S. man loomed ever larger. Behind the figure there were no more blocks. Only horizon. The black legs like pillars rooted to the ground, the head reaching to the sky. Vatzek whispered at Moni not moving his lips.

"You've screwed yourself, Old Whore. Where were your brains? Didn't you know that blackboy there patrols the kitchen when the provisions are unloaded?"

On the right ranged the main path. Only the day before yesterday they had all stood there for the *Selektion*. It would have been easier for him together with the people he knew. Now he will have to go into the crematorium all alone. Suddenly he was seized with terror at the loneliness of it. Like a child too terrified to fall asleep alone in a dark room.

They came up to the S.S. chef. "Take him into the scullery!" he commanded, stepping after them.

At the windows, barrel washers scrubbed the wood of the barrels with a burst of energy, inside and out, splashing water everywhere. Their brawny, upsleeved arms worked with all their might, their eyes stealing furtive glances: Black Death is in the scullery.

Vatzek now let go a barrage of shouting at Moni in an altogether different tone. "Whoreson! Turnips was it you felt like lifting from the basin? Well, it's turnips you're going to get now!" Vatzek waited to hear the sentence of the almighty black potentate.

The S.S. chef stood there, black sleeves crossed on black chest. He studied the fly which had torn out of the web, spoiling his fun for him. Tight-lipped he eyed him, and there was no telling what thoughts passed under the black S.S. cap.

Above the black tunic gleams the steel death's-head insignia. Moni sees it double: like two Mussulman heads . . . This is the way he shivered with cold that time when the Germans came to Kongressia . . The shot Jews lay on the sidewalk in front of their house. Pa snatched him into his arms, carried him into the house, and laid him in his cot in the children's room. The sight of those shot Jews shocks him now more than all the dead and murdered he has seen since . . . Two cooks pass, carrying a full bin of turnips to the cauldrons. There is never even a bit of turnip in the soup . . . The cooks look like well-fed giants. Red, fleshy cheeks. The barrel washers are scrubbing away. What is there to scrub? Aren't the barrels clean? The white scar on the S.S. chef's chin reaches into his moustache. Like Hitler's moustache in the pictures in the windows of the Polish *Volksdeutsche* . . .

The black S.S. uniform gives off exactly the same smell as the big lorries. Not the lorries that bring turnips, but those that deliver to the crematorium . . .

"Give him ten in the ass!" the clenched mouth finally commanded.

The edge of the basin was too high for Moni's rump to bend over at the prescribed angle. Vatzek warmed up, taking a few dry swings in the air with the truncheon over the rump, like a violinist tuning up before the recital. Vatzek pressed Moni's head deeper over the edge of the basin, and still was not satisfied. Finally, he hurried into the peelery and brought back a bench. There. That's better. Now let that whoreson lie there ass up, regulation style. So, it's turnips he was going to pinch!

Vatzek keeps warming up. There is no end to his preparations. Perhaps he hopes that the S.S. chef will take off and he'll be able to save Old Whore. When all's said and done, an old campbird's an old campbird. Vatzek still remembers him when he was Franzl's Piepel. His heart wouldn't let him murder an old campbird.

The S.S. chef does not budge. He stands there, arms folded across his chest, waiting. He wants to get every last drop of the fun. Vatzek becomes furious. His blood begins to boil. Where does he come off suddenly trying to be a philanthropist? He knows that there's no getting out of it now. He'll just have to finish off Old Whore. In that case, let it be over with fast. A fury of hate rages in him. He no longer knows at whom or at what: at the Katzet, or at the Piepel who had made such a damn fool of himself that he, Vatzek, will now have to croak him with his own hands; or at that black whoreson parked there without budging and who Vatzek is fed up with carrying out his orders.

"Lay down, whoreson! Your mother's hole! Turnips? . . . Turnips? . . . Here's turnips for you! . . ."

Vatzek lays the truncheon into him. Flogs, and counts. Raises the truncheon high, aims, and brings it down like a sharp axe into a tree trunk. His teeth are clenched. His eyes gorged with blood. He knows Old Whore will be lying behind the block tomorrow. The S.S. chef does not budge — well, that settles it. Got to finish him off. But do a clean job of it, so he doesn't suffer much afterwards. In that case — in that case — Take that, whoreson, up your mother's hole! Murderously he flogs away, as though not Moni but the S.S. chef were lying on the bench, and Vatzek were now venting all his pent-up Katzek wrath at him: for his three years in Auschwitz, for the girl he left behind at the village near Zamoszc whom the Germans must now be laying . . .

"Turnips? Turnips? Here's your turnips! . . . Nine . . . Ten . . ."

Flogging over.

The barrel washers began fishing the barrels out of the basin in which they were soaking. Now the flogged campling has to be dunked in the cold-water basin. Everything by the book in Auschwitz.

He was dripping as he fled from the kitchen. He ran along the main path. He hobbled through the campling throngs milling around. He no longer saw anyone. He did not know whether the blows were still landing on his body or whether they had let up. He no longer felt a thing. The blows filled his insides, propelling him forward like a coiled spring in a hollow toy. As soon as the spring runs out, the toy will lie on the ground, empty. Dead. The sky frothed at his feet with white spools of noontime smoke from the crematorium smoke stack. The tops of the watchtowers jutted into the sky below. Topsy-turvy S.S. men sat there guarding the clouds. He lay on the ground in the main crossroads, and he felt himself sliding down the sloping block roofs. He struggled up, not knowing whether he was falling or rising. The block inside was a hubbub of new camplings swarming on the oven, in the aisles, in the hutch-holes. He could not remember when and how he had got here. No one paid him any attention or as much as turned to look at him.

He did not feel the wood of the hutch beneath him. He could not remember when he had sagged into it. He did not feel himself lying. He felt himself floating somewhere in space over a painful, endless main path.

Roaring turmoil. Now the block is full, now it is empty. Now he is floating out of the emptiness into the density of a clamorous block. And now – hazy vacuum. Somewhere out of the faraway sky booms reverberate like an oncoming thunderstorm. The booms billow and crash with mounting terror as they roll nearer. Out of the clouds emerges a black S.S. uniform, black sleeves folded across black chest, followed by a cannonade of echoes:

Turnips? . . . Turnips? . . . Turnips? . . .

A panic of tumbling from the triple tiers. A stampede towards the block exit. Block orderlies roaring into the hutches: "Roll-call! . . . Roll-call! . . " How come he didn't hear the gong boom? At the first shout "Roll-call!" an old campbird's feet pick themselves up and run! He struggled to get up, but iron fetters pinioned him to the hutch boards. *Let him have ten in the ass!* . . . Another shred of memory came wafting back to him. That's what happened to him . . . he got ten in the ass. Now they'll be dragging him out to the pile behind the block . . .

"Roll-call! . . . Roll-call! . . .

The block fell silent, empty. Everybody was outside. Block orderlies checking every cranny. Coming to his hutch. They're at him. Grab him by the legs. Drag him.

"Please let go of me . . ." he bleated entreatingly at them, "I'm still alive . . . don't dump me behind the block . . . look, I'm Moni . . . Old Whore . . . red socks . . ."

Evening roll-call.

Everybody is in taut readiness in the assembly areas, breath bated for the arrival of Camp Commandant Rudolph Hoess who is to check if the engravers are looking fit.

Behind them, from the far reaches of one of the camps, carried muffled snatches of sound from a brass band. The air trembled at the clash of the cymbals. Elegy to a day in Auschwitz.

Opposite the eyes, smoke billowed in fat rolls from the crematorium smokestack, unfurling at the feet of those standing in the assembly areas.

The engravers are arrayed near the Office in a separate row. In every respect — Prominents' Prominents. To their left — the kitchen-block heavyweights; to their right — the Office tenderfaces.

Their last roll-call in Auschwitz. As soon as it's over the engravers will be taken to the Political Bureau, and from there — out of Auschwitz. The grapevine has it they're going to be put to work counterfeiting foreign currency.

Hayim-Idl cannot help looking at the trousers on his legs. Brand-new. The dark stripes glow against the grey material. Black shoes, real leather, lacing up over the ankles; hugging the feet so passionately again, like lovers reunited after an Auschwitz separation.

This is the first time his feet are getting the feel of shoes again. The first time since he was brought to Auschwitz. Since that time he was stripped naked, barefooted. When was it all? His memory had not yet healed sufficiently to reach so far into the past.

Engravers. Their last roll-call in Auschwitz. Washed, hair freshly shaven, cleanly dressed they stand there, each with an Auschwitz cap on his head, a striped campling shirt under the striped campling jacket. Hayim-Idl brought his arm up opposite his eyes, studied the sleeve material. Practically a new jacket. Not a button missing. You can button it right up to the throat.

Block Chiefs, kapos, clerks — the cream of the Prominents in camp, the élite of the planet Auschwitz — enviously eye the short row of engravers. They murmur among themselves: Oh, what they wouldn't give to be standing there with the engravers. Each of them muses: Just get out of here! Once outside the barbed wire he'd know how to take care of himself. Not like those ex-Mussulmen standing there. Even outside they're just going to wait around for the Germans to croak them!

The Belgian's jacket isn't buttoned right. He seems to have forgotten how clothes with buttons are worn. There's an extra button at the throat and an extra buttonhole at the bottom. Hayim-Idl reaches out his hand, and without a word rebuttons the jacket like a father helping his little boy, with loving fingertips.

One family. They hardly speak to each other. Stand there in a row – silent. The heart overflows. The eyes look on. The lame mind cannot keep up with the mad flight of the emotions. A short row of camplings standing lined up for roll-call. An awesome mystery veils them. They are leaving this place, carrying out imprinted in their pupils the unfoldings of Auschwitz! Is it really possible?

They! And he, Hayim-Idl, among them! For three straight days Bosker, Block Chief of 14, had sat displayed on the main path propped in a chair with a wooden pole, his feet outstretched before him naked, stripped of the tall black boots. He had been brought back shot. He had already reached the outside of the barbed wire. THE SMOKESTACK IS THE ONLY EXIT IN AUSCHWITZ, the big placard over his dead head had declared. And they, the engravers, are getting out of Auschwitz. And he, Hayim-Idl, among them!

He knows for a fact that they are being sent deep inside Germany where they will be put to printing dollars. The word "dollars" constricts his heart with fear. How does he come to be a dollar printer? But when a man has nothing left but his life to lose, he must even try things which common sense tells him he daren't do. When the Germans began to shoot at the front row of Jews in the Chmielnik woods he got up off the ground, grabbed the baby with one hand and dragged Dvortche along with the other, and began to run.

Against all common sense. Because the Germans had just finished announcing that whoever dared stand up would be shot on the spot. If at least he knew what the inside of a print shop looks like! At home he sometimes used to pass by Rosenthal's print shop. In the summer the grimy window was always open and you could see a boy's back in a blue smock splotched with black ink. He would stand there facing a rattling machine, a big plate that looked like a shiny black moon constantly rising and falling. It had never occurred to him to stop for a moment to watch. How was he to know that that was the very thing that one day would save his life?

Engravers. During the two days of quarantine in the K-B block they became one family. Real brothers. None of them speaks Yiddish, but they could immediately sense Hayim-Idl's love for them. They made him their group leader. He hadn't asked for it. On the contrary — he had resisted. But they made him accept the honor. After all, his name heads the list!

Brothers. Holland, Antwerp, Paris — throw away all those strange, faraway Gentile names and what's left before your eyes is — a Jew. A Jew like you — even though not born in a Jewish townlet like Chmielnik. But each of them had a mother — a Jewish mother just like yours. Which is why they were sent to Auschwitz; which is why they are now here together with you.

They know how deeply he loves them. He will not go lost among brothers. Even if they discover that he isn't and never was an engraver they won't let him down. They'll understand. What is it he wants, after all? To save his life. So he isn't an engraver, does that mean he hasn't the right to live? Nothing shameful in wanting to live. It isn't as if he was robbing anyone. True, the first two or three times he'll have to watch carefully the way their hands work. But then he'll pick it up. That won't be the hardest thing he's had to learn.

Far beyond the barbed wire the Auschwitz camps sprawl before the eyes. But they don't look the same, now. *Faith!*

That's the main thing – faith, the mumble of Hayim-Idl's own lips reaches his ears. An endless crisscross of barbed wire on the mute horizon. Only now they look like fishnets hung out to dry in a fishing village. There is the crematorium smoke. But it is no longer the same smoke. Now it is merely smoke coming out of the crematorium chimney.

Suddenly:

The campling emerged from one of the assembly areas. Breaking ranks, he made a dash for the main path. "Moni!" Hayim-Idl gasped.

Myriad eyes looked on. Auschwitz caught its breath. He ran across the empty main path, heading for the barbed wire. From the watchtowers the machine-gun barrels followed him like spotlights fixing an enemy aircraft. They did not fire, so captivated were they by what they saw. They also want to see, by broad daylight, the encounter of Mussulman and Auschwitz barbed wire. It isn't every day you get to see such a sight here.

He stumbled and fell. A puny boniness lying on the empty vastness of Auschwitz main path. He rose, tottering, and ran on.

"Moni!"

The eyes of the entire camp are riveted on the back of a tiny bone-frame. Eyes of newcomers and eyes of old campbirds, eyes of Prominents and barrels of all the machine-guns in every one of the watchtowers – all now directed at the ember of unfulfilled life that has suddenly flared in full sight of them.

He tumbled into the last ditch. He was no longer visible on the surface. The main path had swallowed him up. An empty stretch. And again he came up. Little spindle-legs wobbling drunkenly, straining to run on but unable. The earth of the Auschwitz main path pulled him down and the unbounded skyline dusking through the barbed wire pulled him on. When all at once: the black convertible of Camp Commandant Rudolph Hoess!

The eyes were still turned to the open gate and the car coming in through it as little arms and legs began to clamber up the barbed wire with frantic rapidity, like a spider scurrying up its web. Human arms. Human legs. Driven by a life and will of their own. Here, in Auschwitz, no one has such free-willed arms and legs. Spent, they freeze to the barbed wire, like a frog petrified in mid-swim. And suddenly, as though galvanized, the body penetrated the thick wall through the opening between two levels of barbed wire.

How did he get away with it? It seems the wire isn't charged with electricity during the day.

Rudolph Hoess stood in his open car. Gaping at the scene, he raised his hand at the watchtowers in signal not to shoot. Now the second foot got through the barbed wire. There he crumpled, lying in a little heap on the narrow strip of ground between the two wire walls. He struggled to his knees. He looked up: another barbed-wire wall! . . . He wanted to surmount it, too. But he collapsed.

Robert, most brutal Block Chief of them all, could not contain his admiration. "Bravo, Old Whore!" he cried out as though to cheer him on. "Bravo!"

Vatzek, kapo of the potato peelery, swallowed the incredible scene. For the first time in the Katzet he felt tears warm in his eyes.

All stopped breathing. As though before the presence of Life manifest. The black convertible drove into the narrow strip between the two barbed-wire walls.

Black boots at his skull. Rudolph Hoess standing behind his head. Auschwitz Commandant Hoess, who had made a personal present of him to Franzl. He made one last effort to move, move and bite his teeth into the black boots. But he fell back.

The Auschwitz sky leaned over his eyelashes. The earth gathered him in like a mother cradling her little one to sleep. Hush . . .

POSTSCRIPT

Rudolph Hoess, the Commandant, has stated that 2,000,000 men, women and children were burned in Auschwitz.

The tragedy of these zeros is impossible to comprehend.

So that the world should know and remember Auschwitz and so that such statistics may never be repeated, I have told part of the story of the two million in the life and death of one small boy.